"YOU'RE ALL IN IT TOGETHER," ALLISON SAID WITH RISING BITTERNESS. "YOU CAN SHIT ON ANYONE YOU CHOOSE TO—OR CHOOSE NOT TO."

"Then why did you come to us?" Nick asked, feeling the man's frustration.

"Because I wanted to shit on Henderson. Gunderstein believes me," Allison said thickly. "Don't you, Gunderstein?"

Gunderstein flushed. Nick became aware, at that moment, of the secret of Gunderstein's skill, the ability to inspire confidence in a source, a method beyond mere tenacity. Everyone was credible. They had reasons. The lie was simply a tool for survival. He was simply a vessel for their justification.

"Yes, I do," Gunderstein replied.

"If you have that much confidence in Allison's story, why can't you persuade him to be quoted?" Nick asked Gunderstein.

"They'll kill me," Allison said, terrified.

Books by Warren Adler

The Henderson Equation
Trans-Siberian Express

Published by POCKET BOOKS

THE HENDERSON EQUATION

WARREN ADLER

PUBLISHED BY POCKET BOOKS NEW YORK

POCKET BOOKS, a Simon & Schuster division of
GULF & WESTERN CORPORATION
1230 Avenue of the Americas, New York, N.Y. 10020

A Word of Caution

There will be those who believe they recognize some of the characters in this novel as persons presently living. Nothing could be farther from the truth. With the exception of well-known public figures and institutions cited by name, all other characters and institutions are purely the creation of the author's imagination. Admittedly superficial bits and pieces of living people and situations have slipped into the crucible of the author's subconscious. But there they have been recycled and disgorged in other forms and configurations. Perhaps, then, the essential message of this disclaimer is that not even a novelist can, or wish to, live in a vacuum. The impact of the mass media is ubiquitous. No one can escape. Which is what this book is all about.

—Warren Adler

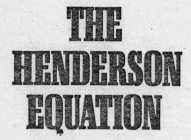

THE
HENDERSON
EQUATION

1

Staring into the vast city room, as it subsided now from the last flurry of deadlines, Nick Gold savored a moment of comparative tranquility. Deskmen and reporters, lifting weary eyes from copy paper, might have assessed his mood as one of self-imposed hypnosis, a kind of daydreaming. News aides turned their eyes away self-consciously, as though fearing their own curious gazes would be an intrusion on the executive editor.

But while Nick's open eyes gazed into the cavernous room, the ninety-one clearly visible desks and typewriters, the clusters of nerve centers through which information had passed from brain to typewriter, from paper pile to paper pile, paragraph by paragraph, through each penciled checkpoint, the image was not registering. The mechanism of his mind was simply idling, lulled by the comforting vibrations of the big presses as they inked the awesome discharge of a Washington day, the distilled essence of a thousand minds.

Cordovan brogues planted at either side of his typewriter table, hands clasped as a cradle for his peppered head, tie loose but still plumb in its buttoned-downed place, Nick kept at bay any irritant wisp of thought that might intrude on his self-imposed tranquility.

His adrenaline would not recharge him until the completed street edition, the freshly inked "practice" sheet, was slapped smartly on his desk by one of the news aides.

The slap of the *Chronicle* falling on his Lucite desk top, like a slap on the butt, jarred him out of his stupor. His long legs unhitched from over the typewriter and curled under the desk as he opened the first section, smudging the ink with his fingers. He covered the headlines with a single glance, as his short-fused temper was immediately ignited by a single word. He pressed a buzzer and waited for the gruff mumble of Prescott, the copy editor.

"Remove *balk,* Harry, as in 'Russians Balk,' lower right, beneath the crease."

"Nit-picking. *Balk* is exactly right."

"It's an old baseball term, Harry. Not precise."

"How about *bark?*" Nick could detect the professional irritation. Copy editors traditionally overreacted to their own myth. They fought over words like male lions over their mates. Nick's temper fuse sputtered. Tread lightly, he told himself. Don't take it out on Harry.

"Give it a try, Harry," Nick said, ending the argument. He peered through the glass and across the room at Prescott, who turned to glare back. Nick smiled and waved, softening the jab. His eye roamed the rest of the page, searching for blips, like a trained cyclops soaking up the neatly inked Times Roman. It was a second look. He had already seen the proofs of page 1, the smudged lines, the silky feel, the still unfamiliar odor of the new newspaper technology. The craft unions had fought its coming for years. They had taunted him with strike threats and slowdowns, sick calls and deliberate fuck-ups.

"I'm no goddamned union negotiator," he had told Myra. "I'm a newspaperman."

"You're the executive editor," she had said gently,

the veneer of layered softness carefully masking the hard flint beneath.

"And you're the boss."

"Your job is to get the paper on the street. Mine is to turn a profit. Neither of us has it all roses."

"But they're being unreasonable."

"Look at it from their point of view. They see technology as the enemy, robbing them of their livelihoods. They see computers taking over."

It was hypocrisy not to accept new discoveries, Nick had thought. It was morally indefensible, if vaguely romantic, like Myra's simplistic view of the *Chronicle*'s mission.

He had listened with rising impatience as she outlined her "views" after Charlie's death, as if in his ten years as Charlie's honcho he hadn't understood. He didn't mind her borrowing the rather naive idea, only the way she stated it; it came out so pedantic and self-serving. Charlie had never expressed it with such self-consciousness. But Charlie had died, his brains soaked with booze, anger, and madness.

"Objectivity must be our first priority," Myra had told him then. "The unvarnished truth. That was my father's only consideration. That's the way Dad wanted it and that's the way Charlie built it." He had listened with impatience. Deference was the proper attitude of a new widow. But the look of triumph in her eyes was clearly visible. Nick had said nothing, his hand whiteknuckled as it held the Scotch glass.

"I need you, Nick," she had said finally. "I know they're all laughing at me." Her father, and then Charlie, had stood between her and the *Chronicle*. Now they were gone.

She had stood up, a sweater thrown lightly around her frail shoulders, practicing humility, he had thought. She was too clever to make changes now, too shrewd. And his view of her was still colored by Charlie's disintegrating mind, the calibration awry. Charlie, toward the end, had seen her as a monstrous enemy, greedy to wrest the *Chronicle* from his hands. And despite the obviousness of Charlie's paranoia, Nick had enlisted in his cause. Was it out of simple friendship, loyalty? Or was Nick, too, secretly covetous of the *Chronicle?* Toward the end she had had Charlie institutionalized, straitjacketed. Nick's last view of him was of a broken, mindless man, hungering for death. Had she known that when she brought him home? Near all those trophy guns. Charlie's death was, Nick knew, his own loss far more than hers.

She did not turn from the window.

"Charlie needs you now more than ever," she had said, invoking the name unfairly, since she knew he could never refuse Charlie anything.

"Charlie's dead," he had answered. She turned from the window to face him.

"And I'm alive," she said. In that moment, he glimpsed the hardness beneath the pose of humility, the chip of granite off the old block. In the way she stood, good athletic legs planted squarely, jaw jutted, the image of her father's portrait in the eighth-floor boardroom, Nick could glimpse both her determination and her frustration. But now no one stood between her and her rightful legacy. Surely, he thought, she had dreamed of standing one day in that spot. Charlie had simply been the means, the conduit, and Charlie had cracked, the victim of genetic poisoning, or so he himself believed.

It was she who had handpicked Charlie years ago, moved perhaps by the same forces within her that she sometimes seemed to despise, her womanliness. To Charlie, his selection had been at first tantalizing, then burdensome, and finally destructive.

Now Nick sensed danger, as if he had suddenly been caught in a shark's scent. Watch out, he told himself. He could feel his breath catch as she came toward him.

"It's my right to be here and I mean to exercise that right," she said firmly, stopping before him, her hazel eyes moist. "We could be one helluva team, Nick. Accept me. Like you and Charlie."

He expelled his breath. The question in his mind was

how long she would need him. Was he simply to be gobbled up like some heavy ripe fruit, eaten to its core and digested?

But Nick had known all along that this day would come. He must learn to see her, understand her, stop viewing her from Charlie's poor vantage point. It was, after all, the price he would have to pay. He must find the key to knowing her, he thought, suddenly anguished again by Charlie's final betrayal, the gun in the mouth, the splattered remains that stained forever the oak panels in Mr. Parker's house, the legacy of his madness. He must learn to accept her, he cautioned himself. She was mistress of his present, his future.

"Charlie built the *Chronicle* out of the strength of my father's mind," Myra continued, as if she had practiced the words. "Out of abstractions. My father hungered for truth. For him, a banker, the printed word was the ultimate conveyance of truth. The power of the printed word was all. Charlie made it begin to happen."

There is truth in that, Nick thought. And he had helped Charlie to build from that beginning. There was credit due her, too, he reasoned, struggling, as always, to view her objectively rather than through Charlie's convoluted prism.

Charlie's first objective had been to make the *Chronicle* self-sustaining, to take it off old Parker's dole. That took fantastic skills, business acumen, horse sense.

"Nothing has to change," she said suddenly, rechanneling the direction of her thought, perhaps ashamed of her immodesty, as if she had shown a strip of soft white thigh. "You take care of the newspapering, just like you did for Charlie in the last days of his . . . his illness. I won't interfere."

"Is that a promise?" he said.

"We'll be a team," she said quickly, ignoring the question. "Nick, we can make the *Chronicle* the most important paper in the country."

"I leaned a lot on Charlie," he had said.

"And Charlie on you."

"I suppose."

"Lean on me, then, Nick. I'm a lot stronger than you might think."

He looked at the frail woman, remembering Charlie's hate. He had watched it grow, had seen its first frail sprouting in the soil of his anger, watched the first buds mature even before Mr. Parker had died, then saw the buds open, multiply, renew, an ugly stalk twisting itself around his friend's guts.

"God, I hate that woman," Charlie had confided to him as the martinis at lunch grew to three, then four, then beyond the counting. And finally Charlie was teetering on the edge of madness, a twilight world.

Once he had found him in a rat-infested walk-up in the heart of Washington's black ghetto. Charlie was lying naked on a filthy, stained mattress in a vile, urine-smelling room lit by a bare bulb, a large booze-bloated woman sprawled next to him in her own alcoholic stupor.

"Take a picture, Nick baby. I want to send it to Myra; a Christmas card."

He had taken the picture in his mind, all right; then, disgusted by the stink in his nostrils, inhaled cautiously as he hauled Charlie from the bed, dressed him, and dragged his dazed body to a waiting taxi. It had not been the first time, or the last, that he had played rescue squad for Charlie in that two-year descent.

The scene and Charlie's words bubbled upward through his memory. From what poisoned stream had come such a deep well of hate, he wondered? Had he missed something about Myra?

"I'm not going anywhere, Myra," Nick said, knowing that he was trapped, like a fly caught in the ink rollers of the great presses.

Her thin hand reached out for his, white and lightly speckled with freckles. Her hair was reddish blonde, but she was letting the grey poke through now, the silver strands somehow belligerent in their glistening validation of age.

Am I surrendering anything? he remembered asking himself as his hand groped out to meet hers, feeling its coolness. He was embarrassed by the sweatiness in his own palms.

"We'll take it from here," Myra said, grabbing his upper arm as well, squeezing it, then releasing it and walking briskly behind her desk.

"We'll work it out, Myra." He wondered if his words were symbols of his impotence, the collective pronoun a sign of weakness. Was he fawning? He became suspicious of his own motives. She was, after all, the boss, he reasoned. He'd simply have to find the strategy to cope with her. If only Charlie's hate had not warped his view.

"I'll keep my promise," Myra said, sensing his thoughts. "I'm not going to throw any monkey wrenches into the works. We'll set policy together. If we have differences we'll use persuasion on each other. No Horatius at the bridge stuff around here."

"I have only one condition," he said, wondering if he sounded courageous.

"Shoot," she said quickly, the enduring shadow of Charlie falling over her chair.

"It's got to be just you and me. No layers of executives in between. No third parties. No bureaucratic bullshit. The always open door."

"Done," she shot back without hesitation. He wondered if she realized what he had meant. It was one thing to have observed the power and influence of the *Chronicle* from the outside and quite another to see it from the inside. Could he explain to her what it meant to be a sculptor fashioning form from raw clay, a painter, palette in hand before the empty canvas? It was like being God. How long would it take her to find that out? Or did she already know?

2

It was not uncommon for a sliver of memory to intrude at odd moments, even now, while he was rereading the editorials for tomorrow's paper. He had edited them brutally, much to Bonville's disgust. Although he sensed that he had been right, the tension over what he had recently observed happening to Myra was making him act erratically. The understandable elation of victory, he had thought at first, a kind of giddiness. After all, they *had* toppled a corrupt President, made him resign, as if his act were an extension of their will. But that was two years ago, and for Myra the euphoria had persisted.

"If we can break, we can also make," she had said repeatedly, although Nick had ignored it. Perhaps it was the environment in which the sentence was uttered again yesterday as they lunched in Myra's office, a tiny dart, projected with a glass of milk in midair. Again he had tried to ignore it, discovering at that moment that it was no longer idle fantasy.

"Let's not get carried away. We can help shape. But you cross a Rubicon when you think you can 'make.'

Shades of William Randolph Hearst. . . . He tried to make himself president . . . he tried to make his girl friend a big star."

"I don't want to compromise principles. I want to help underpin them."

"Hey, Myra," he had said, "sober up." He had wanted to say something about Napoleon getting bogged down in Russian winters, to treat it lightly. Hell, he had felt the same way at times. But he had ignored it and it did not dissipate. It was, in fact, growing stronger in her mind.

That morning she had handed him a list. His eye quickly caught the categorization; all prospects for the grand prize, the presidency. He looked over the list and tried to look thoughtful.

"Who do you think?"

"Too early to take bets." He was determined not to appear to take her seriously, not on this score.

"Think about it. Who stands for what we believe?"

He tried to deflect her thoughts, looking at his watch.

"I'll be late for the editorial conference."

"We'll talk later then," she said.

"Sure, later."

He knew that the tension would make him irritable, would hamper his clarity. Bonville, the least perceptive of the five men in the early morning editorial conference, had ignored his mood. The others had sensed it and backed away from a confrontation on any subject.

"I'd like to embellish my original piece on the defense budget," Bonville said as they poked through an agenda of lead editorial possibilities. Bonville had a hunched, sunken look. He was pale, unhealthy-looking, with an affected way of holding a cigarette, the lighted end thrust upward even when he puffed on it. High cheekbones with eyes inset, skull-like, made him look ascetic, an image he seemed to cultivate, along with the established legend that he was the *Chronicle*'s resident radical intellectual.

"How so?" Nick had asked. He watched Peterson,

his ruddy cheeks palpitating near the jawbone, light blond lashes blinking in nervous warning.

"It seems the moment for sharper attack. Tomorrow, hearings begin and the Defense Secretary testifies. I think he should know we have honed our stiletto. The initial thrust." He paused and looked into Nick's face with a slightly contemptuous sneer. Bonville saw people only as wafer-thin playing cards. Nick supposed he himself was the ace of spades in the Bonville deck. "I think we should come out for a fifty percent across-the-board defense cut."

"You're not serious?" Nick asked.

"Deadly," Bonville quickly replied, pausing and turning now to his colleagues around the high-glossed table, neatly ringed with coffee cups and yellow legal pads.

Nick felt the slight tremor of his lower lip, a signal that anger was stirring. Peterson had noticed. Nick searched Henry Landau's face, stained deep tan by a southern sun. Landau's eyes broke first as he scribbled on the pad. It was his first day back after a month's vacation. He was being cautious.

Landau was his own handpicked managing editor, as Nick had been Charlie's. He had been placed into the empty slot, as Nick had inserted everyone; an extension of his own intelligence, a note on the keyboard. He had been brought in from the competing paper five years before.

Nick had sought talent and perception, guarding against emotional commitment, the thing that he had had with Charlie. Landau was a gamble, a roll of the dice. "I need clarity, intelligence, vision," he had told Landau, hoping that the unspecified requirement of emotional distance would be, somehow, grasped. He had hinted at loyalty as essential.

"I won't be a flunky, Nick," Landau had said in interviews that had gone on for weeks.

"Do you know how to lose gracefully?" Nick had asked.

"Yes," Landau had said cautiously, after a long pause. "The same way I take my victories."

Nick had liked that, and the chemistry had worked better for his self-imposed distance.

"For once, just once," Bonville continued, "let those bastards come in and justify every last nickel of the taxpayers' money. Not just cosmetics this time. Let them prove the cost of every lousy little bullet, every god-damned G.I.-issue condom. It's one thing to criticize like gentlemen. I think we need a much more finite weapon. I think that the *Chronicle*'s asking for a fifty percent cut, *fifty percent,* would put them on their mettle." He looked around him, searching for reactions among the cards. Perhaps, in his own odd method of perceiving, he saw something affirmative. He continued.

"I think we've been too bland. Biteless. We have wasted our national sustenance on adult toys, not to mention the blood of our young men. No, I don't be-lieve that fifty percent is the practical end result in this fiscal year, although I personally believe it to be correct. But the *Chronicle*'s demand of fifty percent would be enough to send them back to the cutting room." He held a black pencil in the air, made a circle, then speared it through its center, a dramatic flourish, signifying finality.

"I think we should attack the defense budget," Nick said evenly, remembering that the assemblage was not a democratic forum, purely advisory to him, "but asking for a fifty percent cut—there's an air of fantasy about it."

"It *is* a bit much," Peterson said, his ruddiness deep-ening. "Frankly, I can't see why we have to be so specific."

"Clear, specific stands," Bonville said, almost in mimicry.

Nick had always insisted on the clarity of specifica-tion. "We don't make abstract charges," he said again now. "We don't bury malicious hints. We don't make unspecific recommendations, unless we clearly label our own ignorance at solutions." Nick had made it a litany. It was amazing how many times it had to be reiterated, repeated, burned into the human brain. He hardly dared to blink his eyes, fearing the betrayal, the ignoring of his caveats.

Peterson had looked at Nick with some slight loss of aplomb, then quickly recovering, he said: "Percentages seem so abstract. Why not simply urge cutting off specific programs?"

"That leaves us vulnerable to attack by the war games buffs," Bonville pressed. "The military science boys. That's just it, the damned war business is not a science at all. For every tactic, there are five opinions on its use. For every strategic scenario, a thousand variations. I don't want to tell the gentlemen of the Pentagon how to play their hopscotch, I'm only interested in the conceptual, the broad picture, the essential stupidity of bleeding our resources in obsolete causes and egocentric internal empire building and bureaucratic bullshit."

You fucking eloquent bastard, Nick thought, the anger finally hissing through the containing membrane. He saw Landau's eyes smiling at him in agreement.

"Bonnie," Nick flashed, his jaws tight, "every time I hear your rhetoric I give special thanks to God for inventing erasers on pencils. You take a perfectly legitimate policy, the holding down of the defense budget within reason—reason, Bonnie!—manageable limits!— enemies do exist, you know, they really do—you take our policy, twist it, exaggerate it, then vomit all over it. Now go back to your cell and write the editorial and if I see one fucking overstep, I'll kick your ass to here and sundown."

He could see Landau looking down at the yellow pad, embarrassed. Peterson flushed and Bonville simply stared in haughty outrage.

Nick was annoyed by his sudden tantrum. Such an outburst was stupid and unnecessary. Ordinarily, handling Bonville was a game, a stretching exercise. He had appointed him to the editorial committee under Peterson because he wanted the outer edges of the Left doctrine to be heard. He had deliberately sought out Bonville, welcoming his sometimes ridiculous intellectual posturing.

"Bonnie," Nick said, seeking to placate the stunned and pouting Bonville, "easy on the acid." He smiled, knowing that the attempt at lightness simply hung in the air like pollution. They passed quickly to other editorial matters.

After the meeting, he followed Landau to his adjoining office.

"I flipped, right?" Nick asked. Landau slipped behind his desk, looking at him through calm brown eyes.

"You missed me," he said, the tanned skin crinkling on his forehead.

"It was a lousy trick to leave me to those jackals. Did you rest up?"

"Fit as a fiddle and ready for love. You look as if you could use a rest, Nick."

How could he explain the necessity of standing guard?

"I've spent the time busting egos. Everybody around here is becoming a hot dog. They all want to write books now."

"It's your monster. Remember, I opposed setting up Wentworth's operation."

Wentworth had been hired as an in-house literary agent in the aftermath of their ultimate victory, the unseating of the hated President.

"I still say it's better to control it from the inside."

"We're a newspaper, not a glory factory. I can smell a book germinating in Bonville."

"It's not germinating. It's hatched."

"You're encouraging their egocentricity, Nick. It's only going to make it tougher on us."

He wanted to explain about Myra, the subtle beginnings of change in her, but he held back.

"You play catch-up. I'll see you later," Nick said.

Back in his office, he started to thumb through the New York *Times,* casting his eye for possible follow-ups, briefly noting how they treated aspects of the news. He found it difficult to concentrate. Things seemed vaguely awry, a distorted image, a modality changed.

Was Myra meddling with the *Chronicle*'s calibration? Making, not breaking. He had himself set the dials, as Charlie had done, years before. Had he really found the balance between power and responsibility? Was Myra suddenly beginning to tamper with the settings?

He tossed away the *Times* and looked over the front page of that morning's *Chronicle,* carefully studying the headlines, then swiftly reading every word. Was their point of view subtly expressed? Were the sentences tight, the words clear, the information accurate? It was, after all, the measure of himself, the manner in which he perceived the world, its humanity and justice; its fairness and outrage; its honor and decency. It was he who had constructed the frame, and while there was great latitude in scribbling on the canvas, the frame was still the frame, quite finite. Let them scribble. Let the ink run. Let the passions roar. Let them write their reviews, express their by-lined opinions, rail away at gods and demigods, but never, *never* could a single errant scrawl go beyond the frame, his frame.

Looking up, he saw a blonde young woman standing in his doorway, a long thin finger raised, like a school-girl asking to leave the room. Beyond her he could see that Miss Baumgartner's desk was empty and that the girl, Martha Gates, had taken the opportunity to get his attention. She had been hired a year before, in the second wave of a staff protest urging more women on board. Nick had responded to keep the peace, although his private revenge for the pressure was to pick the most attractive of the bunch that flooded in on him.

Martha Gates was tall, slim-hipped, with long shiny blonde hair parted in the middle and resting lightly on her shoulders, a picture of madonna innocence, but she had proven herself a damned good reporter.

"Got a minute, Mr. Gold?" she asked sweetly, showing even polished teeth.

"Make it quick," he snapped.

"I've stumbled onto a yarn that's rather sensitive," she said, stepping haltingly deeper into his office. He was certain she knew she was violating the traditional chain of command.

"Apparently the First Lady's assistant, a Mrs. Ryan, is on the take of a foreign lobbyist, a Mr. Kee. It's not that she's in a sensitive spot, but it looks like a clear violation of the White House code of ethics. It seems that Kee and the Ryans have gone on trips together and my informant tells me the trip was paid for in cash by Kee's girl friend."

"Who is the informant?" Nick asked.

"I have this friend who works for Pan American. She's the one that made out the tickets. It's all a coincidence, really. Washington's such a small town. And she has a friend in Puerto Rico at the hotel where they stopped. Actually, it was all so blatant."

The fools, Nick thought. The arrogance of power and position. It was Washington's most rampant disease. Didn't they ever learn?

"I want to do this one myself, Mr. Gold," she said, obviously fearful that the assignment might be given to someone with more rank. He understood.

"All right, Martha."

"I can't tell you how much this means to me, Mr. Gold."

"I'll tell Madison that I've put you on it."

"Will he be angry that I went over his head?"

"I'll square it," he said. She became misty-eyed with gratefulness. "Just check it out. Don't go ape-shit without checking with me."

"Thank you again, Mr. Gold," she said, straightening and going out the door, nearly stumbling over the returning Miss Baumgartner. He watched her approach, the confident stride, the still trim figure of the mid-fifty woman whose sense of importance is not subject to dispute. She wore harlequin glass frames on a beaded security string hanging from either ear beneath her blue-grey hair. He wondered if she knew how it dated her, like his own sleeveless undershirts. In her arms she held the heavy folders of the daily mail.

"The natives are restless today, Mr. Gold," she said,

standing over him, her even, false teeth, too greyish in cast, lined in a tight smile. It was a quirk, he admitted to himself, a comparatively recent aberration, to glance through the hate mail. He couldn't quite understand himself whether it was flagellation, paranoia, or simple curiosity. After years of ignoring these letters he had chosen to see them as part of his regular morning fare.

"They're obscene and meaningless," Miss Baumgartner had protested, "and a waste of time." There was a slight pedantry in Miss Baumgartner's speech.

"Just curiosity," he had answered. Was it somehow a way to escape the sense of isolation, the glass cage? Or to confirm a vague sense of guilt?

He opened the folder and glanced through the heavy pile. The letters had all been opened and stapled neatly to their envelopes.

"Don't forget lunch with Mrs. Pell," Miss Baumgartner reminded him.

"Oh?" He looked up at her. Had he forgotten? "Anyone else coming?"

"She didn't say."

Another blip on the screen. It was not Myra's method to set a date through secretaries. He let it pass, looking over the letters. He picked one from the pile and held it out, reading quickly to himself.

"Commie Bastard," read the salutation. "You fucking Jew Nigger Cunts with your giveaway liberal shit words better keep your assholes tight. Because we real Americans are just waiting for the chance to get you. We watch you all the time, you prick-faced Russian spy fuck. And one night when you least expect, we're gonna get you and strip you and stick a poker straight up your ass until we fry your gut." It was signed "Spirit of '76." He chuckled to himself and shook his head. Wouldn't know if I was doing the job if old Spirit here didn't respond. "Spirit" was a recurrent correspondent, a regular, always the same half-printed scrawl on the same blue-lined cheap paper torn out of a child's notebook. The postmark was always from some different spot in the area, vaguely circular geographically, as if the correspondent had deliberately devised some special method of posting. He put it back on the pile and thumbed through the letters again. He glanced through the first paragraph of another letter, neatly typed.

"Dear Mr. Gold: In the name of Jesus why are you deliberately wrecking the values of country, patriotism, chastity, simple goodness. All we read is bleeding heart dribble favoring niggers. May God have mercy on your soul."

The themes rarely varied. There were piles of postcards, envelopes of all types and sizes. He estimated about seventy-five in the pile, calculating that the yearly haul might be four thousand. Once he had assigned a story on the hate mail of the President. He was careful to urge the differentiation between simple protest, however angry, and pure hate. He remembered being disappointed in the totals; the President's was running ten times heavier than his. Must be doing something wrong, he had told himself.

When he had completed the file—the process lasted less than ten minutes—he thumbed through his regular mail, became quickly bored, and looked out into the city room. A finger went up, perceptible only to him, like a signal in an auction. It was Ben Madison, the Metropolitan editor. Nick waved him in, convinced that they had devised some odd system of telepathy. Like with Jennie. He could always tell when Jennie moved through the city room, however distant from his glass. He could actually feel her presence and, looking up, he knew in advance that she was somehow there, or had been there, just brushing past on her way through. Perhaps she had looked toward him briefly, barely enough to charge the air.

"You were in the city room today," he had always told her later, when they were alone.

"How did you know?"

"I felt it."

Madison lumbered into the office, a big man with huge feet and big ham hands. His face seemed larded, the features thick, but the eyes clear and serious.

"It's Gunderstein. He's pressing away on the CIA story. He wants to meet on it again today."

"Ben. You know, and I know. Two sources of confirmation!"

"He says it's unimpeachable."

"That's not enough."

"Just meet with him once more."

"No, Ben."

"He's driving me crazy," Madison said.

"Why can't he just rest on his laurels? What is this compulsion of his to look under every rock?"

"Just meet with him one more time," Madison urged.

"Not until he can show me two sources." He held up two fingers. "Two."

"It's one helluva yarn."

"Without two sources, it's fiction as far as I'm concerned."

It was, of course, intriguing. Not merely that the spooks were involved in foreign assassinations—that seemed common knowledge—but that Senator Burton Henderson, the great liberal, front-runner for the presidential nomination of his party, was involved.

"Not *Henderson!*" he had exclaimed when Gunderstein had first broached the story to him a few days ago. "In the first place he's a liberal, and no one who ever came out of the spook factory could lay claim to that."

"He was an NSA spook, assigned, attached, or whatever, to the CIA covert operation in Viet Nam in 1963," Gunderstein had answered. The reporter was thin with a pale, sickly complexion, marred by pimples, which further embellished his sloppy appearance.

"My source says that there is reason to believe that Henderson was an essential part of the Diem assassination. It was he who arranged the rendezvous with the killers after the Ngu brothers were given safe-conduct. There is also the allegation that the order was given to him directly by the Kennedy brothers."

"Your source has a great imagination," Nick said.

"I'm convinced it's correct."

"Then confirm it."

"I've been trying."

"Heavy stuff," Nick said. "It would, as the spooks say, blow Henderson's cover. Maybe destroy him politically."

Gunderstein did not respond. This was not his province. His interest was never in consequences, Nick knew, only in the story itself.

"I'd say it was worth pursuit, but don't give me copy. Not now," he had told Gunderstein, dismissing him, watching as his unkempt figure—the hair long and matted, clothes wrinkled, shoes scruffy—slumped out of the office.

Watching Madison now, Nick thought of Henderson's name on Myra's list. He rubbed his chin and looked thoughtfully at Madison.

"We've whipped that CIA beast pretty hard," Nick said.

"It's got a certain fascination, you'll have to admit."

"They argue that if we push too hard we'll be naked to our enemies."

"They're probably right," Madison said, revealing his bias.

"It's their line, Ben. Like a private domino theory."

Lines, he thought. Everyone had a line.

"It's worth pursuing," Madison said cautiously, his eyes watery in their wrinkled chicken-skin pouches. "Besides, the two-source system is tough to pin down in dealing with the CIA. Two disconnected informers are almost impossible to find. They protect each other. And, of course, Henderson emphatically denies any involvement."

"What would you do? His guts are on the line." That word again, he thought. "A revelation like that will blow his constituency. Imagine a liberal candidate with a past like that."

"Yeah," Madison said. "Wouldn't it be lovely?"

"You don't like the man, do you, Ben?"

"I have no feelings one way or the other. Except"—

he paused for a moment, biting his lip—"except that we should leave his politics aside."

"You mean that we should overlook the fact that he's a liberal, don't you, Ben?"

"It shouldn't inhibit our pursuit of the story."

"Do you think it has?"

"I didn't say that, Nick."

"Hey, Ben. We've been together too long."

"Well goddamnit, Nick. We went hammer and tongs after the President. What makes this Henderson any better?"

"We proved our case against the President."

"Well then, let's prove one against this Henderson son-of-a-bitch."

"Because he's a liberal?" Nick asked.

"At least let's not protect him because he is."

"And you actually think this, Ben?" He felt his temper rise. Was he being baited?

"What's good for the goose . . ."

Nick watched the older man flush. Perhaps he was prejudging.

"Okay, Ben, I'll see Gunderstein," he said reluctantly, his eyes lowering to papers on his desk, an act of dismissal. He heard Ben's grunt as he rose from the chair, then walked out of the room without a word. The intercom jiggled on his desk. He pressed a button.

"Delaney," Miss Baumgartner said smoothly. Delaney was the advertising director, the traditional enemy of the editor. Nick enjoyed the perpetual slugfest, the dog-and-cat barkings and clawings. Delaney was exquisitely uninsultable.

"Did you see Carson's review?" Carson was their movie reviewer, nemesis of the producers, acidic and cantankerous, a roaring faggot.

"The theater owners are on my back, Nick. It's the same old story. They threaten to pull their ads out. I have to kiss their asses. It takes time out of my day. If only Carson could offer praise, just once."

"He calls it as he sees it," Nick said, smiling.

"Who knows what that queer sees? Nothing is ever

good. That's not being a reviewer. All they want is occasional praise."

"Carson thinks most of their stuff is shit."

"What does Carson know?"

"We need an arbiter of good taste around here," Nick said, suppressing a chuckle.

"Nick, you're making me vomit. They dump twenty million in lineage in our paper. I'm not tampering with editorial policy. Who gives a shit about the goddamned flicks? I never go. Just tone the fucking fag down. Read today's review. He called Katharine Hepburn an 'over-exploited palsied mummy, a flickering traffic light with two burnt-out expressions: stop and go.' I mean Katharine Hepburn. Nothing is sacred anymore."

"You're too crass," Nick baited, waiting for the predictable explosion.

"Crass? God, how I hate to deal with people who hate money. How can I ever explain to you that editorial copy is just filler, just filler? You guys downstairs are the worst hypocrites. What am I supposed to tell the theater owners?"

"Tell them to pull out and go to the competition." It was the ultimate red flag.

"Goddamnit, Nick. We've got no competition." It was a reflex, a Pavlovian response. He could feel Delaney's long sigh hiss through the line. "It's like talking into a cloud."

"Just tell them I'm an irascible martinet."

"A what?"

"Reading those ads has addled your brains."

"I told them I'd get this kind of shit from you. I told them."

"Well then, your conscience is clear."

"Bug off," Delaney said, hanging up abruptly. Nick chuckled. He knew he had satisfied Delaney's strange code of honor. He'd promised the theater owners he would raise hell, and he had satisfied his conscience. He could almost hear his response.

"I called the cocksucker. He's a stonewall, a hard-nosed bastard. Who reads the reviews anyway?"

It was a game they played, a vaudeville routine. It was always refreshing to think up new scenarios, different variations. Nick also kept in reserve the ultimate squelcher, to be invoked only when Delaney threatened to breach the wall, usually around annual budget time, when they poked into the profit figures.

"All I ask is for cooperation," Delaney would plead in the boardroom, before Myra and the business brass, the ledger boys. "Just bend a little bit. Don't throw that integrity dung in my face." He might have said "shit" if Myra weren't present, a clue to a strict Catholic upbringing, if any were needed beyond the aged choirboy look, the drink-dappled thin Irish skin.

"Christ, Delaney," Nick would reply. "We bent so hard on cigarettes we lost ourselves up our own tush." Delaney would turn scarlet. The *Chronicle* had attacked cigarette smoking, and urged the Congress to ban it from the airwaves. "If we had real integrity, we wouldn't accept cigarette ads, foisting disease on our readers. I lose sleep over that one."

"It's perfectly legal," Delaney would mumble with humility. "Twenty-five million dollars in revenues. Anybody ready to write that off?" There was silence in the room as lips smiled thinly around the table. It was, after all, hypocrisy, even though most of them still smoked cigarettes. But Delaney, the wind kicked out of his sails, would always retreat.

"Caveat emptor," he said to himself, as Delaney's voice clicked off the intercom. The fact was that the *Chronicle* was the only ball game in town. The afternoon paper was in serious decline. It was only a question of time before Washington would be a one-paper town.

Looking into the city room again, he watched Gunderstein working at his cluttered desk. His book on investigative reporting of presidential corruption had made him a celebrity. Now the list of authors on the staff of the *Chronicle* was growing like crabgrass. They must all be talking in terms of sales figures, grosses, royalty splits, movie rights. He waved Gunderstein into his office. Gunderstein advanced, shoes unshined, food stains on his tie.

"My God, you're a slob," Nick said. "Albeit a rich one." Gunderstein smiled shyly. He was almost too boyish to be taken seriously, although he had proven his lethalness. An army of hard-eyed men quaked when his name was mentioned. Some rotted in jail and cursed him.

"It's this Henderson-CIA thing, Mr. Gold. I know I've got something here worth telling." He stood above Nick's desk nervously picking at his pimples.

"If you've got the goods, then why not two sources?"

"I think my one source is enough to start the ball rolling."

"You know spooks that talk. The chances are there is no documentation. They're specialists. They burn evidence. You can't destroy a man on hearsay." He paused. "And there will not be any tapes."

"My man was Henderson's tie with CIA when Henderson was an NSA colonel on special recall duty in Viet Nam. He swears that Henderson was the man responsible for engineering Diem's assassination, on direct orders from the White House."

"It's still a single source."

"But compelling," Gunderstein added quickly.

"It's not the first time it's been alleged. But they've always denied that. Three presidents have denied it. Hunt admitted forging documents indicating that Kennedy had ordered it. That should be enough to finish that allegation," Nick said.

"That's the way they operate. Things are never as they appear. There would have been no document. Hunt could have been trying to authenticate what he knew to be true—that Kennedy did order Diem's death. You know how they would do it—leave themselves plausible denial."

"So there would be no proof."

"If there was, why would Hunt try to create it? Even the Pentagon Papers were vague on the point."

"Then how are you expected to find your sources? Especially if there are no documents, no tapes."

Gunderstein smiled shyly at the reference. "There have got to be others around to corroborate it."

"What you're asking is that we go fishing. Harold, you're a bloodthirsty bastard."

"There's lots of circumstantial evidence," Gunderstein said, ignoring the implication, "and Kennedy was assassinated three weeks later."

"Christ, Gunderstein, your implications give me the creeps."

"Well, you've got to admit it does give the story some added flavor."

"Pure fantasy. Mythmaking. And with just one source—irresponsible," Nick said.

"If you'd just let me run a story speculating . . ."

"You know I can't do that," Nick said. Then he thought a moment, his interest rising. "Will your"—he smiled—"your connection, allow us to quote him?"

"No."

"Why?"

"He's scared. It's the paranoia of the business."

"Won't he point you to other sources?"

"He has, even to Henderson himself. They clam up or simply deny everything." Gunderstein fidgeted. "Look, Mr. Gold. I'll write the story delicately. Once they see it in print it'll flush them out."

Nick watched the young man coolly. He made it all sound so simple. But hadn't it all happened just that way before?

"You see, the CIA . . ." Gunderstein began.

"CIA, CIA," Nick exploded. "I get sick of hearing about it!" Gunderstein ignored the outburst, his brown eyes glistening. Was it Gunderstein he was angry about, his youth, his sureness?

"Good Lord, Harold," Nick continued, calming, "we've attacked that agency for years. We've beaten it over the head. Do you believe we should do away with the damned thing altogether?" Was he overreacting? Worse, did Gunderstein think he was overreacting?

"I don't think my private opinions have any bearing on the matter. It's a story."

Nick stood up, hoping somehow that the act of rising would signal an element of intimidation. The young man continued to pick at his pimples and eye him suspiciously, he thought.

"I decide that," Nick said.

"I know that, Mr. Gold."

Nick sat down again. His gaze roamed over the desk searching for his cigarettes. Without offering one to Gunderstein, he lit up and inhaled deeply, remembering suddenly the first time he had seen Gunderstein. When was it? Five, six years ago. Gunderstein had been a news aide—that damned euphemism for copy boy! Hadn't he worn glasses then, deepening the impression of self-possession, an inert mind? He looked up. The thin abstracted face had fleshed out slightly. Somebody had said he had bought contact lenses. He had always been losing his glasses. When the President had resigned he had become a kind of folk hero. His first stories had broken the scandal wide open. Even the success of the book, the story of corruption and cover-up in the highest place in the government, had left him outwardly unchanged despite his sudden wealth.

"Nothing fazes Gunderstein," Madison had said once. "If a horse pissed on his head, he'd simply flick away the moisture and continue what he was doing."

"I'm sorry, kid," Nick said. "It's just that the source is still too flimsy." Or was it that he couldn't find in himself the same visceral hatred that he had felt toward the President? That, after all, was a labor of love. But this! Henderson was "their boy."

"Keep digging," he added.

Gunderstein shrugged. "I know that the story is responsible. I feel it."

"I'm just not convinced. Not yet." There! He had left the door open. Gunderstein turned and moved away. He could feel his discouragement.

"Harold," he called before Gunderstein's hand reached the door handle. Gunderstein turned. "What do you think of Henderson?" Nick asked gently. Henderson's square features came into focus in his mind.

"I like him," the young man stammered. Perhaps it was the intonation. He recalled a similar phrase from a buried time; a sliver of memory. Nick watched him shut the door and walk toward his desk, a trifle hunched. His eye caught Madison turning instinctively, reading Gunderstein's face. Scowling, he turned and went back to his work.

Nick puffed deeply on the cigarette and punched it out half-smoked in the ashtray. For a moment he looked down at the mangled butt, the tobacco oozing like sawdust from a stuffed toy. It was the sawdust on the floor of Shanley's on East Forty-first Street, across from the New York *News* building, that gave the errant, half-remembered phrase another human environment.

3

"I like him," McCarthy had said, the shot glass dribbling brown Scotch as he brought it to his thin lips and tossed it between bad teeth, down the greedy Irish gullet. They had watched, Charlie and Nick, in a darkened corner of the bar, as the red-faced Police Chief and their managing editor parleyed in a kind of tribal ritual, a bottle of Scotch between them on the table, pouring out shots in turn and tossing them back into their throats, like medicine. Occasionally a roar of laughter punctuated their whispered conversation. It was nearly three A.M. Most of the regulars had already departed, and the bartender, his apron tucked beneath his armpits in the old-fashioned way, was stained with the day's leavings. Even now in the recollection Nick could smell the beeriness—the malt had soaked into the wooden bar—and feel the tension as they looked into the dissipating foam floating on the tops of the amber fluid.

He had still been wearing his G.I. shorts, the kind with three buttons in front and the baggy ass. And he wore the ruptured duck on his lapel. Charlie had promised, in that bone-chilling hopelessness of a Bastogne night, to help land Nick a job on the *News,* where he had worked for three years before the war. Promises made in the face of death and cold were not taken lightly by young men in those days.

For months Charlie had regaled Nick with stories of the *News,* known then as a scandal sheet. Hell, page 3 was a cornucopia of what passed for pornography in those days. Remember the trial of Errol Flynn, the horny son of a bitch? Throughout the muddy hegira through France, the *News* subscription had followed Charlie. Most of the time it arrived torn and when winter came it was sometimes too frozen to unfold. Charlie always looked at the by-lines first.

"Harry Gerritty, that son-of-a-bitch 4F. They've made the cocksucker a rewrite man. I'll kick his ass when I see him." It was only then, after he had reeled off the by-lines, carefully explaining the cast of characters, that he would begin to study the stories.

"They write tight. Listen to this. . . . It's beautiful," and he would read off a story as if it might have been a poem.

Occasionally when they were lucky to find a warm billet with a crackling fire in a miraculously spared French farmhouse, Charlie would talk with feeling about the people at the *News.* They could hear the boom of artillery in the distance.

"Imagine a paper run by a bunch of drunken Irishmen. It was as if they were all deliberately trying to ape those characters in the Hecht-MacArthur play. Some of them still wore hats in the office. Hats! Like in the movies. With press cards in their hatbands. And they still had spittoons around the city room, filled with real spit. And the managing editor, Francis X. McCarthy . . . you couldn't take a shit in New York without him knowing about it. Once Legs Diamond had him kidnapped because he had been pressing the mob too hard. It was said to be the only time in history that a gangster had taken something personally that appeared in print. Old Francis X. had questioned Legs' courage.

It was back in the thirties and the story goes that Francis X. told him to take a flying shit for himself, right there in captivity, in the face of being planted in cement boots. They'd lay the undesirables in a cement tub and throw them in the East River. Now that's what I call a newspaperman."

It seemed natural for Nick to have gravitated toward Charlie in the "repo depo." Weren't they both newspapermen? Nick had been editor of the Ohio University paper and a stringer for the Athens *Gazette*.

"If we don't die tomorrow, I'll get you a job on the *News,* kid. So don't get your ass shot off." It was a gift from God to have found Charlie, Nick remembered thinking, and he was determined to keep alive in the meat grinder of the war. And, equally important, to help keep Charlie alive. Charlie was America's worst soldier, surely too tall and clumsy to survive. Nick was always reaching for his shoulder, pulling him down in a fire fight.

Once, when the Germans had them surrounded, they had been sent out on patrol and returned in the dark after being pinned down by a German patrol.

"Where's Pell?" the Sergeant had hissed when they made it back to their lines. Nick, who had assumed that Charlie was padding behind him in the snow, felt his heart jump. "Where the fuck is Charlie Pell?" It was a confusing time and not uncommon to shoot at the wrong army.

That had been the worst night of his life. He had cried like a baby, the tears freezing on his cheeks. But in the morning a tired Charlie had lumbered back to their lines, falling heavily in the foxhole beside the miserable, shivering Nick.

"Thought old Charlie got a Jerry bullet up his ass, eh kid?"

It had been one of his life's rare sweet moments, to see Charlie's stubbled chin and those glassy grey eyes. He remembered hugging him without shame and pressing his lips to his freezing cheeks.

"Don't worry, kid. You still got that job working,"

Charlie had joked. Even then Nick had sensed the bond between them, now still strong, beyond the grave.

He had kept his promise as Nick knew he would. Nick had gone back to Warren, Ohio, for a month to be with his mother and join in the deathwatch for his father, a doctor in the small town. He had arrived in the *News* city room with a swatch of black crepe still pinned to his lapel, below the shiny ruptured duck.

"Dad died," he had said.

"Tough stuff, kid."

"I did a lousy thing. I told him I wasn't going to med school, that I was going to be a newspaperman after all. He gave me his blessing. I think maybe that's why I hung around."

Charlie had taken him across the street to Shanley's to coach him on how to handle the interview with McCarthy.

"I went straight to the top. I told him you were with the Cleveland *News*. Turns out that McCarthy knew Higgins, the editor."

"Oh, shit."

"Don't worry. I got a rundown on Higgins. Got a good description. They were drinking buddies. When he asks you about him, just say: "That man puts away two fifths a day and is the best fucking newspaperman in Ohio."

"All he has to do is pick up the phone and check me out."

"He won't. You say it the way I've explained and he'll think you've known the man all your life."

Nick watched him standing in the corner of the bar, backlit by the red and green neon sign—tall, curly hair, short-cropped, big ears, a high nose with a little indentation near the ridge where the glasses he hated to wear pinched too tightly, smiling broadly with incredibly even teeth. He patted Nick on the back with a heavy paw. "You're in, kid."

"I'm scared to death."

"You're a reporter, kid. Just do the reporting. Let me handle the rewrite."

They walked back across Forty-first Street, past the loading pier lined with high-backed *News* trucks. Beyond the pier, Nick could see huge metal rollers.

"That's where the rag rolls off the presses. Two million of them a night."

They waited for the freight elevator in the musty corridor, heavy with what were then strange odors. Paper and ink. From that moment it attached itself forever to the hairs of his nostrils, as if a family of bacteria had migrated there for permanent settlement.

In the elevator, Charlie grabbed at Nick's tie, loosened it, and unbuttoned the collar.

"I'm just unstiffening you a bit." When he had mussed Nick's hair slightly, he stood back, an artist surveying the quick dabs on the canvas.

"Not perfect, but it will have to do."

As the elevator door opened into the city room, they got out and Charlie turned to face him again.

"One more thing, kid."

"What?"

"You're a Kerryman."

"A what?"

"A Kerryman."

"What the hell is that?"

"A county in Ireland."

"Kerryman?"

"No, Kerry. County Kerry, dummy. That's where your family is from."

"With a name like Gold? Worse still, my father told me it used to be Goldberg." Actually, he had had an Irish grandmother on his maternal side, northern Irish, he recalled, the hated Protestant Orange. He was an authentic American mishmash, his Semitic father had told him.

"Tell him it used to be Goldic, Gaelic. Get it?" He remembered his stomach had turned as he followed Charlie toward the managing editor's desk, planted imperiously at one end of the city room. His palms had begun to sweat.

"Don't worry. He thinks I'm Irish, too. For a High

Episcopalian, that's really grand fraud. I told him my middle name was Xavier, like his. I didn't know about the Kerry thing till later. Besides, I drink Irish. That's the ultimate identifying clue."

Whatever Nick's misgivings, he had followed Charlie's stage direction to the letter. The thing about Kerry was the clincher. McCarthy spent the first ten minutes of the interview tracing the history of George Higgins and his mammoth appetite for the grape, like an old school tie, the memory warming the older man's heart. From a corner of his eye, Nick could see Charlie peering over his typewriter, tense with expectation.

"Kerry, you say." Nick had, as agreed, injected the subtlety. McCarthy did not notice Nick's bobbing, nervous Adam's apple, or question the Goldic blarney. But there was one moment of panic as McCarthy looked into him with pale blue bloodshot eyes, then shifted suddenly beyond his head to a big wall clock.

"Boy!" McCarthy boomed and a copy boy came running obsequiously. He opened a desk drawer and peeked in swiftly, writing a word on a piece of copy paper and folding it. Nick saw the edge of a scratch sheet. The boy took the paper and hustled away.

"Kerry, you say," McCarthy repeated, the pale eyes turning inward to some embedded memory of the Emerald Isle. He imagined he could actually hear the hint of a brogue in McCarthy's speech cadence. Beyond the voice, the tempo in the city room seemed to accelerate. Typewriters clicked loudly. The cry of "Boy!" echoed in the big room.

"Never trust another Irishman," McCarthy said. "They're all black inside." Nick felt his heart palpitate in his chest.

"But that's what we must have in this business. Black Irish, and the Kerryman is the blackest, a cursed lot," McCarthy said, a heavy scent of booze rushing out with his sudden odd anger. "Stubborn. Tenacious. Vipers. The lot of 'em. We Corkmen hate them more than the devil." He paused. "But we need them, as we need the angels, witness to man's venom." He laughed suddenly, wrote out something on a piece of paper, then handed it to Nick.

"Bring this up to Personnel," he said, dismissing him, opening his drawer again to choose the horse for the next race.

"Like falling off a leprechaun's log," Charlie told him later at Shanley's, clinking glasses in a toast.

But two weeks later he had nearly blown the whole opportunity; and watching the beefy back of the Police Chief as it moved heavily in the chair, Nick saw in its bulk the impending termination of his budding career.

As low man on the totem of general assignment, they had him writing obits and fillers and interviewing an assortment of characters that floated into the city room, as if the paper were a court of last resort. Mostly they were forlorn, defeated remnants of the human chain seeking solace, vindication, or revenge. Or people who had lost something, a son, a daughter, a father, a mother, their pride, money; empty souls spewed up along the city beach. The *News,* a tabloid, written in tight, simple declarative sentences for the masses, had come to be known as the people's press, the literature of the little man. It could be digested in one 20-minute ride from Brooklyn to Manhattan and was the largest circulated paper in the United States.

"There are more of us than them," the city editor, O'Hara, told Nick not long after he had arrived, pointing to a New York *Times* lying like a tattered corpse in his wastebasket. As if to emphasize the lesson, he had spread a penciled cross through "Mr." in Nick's first obit.

"Even when a man dies, he's no 'mister' in this sheet. He doesn't get born 'mister' and he doesn't die 'mister.' " The admonishment seemed to Nick painful at the time, as if a man's dignity were somehow diminished by this final penciled act.

In two weeks he had seen more human misery walk into the anteroom, where a red-faced retired fireman acted as receptionist, than he had seen in the war. There, at least, death arrived with grim certainty. Here it seemed as though death waited in the wings while some mad manipulator injected weird forms of agony before a final demise.

"The woman out there knows who murdered Elwood Johnson," Nick told O'Hara on the first occasion of his being sent to interview one of these unfortunates.

"Who?"

"Elwood Johnson."

"Colored?"

"Yes."

"Ass," O'Hara hissed. He motioned to Donnelly, a grey-headed reporter lounging on the copy bench. "Explain it to old wet ears." Nick repeated the woman's story to Donnelly.

"Colored murders aren't news, kid. We get ten calls a night on those. Who cares?" Donnelly said sleepily.

"Elwood Johnson must have cared."

"We don't report Harlem murders. What's another dead shine?"

"You mean we don't report murders?"

"Oh, we're big on murders. We love murders. But colored murders are hardly news."

"Then what do I tell the woman?"

"Give her a nickel for the subway and tell her to go back to Harlem." Which he did, but not without shame. He got the same rebuff on people who wanted to find a missing relative or friend.

"People are always losing each other. It's not news unless it happens to someone important, a name you know. Like President Truman searching for a bastard son. We're a newspaper, dummy, not a damned catalog."

After the first week he hardened his stance, perfected the technique of the brush-off. Then one day a little Italian with a running nose walked into the anteroom. The city desk sent Nick out for the interview. Mucus was leaking onto the man's lip and his dark eyes kept darting from side to side. He was petrified with fright. In heavily accented English he explained that he had a fruit store on Twenty-first Street that had just been burned down. The man's fingers were encrusted with grime, chapped into frozen stumps from long cold mornings handling fruit.

"They burna my store because I see dem payoffa da cops."

"Who?"

"Da bookie." He looked at Nick as if wary of his youth.

"They take my fruita, too. I see dem taka da money froma da bookie, den dey taka da fruita."

"Who?"

"Da cops." The little man continued. "I tella dem, 'Taka da appla, or oranga. That'sa okay.' Buta dey taka away da bushela full. I say, 'Looka, I donna wanna no troubla.' Buta dey laugha. I say, 'Looka, you getta money froma da bookie, so paya me something. I gotta twelva kids.' Dey laugha. Luigi's justa dumb wop. I foola dem. I writa down da badge numbera. Here." He dipped his shattered hand into a tattered pocket of his stained pants and pulled out a scrap of brown paper bag. Nick smoothed the paper on his knees, looking at the long line of primitive numbers. He felt the man's frustration, his outrage.

"I say, 'You stopa taka da fruita or I tella.' One big cop, he coma and smasha da melons witha da club. I bega dem on da life of da virgin to stopa. Dey coma every day for a week and breaka upa da fruita." Nick felt the man's anger and his craving for justice. "I writa down da badge numbera," the little man repeated proudly. "Then dey burna me down."

"Why haven't you gone to the precinct to talk to the Captain?"

The Italian looked at him and snarled, "You crazy?" Nick felt foolish. He looked at the scrap of brown paper on his knees, finding a special meaning for himself, the power to redress a wrong. Perhaps this explained his compulsion to be a journalist; his belief in the power of the word, the inked word that brought truth and forced justice.

"You sit there," he told the little Italian, surprised

at the authority of his command. He walked back into the city room, and sitting down at a typewriter desk, slid the pulpy paper in the roller. The lead had etched itself into his mind fully composed before his fingers reached the keys.

"The promise of America died on the pyre of Luigi Petrucci's fruit store last night," the story began. Nick pondered the grey words, then ripped the paper out of the typewriter. Would they laugh at his passion? He put another paper in the typewriter, remembering the discipline of the newspaper's style.

"An immigrant Italian fruit merchant today accused the police of burning down his store.

"In an allegation, stemming from his observation of police pay-offs by bookmakers, Luigi Petrucci, whose store is located at 231 West 21st Street, claimed that he was threatened repeatedly by the police when he attempted to protect his produce from their greed." Nick knew *greed* was heavy, unacceptable, but he let it stand.

The story went on to mention the list of badge numbers and alluded to Luigi's fear of further reprisals. When he had finished, Nick put the story under the nose of Baldwin, one of the deskmen, who chuckled as he read it, then tossed it over to O'Hara. After a quick glance, O'Hara squinted over his glasses. Nick slouched on the copy bench, watching him, his arms folded belligerently over his chest. Deny that's news, he said to himself angrily. He heard O'Hara scream for a copy boy and watched the story make its way toward McCarthy's desk. Nick had slugged the story "Gold-Corruption" in the upper left-hand corner.

"Gold!" he heard McCarthy's voice boom. Something in its timbre frightened him; his stance of anger softened like ice melting in a midsummer sun. With a pounding heart he made his way to McCarthy's desk.

"Gold?" McCarthy looked at him as a butcher might observe a fly on a hindquarter.

"Yessir."

"You wrote this shit?"

"Yessir." Only it's not shit, he wanted to say, but couldn't find the courage, his throat constricting.

"You believe the guinea?"

"Yessir," Nick whispered.

McCarthy pondered the story a moment.

"The dumb wop," he said. Nick remembered Luigi's words. McCarthy reached for the phone at his side and dialed a number.

"Hello, you old bastard," he hissed into the phone, watching Nick as he spoke. He paused, absorbing a voice at the other end of the line. "Meet me at Shanley's. Yeah, about eleven." He hung up and pointed a finger at Gold. "You, too."

He had interpreted McCarthy's reaction as vindication. Walking back to the anteroom, he gripped Luigi's arm.

"You got lots of balls, Luigi," Nick told him. "We're going to do right by you."

The little man stood up, smiling.

"I know I comma to da righta place. You a gooda boy." He took Nick's hand. For a moment, Nick thought he was going to kiss it. Instead he held it awkwardly in his rough hands and shook it, tears welling in his eyes. Nick watched as he walked off, bowlegged in his baggy pants.

Later, in Shanley's, over their first beer, Nick told Charlie what had happened.

"You are unquestionably the dumbest asshole I have ever met," Charlie had exploded. "Do you really believe that he'll allow that story to see the light of print?"

Nick looked at his watch. The Bulldog would roll in less than half an hour.

"Yes," he said, firmly but hesitantly. Charlie drained his beer glass and wiped his lips with the back of his hand. "Now, dummy. Lesson one. That telephone was a direct line to the Police Chief. McCarthy is hooked in by private wire. Lesson two. Police corruption is a purely political matter. We don't go after the cops unless there is good political return for the paper. Lesson three. All, well almost all, New York cops are on the take. It's a way of life. It's hardly news in itself. Not to our readers."

McCarthy sat with the Police Chief at a table in the corner, their heads bowed together in intense conversation.

"I can't believe it," Nick said, looking at his watch. "You've got to be kidding. Paying off the police is corruption, pure, unvarnished, raw corruption. I can understand screening the news, but things like police corruption, Charlie, are just too blatant to suppress. I mean we're supposed to be the little man's friend."

"Jesus, don't lay that shit on me," Charlie said, motioning to the bartender for a refill. They both watched as the bartender pulled the tab lever and the amber brew foamed in the glasses. He jerked a thumb in the direction of McCarthy.

"Does that little scene look like an adversary relationship?" Charlie asked.

Nick watched the two men drinking together. Occasionally one of them would explode in laughter. His optimism waned.

"We didn't attack the whole force. Only the corruption of a few."

"The whole thing is corrupt, from top to bottom," Charlie said, downing his beer in a huge gulp.

"But we're the press, Charlie. We can keep them honest by telling the truth."

"The truth? What the hell is that?"

"The truth is"—Nick hesitated—"the truth." He pouted.

"The truth is whatever McCarthy decides."

"But he's only one man."

"He decides," Charlie said emphatically. "Don't assume that his truth is the same as yours."

"But in this case," Nick protested, "it's a clear-cut case of police persecution. The man was injured by the people paid to protect him."

"So?"

"It demands to be told. If you don't tell it, they'll continue to repeat the same damned thing."

"Who gives a shit about one lousy little greaseball?"

"I do, damn it."

"Stop bleeding all over the bar."

Nick felt his anger rising. Charlie seemed to sense it and softened.

"Try to see it from McCarthy's point of view," Charlie said. "He could run the story and embarrass the shit out of the Police Department. But he's a lot smarter than that. He'll just file it away, use it as collateral. Trade-off for a closer relationship with the Chief. Think of all the story leads we'll get, the inside dope. This damned rag comes out every day. Every damned day. What's one poor little guy against that? It's a trade-off."

"It's blackmail," Nick said. "And it's wrong."

"As for your Italian friend," Charlie said, brightening, "the Chief will bust the asses of those cops. But not for the reasons you think. They were stupid."

A nightside reporter came in for a quick shot. He carried the Bulldog under his arm. Nick slid it out from the crook in the man's arm and thumbed through it hurriedly, tearing the freshly inked pages in the process.

"Confirmed?" Charlie asked gently. Nick pushed the mangled paper toward the reporter.

"Confirmed," he nodded. "It just compounds the felony. It makes us all a part of it, accomplices."

"I suppose you're right there. But you'd better harden yourself, old buddy. You'll bleed to death early in this game if you let your sense of justice get in the way of your good sense."

"Never," Nick said quietly, holding down his agitation. "I hope to hell I never get like him." He jerked a thumb toward McCarthy.

"Don't be so hard on him," Charlie said after a long pause.

"God forbid it should ever happen to me," Nick said.

"Or me," Charlie whispered. "Just because I understand how it works doesn't mean I believe in it."

Nick felt the closeness to his friend.

"So you burn as well," he said.

"Yes, I burn too, kid."

When the Police Chief had lumbered off, his heavy, beefy face red with drink and the banked fires of humiliation, McCarthy turned watery, glazed eyes to them. He scowled as if suffering a twinge from a passing pain in his midsection. His lips rearranged themselves into a thin smile. It seemed a signal for Nick to come closer. Charlie followed and they sat down at the table.

"I like the man," McCarthy said, his lips like those of an elephant's trunk squirming toward the edge of the shot glass. The phrase seemed a hurled curse at his own frailty, as if his own humanness was something to be endured. Nick remembered that they had sat at the table for a long time saying nothing, until McCarthy's head, sodden with drink, finally dropped forward on the table.

4

Nick felt the rolled paper in his fingers. He had stripped the shattered cigarette in the ashtray and balled the paper into a dry spitball, as they had been taught to do in basic training. Flinging the little ball into his wastebasket, he mentally swung back into the habit of his day. A news aide put a pile of wire copy on his desk, the first trickle of dispatches from overseas, early stuff coming in from topsy-turvy time zones. He nodded toward the young man, neat and slim in a white starched shirt. He looked over Foster Tompkins' copy filed from India, Calcutta, the ultimate chaos of urbia, a city choking on its own human sewage.

India was back in the news again: a hot spot, inner restlessness increasing, guerrilla activity in embryo, turmoil with Pakistan. He read the dispatch with special care. It told of an interview with the guerrilla commander in a tiny, fly-infested restaurant, in the anonymous teem of the Calcutta netherworld. A picture focused in his mind as he read. The man, Tompkins, was a fine writer, the imagery accurate, the sentences

workmanlike and cadenced. If only the writing throughout the paper were consistently good. A misplaced
metaphor, after all these years, still jabbed him a painful blow. A dangling participle made his belly positively
acidic. Words! Sometimes he felt he was being pounded
by their avalanche, trapped in a dark corner with rocks
of words clunking around him, imprisoning him like the
man from "The Cask of Amontillado." Sometimes he
felt helpless, impotent, a carpenter with a toothless saw,
a clawless hammer.

Oddly, it was only when he read the good writing,
subtle rhythms that controlled the flow like canal locks,
that the pedestrian sentences of the others revealed their
pallor. He read the Tompkins piece and punched the
extension for Phillips, the World editor. The response
was hoarse, indifferent. Busy editors hated telephones
intruding on concentration.

"I thought Tompkins in fine form," Nick said.

"Class tells," Phillips replied. "I just read the piece."

Nick began to think about tomorrow's paper, the beginning. Conception!

At three they would all bring in the budget line, the
assistant managing editors, one for each department,
World, Metro, Sports, Business, Lifestyle, Entertainment, Photo. It was then that they thrashed out the
priorities, budgets in hand, with the day's allocation of
news, feeding on each other, ladling out the soup of the
day, to be poured into the *Chronicle* vat.

It was the moment of his day when suspense began,
absorbing his thoughts. He was already beginning to
cast about for news priorities, building the front page
in his mind from the grab bag of hard possibilities. It
came to him almost by instinct, a built-in sensor embedded in his journalist brain. He had long ago ceased
to bend with the weight of the responsibility. Years of
trusting his judgment had made a friend of it, a con-
fidant, and when it was activated, it cast aside all ex-
traneous elements.

As he worked he was conscious of the impending impact of his product. Millions of eyes were watching,

waiting, all over the world. In foreign, as well as domestic minds, friends and adversaries alike, the *Chronicle*'s words were weighed, the sentences dissected, the subtleties and nuances pondered, little cells of intelligence microscopically analyzed. The *Chronicle,* along with the *Times,* revealed the cutting edge of America's direction in that one pinpoint of time. The idea of it no longer left him humbled, awestruck. Somehow his mind had merged with the ink, a private knowledge. He wouldn't have dared to express it but he had often thought of it as a measure of immortality, his stamp on future generations, the yet unborn who would see it as enlarged pieces of microfilm in the world's archives. Often he would rail against his own flaws, the hodgepodge of personal emotions that threatened his judgment, the frailties that could be corrosive, perhaps the very same concerns that had ultimately destroyed Charlie. The telephone rang, recalling him.

"Lunchtime," Miss Baumgartner's cheery voice said, intruding.

Remembering, he wondered what Myra had in mind, his curiosity whetted again, a tug of uncertainty strained for attention. He got up, straightened his tie, and smoothed down his hair. He looked at a reflection of himself in the glass wall. Then, putting on his jacket, he passed through the door into the city room clamor which the glass room had partially deflected. As he walked toward the elevators, he caught a glimpse of of Gunderstein, his head pressed against the telephone, a gangling, ear-flapping bloodhound absorbed in the scent. Had he been fair with Gunderstein? Annoyed at his own questioning, he waited briefly for the elevator, nodding to others who waited, conscious of the nervousness his presence created.

As he waited, he was tempted to push off to the Lifestyle section, tucked away down a long corridor in what was once the old building. If Margaret weren't the editor, he reasoned, a simple excuse might cloud the transparency: the yearning for Jennie, a brief look at her. Even though Margaret carefully concealed the

ex-wife relationship with an attitude of tough professionalism, well deserved, he would see her accusing
contempt, a brief flicker in the eyes, an arched brow,
an uncommon movement of the head. They had lived
together for nearly ten years, an eternity, which sometimes seemed so brief. Some mornings he would awake
and sense her sleeping beside him in that curled way,
buried beneath the covers. It was not a longing, he conceded, just a brief memory of an old habit. She had,
after all, shared the years of his youth and their union
had produced Charmagne, troubled Chums, misplaced
in the generations.

"Don't call me a hippie, Dad, that's absurd, a decade
old," Chums had said to both of them.

"Well, what do you call it? You've left school. You're
rootless, unmotivated. God knows what garbage you're
putting into your system and, not that it matters, you're
worrying your mother and me to death." She was lying
on a bare mattress in a room in a big old San Francisco
house, a commune. "Even this whole scene is passé."

"Not to me," she said.

"There's no logic in it," he argued.

"There is to me. I see no logic in *your* life."

"I'm not being self-righteous, Chums," he said, softening. There was a twinge of guilt. I was a lousy father,
he thought. I loved a newspaper and old Charlie. But
hadn't he once loved her mother? Even when they had
told her she was a child of love it was too late to matter. Chums knew she was a victim. That was two years
ago, the last time he had seen her. He missed her. They
still accused themselves over it, if silently. It lay over
them like a cloud every time their eyes touched. And
he saw Margaret daily; at the three o'clock budget
meeting, other places in the office, around town.

Was it poetic justice for Jennie to have fallen from
the sky into the Lifestyle section? It was ludicrous for
a mistress to be working for an ex-wife. Margaret had
changed her name back to Domier, proud of the French
heritage, which "Gold" had obscured.

"Shit you say," Jennie had said, showing a stunned look by the revelation. "Your ex-wife?"

"None other." They were sitting at Sans Souci having a quiet dinner. He had put his glass down as if he had been overcareful to choose the right moment.

"You dumb bunny," she said, laughing. "That's the first thing they tell you. You think it's a secret?"

He didn't really, but he wanted her to hear it directly from him.

"Am I in for revenge, mental torture? She's bound to find out about us."

"If I know Margaret she already knows. It was too long ago to matter. We're actually almost friends again. She'll judge you professionally, though." He hesitated. He had, after all, been rewriting her copy before Margaret saw it.

"I'll get better, Nick, you'll see."

"Sure you will."

She pouted. He sensed that she was feeling uneasy about her dependence on him.

"I don't know what happens to me when I sit down at the typewriter."

"You'll loosen up. It comes with experience." But he knew better. Talent could not be taught.

"Teach me," she said, stroking his thigh under the table.

It was a fair trade. She gave him her youth and he rewrote her copy.

Now he was holding down temptation, keeping his legs from moving down the corridor for a brief glimpse of her oval face, a trifle small, with deep-set dark eyes. Up close, he could see the tiny flecks of yellow in them. Margaret had not mentioned it once, although he was certain it was the chief gossip at the *Chronicle,* the old pen in the inkwell routine.

In the elevator, he smiled at the memory of the morning. Sitting on the edge of the bed, he was pulling on his socks, feeling her watchful eyes, then her fingers groping at the band of his shorts.

"I never have enough of you," she had said, blatantly

groping inward and downward, gently forcing him to erect. His eyes had turned to the bedside clock.

"There's time," she said. He had stood up, socks tight to his knees, playfully escaping as she snapped the band. She had slid her legs over the side and held him in the vise of her naked thighs. Then he had not wanted to escape as she reached for the hem of his shorts and pulled them downward, gentle hands caressing him, the sense of time fading as he let her feel him, kiss the small of his back. Finally, he had turned toward her, swelling as her lips soft and greedy gave him pleasure, teased him with sensation. He had looked down at her dark hair, the face turned slightly upward, pale in the white early morning light. She groaned lightly, the sound titillating, goading the passion. His hands tightened on her head, as he moved her away and, bending, kissed her moist lips deeply, tongues joining.

He had remained standing as she had angled her pelvis toward him, positioning her lissome body to receive his manhood, which plunged into her as he shifted his weight, watching as the hard organ plunged into her lightly haired softness, exquisitely tender and wanton. The chronology of their lives narrowed, youth returning like a rose blooming in Indian summer. He had wanted to show gratitude for this gift of joy. Consciously, he prolonged the joining, watching her eyelids flutter with pleasure, as her body squirmed joyfully, spitted on his hard flesh. Was it the knowledge of his age that made it so exquisite, made each time with her better than before? He had lived for three decades before she was born and she was three years older than Chums. Had it ever been this good with Margaret?

When he finally came, it seemed deeper, a thunder inside him, an aliveness that made all the spendings of his youth seem wasteful, casual. It was as if each time would be his last, a hint of death in the air, assailing him with its unescapable promise of mortality.

"My God, if only I could express what it means to me," he had told her.

"Believe me, my darling. I got the message."

It was new to him, the lingering over brief pleasures in the middle of the newspapering day, the conscious mulling over of relationships beyond the orbit of the *Chronicle*. Rarely had other passions competed with his involvement with the paper. Was his power of concentration corroding under the joy of it?

The elevator door slid smoothly open on the eighth floor, the act drawing him swiftly back to his concern over just what, if anything, Myra was up to with her list of candidates. He was certain it would emerge sooner or later. He moved into the heavily carpeted floor, a cliché of executive imperialism. There were constellations of chromium—lamps, trims, desk legs— primary color abstractions which hung on carpeted walls like clear, sure-sighted eyes. Even the model of the new building, now built, still displayed in a glass case and shown so proudly by Myra, had prompted a kind of mental nausea. It was purely a difference of taste, although even the *Chronicle*'s resident architectural tastemaker had laid in some tender knocks. He had called the corridor leading to Myra's office the Appian Way, and her office itself "subtly intimidating, suffering perhaps from a slight, ever so slight, case of sanctum sanctorumitis." She had been outwardly amused, or so it had seemed to him at the time.

He winked at the two tall female secretaries who framed the double-doored entrance to Myra's office suite. Bookends, he thought, as he brushed past them, their coolness and efficiency bristling in the air.

It was strictly an illusion, a decorator's fantasy, inspired by Myra's own effort to show the authority of ownership. It was he, Nick, who ran the *Chronicle* while Myra played at the abstraction of running it, knowing that her real power was only by veto, which, so far, she had dared not exercise. She sensed, it seemed, that her ability had been stunted by her father's stubborn belief that the art of newspapering was better left to the male mind.

Myra was sitting at the round table near the window, slats of sun spearing the yellow napkins planted stiffly in sparkling glasses. He seemed to have walked into the middle of a private amusement, catching the end of a girlish laugh. Myra, still smiling, turned to him as he came toward the table. In a corner near the bookcases a tall man effortlessly posed in a vested pinstripe grey suit, a rounded glass in his hand, the large sky-blue dots in his deep olive tie an obvious clue to his conscious sartorial image since the color was a perfect match to the eyes. It was a faintly familiar tableau, like a Vermeer with the people in modern dress. It was Senator Burt Henderson.

Nick dreaded the inevitable small talk that would mask the essence of the intercourse to come, a kind of ritual fencing, so finely honed in the Washington ether. There is a growing effluvia in this place, Nick thought, consciously holding the lid on the jack-in-the-box anger that had plagued him all morning. It was the discovery of the guest that galled him most, the irregularity of Myra's not having announced him in advance.

"Nick," Henderson said, holding out his politician's hand, the flesh firm with ingratiation. Nick felt its strong, tightening grip. They had met on numerous occasions, especially in the days when Nick circulated more freely in the years after Margaret, the time before Jennie.

"Where the hell have you been hiding?"

"In my glass cage, where else?" He watched Myra exhibit a tiny frown. He should make an effort to hide his pique, he cautioned himself.

"Burt called this morning. He had something he wanted to discuss," Myra said. Henderson lifted his glass, skimming off a sliver of the surface. A maid came quietly into the room with practiced unobtrusiveness and placed a martini over rocks in front of Nick. As he looked into its glistening viscosity, his caution heightened. Not that placing the accustomed drink was unusual. Was it the absence of an eye signal from Myra, the flicker of a lid, or, perhaps, the trifle too swift delivery? His fingers closed around the coolness of the glass.

"Always willing to hear from Burt," he said. He

could feel Henderson gathering his force, the assimilating of all he knew about Nick. It was the traditional way the powerful approached the more powerful, measuring the thickness of the ice before each cautious step. With men like Henderson, who exuded practiced media charm, Nick imagined he could see the gears mesh, the mask reassemble like electronic markings on a computer console.

"He was telling me the joke about the one-eyed man," Myra said, her grey hair a trifle bluish in the brightness, or was it the blue dominance of Henderson's eyes, which peered out, flaunting this gift of genetic mutation?

"As the fellow said to the one-eyed man"—Henderson lifted a finger—"Eye . . ." Nick granted him a small laugh, he hoped politely. Henderson stepped out of the shadow to the sun-washed table and sat down before the iced silver fruit cup.

"This thing with India is getting ominous," he said, switching easily to a more serious note. "Christ, if India begins to blow it will be an absolute horror."

"All those people," Myra mused, her voice trailing off.

"We'll be assailed by our usual helplessness and our sense of guilt about it. If anything was inevitable in this world, it was an Indian eruption. The pressure cooker was taking too much pressure," Henderson said in his most impressive senatorial invocation.

"What would you do?" Nick said, his journalist's mind prodding the question. Henderson raised his blue eyes, aggressively secure.

"Not one damned thing," he said. "For once, just once, I would embark on a program of belligerent non-involvement. India is a quagmire to beat all quagmires, a self-righteous leadership fostering a policy, a deliberate policy, of impoverishment as a form of population control."

"Everything else seems to have failed," Myra said. "Fertility is choking them to death." Nick watched Henderson's mask assemble into deep concentration as Myra spoke. Surely he was fawning, using the weapons of his male arsenal. Couldn't Myra see the transparency? He wondered vaguely if he was the only one in the city, in the world, who could really see the sham, the bare bones beneath the transparent skin.

They picked at their fruit cup. He imagined Myra's eyes had locked briefly into Henderson's. Nick's antenna bristled with reception. There is a conspiratorial stink here, he told himself.

"Burt has alluded to something we're working on," Myra began, patting her lips with the yellow napkin. It seemed a signal to begin.

"Oh?" Nick said innocently. He was determined to remain close-lipped. It was not unusual for him to receive appeals. Hell, it was a way of life in this business. Over the years he had developed stock answers, such as "Facts are immutable."

"Nick calls the shots," had always been Myra's stock response when confronted by appeals. "We have an agreement." But this was different. And Nick felt it.

"It's this CIA thing, Nick," Henderson began, hurling himself over the gulf of small talk. He paused. Nick caught his flash of panic, quickly doused. The expected response not forthcoming, Henderson was forced to continue.

"Gunderstein is on my back like a leech. He calls. I deny the implication. He calls again. He calls everybody. This has been going on for weeks. At the receiving end it's like a persecution, a terrible harassment, like a fellow sitting under the guillotine, waiting for the blade to fall."

Nick watched him as he spoke, sensing the discomfort. He had seen it many times before. He felt Myra's deliberate avoidance of his eyes.

"Either run the story, or get off my back," Henderson said. Surely he had wanted to say: Shit or get off the pot.

"You know the Jews didn't kill Christ, they worried him to death," Henderson said. Nick pushed aside the offensively heavy hand of ingratiation. Didn't Henderson know the allusion only made matters worse?

"I never suspected that you saw yourself in that role," Nick said. Myra looked down into the poached fish that the maid was putting in front of her.

"These confrontations are always difficult, especially from this end," Henderson mumbled. He was right, of course. Nick softened. The real issue wasn't Henderson at all.

"I know, Burt. The story hasn't run because I have not been satisfied. It's a one-source story. The pattern is familiar. A subject grips the public imagination. This year it's the CIA, the spook business. One thing leads to another. We carried the story of those assassination teams, set up through CIA, that supposedly rubbed out foreign officials in the sixties. We hedged on it carefully, despite a leaking sieve within the agency. Then comes the second wave, the confessions, the compulsion of bottled-up guilt. Now the lights are on and the clothes off; it's open season on confession. And when you've got a star bloodhound like Gunderstein, he follows all the scents. He's got a source. He's tracking down another. The source tells him you were involved when you were in the army . . ."

"Involved in what? Specifically what?"

"In the assassination of Diem."

Henderson shook his head and sighed. He directed the focus of his controlled rage at Myra.

"You see," he said, "it's positively defamation, irresponsible. I deny it categorically. It is a patent attempt to destroy my political career. And I resent it." He was emphatic but in full control. Only a slight flush beneath the winter tan revealed the obvious internal turmoil.

"The man's name is Carter Allison." Nick searched Henderson's face for a clue. Nothing stirred to embellish the hint.

"I never heard of the man. Nick, it's like the McCarthy era. How far does the press have to go to flex its muscles? Really, Nick."

Myra remained silent, her eyes still on her plate as she picked at her lunch.

"I told you, Burt, I would not run the story until"—
he checked himself—"unless it's confirmed by another
unimpeachable source."

"Damn it, Nick. Take my word for it."

"Your word?"

"I think my word has credibility. Have you lost all
faith?"

"In the word of politicians? Is that the question
you're asking?"

"No, Nick. My word."

"You know what you're asking?" A danger signal
had gone up in Nick's head. He was clever, this Henderson. He was prodding him to confess a bias, to articulate
it in front of Myra with him as witness. He saw the
looming trap and side-stepped.

"Of course."

"I always start out disbelieving news leads. It's a
habit of newspapering," Nick said, amused at the irony.
"But I have been known to be disappointed."

"What the press will do finally is to run off everybody with political aspirations. Who the hell wants to
submit to your magnifications? You start off with the
built-in bias that every politician's heart is overflowng
with mendacity." Somehow, now that he had side-
stepped, the admonition had lost its sting. "And you
proceed from there. In my case, I am a victim, a
speared fish, thrashing about on your point." He raised
his blue eyes to Nick, the sun glistening from their surface.

"There's got to be some compassion. I'm asking for
mercy, man."

"If I thought in those terms," Nick said, "I'd go nuts."
He looked quickly at Myra, the allusion to insanity both
involuntary and indelicate. Myra had raised her eyes
and looked at him impassively. It was a three-cornered
conversation between faces on cards, the queen of
spades talking to the king of clubs and the jack of dia-
monds. Did they see him as he saw himself, the jack?
Jackass might be better. Did they think he could not
smell the conspiracy?

"Either print it or be done with it," Henderson said. "I don't want to live in the shadow of the knife." It was, of course, a display of bravado, macho. Nick could see the shiny colonel's eagle, the glistening boots, the blue glaze under the helmet liner. A flash of memory of his army days intruded. "Now that is a leader of men," Charlie had sneered at their battalion commander, square-featured and confident, with the Arrowshirt look of that era.

"Nothing is that clear-cut, Burt," Nick responded.

"It is to me."

"Only an irresponsible newspaper would already have printed the story."

"And it would be libelous," Henderson snapped.

"Would it?"

Henderson squirmed visibly. Was he getting at last to the soft underbelly?

"Or filled with half-truths."

"Like what?"

"Like I was recalled by the National Security Agency for a brief time in 1963. That's on the record. I have a certain expertise in intelligence data. I was with Marshall in the Chiang-Mao negotiations. Hell, I was just a kid. And I was on MacArthur's staff in Korea. Let's face it. I'm vulnerable. I was, in a sense, a spook. It's quite in vogue now to knock such an involvement and that alone would murder me with my constituency."

"It would hurt. I'll grant you that," Nick said.

"But I was *not* mixed up in any assassination teams. Whatever the hell they were. Believe me, Nick. That's pure fantasy. Rubbish. Take my word for it."

There it was again, Nick thought.

"Allison told Gunderstein you played a significant part in the whole Diem action."

"He's a goddamned liar. Whoever he is. Bring him here. Let him confront me." Henderson isn't really the issue at all, Nick reminded himself as he watched Myra light a cigarette and blow smoke out of both nostrils. He reached into the silver cigarette dish, slid out a long-filtered brand, lit it, and inhaled deeply. Henderson's pain seemed distant. Was this Myra's handpicked man? Would the little list have all the other names crossed out? What did Myra believe? Was this Henderson's test or his own?

"Believe *me*, Burt," Nick said, "I don't take the matter lightly."

"I know that, Nick," Henderson pressed, "that's why I thought I'd take this direct route. I'd have a tough time getting up from the mat even if you hedged the story. You acknowledge that in today's climate it would hurt me badly. In political terms, it would kill me with the kids, a whole generation of kids who came of age in the middle sixties. You see, I too take my responsibilities seriously."

"I'm quite aware of that, Burt. I'm also very much aware of your presidential aspirations." He looked at Myra.

"I've made no bones about it. I'm not ashamed of my ambition."

"I never met a politician who was." He wished he had checked that, the implied cynicism was, in its way, an admission of bias. Were they outfoxing him? A maid cleared the table in silence then brought a carafe of hot coffee. They remained silent as she poured. It was revealing to see their distrust even of supposedly "safe" retainers. Surely the maid had silently absorbed conversations like this before. Would she one day write her own book, Nick thought, her own revelation of power from another vantage, through another lens? "But I heard them say it," she might say to a book editor. "I was there. They thought I was merely a picture on the wall."

"This isn't easy for me, Nick," Henderson said, when the maid had gone. "Call off Gunderstein. Take me on faith. This one time. Christ, man," he looked at Myra, "I'm on your side."

It was, of course, ideologically accurate. He wanted to shout: "You're not the issue!" Myra was eloquent in her silence.

"It's not as simple as all that," Nick said. "There are ecological problems."

Henderson seemed confused. Power is power, he must be thinking. Nick preempted the expected response.

"I've got to let Gunderstein play it out. If there's no truth in it, he'll come up against a blank wall and that will be the end of it."

"There is no truth in it, Nick. I swear it."

"You've got to be a newspaperman to understand."

"You make it sound like there's some special mystique about it.

"There is."

"But, Nick, I'm vulnerable. I have enemies, especially at the right end of the political spectrum. They want my ass. They'll pay for confirmation, if necessary. Put out the right bait and they'll find a fish for the hook."

"Gunderstein will see through it."

"I'd hate to stake my career on a newspaperman's ambition." It was Henderson's bias now. For the first time since he had come into the room, Nick felt the raw power of his own position.

"This time you'll have to trust *me,* Burt. You'll have to have faith in my instincts."

"I never said I didn't." Henderson was defending now.

"He's right, Burt," Myra said suddenly. He had flushed her out. She was telling him not to press.

"He lives by story values," Henderson said. It was a mild protest. "I live by image. That's not necessarily compatible."

"That's the name of the game," Nick went on. "We're not only the victimizer. Sometimes we're also the victim."

"Of what?"

"Of the image-maker's bullshit. If we let down our guard, we blow our credibility. That's what I mean by ecology. We're very sensitive to words around here. If I get too heavy-handed, they'll get suspicious of me, of my—" Nick paused—"let's call it integrity. They know

the parameters. If I sidestep the subtleties, they'll buck.
I've got a constituency, too." It was a lecture directed
at Myra. He watched Henderson watching Myra, who
had slipped back into impassivity. Sipping his coffee,
Henderson suddenly drained his cup and placed it down
again, soundlessly, on the saucer. The act seemed a
symbol of finality, as if his persuasiveness had failed.
Despite it, his coolness commanded respect.

"If there is no credible confirmation, it's dead. That's
as far as I can promise. I'm hardly an enemy. I'm not
searching for anything."

"You wouldn't know it from where I sit."

Henderson glanced at his watch to cover his desire
to leave, having seen that he was making little headway.
As he stood up, Myra followed, came around the table,
and put her arm in his. Nick remained seated as Henderson held out a firm hand and joined it to Nick's, pumping it with undiminished vigor.

"I suppose I should understand," he said.

"Don't sweat it," Nick said. He wanted to mitigate
the man's anxiety by assuring him that rarely do words
slip through the net, his net. But he felt Henderson
might see pomposity in it, bravado, and it would make
matters worse. His eyes followed them toward the
door, where Henderson bent to kiss Myra lightly on
the cheek.

"See you at the game Sunday," he heard Myra say.
In its way it was more a confirmation than the physical
closeness, the ritual of the touching of the flesh which
revealed nothing. But this thing with the game. That
was the stuff of which myths were made.

Each Sunday the Redskins were in town the owner,
Henry Bloomington Swopes, paid court to Washington
power. It was no coincidence that Swopes was the
lawyer for the *Chronicle*. Power clusters together like
peanut brittle, Nick had thought on the occasions he
had attended, which was most of the time. Myra had a
standing invitation to bring a half dozen guests and
therein lay the trappings of rank. Like the elegant ritual

of a Japanese sword dance, a day in the owner's box followed the scripted scenario to the letter, complete with stage directions.

One arrived nearly two hours before the game at the private dining room behind the owner's box. Guests came dressed in chic football-viewing togs fresh out of the latest "W" pages. The sense of with-it-ness hung in the air like perfume, oversweet and, in a special way, intoxicating.

A feast was provided, rustic, but elegant in its casualness and presided over by Swopes with a boyish charm which masked the ritualization of the set piece, a tableau arranged around Myra Pell, the Queen Bee who, even Nick grudgingly admitted, played her role with superb style, with just the right measure of blue-blooded humility. Conscious of her favor, guests would bask in the glory of proximity and like obedient supporting players, allow the Queen the best lines.

To the practiced observer of the Washington Scene, the primary action was played out during the game itself, when royalty exhibited itself in the imperial box as the gladiators performed for the multitude. In the magnified eyes of the binoculars, one might speculate, draw conclusions, derive hints of who might be in the running for special favors and, conversely, who was in decline. Even the late dishonored President had attended, measuring his power against theirs, concluding, wrongly, it turned out, that he held the better hand.

Myra closed the door softly after Henderson and came back to the table where she sipped the dregs of her coffee, holding the cup with a light, delicate touch in shapely fingers.

"You could have at least given me fair warning," Nick said.

"You might have talked me out of seeing him."

"I would have tried."

"Believe me, Nick, I agonized over it." She sipped her coffee. "But all's well that ends well. It turned out better than I thought it would."

"How did you think it might have gone?" Nick asked. Did she have it in her head to be a matchmaker?

"I thought you'd display some of the Gold temper, get your dander up, become self-righteous. I'm proud of you, Nick."

He felt her attempts at manipulation and, now that his guard was up, he listened closely. He felt in himself an echo of Charlie's anger, the cutting edge of his madness. "The devious bitch," Charlie had erupted. But was it really deviousness? Her strategy was almost transparent. Surely she knew that, and had orchestrated this charade as an oblique confrontation.

"How else could it have been played?"

"You could have accused me of deliberately trying to get you to kill a story."

"I'll reserve judgment on that."

"You still don't believe him then?"

"Do you?"

"Why do you always answer a question with a question?"

"It's my Semitic background."

"And your newspaperman's natural tendency. Your cynicism is showing."

"So is your starry-eyed innocence."

She smiled thinly at first, then broadly, displaying her cared-for, even teeth. Like her hands, smooth and tapered, her teeth were distinguishing characteristics, oddly youthful in her aging face with deepening crinkles around the eyes.

"I'm not innocent, Nick," she protested. "Intuitive perhaps, but not innocent." No, she was not innocent, Nick thought, remembering Charlie again. She lit a cigarette, puffing deeply.

"You believe him then?"

"Yes, I do, Nick. Call it a gut feeling if you won't go with intuition."

"Is there a difference?"

He wondered if there was a romantic interest in Henderson, an errant thought quickly discounted. Myra's sexuality had been sublimated, he had concluded, long ago, its fury spent, if Charlie's graphic early descriptions were to be believed, on Charlie.

"The woman's insatiable," Charlie had told him in the early days of their marriage, and he had hinted at it during their courtship. Could it flicker again, Nick thought, recalling the morning with Jennie? Yes, it was quite possible for love, whatever that was, to intrude, even in midlife, gathering heat in the ashes. He must watch for signs in Myra. Henderson was certainly attractive, confident in his manhood, ambitious enough to use that route as a last resort.

"I believed him," Myra said.

"He was believable, I'll grant you that. It's his dominant quality. It's also the trained response of the clandestine service. Unfortunately, I have facts to contend with."

"Like what?" Myra asked, a trifle too swiftly, a brief frown lining her forehead, then disappearing.

"Allison's so-called confession. Gunderstein's instinct."

"Even you admit that you're not convinced."

"I have to go with Gunderstein's track record. Hell, Myra, he is, after all, a star in the *Chronicle's* crown. We went with his instincts before."

"Also our own."

"True."

"We knew he was on the right track before. We encouraged him. We put all our strength behind him. We were committed from the beginning."

"We were dealing with an acknowledged enemy, with ideological differences. That's a hell of a motivating factor."

"At least we both agree that Henderson's a friend." She drew deeply on the cigarette again, then added quickly, "He stands for the things we believe in. He has compassion, decency, a sense of morality. The country needs that kind of leadership, Nick. He's our kind of guy."

"That's beside the point."

"That *is* the point." She punched out her cigarette in the ashtray, a trace of frustration in the act.

"You really believe we're persecuting him?" Nick asked, measuring his words carefully.

"I think he's entitled to a quick resolution."

"Either way?"

"Either way."

He was seeing her differently now, as if the light were shifting in the prism of his lens. She did, after all, have the power to order him to shut the tap, a privilege she had never invoked. Was he prepared to walk away from this, all this? His sudden vacillation frightened him. Her message came through quite clearly. All subtlety was dissipated, her direction confirmed. He slapped both his thighs.

"Well then, let the chips fall where they may." And let the best man win, he might have said, completing the cliché.

"I never implied otherwise," she said, lighting another cigarette. He watched her grope for control, then turned his eyes away.

"I trust your judgment, Nick," she said, a hint of pleading in her voice. "Just as Charlie did." She paused, letting the reference to Charlie take effect. "You believe that, don't you, Nick?"

"Yes," he said after a while, but his long pause had added a note of tentativeness which she ignored, perhaps hoping to dispel the tension. She stood up and went behind her large desk. Opening a drawer, she took out a hand mirror and patted her hair.

"You are coming to the game Sunday?" she asked, examining her face in the mirror.

"Yes."

She turned away, a finger poking at an eyelash. Then without looking at him she said, "And bring Jennie."

"Jennie?" He had no time to control the reflex. She had caught him with a dart outside his field of vision. Rooted to the spot, he waited for more to come.

"Come on, Nick. Isn't it time you came out? It's no secret, you know."

He remained silent, turning to go, a stammer caught on his tongue. He felt her eyes on his departing back.

"Don't be so damned inflexible," she called after him, her meaning unmistakably clear.

5

In the elevator, he felt the anger glow inside his gut. He looked at the bank of buttons and pushed "B," hoping that the cab would descend without interruption. But he was not to be spared. On the editorial floor, Bonville emerged, his thin face scrupulously searching Nick's in his myopic way, as if investigating for skin blemishes.

"I've put the defense copy on your desk," he said, insensitivity proclaiming itself in the face of Nick's obviously distraught look. "Landau said he wouldn't put it in type without your final okay." The word *okay* was belched out with contempt.

Nick grunted and looked above Bonville's head to the lighted floor signals. When the elevator opened at ground level, Bonville stepped aside, an obvious act of deference, a deliberate nurturing of arrogance. When Nick didn't move, he shrugged, the beginning of a sneer arranging itself on his features as he proceeded out of the elevator cab. Nick made a mental note to rip the hell out of his editorial, already convinced of his suspicion that Bonville had reached far beyond the agreed-upon parameters.

On the basement level, Nick stepped out into a massive forest of heavy paper rolls, the pulpy smell heavy in the air. Vaguely recognized by the workmen who handled the paper, he walked down the long corridors, like trails through a forest. He hadn't been down here in months. He wondered why he had come here now, a small figure roaming in the midst of these oversized cylindrical stumps. Perhaps he had come seeking recall for some moment of time past, hoping like Proust to find some epiphany in the scent. Was he looking for Charlie in these groves? When he had traversed the long length of the area, he found an exit and mounted a metal staircase, his leather soles clacking on the steps. Opening a door on the next floor, he found himself confronted with the skeletal massiveness of the press, a vast superstructure laced with latticed stairwells. There was an awesomeness not only in the technological puzzle of the devices but in the size of the huge rollers. Even the sounds of tinkering seemed portentous, tiny signals heralding the cacophony, as the oiled and inked maws waited for the ingestion of words. He felt humbled in its presence. Did the captain of a huge ship derive the same humility facing its complicated entrails, knowing in his heart that despite the dependence on technology, despite the crew, despite the exigencies of weather and the unpredictability of the ocean, the ultimate responsibility of all lives depended on his own fallible judgment?

In the end, what was all this technical acrobatics in the face of man's will and spirit? Just another pile of shaped alloys, a junk shop of potential ruins for future scholars of antiquity. The smell of ink permeated the huge cement cavern, reassuring somehow, like the paper rolls below, a clue, perhaps, that man could still perceive the power of it and in that perception was, therefore, still in control. Could Gutenberg have imagined it back in that German cellar? The power of the word! Of course Gutenberg knew, beginning symbolically with the Bible as if to confirm the reverence of his pursuit. A wrench fell nearby, clattering to the cement floor. He looked up and saw a man, oddly hatted in the special fold of copy paper, the badge of the pressman. The man shrugged in apology.

Nick retreated to the stairwell and moved upward, pausing briefly on the next level, from which the stacked and folded papers would in a few hours fan out over the world, bound in wire, loaded into trucks, carrying the word, a mirror of the world, his world, in that moment of time. His faltering confidence returned as he moved upward still another floor to where the words were processed, the shrinking bank of linotypers cranking out their metal slugs of words, thrashing arrogantly in the last throes of obsolescence. He walked past the ungainly machines toward the area where the new technology was encroaching, where the new word-processing equipment was in smooth action, keyboards clicking out the sentence visible on their electronic consoles. He was more recognizable here, and he nodded to familiar faces when eyes strayed from the consoles as he passed. He had fought hard for the installation of the new equipment, despite the unions and his own impatience with their reluctance, bucking all the way through the long negotiations that had, toward the end, interrupted the flow of words. An army of editorial workers sweated over tapes, the photographed type, the paste-up. Lines of people stood along the proof racks, fitting together the ads, pasting, reading, proofing—an endless process. He watched the clock as the hands moved relentlessly toward imposed deadlines, finite time that controlled the rhythm of his life. The clock was so embedded in his head, he did not need the graphic view of time to respond. He ducked quickly through a door and pounded upward toward the editorial rooms, swinging open the door to the brightly lit center of his life.

His brief tour had refreshed him, validating once again his relationship to his work. It was a ritual that Charlie had woven into his own life in the days when it was possible to know by first name even the humblest paper handler, the shiest typesetter.

"We are all cogs," Charlie had told him. "Never forget that." Surely even Myra had felt the same sense of awe. Of course, there was a mystique about this business. Henderson's allusion was the instinctive reaction of the outsider who saw only the power of it, the muscle itself encased in the supple skin, not the blood and tissue that fueled it.

The city room was teeming now, the typewriters clacking in wild crescendos, counterpointed by the persistent ringing of telephones. He headed for his glass cage past lifted eyes.

"A half hour to budget conference," Miss Baumgartner reminded. He waved at Landau as he passed. In his corner Gunderstein typed, engrossed in still another telephone probe.

Bonville's editorial nagged at him from the top of the Lucite desk. Pencil in hand, he began to read it hurriedly, emasculating the persistent line, sculpting it to the proportion of his own vision, feeling joy in the doing, flexing his power. When he had finished, he waved to a news aide who responded quickly and took the copy from him.

"Bring it to the editorial copy desk," he commanded. The young man took it and left quickly. Picking up the phone, Nick punched out Jennie's extension.

"Get ready, kid, we're having a coming out party."

"A what?"

"A coming out party. We're going to the ball game Sunday. The royal box."

"Nick. Are you all right?"

"It's a command performance. By order of the queen."

"As a twosome?"

"A dynamic duo. You and me, babe."

"Christ, Nick. I don't think I'm ready for it."

"Then get ready," Nick said, his voice lowering. "It's the moment of truth."

The tour of the plant had dissipated his depression and hearing Jennie's voice had exhilarated him.

Despite ominous signs in the heavens, he told himself, all was still well on the planet. Not that he had discounted the blip on the radar screen. Myra was, unquestionably, moving into a more militant phase of her management, her confidence buoyed by the paper's recent string of phenomenal successes.

Looking back now to his nine years as executive editor, the years before that when he had walked gratefully in Charlie's shadow, he applauded his, their, instincts in building a sturdy ship with a tight tiller that responded only to their special touch. The mechanism was a complex, Rube Goldberg concoction, each part oddly fitted by his and Charlie's own hands. At each terminal of movement, where the joints fitted smoothly together, Nick had carefully honed his own special fittings. Landau, managing editor; Madison, Metropolitan editor; Domier née Gold, Lifestyle editor; Peterson, Editorial Page editor; Prager, Sports editor; Phillips, World editor. The others he had created—like Gunderstein, even Gunderstein, and all those special correspondents burrowed into the White House, the Hill, the Defense Department, the Treasury, and into every major foreign capital of the world. A single faulty part could injure the whole.

And he was the fuse, the spark of connection through which the special energy flowed. It was quite true, he told himself with candor, that the fuse was replaceable, but not so simply dislodged, and if dislodged, not so simply replaced, and if replaced, not exactly replicated. Try extracting a note from a Bach fugue and watch the symmetry, the special balance, fall apart, he reasoned. He found security in that, despite Myra's power over his future. The question was: did Myra understand the actual limits of her power? Only he knew where all the pieces fit in this intricate mechanism. She was clearly changing, moving into a new dimension. He would have to watch her carefully.

Playing favorites was an old newspaper game. It had

destroyed Hearst, bringing him to the final abyss of his own megalomania. It was not enough for Hearst to want to make presidents; in the end he had wanted to *be* president. The ultimate power trip. Surely Myra could be deflected with such sound examples. But hadn't someone tried to dissuade Hearst?

The logic of his arguments, by then, had softened his suspicion. There was, after all, some good horse sense in the old girl, as the matter of himself and Jennie had testified. It was futile to be clandestine. His initial instinct, as his love for Jennie became apparent to himself, had been that it might diminish him in the eyes of the people at the *Chronicle,* a revelation of vulnerability. His was an example to be set. A newspaper was no place for interlocking passions. Emotion, especially that one, could distort judgments.

But despite the relief of their impending "coming out," Nick, with that persistent questioning of questions, determined to watch for minefields ahead. Better to be cautious than exploded, he thought, remembering arduous detours in France to avoid the tricky patterns of German mines. Why had Myra chosen exactly that moment to tender the invitation? Was she simply playing on the insecurity of a man in love with a girl thirty years his junior? Was this in Myra's mind when she released her well-aimed dart?

"Don't be so inflexible," she had said, another echo to his journalist-trained ears which trapped the inner monologue. Listen to what she is saying, he reminded himself.

6

The Parker house on Massachusetts Avenue, a William Hobson Richardson travesty with turrets and cupolas, was a landmark even in the old days. In a city that made architectural judgments of people's worth and eccentricities, the house was a fitting residence for a banker turned newspaper owner. Mr. Parker, George Albert—it was his statement of himself to have others think of him in terms of three names—was solidly built, a pocket watch and Phi Beta Kappa key always displayed on the vested, large expanse of belly. If this wasn't enough to make his antecedents suspect, there were always the pince-nez glasses and the high black shoes that attested to his resistance to contemporary styles, as if pre-World War I were his permanent era. Nick's first brief view of him with the oak paneling as background in the library of his home, standing near a crackling fire, one hand on the edge of a leather winged chair, dark pinstriped vested suit, pince-nez removed but visible in the fingers of his right hand, had given him a completeness of view that subsequent casual encounters could never erase.

"Father, this is Nick Gold, a newspaperman friend of Charlie's," Myra had said, as if the identification as a newspaperman were necessary ingratiation.

"Ah yes," Mr. Parker responded. He was preoccupied. But Myra had planted a kiss on his cheek and the old man responded in kind. To Nick, it had been a brief photograph, a flicker of the lens. He had no idea that more than a quarter of a century later he would be contemplating that still clear print.

He had been invited down for the engagement party. By then Charlie was in the Washington bureau of the *News,* a post granted as therapy by McCarthy after Charlie had been found drunk and spinning on the huge globe in the lobby of the New York building. Somehow the air of Washington had worked a cure. Charlie, sensing the destructive power at work, went on the wagon, and his letters to Nick testified to returning health and an interest in Washington that absorbed his energies.

"This place is a howl," he wrote in a clipped, hurried prose beaten out between deadlines on thick, pulpy copy paper in pica type with capitalizations rampant. "Attended my First Presidential News conference. Harry is a feisty bugger, a Real hayseed, but lotsa moxey. I didn't have the Balls to ask him a question although They tell me that some of the questions are Rigged in advance. Personally, I think that's Horseshit, but old hands here say that FDR, who they call his Imperial Highness, used to plant questions among friendly newsbuffs to get a point across. Anyway, I feel damned good, now that I'm off the Goddamned juice. It was a good Move, getting down here, even though I Bucked like hell. I miss you, you old Bastard. You'll probably go to hell on a sled now that I'm not around to Blow your nose. Oh yeah. I'm getting laid a lot. There's lots of girls down here from Pennsylvania and Ohio. The girls from those dumb shit towns (like the one you came from) Fuck the best. Don't take my word for it. It's been validated by big Shirley. She runs a wonderful little cat house on 16th Street. The Best whores come from Ohio, she says. I said I know that, because I know you."

He was considered a political maverick by the *News* desk people who began to detect Democratic bias in his copy, definitely too Left for the *News* Republican posture.

"I'm surrounded by Paid Republican agents, snobs," he wrote to Nick. "They say that Truman is on his way out anyway, so why the fuss. Nick, you just can't believe this place. They actually run the country from Here. It's a Land of Pygmies, with occasional Giants like Marshall. I interviewed him the other day, the old Commander. Never realized what a tall man He was. And I really admire Acheson. God, I love it here. Except for not having you around, old Buddy. I'm as happy as a pig in shit. Met a girl, too. Her father's the publisher of the *Chronicle,* a hind-tit paper, which after meeting him, I'm convinced has Integrity. The old man drips with it. He scares the shit out of me. But Myra, that's the gal's name, dotes on him. You should see the House they live in. It's as big as a Fucking Embassy. They entertain a lot and I'm hobnobbing with the Rich and Powerful. I'm kissing a lot of asses, Nick. You should see me. You'd piss in your pants at me in a tux. I think I'm in Love with Myra."

The letters began to be more infrequent and except for an occasional brief conversation on the telephone, Nick hardly heard from Charlie at all. By then, Nick was immersed in his own affair with Margaret, who had just been promoted to assistant movie reviewer. It was mating time for both of them, a time when male friendships pale.

"I'm engaged," Charlie finally wrote. "She's one hell of a gal. I've become pretty fond of the old man, who's trying to get me to quit the *News* and come work for the *Chronicle.* It's a stuffy old rag and I hate the thought of being the Son-in-Law, but Myra's working on me as well. I think I'm about to surrender. We're having an engagement bash at the old homestead, where I have become a regular moocher. I practically live there. Let's face it. I was born for Luxury. They change the Fucking towels twice a day, not weekly. That in itself is a cultural shock. As for you, you Bastard, I'm expecting you down here for the Bash. Just hop the Congressional Friday night and we'll pick you up in Myra's Lincoln. Prepare to be impressed. We'll put you up in the Mansh."

He had, of course, jumped at the invitation.

His first glimpse of Myra was at the wheel of a big cream-colored Lincoln with the Capitol in the background, a glistening whiteness in the Washington sunset. Even seated, she was clearly tall and slender, with long athletic legs. Her delicate white fingers clutched the big wheel as he slid in beside Charlie.

"So you're the famous Nick," Myra said.

Myra had driven them through the city, pointing out the Capitol, the Senate Office Building, the old House building, the Library of Congress. The big car rolled quietly through the Mall, past the National Gallery and the turreted Smithsonian and on into the deepening glow of sunset, the Washington Monument soft and pink in the reddening sky. Swinging into Fourteenth Street, she moved the car expertly through traffic, then turned onto Pennsylvania Avenue to give him a special view of the White House. By then the lights had gone on and the fountains danced in front of the Georgian porticos.

"There she is," Charlie had said, "the big house."

"Is Harry home?" he had asked.

"Up there," Charlie pointed, "on the third floor."

"It's beautiful," he had said, a lump forming in his throat. They remained silent until the car drove into the driveway of the Parker house.

Despite a certain amount of wiseacre banter, Charlie seemed genuinely changed, more secure, happier, the bad memories gone. Because he loved Charlie, he could welcome his friend's good fortune while feeling sadness at the ending of their youthful chapter.

Charlie had taken him through room after high-ceilinged room to a large Tudor-styled, beamed billiard den, a kind of clubby relic of a life-style only lived by those of Mr. Parker's age and station. On one wall a heavy oak credenza exhibited hunting guns, ominous in their splendor of shined gunmetal and stocks, and one of which, years later, would explode a shell in Charlie's troubled brain. In his memory, Nick had always invested them with a kind of inner life. Had they been so lovingly cared for all those years so that they could be used with such abruptness? Who had taken such care?

At dinner that first night, Mr. Parker sat at one end of the big oak table in the dining room, his pince-nez shining in the glare of the chandelier, his hands gripping the carved arms of an antique throne-like chair. Charlie and Myra sat on either side of him, their heads turning attentively to the old man's conversation. His speech was crisp and measured, each statement imperiously delivered; he was a man accustomed to power and to dispensing wisdom. The setting itself embellished the characterization, the exquisitely set table with its glistening silver and crystal, the high plaster-sculpted ceiling, the costumed maid who moved silently around them placing steaming dishes soundlessly on the lace cloth. In this setting any voice but Mr. Parker's sounded tremulous and tentative. If Nick had any early suspicion that the scene had been staged solely for his benefit, to impress Charlie's bosom friend, it was quickly dispelled. This was Mr. Parker's authentic world, the self-realization of a willful mind, now in the process, obvious to Nick, of bestowing the mantle of succession on Charlie Pell. It had been explained earlier by Charlie, so casually that it seemed of little consequence, that Myra's mother had died years before.

Mr. Parker, Charlie had told Nick, could trace his line to a branch of the Brahmin world of Boston, and before that to acquisitive Tories who had persisted in service to the Crown, leaving their seed to begin again in the dregs of atonement. Perhaps the old guilt was still residual ten generations later in Mr. Parker's fanatic approach to the democratic ethic. The early family acquisitiveness stacked wealth upon wealth until other generations seemed invisible behind the pile and working in the family bank in New England seemed a pallid way to spend one's life. To Mr. Parker, service had more lure than greed, and he was one of the first traitors to his class to side with Roosevelt in 1932. In Charlie's initial explanation, told as Nick watched Charlie shave before dinner, the old man had been appalled by the nation's leaders' failure to cope with the Depression and had, through observing the pain of it at second hand, become committed to people's needs. Roosevelt had appointed him Undersecretary of Commerce in the early days of his first administration.

Government and politics had left him singed. The old Tory strain could not compromise with venality, no matter how well intentioned, and he was soon left with only his integrity and a firm conviction that the real enemy of America was a diminution of the values of Jefferson. Materialism without values, he perceived, was the thickening destructive wave in the distance. But it was frustrating to preach ethics in abstraction, in the face of all those empty bellies. Because of his wealth he had been able to maintain an important salon and, despite the ineffectiveness of his wife, owing primarily to shyness and later to illness, he could still attract to his lavish home the cream of Washington society, not only the idle blue bloods, but the people who held the levers of power.

But for a man like Mr. Parker, Charlie had indicated, it was like pissing into the wind. All that socializing had only left the old man adrift on a sea of good liquor and victuals and willing gullets, hardly offering anything constructive. He began to seek a more effective way to amplify his ideas. By then, he was more than simply a traitor to his class, he was a renegade, a stickler for truthful presentation of existing facts. Having seen the politician and his sinister ways of manipulation, the old man's faith now resided with the people as the only force available in the democratic context to control their own destiny. Even Charlie seemed willing to suspend his newspaperman's cynicism in the face of Mr.

Parker's somewhat naïve singlemindedness, since, by the time Charlie had arrived on the scene, Mr. Parker had found his voice in the *Chronicle* and his criticisms and ideas were beginning to find their way to the target.

Ten years before, Mr. Parker had bought the bankrupt *Chronicle* at auction, a low fourth on the hierarchy of Washington newspapers, and since then, had poured in millions to sustain his voice. If the dent to his fortune had left him somewhat bemused and perhaps guilt-stricken, at the least, disloyal to the ancestral line, he could take comfort in the calm purity of his vision. All this could be inferred from exposure to the man, even during the brief weekend, with gaps of his life filled in by Charlie's excited explanations.

"The press is the last bastion," Mr. Parker intoned, his impatience with small talk foreshortening the usual introductory trivia. "Hitler knew it and went for its jugular at the first opportunity. Lenin was luckier. The czars had already corroded the effectiveness of the press. The future of America rests on the First Amendment."

It sounded to Nick like something written in a textbook. The *News* had taught him a harsher reality.

"Objectivity," Mr. Parker said, lifting the first wineglass of the meal, "that's the ticket. The press must wring out all emotions, squeeze it out of the pulp like water from a wet mop. Objectivity." He let the word roll on his pallet like the taste of the wine. "Trust the people to discern the truth. That's the heart of the system. Leave opinion to the editorial pages. That's the appropriate place to give one's views in sober, reasoned fashion, based on logic, after weighing both sides of any question."

Nick watched Charlie as he listened to Mr. Parker. He had expected signs of exasperation, an eye lifted briefly to the ceiling, a bite of the lip. But Charlie seemed oddly absorbed as if he had been actually listening with all his brain cells.

"Impossible to achieve, Mr. Parker," Charlie said suddenly, giving Nick his first clue. Myra, conditioned to the debate, also watched its progress with some concentration. "You can't totally eliminate personality from the reporting of the news. Somebody has to register the facts. Somebody has to fashion them into words. Somebody has to write a headline. That's three different lenses, not to mention the way it is presented graphically on the page by still another person. At the *News* . . ."

Apparently the mention of the name was enough to bring a light flush to Mr. Parker's cheeks.

"That's a panderer, a garbage dump. What happens in the pages of the *News* takes place in Captain Patterson's pygmy mind."

"But he's dead."

"From the grave, then. That's not a newspaper."

"Please don't take offense, Nick," Myra interjected. "Father's insult is purely generic."

"Not necessarily," Mr. Parker said, trying but failing to smile broadly. No one, not even Myra, could trifle with his obsession.

"Every man who works for the *News* bears responsibility."

"Like the Germans," Charlie said, shrugging his shoulders.

"Exactly, Charlie."

The maid brought trays of steaming food, which they ladled ceremoniously onto their plates. The old man was silent for a few moments, chewing carefully, absorbed in his own thoughts. Midway through his dinner, Mr. Parker began again, fork in midair.

"Personality," he said, as if it were a chapter heading, like "Objectivity" earlier. "It will ruin journalism. That's why the *Chronicle* has no by-lines on its front page. I will not have personality dominate the news. It is not fair to the people. By-lines are merely an excuse to editorialize, to bring the news into the realm of personal opinion. We have a high responsibility to unbend the truth, especially in Washington, where the truth is in short supply."

"But it makes for boring reading," Charlie said, firm but respectful. "It's too reasoned, too juiceless. The competition is not building stories in pyramids the way the journalism textbooks teach. And we are competing, for attention. It's not enough that we've got to fight other newspapers for the reader's interest, but television's beginning to happen. And life itself is getting more frenetic."

"Exactly why we need a newspaper, at least one, that subjugates personality, that tells the straight story. The people must be given a chance to form their own opinions, to get the facts without bias." He was silent for a moment as he finished the food on his plate.

"Bias," he began again with his peculiar pedantry. To Nick, the method of presentation was contradiction in itself of the old man's point of view, since his personality dominated his own presentation. "Most, I say most, newspapers in this country reflect the bias of their owners in their news columns. Study the way the Washington *Post* or the *Star* present their news, the Scripps chain; even the failing Hearst newspapers roar out their bias as a kind of tribute to crazy Bill. And McCormick. There's egomania for you. And Cissy Patterson. Her personal prejudices still reek from the pages of the *Times-Herald*. Go from city to city and see if it isn't true. The process of disseminating information is the product of only a few obsessed minds, the bias of power and personality." He seemed to be trying desperately to convince Charlie, a special clue, it seemed, in assessing what was obviously so tantalizing to Nick's friend.

"Mr. Parker," Charlie said slowly, uncommon to his style, searching for a diplomatic path. He was walking on eggshells here.

"The name of the game is circulation. Without circulation, readership, you're working the tiller of a doomed ship." The nautical reference seemed another hint to Charlie's new life among the swells, confirmed later by pictures of sailboats in the library. "You can't run a mass media enterprise for the happy few, unless you run it as a hobby." It was a cutting reference, since Nick could almost feel Myra wince. "In a way, the *Chronicle* reflects your own bias. I don't necessarily mean ideological, although the editorial pages leave no mistake about where you stand personally. Even the objective truth as you present it is, after all, only your objective truth. We're dealing with an onrushing river of facts, plucked at random by your reporters as they ride the tide. It only appears to be objective in the heat of the moment, within the time frame demanded by your headlines. It's only an ideal."

Mr. Parker was listening carefully, an ear cocked, as if he were probing Charlie's words, picking through them like a man searching for something. When he did not speak, Charlie continued.

"I'm not saying you should pander like the *News,* but you've got to make some compromise with the public. Besides, the idea that all you have to do is tell both sides of a story and the public will react with reason, is naïve. It assumes that the public has a balanced brain and is waiting patiently to weigh both sides of any given question. In the first place, the public has little patience, and little time, to steep itself in the questions. They may not even be paying attention. And you don't just run a newspaper for only the informed few."

Mr. Parker nodded as the plates were cleared.

"The New York *Times,*" he began. "There is the closest thing we have to an objective newspaper."

"And even that has bias in its news columns."

"That's because they've let personality interfere. The by-line again. I can remember when the *Times* had few by-lines on its front page. You could trust its consistent vision, then."

"I think it took the only road open to it, a compromise," Charlie said. "The *Times'* bias is in what they leave out, not what they put in."

"Exactly," Mr. Parker agreed for the first time. " 'All the news that's fit to print.' Who decides what's fit? There's the personality factor."

"You just can't eliminate the humanness from people, Mr. Parker. Especially people who control information. It's one hell of a newspaper no matter how you slice it."

Mr. Parker concentrated on his dessert. He was silent for a long time. Myra's eyes kept moving from him to Charlie. She was a silent victim of the male supremacy in the room, and in retrospect Nick realized the scene provided a clue to later actions.

"Do you think Truman is finished?" Nick asked, feeling the obligation of the guest to pay for his dinner with some participation in the conversation.

"It looks that way, although he's a tough old bird," Mr. Parker said. "I'm inclined to support him."

"Only because he's as contrary as you are, Father," Myra said.

"Any man that's smart enough to defer to Marshall and Acheson cannot be all wrong."

"He seems such a pygmy next to Roosevelt," Charlie said. "That's his major handicap, that damned comparison."

"You see how we make our judgments," Mr. Parker said quietly. "Personality dominates. I worked for Roosevelt. I'd sooner play poker with Truman."

"Father did play poker with Roosevelt," Myra said.

"Precisely why I'd rather play with Truman." For the first time, Nick saw Mr. Parker laugh.

After dinner, Mr. Parker disappeared for the rest of the evening.

"He's gone to the paper," Myra explained.

"He's afraid that if he didn't read every word before it hit the street, his damned objectivity would suffer," Charlie said.

"Objectivity," he mimicked Mr. Parker.

"I'm worried about him, Charlie. He's burning himself out over that paper," Myra said, a frown darkening her face.

"It's an impossible burden," Charlie said, reinforcing her observation. "The burden of truth."

"He's stubborn," Myra said. A telephone rang in the distance. The maid came in and called Myra. She stood up.

"Hey, fellows. Tomorrow's our engagement party," she said, getting up.

"It'll be quite a bash," Charlie said. "Everybody will cover it except, of course, the *Chronicle*."

"Not objective?" Nick asked.

"Not objective."

Nick and Charlie sat in the huge living room, near a grand piano on which perched a forest of photographs in a variety of gilt frames, mostly family pictures with famous personalities. There was a picture of Mr. Parker, Myra, and what was certainly her mother, with Roosevelt. Charlie's eyes swept the long room.

"Well, what do you think, old buddy?" Charlie asked. He seemed back in familiar character.

"I think you've stepped in shit."

"Not bad, right?"

"Right."

He leaned back on the soft upholstered chair in which he was sitting and put his hands behind his head, elbows up, a pose of contentment which did not quite fit the uncertainty that Nick caught in his eyes.

"What do you think of Myra?"

"She's lovely."

"She's got this thing about her father. A kind of worship. It bothered me at first, but as I get to know the old boy, I'm beginning to feel the same way. He's obsessed, as you can see. The paper's taking a bad financial licking. Myra says he's already poured in five million. Five million! Now there's an expensive obsession for you."

Nick looked around the room.

"It seems that there's lots left."

"Who knows? They don't discuss money around me," he sighed. "They don't discuss a lot of things." His eyes glazed over for a moment.

"He wants me to go to work for the *Chronicle,*" he said suddenly. "Imagine me as the Son-in-Law. We'll be at each other's throats in a week. I keep refusing."

"What does Myra think?"

"There's the problem, at least I think it is. He's a man that puts great stock in his life, tortures himself inwardly about the continuity of his precious expensive hobby. He doesn't believe Myra can handle it."

"Handle what?"

"The running of the paper. It's hard to imagine these old rich types. They see double vision. Look back and forth in time. He sees the continuity of the *Chronicle,* his half-baked idea of a newspaper continued into the future *ad infinitum*. But he has no faith in females. Was disappointed in his wife, but loved his mother. Freud would have a field day with his libido. They're plotting to have me take over. I'm the compromise candidate."

"That's fantastic, Charlie," Nick said. "My God, it's like having the biggest electric train on the block."

"In effect, I'd be working for my wife. He has too much faith in bloodlines to ever will the stock outside the line. He'd expect, of course, that we produce sons." He stood up and stretched. "Come on, let's take a walk."

They walked briskly down Massachusetts Avenue, past stately homes, many now converted to embassies. The night air was soft, warm. They passed over a bridge, below which traffic rolled quietly through Rock Creek Park.

"What do you think?" Charlie said again, dropping a cigarette onto the grass in front of the British Embassy and punching it into the ground with the toe of his shoe. Nick felt the weight of responsibility. It was a burden he wouldn't accept. He remained silent. Charlie looked at him and shrugged.

"Do you love Myra?" A question with a question. Now it was Charlie's turn not to answer. He punched Nick on the upper arm.

"It's great to see you, kid. I really missed ya."

The engagement party itself was in keeping with Mr. Parker's life-style, the kind of party a doting father would throw for his only daughter. Flashbulbs popped as Washington's high and mighty paraded, tuxed and bejeweled, into the great hall of the big house. Nick recognized famous faces. But he was not experienced in party talk and preferred to stand aside and observe the scene. He watched Mr. Parker, an always imposing figure, his huge girth bound by a purple cummerbund, greet his guests and move through crowds of familiar faces, touching hands, kissing cheeks.

To unaccustomed eyes it was a feast of power, and Nick remembered thinking how much of his own destiny was affected by the decisions of these men.

Charlie occasionally took respite with his friend, identifying the cast of characters with an amusing running commentary.

"That hayseed is Barkley. He's the Senator who outfoxed Roosevelt. He loves filthy stories. They always take place in Paducah. And that's Senator Taft, the balding fellow with the hair pasted over the knob. And there's Perle Mesta, our hostess with the mostest, and the Cafritzes, if you like to count Jews." Myra came over and planted a kiss on Charlie's cheek, looking radiant in a pink chiffon dress, like a girl at her first prom.

"Love you," she said lightly, taking him by the hand and leading him through the throng, as if on a tour. If there was any hesitation on Charlie's part, Nick knew then that all that glitter was seductive, beyond his capacity, anyone's capacity, to resist. There was, after all, much to learn about these people in this environment, and since they exercised a control over destiny, they were certainly worthy of greater inspection.

"It's a zoo, old buddy," Charlie said later, when the dancing had begun and the great and powerful moved to the odd beat of Lester Lanin. It was unlike any rhythm Nick could remember, a special beat, as if even the music had to be refashioned to conform to the exotic tastes of the elite. They had moved through French doors to a stone patio which jutted out into a well-trimmed garden. People huddled in conversational tableaus, intent in their discussions, trading confidences. To Nick, other people's conversations always seemed somehow more important to them than what he could muster; weightier. In the soft shadowy light of the garden, that impression was magnified as important looking men and women, elegant and mysterious in the night, pondered fateful decisions in whispered tones.

"You seem to have found yourself in the eye of the universe," Nick said, and immediately had the impression he was also posturing.

"I think your description, like your prose, old buddy, is a trifle purple."

"Really, Charlie, I'm as impressed as hell. Christ, these people are just names in a paper to me. I've tried all evening to be superior to it. You'd think a reporter would be more blasé about it. I have to admit I do feel a wee bit inconsequential with all this brass."

"They all squat to shit," Charlie said. He lit a cigarette, the light blazing briefly across his square, handsome face, the jet black full hair curled naturally over the edges of his high forehead. The flame caught glints in his myopic eyes, alert and perhaps fearful. Or was that just the effect of the flickering light?

"Doesn't it scare the hell out of you, Charlie?" Nick asked. He knew even then that it was an echo of something he might have said through half-frozen lips, crawling in the mud along a French hedgerow. Images of the war were locked into his perception. Charlie caught the reference, as Nick had known he would. The ambience of friendship had not deteriorated during their separation.

"Not if you whistle loud enough," Charlie said, slowly puffing on his cigarette.

"The old man's passing the relay stick, Charlie," Nick said. He wondered then if there wasn't an element of envy in it.

"Yeah," Charlie said. "I like the dotty old bird." He inhaled deeply, then blew the smoke from his nose. "Do you think I'm a goddamned phony, Nick?" Nick felt Charlie's eyes bore into him through the shadows.

"You've got a lot of faults, my friend. But phoniness isn't one of them."

"It's just that I feel that I'm hiding my flaws deliberately, knowing what he has in mind for me."

"It's a temptation not to be sneezed at."

"You think I'm selling myself out?"

"How the hell can I answer that one?" Nick knew

that he was evading the answer. "The real question is: Do you love Myra?"

"Yes," Charlie said. "I suppose that is the real question." They were silent for a long time. Strains of the music floated in the air. "I wonder what the hell they see in me?"

"I've wondered about that myself," Nick said, remembering the first time he had seen him, the gangling, sloppy soldier tossing his C ration into a puddle, defiant in the face of his own hunger. "Let them eat shit," he had hissed. Nick hadn't even stopped to consider, but had tossed his own ration into the same puddle, the act stupid in itself but validating the powerful chemistry of Charlie's personality and its irrevocable effect on Nick. Perhaps Mr. Parker and Myra had felt the same compulsion.

"But you can't tell by me, baby. I'm a fan," Nick added.

"I knew better than to ask a dumb bastard like you. Boy, have they bought themselves a peck of trouble," Charlie said. Perhaps he was remembering his trip around the globe in the lobby of the *News,* the pain of the aftermath. Or perhaps it was a burst of clairvoyance as he looked into his own future and the madness that he must have felt lay in his tissue waiting to mature.

"If I could only be certain I'd be making the right move. There are a lot of problems with it."

"Like what?"

"I'm not sure," he said mysteriously. "Ah, what the hell," he sputtered, flicking the lighted butt onto the trimmed lawn. Nick watched its glow fade into the darkness. "Maybe the die is cast," Charlie said. "Besides, I like the idea of taking these bastards on."

"Now there's objectivity for you," Nick said.

"The old man's right about them, Nick. This place is a pit of self-delusion. Somebody has got to keep them on the straight and narrow. Can't you just smell it around here?"

Nick breathed deeply, sniffing only the perfumed air. "Yeah," he said.

"Oh, there you are," Myra's voice, high-pitched, faintly irritated, called from behind them. "Dad wants you to meet some people." She put her arm through Charlie's.

"I was just talking to old Nick here, Myra. We were reminiscing about bachelor days in New York."

"I'll bet they were quite racy," she said.

"Obscene." Nick watched him resist her pull.

"Come on, Charlie," she said, "give father a break. He's doing it for us, you know."

"Go on, Charlie," Nick said, "I'll be fine."

Charlie remained silent for a moment, stubbornly rooted. She pulled at him again, almost throwing him off balance.

"Don't be so inflexible," Myra said petulantly, as Charlie yielded and followed obediently on her arm, like Alice proceeding through the looking glass.

7

When Nick arrived at the budget meeting they were all sitting around the polished table, reviewing their papers. His eyes swept their faces: Landau, Peterson, Prager, Madison, Phillips, Dover, and Margaret, with her persistent upsweep hairdo that defied all style changes.

There was always tension at these meetings, with each editor presenting his story ideas for final inspection, ready to defend his judgments. It was, as he had lectured over the years, the moment of truth, the final screen of the information and events that they had chosen to record of that day in time, for all posterity to ponder. The daily meetings had taken on a special rhythm, the agenda fixed by the priority of his own interests. The consideration of the sports budget was always first, only because it was the least likely to be amended since Prager, consistently bucolic, sensed his advantage over the rest of them, both in knowledge and interest. To the rest of them, sports held only marginal interest, although they enjoyed the spectacle. To Prager it was a total world, as it was to many thousands of their readers, a gospel to be absorbed, passionately gobbled up, a religious experience. Prager dominated like a monarch, a man with monumental prejudices, favoring players, owners, cities, countries, even types of sports. He hated tennis because it had become the province of the new effete and doled out its coverage in niggardly doses. He had been Charlie's choice, and a wise one. Despite Prager's abrasiveness, he had kept the sports pages a gallop ahead of the rest of the *Chronicle* in accuracy, variety and interest. None of the others dared question his authority over his domain, although any of them would have given a month's pay to see his superiority dented. Instead, they took refuge in humor, salted by Prager's total inability to understand them.

"Don't you think you're going a little ape on football?" Nick mumbled, a deliberate barb.

Prager lifted his eyes to the ceiling, tapping a pencil. "It's the season. You want me to feature the tiddledywinks tournament?"

Nick watched the tight smiles respond. Nobody would dare chuckle.

It was a source of amusement to watch Prager at the Redskins' games and observe his reluctant and disdainful greeting. He would never ever set foot in the owner's box, dismissing Myra and her guests as dissolute members of the ruling party, utterly contemptible.

Nick passed over the Sports budget with perfunctory attention. To look it over with a lack of comment would have somehow been interpreted as a deprivation. Next he passed on to Margaret's budget. His eye caught the line, "Interview with Norman Mailer—Jennie." He had actually rewritten the first five paragraphs of the piece in its entirety, much to Jennie's chagrin. She was protesting more and more. Although this morning her irritation had seemed to disappear.

"Might be a good idea to increase your coverage of the Indian ambassador," Nick said to Margaret. "The action seems to be shifting to that part of the world. Besides we've given the Iranians enough of a play."

"They throw better parties," Margaret said. "More people. Better picture stuff. Christ, Nick, the Indians are insufferably self-righteous, besides being boring."

"Maybe if we covered them, they'd get the message," Nick said.

"Nothing like a dose of exposure to motivate their media sensitivity," Landau said.

"Check it out, Maggie," Nick said, looking up as Margaret scribbled on a notepad. "And you should know I got a scream from the advertising department on Carson's review. Delaney really roasted me."

"You get it only occasionally, Nick," Margaret said. "I get it daily. You should see the stuff I pencil out. Whenever he throws a bouquet to one of his pretty boy favorites, we go into psychodrama. Probably increases his venom with the other gender."

"I like his stuff," Peterson said quietly.

"Screw the advertising department," Madison said, his voice booming, accentuating the perennial bone of contention.

"They pay the freight, people," Nick said. It was the traditional answer. He looked at the clock and pored over the Metropolitan budget.

"Watch the mix, Ben."

It was almost a daily complaint, inevitable in the coverage of three jurisdictions: Virginia, Maryland, and the District of Columbia. And as they expanded circulation, it was becoming increasingly difficult to expand the county coverages. Even the split runs had not solved the problem.

"It's a bitch, Nick. I need more reporters. It's becoming unmanageable. It's like covering three different countries."

"Compress the stories."

"We're trying, Nick. Then I get flack from my own guys. There's just not enough space."

"There will never be enough of that commodity," Landau said. They went down the list of stories, discussed some, passed through others quickly.

"We should editorialize more on the Metro system," Ben suggested. "The jurisdictions are trying to turn off the money tap. It's purely racial, in my opinion."

"What do you think, Pete?"

"We've got one in the works."

"And Maggie, you might search for a new angle for Lifestyle."

"We've covered everything on it but the commodes."

"That might be a hell of an angle," Nick said. They could see he was serious. He watched Margaret nod her head.

"Maybe, Nick. Might find some innovations there."

"Computerized johns," Landau said. Prager snickered. Nick could feel his impatience.

When he got to the budget from the national desk, his eye flicked over the list and stopped suddenly, a red flag wildly waving in his mind. He noted the neatly typed line, "Henderson health bill—Grinnel." Grinnel was their senior Senate man.

"What's the Henderson piece?" he asked, trying not to show the flash of anxiety. He looked at Madison, who averted his eyes.

"It's a Senate speech, supposedly major. It's Henderson's pet project. Universal health insurance," Arnold Dover said. He was a quiet man, the least prepossessing of those around the table.

Nick searched his mind. Hadn't they covered it recently?

"Anything new in it?" Nick asked.

"Not really," Dover said, his eyes darting toward Landau. It was, after all, a pet project which the *Chronicle* supported editorially.

"We just had an editorial on it last week, complete with bouquets to Henderson," Nick said, remembering.

"That's right, Nick," Pete agreed.

"We'll overkill it with support," Nick said, his tone argumentative. They must see he was making a stand.

"It seems appropriate," Henry Landau interjected.

"Christ, Henry, you're just off vacation." Nick had meant the implication to be unmistakable.

"It's clearly in keeping with our policy of support," Landau argued, his deep tan masking a flush.

"It's only a Senate speech, a contrived media happening. If we resort to that kind of coverage, we'll blow our integrity."

"Every time Henderson passes wind, we cover the bastard," Madison said, his private view intruding.

"Was it contemplated as a front-page story?"

Landau swallowed deeply. "I saw it as front page, yes. Lower left with a two-column head. Frankly, Nick, I think it's an important story."

"Would you like to review it, Nick?" Dover asked, perhaps feeling that the passion expended seemed disproportionate to the issue. But then Henderson had always been good copy.

"Yes, I would, Arnie," Nick said. He was groping for control now. Was he having a slight attack of paranoia or was Myra's hand clearly visible?

"I don't understand all the fuss, Nick," Landau said. His rest, so obviously refreshing, had them all at a disadvantage. Perhaps Landau was simply an innocent victim of this uncommon tactic on Myra's part. But it was enough to raise Nick's antenna.

"Let me see the story," Nick said, determined at least to keep it off the front page. He passed over the issue and continued with the meeting, but the idea persisted in his mind. He'd need time to examine this new wrinkle.

Surveying again the faces of the people who sat around the polished table, he could envision a scenario of conspiracy. It seemed obvious, circumstantially, at least, that Myra was making an attempt to force her will on the *Chronicle,* which, in the final analysis, meant forcing her will on him, the last screen through which the information must pass. In theory, it was her right to do so since she held the controlling stock interest, the corporate majority voice. It was, after all, a business which made no claims to democratic processes. But even monarchs could be captives of their courts and, following Charlie's lead, Nick had built layers of protection to cushion blows, absorb shocks, even allow for occasional breaches. Both he and Charlie had chosen their people carefully, although that did not insure perfection. People had needs, yearnings, dreams, conflicting motives, levels of ambition, different strategies. As a conscious puppeteer, Nick knew only that the voice of the *Chronicle,* with all its tones and dialects and impressions, must be his own.

Looking back now to that first moment of exposure to Mr. Parker and Myra, he could understand the inevitability of Myra's challenge. It came as no surprise, except for the manner in which she had marshaled her forces. At least her objectives were clear. She would try capture first, conquest without pain in the guise of shared power. If that didn't work, she would attempt envelopment, containment, a choking off of authority. Barring that would come the frontal assault, a battle in which she knew the Pyrrhic victory would leave the foundations in ruin, a price perhaps too high, although she might calculate that it was worth the gamble.

But if the strategies were clearly outlined, the question of her motive was less clearly defined. Was it, after all, inevitable that power once tasted increased the appetite, feeding upon itself? Was it, then, a mistake for him to have conspired to go after the jugular of a President, however deserving? Was he merely a willing tool of hers, or she of his? Had it left them with the kind of power that was unmanageable? Was she now testing how far the *Chronicle* could go? Was he, after all, defending a moral principle or his own power over other men? Was Henderson, inside his cool blue eyes, cringing in fear? Nick thought of Charlie's battle to stay free of Myra. But how much of that was the product of his madness, the warped focus of a deranged mind? Was she, at long last, making her move? If that were so, then everyone around the table was suspect, all possible agents.

After the meeting broke, Margaret followed him back to the office, exercising, as she had rarely done, the prerogative of the ex-spouse. He knew that his concentration had been deflected as the meeting had progressed. They had, in a sense, worked around him, conscious of his darkened mood. But only Margaret, with the benefit of their shared experience, could see beyond the public face, closer to the pain.

"You've got a bug up your ass, Nick," she said, when she had closed the office door behind her and perched stiffly on the facing chair, inspecting him. He remembered being once titillated by her profanity, so unique, almost charming in their generation.

"Change of life, I guess," he said. He could tell by the way she was making up to hide the wrinkling on her thin skin, that hormonal imbalance could be a credible excuse.

"Bullshit."

"Well then, the usual pressures. Maybe I can't take them the way I used to."

"More than that, Nick," she said. Her gaze seemed always magnified when she concentrated hard to see inside of him.

"I'll work it out," he blurted.

"Nothing I can do?"

"Nothing."

He searched her face for any trace of doubt. He had lost the habit of confiding to her. He felt the sudden heat from an old ash.

"Really, Maggie, I'll work it out," he said gently.

"Sorry for prying."

"Hear from Chums?" he asked, as if it were necessary to validate their link.

"Not a word."

"How long has it been?"

"Three months now."

"My God."

The shared concern for Chums generated sadness, the living symbol of their failed marriage. They had ceased recriminations years ago, sharing blame at last, along with the newspaper business, the principal debaser of their parenthood. Margaret got up from the couch, straightening her topheavy body, once the source of his pride. Middle age, like retribution, had settled the fat in her breasts. They had been her dominant physical charm and getting his hands on them was once an obsession, he remembered.

He had observed her peripherally at first, slim-hipped and large-breasted, as she moved in a graceful glide through the city room on the way to her desk in the feature department, a glass-walled section housing the columnists, the drama and movie critics, the society and financial editors. With skin as white as alabaster and red, upswept hair shining in the bright fluorescent lights, she was, amid the physical shabbiness of the motley band of newspaper types, a fresh rose in a sea of weeds. Having spent the last two years of the war as a copy "boy," a direct effect of the manpower shortage, she had forgone college in an effort to break into the newspaper business. The war had caused an imbalance in the sexual mix and she had seized the opportunity to storm the male fortress. By the time the boys started homeward from Europe and the Pacific, she had served her apprenticeship on the copy bench and was already seeing her occasional by-line over reviews of the "B" pictures.

It was not uncommon for busy eyes to rise as she passed through and soon he was joining in the staring and fantasizing in the trail of her body as she moved.

"Now there's a pair of headlights," Charlie had said, whistling lightly, a sound she must have heard; later Nick learned that she had secretly enjoyed the attention. To Nick, whose knowledge of women was confined to the demeaning "bam-bam, thank you, ma'am" variety of relationship in the makeshift cathouses of war-scarred Europe, Margaret Domier represented the epitome of unattainability. And although the men watched her, the blood, like his, he thought, surging in their genitals, she maintained the kind of professional coolness that could defuse them. As for Nick, even though they had begun a casual acquaintance, he always felt himself flushing in her presence, perhaps because his fantasies had by then been prompting him to masturbation and, unique to the era, massive guilt feelings.

He had wondered if others were sharing the recall of her covered breasts, imagining them lying warm and full, nipples pink and gorged, in the restraints of her brassiere. It was the years in which the mass media, preliminary to *Playboy*'s institutionalizing the phenomenon, was proclaiming the American male's hang-up with mammaries, and he assumed his case was of the galloping kind, investing him with the burden of imagined sexual aberration.

If it weren't for the massive snowstorm of 1947, which dumped twenty-six inches of whiteness, the last time in memory that New York had ever appeared so clean, he might have continued his masturbatory fantasies without abatement on through middle age. As it was, they were both working late on stories, she on a movie review and he, oddly, on the weather roundup, a sidebar on transportation tie-ups that was to be re-plated for the two-star edition. The office was nearly deserted when he dumped his finished story in front of the night city editor and moved toward the time clock. Margaret had just punched out and he found himself walking beside her along the corridor leading to the elevators.

"I'm supposed to catch a flick tonight, but I'd better

get home," she said. She was living with her parents in Borough Park then. "Besides, it doesn't much matter. I could rewrite the *Variety* review."

"That's cheating."

"Better than being caught in the bowels of the New York subway system freezing my ass off." The reference embarrassed him.

"No sweat with the subways. I just spoke to them."

"What about later?"

"They swear the system won't break down."

"That a guarantee?"

"I give it my personal blessing."

She looked at him curiously, as if seeing him for the first time. He felt the interest, sensed the moment.

"I'll make a deal," he stammered. "Take me to your movie and I'll take you home."

"Isn't it out of the way?" He was living with Charlie in a walk-up apartment on Second Avenue.

"Not at all," he lied. He hoped she wouldn't ask him where he lived. It was a gift, he mused, watching her button up the top buttons of her cloth coat over those tantalizing, bulging mysteries. She was silent as they went down in the elevator and walked through the lobby, the big globe circling on its pivot, with a protective chrome safety railing to enhance its veneration. In the street the snow was falling thickly, the drifts heavy. But with the feel of the crystals on the skin, and the clear smell in the air, there came an odd refreshment. It was a night to be out in, he had thought.

"What the hell," she said, tucking a hand under his arm. He imagined he felt the softness of her breasts pressing against him. They walked up Forty-second Street, following a beaten trail, their booted feet crunching in the fresh snow. He felt his heart leaping with the excitement of her nearness, embellished by the pride he felt in having the guts to ask her to be with him. They walked slowly, savoring the falling crystals which dropped gently on their skin. In the lobby of the New York State on Broadway, they brushed the snow off their faces and clothes. Her cheeks were red with the glow of the cold and the delight of the sudden warmth.

In the darkened theater he felt her closeness, his concentration difficult as he sensed her breathing in the rise and fall of her chest. She was restless, perhaps writing her review in her head as she watched the contrivances of the John Wayne horse opera, mounted in gloss, clichés abounding, the music in stirring accompaniment to the lingering long shots of the Western landscape. It was odd that he could never remember the name of the movie, only the impossible happiness he was feeling, waiting for her restlessness to brush her body against his, contemplating ways in which he could move closer, trembling with impatience for the next touch. He never found the courage to reach for her hand or slide his arm along the back of her seat. When the picture was over and they filed back toward the exit, he discovered that his shirt was soaked with perspiration. By the time they had ordered waffles at the near-empty Childs restaurant across the street, he had determined that he was in love and he could barely find the strength to lift the syrup-drenched confection to his mouth. Mostly he watched her lips move, noting the crookedness of one of her teeth, a charming flaw, as she recounted her opinion of the movie.

"Pure escapist," she said. "When you've seen one John Wayne, you've seen them all."

"Will you roast it?" he asked.

"No," she said after a pause. "I'll judge it strictly in terms of our audience. The yardstick will be whether it's a good John Wayne or a bad John Wayne."

"And the conclusion?"

"It was a good John Wayne."

"How many stars?"

"Three, easy."

"That's pandering."

She looked up at him, a speared waffle segment in midair. "Don't confuse me."

He felt himself trying to make an impression, assuming a flippancy that he hoped she might appreciate. Above all, he wanted to be noticed, remembered, flagged down by her consciousness. The subways were running on schedule, although the drafty stations were freezing and the wait between trains was long because of the hour. They had to change, finally arriving at her station in Brooklyn after midnight. During the long ride he had searched his repertoire for ideas that might interest her, compulsively seeking ways to keep the conversation going. He got her talking about herself. Her father was a longshoreman and she painted verbal pictures of a heavy, brutish man, sitting around the house in an undershirt, with a cowed mother who worked as a waitress, and, herself, the defiant daughter.

"My father is always mad at me," she said. "He can't understand my interest in being a newspaper-woman, among other things."

"Like what?"

"Like I'm a renegade Catholic. When I stopped going to confession he let me have it. I finally told him I got tired of the fat priest asking me where I touched myself. When I was through he was sorry he had asked. He's a good old bird, though, an overgrown kid."

"My father was a doctor. I hardly saw him when I was growing up. I only found out about him through his letters to me in the army. By the time I knew about him, he was already dying. He was a marvelous writer. I've saved all his letters."

He was conscious that he was saying things that could only be said to someone trusted, a gift from oneself, the private revelation reserved for special ears.

"What was it like, living in a small town?" she asked. He was overjoyed that he had, at last, engaged her. Perhaps it was the special way she asked that hinted of a deeper interest on her part. He felt its beginnings. No one had quite asked that question in precisely the same way, even Charlie, who considered Warren, Ohio, a kind of purgatory.

"Like living in the bosom of one big family." The reference made him hesitate, smiling inwardly at himself. "You knew pretty near everybody and since I was the doctor's son, I had a special status. My mother took this status quite seriously. She still revels in it. There was a special role, too, in having married a Jew. There's a mystique about Jewish doctors, a kind of prejudice in reverse, as if the Jew doctor were somehow smarter, more competent."

"Was it true?"

"Yes."

By the time the ride was over, he had reconstructed his life and she hers, hardly conscious of the screening process that might have made the related images less meaningful. On the long walk to her apartment building in the deepening snow, he sensed that they had become closer. Despite the snow and the difficulties he would have in returning to Manhattan, he wanted to prolong the closeness.

Sitting on the hallway steps outside her apartment, shivering in the unheated hall, they continued to talk, whispering. He felt her warm breath against his cheek. Finally she stood up and leaned against the wall.

"It was great fun, Nick." He looked into her eyes, deep in shadows, staring silently, feeling clumsy as he pressed his body against hers, searching for her lips. He had moved cautiously, hoping for some flicker of matching effort on her part, which came, surprisingly, as she lifted her face to compensate for his height, pressing her lips against his, her mouth slightly open. His tongue tentatively reached for a caress from hers, which responded, making his heart beat wildly. He felt her contours through the thick coat. Enveloping her in his arms, he pressed his mouth harder against hers, until he could feel her beginning to gasp for air. Never before had a kiss had so much meaning. When they had disengaged, she turned away quickly and without another word put her key in the apartment lock and let herself in. He stood there for a long time before he went back into the snow. He had all he could do to prevent himself from throwing himself frontside up into a snowbank and letting the crystals fall into his opened mouth. Instead, he made snowballs and flung them against the sides of cars. It took him three hours to get back to Manhattan. The subways had been disrupted after all.

8

Nick had always characterized himself as analytical, probing, with a mind that perceived life with some logic and sought truths with scientific curiosity. Yet he could not put his finger on the precise motivating factor within his makeup that insisted on his being a journalist. Perhaps it was a genetic transference of his father's pursuit of medicine, essentially a similar game of hunt and find, although newspapering made little pretense to the scientific method.

It was only a wild guess on his part, although there were writers alleged to be in his father's line dating back to Europe and his mother had a great-uncle who had once owned a weekly paper in a town near Toledo, Ohio. But since he could never find an answer in his ancestry that totally satisfied him, he thought instead that he had a special gift, a rare enthusiasm for the written word. Hadn't it been discovered early in his life by a fourth grade teacher? She had said to him that he had a real flair for composition, a spark that ignited soaring expectations in his parents' hearts and encouraged them to encourage him.

This encouragement, which came in heavy doses, made him bookish, and by the eighth grade he was becoming insular and shy; the world of the imagination, characters in library books, seemed more exciting than people who lived in Warren. How many exploding fantasies and ambitions are spawned in the public libraries of small towns? In Nick's case, after books, it was in the newspaper section of the library, where the papers hung neatly on wooden rods. Perhaps it was also the serenity of the reading room itself, the huge globes that hung on long heavy linked chains from the white ceilings, the polished tables and wooden chairs, the smell of books and newspapers. Each turn of the newspaper page brought portents of excitement, panoramic views of cataclysmic events, stirring passions, rages, humors to his young mind. The progression from the Columbus *Dispatch* to the Chicago *Tribune* to the New York *Times* began slowly, then accelerated, and soon he was comparing the way each newspaper said things and perceiving similar events in different ways. Then, suddenly, the library phase was over and the high school newspaper became the obsession. This first boldface by-line, misspelled as it was, was an event greater than his first long pants, which in the early thirties was an otherwise unmatched event.

Explanations about why he pursued the newspaper business with such passion never seemed, somehow, to hit the mark. He liked to think he had a natural talent for it, an insatiable curiosity, and a special flair for presentation, although in those days he still built stories like pyramids with the five W's always intact in the lead. Under the by-line, though, he couldn't resist the snappy lead and once looking over his high school clips which his mother had saved, he was quite impressed with the way he turned the phrases. You were a precocious bastard, Nick, he would tell himself, as he pored over his mother's musty shrine. Unfortunately, the old newspaper clips, yellowed and crumbled, would hardly stand the test of time. It had taught him how transitory newspapers really were.

A life is a series of converging vectors, Nick had decided in recalling his own. If he had not been drafted after college, he would not have met Charlie. And if Charlie had not been the peculiar blend of himself, the magnetizing force that could never be adequately explained, Nick might not have been attracted to him. In the end, the contrivance was Fate, which could have killed one or the other off in the random ways of war. There was, of course, no end to that kind of speculation, but somehow Nick could relate all this sudden interest in the why of his life to his burgeoning love for Margaret. Love was apparently the time one looked inward on oneself, searching in all the dark corners, a kind of spring dusting process, uncovering obscurities, discovering misplaced riches. Love, as Nick discovered then, was only corny if you weren't in it.

But now that love had come the real insecurities also began. Was it to be unrequited or returned? Was he doomed to heartache and despair or was there hope ahead, the promise of unbounded joy? On that first day after the movies and the snowstorm, and the first reaching out, he had come into the office earlier than usual. He was determined to get to his typewriter early, before prying eyes might accidentally see what he was writing. He wanted desperately to tell Margaret how much the time spent with her had meant to him. After all, the typed word was the operative mode of expression and surely Margaret was sensitive enough to understand that some things could only be said properly on pulpy copy paper.

But midway through his outpourings, being the only reporter around, he was sent out to cover a traffic accident on the West Side Highway, and soon became too absorbed with facts to allow the intrusion of any other sentiment. Maybe this was the thing about the newspaper business, the total absorption, the need to press against time, the concentration on acquiring information above all else. He had always seen that moment as a special intrusion, a harbinger of the destructive force of pressed time, the compelling necessity to feed the maw of the presses at fixed moments, whatever the human consequences of this timetable. *Deadline,* even as a word, was pregnant with depravity.

When he eventually returned to his love letter from the bloody sights of the highway accident the sweetness seemed gone from his typewriter. The fires of love still blazed, but the muse had failed.

There was a water fountain beyond her office from which, when you dipped your body to line your mouth with the spigot, you could see into the large glassed-in feature room where Margaret spent her time. That day, like a man with an insatiable thirst, he paraded back and forth from the water fountain waiting for a glimpse of her, which never materialized. He learned later that she had been out watching movies, but the sudden emergence in himself of the possessive state had made him seethe with anxieties, insecurities, jealousies.

When she finally did return to the office, he was exhausted with uncertainty, fed further by her seemingly casual interest as she lifted her head from the typewriter and waved, pleasantly enough, to his mooning face staring from the other side of the glass. The very aspect of pleasantness, so kind and unassuming, so bland, could only be a heatless flicker to his inflammable inner tinder. Had he misread her the night before?

Fearful that he would betray the vulnerable softness in himself, he was quick to assume that he was merely the newest victim of unrequited love, and he deliberately changed his tactics. His first strategy was a withdrawal. He decided to ignore her, only to discover on still another trek to the water fountain that she had left for the day.

"What the hell's the matter, Nick?" Charlie had asked. The loss of self-possession was obvious.

"Bellyache."

"Where the hell were you last night?"

"Around."

"Okay, don't tell." Charlie had his own problems then.

When he met Margaret in the city room she smiled at him almost too broadly and their exchanges were bantering and, on his part, cautious.

"How's the mooin pitchers?"

"It was a bad week. The ants in my pants are getting restless."

He searched her eyes for the remotest sparkle of returned affection. God, he loved that woman, he was certain. Near her, his body trembled and his tongue froze in his mouth. What had he done? What was there in him that she could not find equally as fascinating as he found in her?

The pain was the more excruciating in the face of the Christmas season. New York bloomed with Christmas preparations. Park Avenue was blazing with colored lights, festooned in its annual trail of huge Christmas trees. Santa Clauses stood on street corners collecting money in their chimneys, looking jolly with rouged cheeks while they stamped their feet in the cold.

Perhaps it was simply the agony of unrequited love that embellished his introspection, but that Christmastime, he seemed to look out upon the world with a heightened sense of observation.

"Remember two years ago, Charlie?" he asked. They were huddled up in their coats against the freezing wind as they walked back to their apartment. Charlie's nose was running over his upper lip.

"How can I forget?"

"It was a bitch. We're lucky we lived through it."

"I hope you're right."

He looked at Charlie.

"Yeah," he said. "We'll have to see if it was worth the sparing."

"Shit."

It was a hurled curse out of context, a hint of anxiety which did not surface until a couple of days before Christmas Eve. Absorbed with his own problems of apparent rejection, Nick didn't see what was happening to Charlie.

At that stage in their friendship Nick knew little of Charlie's early history. Charlie had been brought up in modest suburban circumstances in the days when suburban life was a genuine symbol of WASP superiority, even without the frills of wealth. Nick had pieced together a picture of a scrubbed American family living in a modest house with porch and faintly squeaky screen door, neatly painted and shingled and looking out on a broad elm-lined street, a three-block walk from the quaint Long Island railroad station. From the details of the half-sketched picture, Nick could summon up images of the old swimming hole, smoking corn silk back in the shed, bamboo fishing poles, bubble gum cards, even an American flag fluttering on a pole in front of the house on legal holidays.

Growing up in Warren was like that, and in Nick's frame of reference his first mental picture of Charlie's younger days was a hangover from his own happy childhood. He could not imagine childhood without warmth and serenity, and it wasn't until Christmas dinner in the Pell house in Hempstead that he finally saw the inside of Charlie's anguish.

Charlie's invitation seemed frantic.

"You've got to come with me," he had commanded.

"Got to?"

"Please, Nick. I just can't do it alone. It's been five years since I've been there for Christmas. I need a little moral support."

"You sound like it's some kind of hell."

"You don't know the half of it."

In the train, Nick sat closest to the window, watching the flat landscape recede, the now barren farmland interspersed with tiny towns looking neat under the snow blanket. He felt Charlie's restlessness as his friend crossed and uncrossed his legs and slumped in his seat. He was silent for most of the trip, until near the end when he finally spoke.

"My mother's mad, Nick," he said.

"Mad?" He had thought Charlie had meant angry. "At you?"

"Mad, mad. Balmy. Nutty as a fruitcake." Nick turned from the window and looked at Charlie. There was no humor in the retort at all, despite the bantering cadence of his response. "We'll all be playing a little game. The idea is not to notice how nuts she really is. Keep an eye on my old man. He'll give you the cues." Nick didn't answer, contemplating the possibilities of an eccentric afternoon. Charlie sighed and shook his head. "It'll be grim, kid."

By the time they reached Hempstead, the train had emptied and they had little trouble finding a rickety thirtyish vintage cab outside the station. Nick could feel Charlie grow more tense as the ancient taxi rattled through town and past the deserted shopping area with the Christmas decorations tinkling in the wind. The cab pulled up in front of a white house, carefully maintained, as if the owner had taken special care to keep it shined like a prized jewel. To Nick it looked bright and cheerful enough, a picture postcard quality.

After the cab had crunched away through the white, clean snow, Charlie stood for a moment surveying the house, his eyes growing moist.

"A pretty little place," Nick said. Charlie turned his face away and sniffled, brushing the back of his hand across his nose.

"Don't let it fool you," he barked, kicking up a mist of snow as he strode up the wooden steps to the door and banged the polished brass knocker.

A thin, cadaverous face appeared, as deeply lined as if a sculptor's tool had sliced deep ruts from the man's high cheekbones down to the chin. He was dressed in a dark blue suit, shiny with use, surely his best suit, with a white shirt and tightly knotted tie; a gold collar pin passed under the knot, tightening a frayed collar. There was a vaguely familiar hint of Charlie in the way the man carried himself, although that aspect of him seemed lost to the impression of a kind of withered plant. There was no display of affection between father and son, only a lightly clasped handshake.

"This is my friend, Nick Gold," Charlie said. Nick put out his hand and was conscious of a valiant attempt at a forced smile. But the older man retained a puzzled look, keeping his arm stiff, leaving Nick's proffered hand stuck in the air.

"I didn't expect . . ." Charlie's father began.

"It's all right," Charlie said. Nick observed that they were talking in whispers. They followed the older man through a long uncarpeted corridor, the wood brightly polished. It squeaked lightly as they walked. Nick noticed a sparsely set dining table. Shades were drawn, casting shadows, the bright day shut away except where shafts of white light struck inside where the shades were not snugly fitted. They walked into a parlor lit by low-wattage bulbs under old-fashioned lampshades. Nick's further observation of the room was interrupted by a sudden change in voice pitch as Charlie's father, straightening, began walking with an exaggerated gait, like an actor coming suddenly onstage.

"Charles is here, Princess," the man said. He had directed his falsetto, cheerful voice to a hideously white-masked woman sitting stiffly on a wing chair. Charlie flashed a troubled gaze at Nick, as if urging him to patience, obviously embarrassed by the sight of the strangely made-up woman. Charlie's mother's face looked like that of some strange rag doll, the lips exaggerated in a bright red cupid's bow, eyebrows shining in a long thin line, eyes deep in mascara, the stark white forehead ringed with little red curls. But it was the white makeup, so beyond humanness, like a character in mime, that held the interest. Nick watched her with fascination as one might observe a freak in a circus sideshow. The woman was obviously demented. Mad, Charlie had warned.

"Hi, Princess," Charlie said, smiling and bending over to kiss a pasty cheek. A tiny white hand lifted itself weakly to Charlie's shoulder. "Here's Nick, Princess,"

Charlie said, struggling to maintain his role in the charade, winking, a signal for Nick to follow his lead.

"Wonderful to meet you, Princess," Nick stammered, feeling difficulty in assuming the role. The tableau of the frail painted woman, dressed in an old lace gown, years out of style, and the two men, father and son, casting themselves as characters in her confused fantasy, told the story of their pain in a single glance.

"Did he put his bicycle in the garage?" she asked. Her voice seemed calm as she directed the question to her husband.

"Yes, Princess."

"And have you washed your hands?" she said, this time to Charlie.

"Yes, Princess," Charlie answered.

"Such a good boy," the woman sighed. "You should have seen his report card."

"Yes, Princess. His teacher said he's the smartest boy in the class."

"We've made a wonderful Christmas dinner," the woman said, a flash of lucidity, it seemed, if one closed one's eyes. "We've roasted a beautiful chicken and, if you're a good, good boy, we have strawberry tarts."

"How lovely, Princess," Charlie said, moving his hand to signal Nick to respond. It was apparent he was quite familiar with the stage directions.

"Lovely," Nick said. The word stuck hoarsely in his throat.

Charlie stepped back and dropped heavily into the couch.

"Are you in Charles' class?" the woman said, turning her shadowed eyes to Nick.

"Yes," Charlie's father replied, frowning at Nick. It seemed essential that they find him a role.

"Do you like Mrs. Peters?" the woman asked. Nick felt sudden moisture bursting into his armpits, sliding coldly down his sides.

"She's . . . terrific, Mrs. . . . ." Charlie tugged at his sleeve. "Peters," he said quickly. He could sense Charlie's father's relief.

"Do you get good marks?"

"Not as good as Charles," Nick replied. He felt the pain of the two Pell men hanging heavy in the room.

"Mrs. Peters says that Charles is the smartest boy in the class," Charlie's mother repeated.

"We're very proud of that. Aren't we, Princess?" Charlie's father said, his eyes fastened to her face, quick to react.

"Are you wearing clean underwear, Charles?"

"Of course, Princess."

"It's Christmas," the woman said. "Little Jesus will be so happy."

Charles, Nick noticed, held himself tightly, unsure of his performance. Nick dared not look too obviously at his friend's embarrassed face, lest he see the full extent of his unhappiness. The conversation continued along the same track, recapturing past moments, lived through as in a cycle, as if time had become suspended somewhere, an endless wheel, in Mrs. Pell's corroded brain.

"You should take your nap before Christmas dinner, Princess," Charlie's father said after the conversation had grown repetitive. She put out her frail arm and Mr. Pell took it, gently half lifting her. She rose unsteadily and he led her out of the room. They could hear them rise slowly on the staircase, the wood creaking in the silence of the darkened house.

When she had gone, Charlie looked helplessly at Nick. He reached into his pocket and slipped a cigarette from a crumpled pack. Lighting it, he inhaled deeply and blew the smoke angrily out of his nostrils.

"Weird, eh, Nick?" he said, his agitation apparent now as he came out of his role.

"How long has it been?"

"All my life, it seems. Actually I must have been about ten when the final snap came."

They sat silently in the dark, oppressive room. A piano stood in the corner, the wood shining, a lace doily stretched across its top on which a vase stood with paper flowers. Nick was sure Mr. Pell had kept the piano finely tuned. The creaking stairs signaled the return of Mr. Pell. He came, lips in a tight smile, as if a weight had been removed. He seemed to unwind into normality.

"How are you, Son?" he said quietly. Nick felt like an intruder.

"How long can it go on like this?"

Charlie's father's eyes looked warily at Nick.

"It's okay, Dad," Charlie said, "I don't care if Nick hears."

"I'm sorry," Mr. Pell said. "We never have visitors."

"She should be put away," Charlie said. He stood up and paced the room.

"Never," the father said.

"It's a lost cause. She's getting worse. You're pissing away your life."

"That's my business."

It seemed a familiar, ritualized exchange.

"She's worse than ever," Charlie said. His fingers felt the lace doily on the piano. "It's wrong."

"You're away," his father said. "What does it matter to you?"

"Christ, Dad." Nick watched as his friend's fingers tightened on the lace. "I can't stand to see it."

"You don't come that often."

The two men glared at each other across the room.

"I don't know how you stand it," Charlie said gently, in what seemed a grudging acknowledgment of his father's courage.

Later, they sat around the dining room table on which Mr. Pell had set three places. When he had gone into the kitchen, Charlie said, "He has to feed her. He won't do that in front of strangers. He probably has her sedated."

"I had no idea, Charlie," Nick said.

"Who could possibly have any idea? He's made it a way of life. It was bad enough growing up with it. I hate coming here."

It was obvious that his father had taken great care to prepare a fine dinner. He brought the roast in and silently carved it, serving his son first. When they were all served, the vegetables and potatoes passed around, his father asked, "How's the newspaper business, Charlie?"

It seemed to open a new phase, the simple, quite normal curiosity of an interested parent. Charlie's response seemed overzealous, detailed, as if he were writing the older man a letter. The responses were long, embellished with tiny asides, a litany of his life. It was a display, prodded by compulsion, to tell everything, to paint a finite picture of a son's life, as if it were happening to another person. Only a genuine feeling of love, Nick thought, or guilt, could prompt such an outpouring. He was hardly that informational with his own mother. Nick had been curious that Charlie had brought no Christmas gifts. This was the gift, the telling of his life, and the father knew it, soaking it up like a sponge.

Nick could see the joy it gave the older man, hopelessly out of touch with anything beyond the closed world of his wife's madness and his own charade. It validated all he had felt for Charlie, the measure and texture of his admiration, perhaps his love. After dinner they drank coffee and smoked. He noted that Charlie glanced at the grandfather clock that stood in the corner of the dining room, a watching face. The father saw the surreptitious glance and his face clouded over again, the ruts in his cheeks deepening.

The light around the edges of the shade faded and soon they were standing at the door again for a farewell that on the surface seemed as tepid as the greeting they had received earlier. But having received a greater knowledge of both men during the afternoon, Nick could observe the deeper emotions behind what earlier had appeared a joyless response. The handshakes were still weak, lifeless, but in the touching of their flesh, Nick could understand what father and son really felt, a shared pain. Charlie looked upward as they moved through the short ritual of their farewells.

"Kiss the Princess for me," he said, and soon they were crunching through the snow in the starlit night toward the ancient taxi that now waited at the curb.

Before he stepped into the opened door, with Nick already inside, Charlie turned once again toward the neatly painted house, maintained with such meticulous care, as if in its preservation his father might find some meaning to his hellish existence. When he turned again, tears streamed down from his eyes and he held a hand over his mouth to mask his sobs.

9

The visit to Charlie's parents had thrown his friend into a deep depressive silence, an impenetrable introspection about which Nick dared not speculate. It could not be easy to simply file away the memories of that house, that childhood, that imprisonment. Attempts to jolt Charlie out of his cocoon of noncommunication floundered on shoals of indifference. If he had been looking for landmarks at the time, if he had had the talent of clairvoyance or the absolute knowledge of subsequent events, he might have spotted the beginnings of Charlie's liquor problem. Not that, even then, it would have been an obvious clue. Drinking was so enmeshed into newspapering, especially at the *News* with its odd crowd of Irishmen, that signs of sclerosis, bulbous noses, and the red crust of skin blemishes across the center of a face were worn like badges of honor, and a man's worth was measured by quantities of alcoholic consumption.

To be falling-down, raving, screaming drunk was an aberration to be understood and endured, provided it was done only periodically. It was understood that for any man, life could sometimes become so unendurable and preposterous that such a state was a prerequisite for coping with its horrors. A man in his cups was an object of veneration, a troubled soul for whom a whiskey was the only succor.

Special honors went to men like McCarthy who could imbibe in quantities measured in fifths until their senses finally rebelled; the length of a lucid frame of mind was important. There was also a measure of character in the time needed for the head to clear; McCarthy shined here as well, returning to the scene the next morning able to function, the tremors controlled by the day's first hair of the dog. It was not uncommon even for Nick and Charlie to stumble homeward, like two awry bookends, after a night of drinking at Shanley's long wooden bar. In that environment, inebriation was positively encouraged. It was, after all, the sign of the complex man, a soul of many humors, a mind in turmoil, which only the god of the grape could soothe.

It was, therefore, not unexpected for Charlie to seek the solace of booze. He was, after all, under the eye of of a watchful friend whose duty it was to carry him home, remove his shoes, and clean him up the next morning, pouring the first amber drop into the shot glass. In that world, it was seen as taking the cure. Knowing the illness, Nick was all the more solicitous. Unfortunately, there was a kind of conditioning involved for a massive bender for which Charlie's constitution had not been prepared, and the morning-after recoveries were far too long to escape notice. By noon it was obvious that Charlie couldn't make it through the day.

"Take him out," the city editor had whispered two days later, watching Charlie's head slump over the typewriter. Nick led Charlie out of the city room, down in the elevator, propping him finally against Shanley's bar where he was allowed to nurse the devil in glorious privacy in the care of the bartender, expert in this kind of babysitting.

But while this was accepted procedure, after three days Nick began to worry. Perhaps it was this that shook his resolve not to pursue Margaret, made him careless about his own vulnerability as far as she was concerned. Certainly it made him less shy, even crafty, as he followed her one day to the Automat on the corner of Forty-second Street and Third Avenue. Drawing a cup of coffee from the tap, he brought it to her table.

"I'm having one helluva time with Charlie," he said as an opening gambit, hoping she would sense his need to unburden himself.

"That's pretty obvious."

"He's got troubles. Big ones."

"Common afflictions," she said, indifferently, without sympathy.

He watched her face, the cheeks moving as she daintily bit into a sandwich. Was he soliciting her pity? A new ploy. He had expected her to inquire further. Instead, she silently chewed her sandwich, washing it down with coffee. He searched her eyes for some hint of interest.

"Did I offend you the other night?" he blurted.

"Of course not, Nick."

"Then why the indifference?"

"Indifference?" Her eyes widened. She was silent a moment and put the remains of her sandwich back on the plate.

"I'm not indifferent, Nick."

"You're not?"

"No. Surely you can see that."

"I can't. I really can't. I know that I'm not indifferent to you, not after the other night. I really felt we were approaching something."

"I know, Nick," she said, dropping her eyes.

"Well, then," he said, rejoicing in the admission. He knew again that he was in love. She paused, sipping her coffee, watching him.

"I'm not looking for that kind of relationship, Nick. I'm not ready for it."

"You mean it requires some kind of apprenticeship?" He was conscious of his sarcasm.

"No, I don't mean that at all."

"Well, then, explain it better." He felt his pressure on her. Was she teasing him?

"It's just not a priority in my life, Nick. It can only interfere with my career. Frankly, I'm frightened of any entanglement. Nick, you just don't know what it means being a woman in this business. There are lots of pitfalls."

"I hadn't realized you were so ambitious."

"That's exactly how a man would react," she said sharply. His eyes dropped to her chest. He felt a vague tug in his loins.

"I didn't know it had a gender," he said.

"I *am* ambitious, Nick. I took advantage of the war, of the boys being away, and I don't want to yield my position. Can't you see how vulnerable I am?"

"No, I can't." He hadn't suspected. It seemed far from his own frame of reference.

He hadn't imagined that there were other reasons, beyond simple human chemistry. It was, for him, a totally different way to view things. She was telling him that she cared for him. What was there beyond that? It was difficult for him to comprehend. Ambition was a male province, he reasoned.

"I'm determined that nothing get in the way of my chances to make it in this business."

"What has one thing got to do with the other?"

"A lot."

"I'm confused," he admitted.

"That's because you're a man. I know what I'm talking about, Nick. I'm prepared to make whatever sacrifice is required. I don't want to get trapped."

"By what?"

"Biology. Tradition. The way I look at it, I'm lucky to be where I am. I don't want to blow it. If I had started just three years later, I'd be competing with the boys coming back from the war. Who the hell do you think would be getting the promotions? As it is, I begged them to put me on the street. Not that I'm unhappy being a movie reviewer. They can see that as a woman's place, that and writing about garden parties or weddings. I consider myself damned lucky."

He searched his memory for names of women reporters. There was one at the *News,* a tough old bag.

"There are lots of women in this business," he mumbled, conscious of his attempts to twist reality.

"Bullshit."

He looked at her and smiled.

"All right, I concede that it might be slightly tougher for a woman."

"Slightly," she sneered.

"But that doesn't mean you have to crawl into a shell. Why deny a perfectly human reaction? Margaret, I care for you. To me that's important, very important. I can't see how that can possibly interfere with your career."

"Poor Nick," she said, "you just don't understand. I care for you too, Nick."

His heart leaped with joy. "So what's the problem?"

She shook her head. "Men," she said. "Why are you all so obtuse?"

He put his hand on top of hers, feeling its warmth against his flesh. "Hey, in a few days it'll be New Year's Eve. I've been assigned to cover it. Why not tag along? Unless you've got something better to do."

She looked at him for a moment, shaking her head and laughing, the tension broken. "What the hell?" she said.

"Sure, what the hell?"

Later he had gone back to Shanley's to fetch Charlie, incoherent by now. He hailed a cab and maneuvered him into it, cursing his responsibility. Charlie's problem was becoming a burden to him. Compassion for his friend was wearing thin.

"It's time to stop this shit now," he said firmly, pushing Charlie, fully dressed, into the shower.

Contemplating this renewed burst of feeling for Margaret, loosed now by the possibilities of reciprocity, left Nick little time to play crutch for Charlie. And, perhaps, seeing its abrupt loss, Charlie responded by taking the first weak and awkward steps by himself. It wasn't that he went on the wagon. The next morning he was still nipping at the bottle to steady himself, but he was able to function through the day.

Covering New Year's Eve for the *News* was, in itself, an anomaly. The year actually changed sometime between the publication of the two-star and the three-star, and the story of the festivities was more a tradition than a necessity, causing havoc on the tenses. Fleets of photographers were sent out early to the city's most exotic night spots to set up New Year's Eve pictures. The pictures were always stilted, since the principals had been gathered either from the street or from among the booze-soaked regulars at the bar to whom New Year's Eve meant only that liquor sales would continue for an extra two hours, till six A.M. A reporter could write the first roundup by rewriting last year's story, then calling in changes as the evening progressed. Even that was fully predictable and the reporter was allowed to map out his own itinerary.

Thus, Nick and his companions could pursue a freeloading hegira. Naturally, considering that it was his first date with Margaret, he took special care to choose carefully. He had also prevailed upon her to find a date for Charlie, who reached New Year's Eve in reasonable control of himself

Since Nick was the only one of them actually assigned to work that night, it was decided that they would all meet at Shanley's for a hamburger, lining the stomach before the impending trek. Their first stop after Shanley's was to be Sammy's Bowery Follies, one of the city's most popular freak shows.

At Shanley's, Nick and Charlie sat at one of the tables in the rear, waiting for the girls to arrive. Charlie was drinking beer in deference to the evening's sexual possibilities, and spent the time rolling bread balls on the checkered tablecloth. For all his wise-cracking bravado and his rugged and disheveled good looks, Charlie was not a ladies' man, although he enjoyed creating for himself the role of great swordsman. In Europe they had both stood on the same cathouse line, more as a badge of male macho than a provoking necessity of the sex glands.

Sweeping into Shanley's, her wonderful breasts jiggling promisingly in her open coat, Margaret was followed by a somewhat less prepossessing girl. Charlie glanced at Nick with that desperate look of letdown, the unfulfilled dream, a hint of disaster yet to come.

The girl, whose name was Edie, was tall, big-hipped, her face beginning to puddle into fat. Margaret made the introductions and they sat down and ordered their hamburgers and french fries. The sight of his date for the evening had caused Charlie to switch to hard booze.

"Edie's a nurse," Margaret said. "She works at King's County Hospital."

"We work odd hours," Edie said, bending her head over the foam of the beer. "I'm lucky to be off." Charlie drank his booze from a shot glass, chasing it down with beer.

"Do you take a Hippocratic oath?" he asked.

"As a matter of fact we do, a sort of adapted version of the one the doctors take."

"Do you believe in it?"

Nick could see the beginnings of drunken belligerence. Edie looked helplessly at Margaret, who shrugged, signaling neutrality. Nick reached for Margaret's hand and held it tightly, reveling in its yielding warmth. He felt too much joy to be bothered as Charlie pressed on about the nursing business as if he were seeking to draw out of the girl something he might attack.

"Yes I do," she said. "I wouldn't be a nurse if I didn't."

"Does it bother you to see all that human misery?"

"Of course."

"Don't you feel ghoulish?"

"Of course not."

"Do you see lots of hopeless cases?"

"There is always hope."

"I can tell you're a Catholic."

"Edie and I went to parochial school together," Margaret offered, turning her eyes from Nick's. "Only I'm the renegade."

"You mean you believe all that Catholic crap?" Charlie asked. He had ordered another shot.

"Of course," Edie answered brightly.

"Everyone to their own opiate," Charlie said.

"To each his own," Edie retorted.

"Margaret?" Charlie asked. The smile took the edge off his sarcasm. "You brought me a saint. What a great gift for the New Year. A healer, a believer, balm for the savage spirit."

"I see you've got a flair for poetic expression," Edie said, revealing her toughness. Nick knew then that she could handle Charlie.

They finished their hamburgers and hailed a cab. Nick sat between the two girls, his arm around Margaret's waist, feeling the joy of being so close to her. His confidence in the promise of the evening began to grow. Now he was sorry that he had dragged Charlie with him. He determined to ignore him. Nothing, he vowed to himself, would destroy the specialness of this evening. He was in love, he assured himself. All disruptive factors paled beside this knowledge. He pressed his lips into Margaret's neck.

Sammy's Bowery Follies used the aberration of alcoholic addiction as a form of entertainment. Men and women, grown uncannily alike with the bloat of wine—apparently a wino was able to sustain greater longevity in his addiction than whiskey drunks—actually performed a show for the benefit of the curious uptowners who flocked to the place. It was certainly worth a good picture and the photographer had apparently set up his shot and left. A little man with a big paunch showed them to a table after Nick had identified himself. They ordered a round of drinks. Charlie ordered a double Scotch.

"It's weird," Margaret said, looking at the odd people.

"No more weird than the rest of life," Charlie pointed out.

"I agree with *you*, Margaret," Nick said.

He held Margaret's hand under the table, his thigh pressed against hers. Lifting his glass, he clinked it against hers.

"Let's order champagne," Nick said. "The occasion calls for champagne. It's New Year's Eve." He motioned to the proprietor.

"You got champagne?"

"Champagne?" He yelled across the room to a fat toothless woman strumming a piano. "Hey, Fanny, we got any champagne?"

"Yesh," she giggled, her booze-burned throat hoarse but still strong. "We just made a batch in the back room."

"How'd you make it, Fanny?" a man shouted from the bar.

She put one hand over a huge breast and squeezed it.

"And I've given it my best year, baby," she squealed.

The proprietor brought over a bottle of New York champagne and an ice bucket. Popping the cork, he poured it into glasses. They watched it bubble, lifted their glasses simultaneously, and clinked them.

"To 1948," Nick said. He was feeling warm, festive.

Edie looked at her wristwatch. "We've still got two hours."

The girl at the piano began to sing a medley of lewdly rearranged Cole Porter tunes, to the accompaniment of howls from the bar. Soon they all had the giggles and the champagne was gone. Even Edie had loosened up a bit and appeared to be enjoying herself, although Charlie could not seem to shake his sardonic mood, visible in the way he smoked his cigarette, holding his hand stiff, the cigarette locked between the two wrong fingers. Nick went off to call the rewrite desk and fill in the color for the next edition.

"You lucky son of a bitch," the rewrite man said.

"Tough shit," he replied, exhilarated by Margaret's presence and the effects of the champagne.

They left Sammy's Bowery Follies holding their glasses, with Nick tucking another bottle of champagne under his arm. Hailing a cab, they arranged to hire the man for the evening, pooling their meager funds of about thirty dollars and sealing the deal with the driver in champagne toasts. They stopped at El Morocco, the Carnival Club, then Billy Rose's Diamond Horseshoe.

By the time they arrived at the Diamond Horseshoe, Charlie was staggering, leaning against Edie who was also slightly tipsy but still in full control. The nightclub was jammed. Noisemakers filled the air with deafening blasts. Streamers sailed through the smoke like rockets. Nick was in love, feeling gay, happy, light-headed. Hell, it was 1948! He had lived through a war. He was working in his chosen profession. He had a great friend and he was in love with a girl and the future stretched out before him in an endless verdant landscape. No New Year's Eve could possibly match this one, he thought.

The music grew louder. The din of voices accelerated. Then the orchestra began the strains of "Auld Lang Syne" and he and Margaret stood up and kissed, their bodies hungering, lips parted, tongues deeply entwined. Around them the celebration reached its final intensity. Even Charlie and Edie were locked in an embrace.

"I love you, Margaret. I love you more than anything I can think of that exists in the world." He was conscious of the clichés, the platitudes, but could not find better words. Margaret was silent. He could feel tears stream down her cheeks.

"Why cry, darling?" Nick asked.

"I'm not sure how happy I should be." She seemed helpless and vulnerable in his arms. Sensing this only increased his feeling of strength, of confidence.

He felt the surge of his manhood, the meaning of its mystery.

"We're going," he said suddenly to Charlie, who looked up drunkenly and nodded.

"We'll be fine," Edie said, tentatively watching Charlie, whose head wavered.

"We're going to the apartment. Meet us later," Nick said. He smiled thinly, admiring his courage, watching Margaret turn away her eyes in embarrassment. Outside the streets were jammed. Times Square was the center of the universe on New Year's Eve, the great symbol of American optimism that the passage of time would make all things better. They couldn't find their cab in the crush and walked instead, the air clearing their heads as they strode with arms around each other's waist.

He had spent the morning, before he went to work, cleaning and dusting the apartment, even washing the windows and the woodwork, banging the dust out of the upholstery, buoyed by the hope that somehow Margaret and he would make it back together. The moment they were inside the apartment, the consciousness of self-realization goaded him into a swift, lustful, strong embrace. They stood in the center of the living room, too greedy for each other to take the time to remove their clothes in logical sequence, and she was still wearing her coat when he had removed her brassiere, the first priority of his obsession. He felt the naked breasts in his hands wonderfully firm, the nipples straight and hard. He could not let her go even for a moment, his right hand fondling her breasts while his left reached down her back, insinuating itself beneath the elastic of her panties and down to where her buttocks parted. Standing there, tongues entwined, still in their coats, the wonder of her flesh in his hands, he could feel the strong shudder of his own ecstatic orgasm as its force consumed his body with joy. She must have felt it too since her body pressed closer as his raged against hers. He could barely catch his breath, wondering if she had shared the experience.

The orgasm by no means spent his passion and when they had at last undressed properly and slipped between the cool sheets of the bed, clinging to each other, he could not believe his happiness. The light from the living room was enough to spread good visibility in the room and, assured that her modesty would not be offended, he slid the sheets down and looked at her wonderful breasts, more beautiful than he had imagined. He squeezed them gently, fondled them, rolled the nipples gently between his lips, then seeing her special joy in it, he rubbed the tip of his erected penis around the nub of each nipple, giving equal time to each breast, until her response in reaching out to his erection and taking command of the process induced him once again to a raging orgasm, only this time he could feel the mutuality of their spendings, a delight never to be replicated in quite the same way. They rested, smoked cigarettes, and talked in hushed tones about their aspirations, exploring their feelings.

"You can't conquer biology," he had told her proudly, as if he were imparting a great truth.

"I guess not," she said.

"You see, it's not so easy to control how you feel."

"Not easy at all." She paused. "But I still intend to fight this thing. It just isn't going to louse up my priorities."

Perhaps it was the implied challenge, but he was reaching now for her clitoris, gently playing with it until her response became obvious and he was consciously exciting her, taking his time, fondling and sucking the fantastic breasts, watching her eyelids flutter with pleasure, kissing her body with open lust. He put his finger deeply into her tight vagina, wondering if she was a virgin, hoping in his heart that she was.

He had carefully placed his condoms in the little end table beside the bed and, clumsily reaching for them, opened a package and watched her eyes as she sneaked a look at how he was rolling it over his erected member.

"Please be careful, my darling," she whispered. The joy of knowing he would be first seemed to enlarge his soul. Certainly it increased the immensity of his penis as he gently inserted it into her and felt her tightness as she struggled to fulfill the connection, surely feeling the mystery of this, her first joining, a special gift to him, a validation of her commitment.

As his body moved deeper inside her, ignoring her brief outcry of pain, he could feel the singlemindedness in her, her determination to complete the offering, as if he were merely a participant in some ritual known only to her. It was an evening rich in wonders. Later he would contemplate this memory as a point of beginning, a joyful assertion of himself, knowing that to her it seemed always a moment of weakness, a kind of self-betrayal. And yet, between them, it represented the only sustained tangibility left in the shambles of their marriage, greater than Chums, since from that evening onward all was downhill in their relationship.

He had fallen asleep in her arms, still entwined in their connection, when the telephone stirred him to consciousness. Through the rent in the windowshade, he could tell that dawn was beginning. At first he could not recognize the voice.

"It's Edie," she said finally. He had not understood what she had been saying. "Charlie is very drunk. He's sprawled on the revolving globe in the lobby of the *News* building. I think you better come."

"My God." He sprang out of bed and slipped into his clothes. "It's Charlie," he told Margaret, who was stretching awake. "He's drunk on top of the world."

"What?"

He bent over her and kissed her deeply on the mouth. "I love you. I truly love you."

"And me you," she said.

He ran through the streets and found Charlie, sprawled on the top of the revolving globe, his jacket caught on the axis, as if he were impaled.

With the help of the security guard, who had been unsuccessful at initial attempts at dislodgement, he detached Charlie and carried him into the street.

"He's really a nice fellow," Edie said. "Something seems to be eating at him."

"That's obvious," Nick said. He was annoyed at the intrusion. Edie looked uncommonly pale in the early morning light.

"He kept pressing me about mercy killing. He started to get really nasty about it."

"You mean he accused you of something?"

"I couldn't tell." She held out her hand and he shook it gently. "Even though it ended like this, I had a great time."

"What made him do it?"

"He said he wanted to screw the world." She smiled nervously. Such language was obviously not a common practice with her. He watched as she got into a cab. He never saw her again.

10

Henry Landau's tan seemed to be fading quickly as he stood before Nick, his eyes narrowed, betraying a hint of confusion. It was difficult to think of Landau as conspiratorial, Nick thought, determined nonetheless to stay on his guard. Deceit was a wily bastard, he had learned. It could stay frozen into the landscape like a poisonous snake, camouflaged, ready to squirt deadly venom when one least expected it.

"Maybe I missed something," Landau said, "but the Henderson thing seems blown out of proportion."

"Frankly, I hadn't meant it to be." Nick forced himself into a semblance of outward calm. He reached for a cigarette, lit it, and puffed deeply, letting his gaze slide over papers on his desk. He hoped it would make him appear less tense, distracted, as if the Henderson thing had passed.

"Dover gave me Grinnel's Henderson story." Landau put it on Nick's desk. He had let it drop from a higher distance than might be polite. "It seems perfectly sensible to me," Landau said. "The health bill idea, as we all agree, is a great one. Our editorials say so, at least. And Grinnel, as you'll see, wrote the story as if it were an opening gun of a new attempt at passage. Essentially the news value is in the timing."

Nick looked down at the copy on his desk. "I'll look it over."

"It's getting late, Nick," Landau said. "Do I count it in or out?"

Was Landau putting pressure on him? Nick looked up at the tanned face and forced a smile.

"I don't want us to go out on a limb. Gunderstein's working on a story that might be quite damaging to Henderson." Nick watched Landau's reaction.

"I heard."

From where? Nick wondered. From whom?

"So you see . . ."

"No, I don't," Landau said. "What's one thing got to do with the other? Gunderstein's story is one thing, and besides it's far from being proved out. But the Henderson speech is quite real. What you're doing is establishing a line on Henderson. Next thing you know we'll have to hand out lists as to who we approve of and who we're against."

Perhaps it was the reference to lists. Nick remembered looking over Myra's list. What was happening here? Was Landau simply being clever, playing with him, manipulating him? Was he Myra's agent?

"Henry, let me ask you a question," Nick said cautiously, pausing briefly. "How do you feel about Henderson?"

"Feel?"

"That's it. Feel."

Landau hesitated. *"Feel* implies an emotional response. I don't think I'm in a position to answer the question on that basis."

"Suppose I put it another way, Henry." Nick knew he had bungled the trap, but he pressed on. "Do you favor Henderson's candidacy?"

"He hasn't even announced he would run."

"What has that got to do with it? In this town everybody's always running." Landau appeared to feel foolish, fighting anger.

"What the hell's come over you, Nick? I think you're somehow trying to accuse me of favoring Henderson's candidacy. You know me better than that. Such an implied accusation is patently absurd. I don't give one shit about Henderson. He's not even the issue here."

He was sorry he had baited Landau. But he felt he owed it to himself to see how far the battleground had spread. Even if Myra had somehow insinuated herself with Landau it had been too brief an attempt, too restricted, to do any real damage. Myra could be marvelously subtle, even during a chance meeting in an elevator, a simple greeting in a corridor. Words and mannerisms are weighed carefully when they emanate from powerful people, Nick knew. She also had, he admitted, the ability to project the charm of personality, a fuse cap which she could add to the stick of dynamite which was her power over them all. Because of this alone, she could reach people, manipulate them by her favor and, perhaps, be manipulated by those who sensed her vulnerability, her thirsts, her needs. There was simply no way to shield her, warn her of those who had designs on her largesse. If he let down his guard for a single second . . .

He was conscious now of his own sense of tactics. The issue of Henderson was in the air now. It could never again be approached casually. Responses would be weighed, words measured, intonations calculated. It would spread like an infection through the other editors, downward to the assignment editors, the desk men, the reporters. He had sent his message. And, judging from Landau's reaction, it had been received.

As Nick read the story, he was conscious of Landau standing over him, fidgeting. He was not really reading the story. The contents, the thrust, were obvious, the reportage competent. Grinnel was a pro. Landau's irritation had pointed the way. He would let them run the story, give them their Pyrrhic victory, but he would keep it off the front page. His power over the front page was too precious to squander.

"You're right, Henry," Nick said, "it's got good value."

"Then we can run it?"

"Yes. But I really don't think it's front-page stuff."

"Well," Landau softened, "you're the boss."

"If you really feel strongly about it, Henry, lay it on me."

Nick could afford to be magnanimous now. He knew that Landau would back off, which he did.

When he had left, Nick swiveled back in his chair and rested his head against the cradle of his hands. He looked out into the city room feeling its rhythm, like a surging, foaming, high tide, as the first deadline approached. At this hour—it was nearing six—the tension seemed to build. People moved swiftly through the room as in a revved-up movie projection. Under normal conditions, as if normality could be defined, he might have stolen a moment to depressurize. He felt tired, strung out. Perhaps age was taunting him after all, despite the morning episode with Jennie. He had always secretly snickered at references to the male menopause with its implications of psychological changes and subtle chemical imbalances, the slowing down of the blood. At least with women the evidence was conclusive. The period stopped. Estrogen ebbed. He speculated on how deeply the changes were affecting Myra. From where he stood, he could see a profound difference in her, this sudden greed for more power. Was it a compensation for the final curtain on youth? They were both about the same age. He wondered if she still had a sex life. Odd, that he had never thought about it for years, having decided that after Charlie's death there had been a renunciation. Surely it had actually happened years before, as if Myra thought of it as trivia, a petty self-indulgence that sapped energy. Earlier he had wondered if Henderson had somehow rekindled her desire, but he had rejected the thought. Too out of character, from what he had known of Myra in the last few years. Hadn't she herself admitted her passage into neuterdom?

"I've had enough of this man-woman nonsense," she had said on the day after Charlie's funeral. "I've been cured of that frippery. We've got other fish to fry."

It had been said with such passionate finality that he had assumed its truth. But Jennie had taught him that love, or whatever it was, could still lurk in middle age, a hidden force ready to recharge the blood.

He punched his intercom and asked Miss Baumgartner to bring him some black coffee. The effects of caffeine, at least, were predictable. When she brought the steaming container, he asked her to summon Gunderstein, whom he could still see hunched over his typewriter, picking his pimples.

"I've been thinking over this Henderson business," Nick said when Gunderstein had come in and slumped in a chair, his unshined shoes splotchy and stained, like those of a house painter. His lensed eyes betrayed his surprise. "I'd like to explore it further."

"Well, frankly, I've been doing that all day. I seem to hit nothing but dead ends."

"Has it destroyed your confidence in the allegations of your informer?"

"Not at all. The man's story is quite credible. It's the other sources that are tough to come by."

Nick watched Gunderstein's face, scrofulous, pasty, the unhealthy pallor a clue to the obsessed man within.

"Could you set up a meeting?" Nick asked. He wondered if he was sounding casual enough. "I'd like to see for myself. Get a feel of it." The very idea of *feel* had the ring of hypocrisy in the light of his previous discussion with Landau.

"I don't know," Gunderstein said. "The man is awfully cagey." He thought for a moment. "Perhaps he might come to my place."

"See what you can work out."

Gunderstein shrugged and edged his rumpled body upward out of the chair. "I'll try," he said. Before he reached the door, he turned and faced Nick. "Does this mean that if the man passes muster we might run the story?"

"I'm not sure, Harold," Nick said.

"Will tonight be okay?"

"I'll be available," Nick said. Gunderstein, Nick knew, had a similar fetish about procrastination, an affliction of the news business which demanded immediacy in all things.

As Gunderstein left, Nick glanced into the city room, catching Ben Madison in mid-turn as he moved back into the familiar hunched position. What had Madison assumed from this second visit with Gunderstein?

A news aide came in with a pile of page proofs. Nick took comfort in the new chemical odor that reeked from the sheets as he pored over them. He picked up the phone and called Nichols, the photo editor. "That page-four shot has a bad crop."

"I saw that, Nick," Nichols answered. "It's already fixed."

Details, Nick sighed, proud of his ubiquitous eye which could snare the slightest imperfection whether it be misnumbered dates or wrong fonts. Often he would catch these imperfections after they had passed through an army of double-checking. For years he had kept a file of pornographic misprints, like "shit" for "shot" and "cunt" for "can't," and was forever on the alert for a disgruntled typesetter who might be seeking some uncanny word-vengeance to blow off steam. Like the famous recipe for apple pie that began with the lead-off head on the food section "The Prick to a Fart Apple Pie," instead of "Trick" and "Tart," which had slipped through the street edition to become a collector's item. He was proud of his ability to absorb himself in minutiae of proofing, to be able to spot a break in the rhythm of the presented information, as if the cells and tissues of the *Chronicle* had merged within him. He had learned to trust his judgment. Was it possible he was always right on the money or was he merely being victimized by the power in his hands? He had never dared breathe even a hint of this feeling to anyone, lest they accuse him of egotism or self-possession. Instead he had honed for himself a role of modesty, where manipulation and even despotism could be carried out under the guise of fairness and persuasion. To have discovered this knowledge in himself, he reasoned, was a sign of maturity, of having succeeded in coming to grips with his power over others. Being brutally honest with himself, he saw Myra's muscle flexing as a challenge to that power, a challenge that needed to be bottled without mercy. He dreaded to contemplate what the *Chronicle* might become in the hands of someone less aware, more obsessed, for example, with ideology than credibility, with forcing ideas, instead of insinuating them, in seeking power merely for the sake of exercising it. The day the *Chronicle* lost its suppleness and subtlety was the day of its demise, he knew. He must, at all costs, protect it from that fate.

The phone intruded on his proofing. It was Gunderstein.

"He'll be at my apartment at Four thousand Mass, six D, at eleven."

"I'll be there." Nick made a note of the place and time. It would hardly be an inconvenience since he lived at Foxhall, less than a quarter of a mile away. He remembered to call Jennie. They had an "arrangement." She lived across the street from him in the Berkshire Apartments, but as their relationship had evolved, her one-bedroom apartment had become simply a dumping ground for dirty laundry and an occasional refuge when she needed to be alone, a condition he respected and sometimes welcomed.

They had often joked of how her apartment had become simply a front for respectability and, as he had learned earlier that day, a rather flimsy one at that.

"I'll be late," he said into the phone.

"What's up?"

"I'm going out on an interview with Gunderstein."

"Who is he after now?"

Her questions were always sharp, incisive. He could

never understand why she could not translate the apparent insight into her writing.

"A Senator—Henderson."

"Well, that's a relief. I thought it might be God."

"He'll get to that some day."

She was always probing. It was a relief to have someone with whom he could unburden himself, and she listened to him with keen alertness.

"I thought he was the fair-haired boy," she questioned.

"That's the problem."

"I'll be covering a story tonight, too. Judy Barton is sick and Margaret asked me to cover an embassy thing. The British are having a small to do. Veddy posh and exclusive."

"Ought to be fun!"

"Anybody who is anybody will be there. Lots of big politicos and media heroes. I think I'll do a real bitchy piece."

"Wonderful."

"I think I'll deliberately show up tacky. It's so much fun to be tacky and still have everyone kiss your ass."

"We sending a photographer?" Nick asked. It was a professional reflex.

"But, of course. We've got a heavy list. Margaret's got a bunch of kinky requests. All opposites. A big Jew with a big Arab. A Russian with a Chinese. A Republican with a Democrat, contenders, that is. They'll all be there. Ambrose, Carter"—she was reading from a list—"and Henderson."

His antenna went up. "Any specific shots?" he asked.

She hesitated a moment. "Never could understand your ex's scrawl. It looks like Rockefeller and Henderson."

"When did she give you that assignment?" Nick asked.

"She gave it to Judy yesterday. I just pulled it out of the files."

"I see."

"What's that supposed to mean?"

"Nothing," he said quickly. But it had been too late. He knew her curiosity had been aroused.

"Anything I should know about, Nick?"

"It's nothing."

"Nothing you say is ever nothing."

"You overrate me."

"Is that possible?"

"Not really," he said laughing, hoping he had placated her innate curiosity. He pecked a kiss lightly into the phone, feeling silly. "See you later, alligator."

"Oh, Christ. You are an anachronism."

"Be careful. I'm sensitive about my age."

"You'd never know by me." She hung up, leaving him vaguely suspicious. Surely not Margaret. He shrugged it off. He was reading things into things, overreacting. He continued with his review of the major news pages, losing himself again in the minutiae. He made further angry corrections in Bonville's editorial with heavy penciled strokes. His thoughts returned to his conversation with Jennie; not Margaret, he assured himself—or was he getting paranoid?

11

As he worked he could sense the ebb of energy in the city room, the phased disappearance of the reporters, deskmen, news aides, secretaries; the lowered din as the telephones rang only sporadically. Looking out, he saw the room strewn with debris, Styrofoam coffee containers, potato chip wrappers, wastebaskets overflowing with cast-off soggy copy paper, ashtrays choked with crushed butts, the residue of a frenetic life. And so, he thought, staring into the emptying room, remembering the old daytime radio soap operas, we leave the *Chronicle* now, having created another day in the life of the world, another fantasy on which souls might masticate, another moment in time, frozen, cast into a preconceived shape, mostly of his vision. He could not understand why his mind was suddenly thrashing about in this groping way. Perhaps he was trying to think through what seemed to be happening, as if it were essential to his future movement through an untracked trail on a now frozen pond. Where lay the thin ice?

If he were to believe the writers who polluted the "with-it" parasitic rags with their voluminous outpourings, he, and all the hierarchy of the *Chronicle,* stood at the pinnacle of a kind of "mediacracy," a new elite of mythmakers. They had replaced the creators of the other fantasy arts, the authors of books, plays, and movies. Perhaps conscious of that, he had carefully avoided the company of these so-called peers, avoiding at all costs the little "in" parties, the private entertainments held mostly by the frantic group of sages who wrote syndicated columns, many of which appeared in the *Chronicle,* and the stars of the new personal television. Intermingled with the mythmakers were their creations, the power seekers who knew themselves to be media happenings, like Henderson. Handsome Burton Henderson, master of both hard and soft news. Here he was today, for example, galloping into print in the news section and already on deck for a picture in Lifestyle. All this happening right under Nick's nose. What kind of monsters had they made? If he was only vaguely sure before, he was now becoming more and more convinced that something was radically wrong with the system that he had helped create. Upstairs, sitting in her manicured office, holding court for the high and the mighty, Myra was actually beginning to believe her own invulnerability, the ultimate power trap. Her father's whole thesis of objectivity was crumbling under the weight of the new media power. It had long passed objectivity. Personality had won and he, Nick Gold, had smoothed the way for its final victory. Was it possible that the *Chronicle,* in whose maw so many lives had been chewed up, was wrong? Wrong in the way it showed people their world, wrong in the way it brought the fantasy into focus? Wrong in the expectations it offered? Wrong because they had been so sure they were right? Wrong because somehow they were the only eye left on the top of the mountain?

He could not tell how long he had sensed that this was happening, or even understand why he had pulled away from the self-serving cluster of mediacrats, who saw themselves as the keepers of the holy grail or, at the very least, enjoyed the idea that other people thought so.

Perhaps this was why he determined to keep his affair with Jennie secret. He could rationalize his breaking away, turning down invitations to the little soirées, the private pool parties, the silly tennis tournaments, the dinners for eight in Myra's town house, the "oh-so-with-it chic-talk," the behind-the-scenes revelations of the secretaries of State and Treasury and, of course, the power handlers at the White House. It dawned on him now why Myra had asked him to bring Jennie "out" to the Redskin games, have her be part of the gang, a regular attendant at the royal box. He'd no longer have an excuse to hide. Myra would draw him back to their orbit, immerse him, smother him.

The vibrations of the big presses began to be felt and he waited expectantly for the first copy of the street edition, which always arrived in tandem with a sinking heart, the terrible possibility that the stories would all be different from those that had been sent down to the composing room. It was a recurrent expectation, always frightening, and it was with a sense of deep relief that he viewed the familiar front page, exactly as it had appeared in proof.

When he had given it a final going over, he left the city room with a wave at the "lobster" crew who had settled into their own special ambience, waiting for morning, some hoping that the night might be eventful, others content with inactivity, using the time for activities like writing books, now the *Chronicle*'s major occupational disease.

The November chill signaled the first stirrings of a Washington winter, as erratic as its political environment. Nick walked swiftly, his ears alert, listening for footfalls at his rear, a habit he had developed but felt was reprehensible, in the light of the *Chronicle*'s avowed position that crime was an aberration resulting from a deprived environment—a noble thought which offered little comfort for a mugged victim. He had felt it politically important to maintain that stance, as if to breach it would open a huge cleavage for the law-and-order superconservatives to pour through, destroying the *Chronicle*'s credibility in the liberal community, its carefully nurtured constituency.

In front of the Mayflower he hailed a cab and watched Connecticut Avenue recede. Swinging around Dupont Circle, the cab rolled swiftly down Massachusetts Avenue, past Embassy Row into the land of the powerful, the magic ZIP code 20016 where lived the movers and makers, the privileged sanctuary of the elite that bridged the gap between Georgetown and Chevy Chase, through to Potomac, the last stronghold of the close-to-town landed gentry.

The cab dropped him in front of 4000 Massachusetts Avenue where he walked through the security maze. He could actually feel the television cameras watching him. Despite the fact that the *Chronicle* had one of the most sophisticated security systems in town, the act of surveillance, especially in what could be described as a social context, was repugnant to him. He wondered if any such devices had, as yet, found their way to Warren, Ohio. Properly announced through the switchboard, he went up the elevator, through the corridor smelling faintly of cabbage, the eternal symbol of apartment living, to the waiting pimpled face of Harold Gunderstein standing in the doorway of his apartment.

Gunderstein, his tie awry, his shirt puffed out of his belt, two sizes too big, the pants stained and creased, seemed to be the embodiment of the cabbage smell, the source of its emanation. But inside the apartment, other odors assailed Nick. Books and papers were piled everywhere, in little mounds Stonehenge-like, on every available surface. Remnants of food were everywhere, stale sandwich bits, dried pickles, milk-crusted glasses, empty beer cans. Considering the high rent, a sop to his newfound riches, Gunderstein's apartment interior seemed incongruous, a nest of poverty. It was a fitting complement to his image. Where else could a rich slob live?

"God, what a shithouse!" Nick said, as if it were the expected social grace.

"The maid comes tomorrow." Gunderstein shrugged

apologetically. He was wearing glasses now, the cosmetic of the office discarded, and he looked as Nick remembered him years ago. Nick followed him into the living room where a paunchy man sat on a brightly colored couch, holding a tumbler of whiskey.

"This is Carter Allison," Gunderstein said. The paunchy man held out his hand, showing brown teeth and dimpled cheeks. He had once been boyish, now gone to seed.

"Sounds like a stage name," Nick said, conscious of ingratiation.

"I can assure you that it's my legitimate baptismal name. The middle name is Blandish. There was once a Lord Blandish, I'm told, but I spring from Maine potato farmers."

"I've filled Mr. Gold in on all you've told me, Carter." They had obviously reached some plateau of relationship. It was odd how Gunderstein would evolve so quickly into a first-name basis with a news source; as if he had merged into the information.

"You don't believe me," Allison said, glaring at Nick. One couldn't tell whether it was a question or an answer.

"I didn't say that," Nick answered, assuming it a question, watching Allison's growing anxiety. Gunderstein poured another drink into his glass from a nearby opened Johnny Walker Black.

"Well then, why don't you run the story? It's the truth. I know it's the truth."

"It's just that we haven't been able to confirm it to Mr. Gold's satisfaction," Gunderstein said. "The *Chronicle* has a two-source policy."

"You'll never confirm it. They're too clever. Besides, the men who gave the order are dead."

"He means the Kennedy brothers," Gunderstein interrupted.

"That's pretty heavy stuff."

"It didn't seem so at the time," Allison continued. "Just a routine action. It was almost fun. I was actually just a garden-variety CIA analyst posing as an embassy

clerk, low on the totem pole at that. But I did know the
language and in those days there were few of us around.
My mother's"—he paused, perhaps recalling some rare
sentiment—"second husband was a French businessman. I grew up in Saigon and could speak fluent Vietnamese and French, a perfect mark for the CIA re-
cruiter who found me at Berkeley." Gunderstein poured
more whiskey into the man's glass. "I met him only
twice. Both times in the public lavatory of a broken-
down Saigon hotel."

"Real cloak and dagger," Nick said sarcastically.

"It didn't help my career one way or the other,"
Allison said sadly, the stink of his bitterness like a hot
gust in the room. "I was simply told by my superior to
provide information. It was hardly intelligence. Most of
the stuff could be found in the newspapers and on the
street. Any pimp or bar girl could supply it."

"What kind of information?"

"Diem's enemies. Believe it or not, all I did in my
two years of official duty in Viet Nam was to keep track
of the enemies of the Ngu brothers. It was quite simple,
really. They had so many. They were horrible people,
turds, both of them. I could have given it to him over
the telephone, but they thought that was too dangerous.
What was the name he used? Mr. Marshall. These
military types have absolutely no imagination. I might
have suggested Smith. That at least has some authentic-
ity to it. Or Jones." He laughed, showing his bad teeth.

It was easy to define the man's motivation, Nick
concluded: frustration, empty dreams, a life unfulfilled,
translated now into jealousy and hatred—a classic case.

"It was dark in the lavatory," Allison continued. "We
sat in separate stalls whispering. I can still smell the
place. All I could think of was getting out of there."

"You didn't see his face?" Nick looked at Gunderstein.

"Not the first time, although his voice made a special
imprint."

"Go on."

"He was quite clever and I didn't really know what

he was looking for until a few days later. By then, of course, it was over."

"You mean the assassination?"

"Of course. You see, he was searching for someone who could pull the trigger, probing possibilities. Apparently he had some preconceived profile. He wanted someone who had enough motive, hatred, to pull the trigger. Someone who could be tipped off to the Ngu brothers' exact whereabouts at a preset time, with enough balls to do the job."

"And you found the man?"

"I said it was easy. I found many. You could have thrown darts at a wall of names. It was almost an honor. I found him a good prospect. A commander of an armored unit, not very high up. No paper passed between us, just words. He was a persistent cuss."

"But you never saw him?"

"Let me finish. I said I met with him twice." There was a well of belligerency in the man, as if he had withdrawn into himself, within some mental fortress. Perhaps he saw the challenge to his credibility as further humiliation, new evidence of his manipulation by unseen forces. "It was during the night of the actual coup. There was fighting still going on in the Palace. This time he used the telephone. He knew spook talk and I understood him. It was quite clear: same station. Off I went to the fleabag hotel, directly to the shithouse, sitting down in the foul place. I could hear him breathing beside me and could see his shoes from under the partition. Apparently the first name I had given him had fallen through and he probed for another, a similar profile. I tell you it was easy. I came up with another name quickly. He made me spell it again and again until it sunk in. I knew by then that it had something to do with the Diem thing. It's funny how silly this sounds in retrospect. Grown men sitting on the crapper plotting a killing. It's hilarious when you think about it."

"I'm sure it's given you great moments of nostalgia," Nick said. There was something grating, offensive, unclean, about the man.

"I was sitting in the stall nearest the sink," Allison continued, "and someone had come in and was waiting, which made it impossible to continue talking. The man told me to stay where I was and he got out instead. I heard the water in the sink begin to run and splashing noises. There was a crack in the thin wood of the stall and, in the dull light of the small electric bulb over the sink, I could see the outline of his profile quite clearly. His collar was open and he was washing his neck. I was so close to him I could almost touch him and somehow his dog tag got loose and, by the glint of that light, I could actually see his name, Burton Henderson, as clearly as I can see your face. He turned toward me only once and I could also see his eyes, incredibly blue. He was a handsome bugger. When the man who was using the other crapper left, he got in the stall again, and I had to repeat the prospect's name. It was getting unbearable in there. I remember pleading with him to let me get the hell out of there. Finally, I left. As far as I know he was still sitting there in that Oriental stink."

"Are you sure this Senator Henderson is the same man?"

"Positive."

"Then why can't we confirm it?" Nick said, turning to Gunderstein.

"I've tried. I've badgered the CIA and as many old Viet Nam hands as I could find."

"They couldn't confirm it," Allison said. "This operation was strictly outside the chain of command. There wouldn't be a single document on the subject, not a breath. I'm the only connection."

"And the Viet Nam commander who led the assassination team?"

"Long dead. They saw to that early in the game."

"That's the trouble with you spooks. You see some sordid conspiracy everywhere."

"Monkey sees as monkey does," Allison said, his tongue heavy now.

"So it can't be confirmed. All we have is your word," Nick said, wanting to add: And that's not very much.

But Allison was alert to the implication. He was drunk but apparently his mind was still clear.

"And I suppose you don't put a high premium on that."

"Now that you mention it." Nick shrugged.

"It wouldn't matter, anyway, Mr. Gold," Gunderstein said, "he won't be quoted."

"Why not?"

"It's a lousy life, but the only one I've got. They'll stop at nothing."

"They?"

"Powerful men stop at nothing. And what could be sweeter, more tantalizing than revenge? The Kennedy brothers for the Ngu brothers. Old boozy Carter Allison for handsome Burt Henderson. I know my equations, Mr. Gold."

"Kennedy was shot exactly three weeks after the Ngu brothers," Gunderstein said. "He's frightened. And I can't confirm it. If only you'd let me write the story without using the man's name . . . I think I'd be able to flush out another source."

"I'm telling the truth," Allison said, finishing the tumbler full of whiskey, quickly replaced by Gunderstein. "Henderson was an NSA man, a retread, called in just for this purpose. He also had some knowledge of the language. And he was in Viet Nam during that period. All that is a cinch to confirm."

Gunderstein nodded.

"Purely circumstantial," Nick said. "You're accusing the man of engineering an assassination."

"I'm more than accusing. I'm insisting," Allison said, his face flushing, his eyes narrowing.

"I think this story is like cotton candy. It melts in the mouth," Nick said. He stood up and began to pace the room, making detours to avoid knocking down piles of books. "There's simply not enough to go on. We've no moral right to accept this . . . this hearsay. It would destroy Henderson's career."

"Moral right," Allison sputtered. "You'll make me ill. If I thought I was getting into the area of moral right, I'd never have opened my yap. You guys are newspapermen, aren't you? Since when do you guys deal in moral right? I'm giving you a story. I'm telling you that your hero Burton Henderson is full of shit, a fraud. All you pinko bleeding hearts. You think Henderson is all nigger lover, all heart, and you plant kisses on both his cheeks. It makes me want to vomit."

"We're certainly not a conduit for revenge," Nick said, sitting down again. He was conscious of having a strong desire to bait the man, to push him into some vague admission of dark motives. Allison emptied his glass and looked helplessly at Gunderstein, who turned away in obvious embarrassment.

"There isn't a shred of hard evidence, Allison," Gunderstein said sadly. "I've tracked it everywhere, the CIA, the NSA, old Nam hands, even Madam Nhu who I reached in Paris. Oh, there's a general undercurrent of agreement on the CIA's role, but Henderson is not in it. And that's the story, Allison. You've got to see Mr. Gold's point. He wants another source of confirmation. You can't really blame him."

The man's bloodshot eyes sought Nick's. Why had he come? Nick wondered. Was he really hoping that the information would be more conclusive? Of course he was, he assured himself, dismissing, as Allison had done, the moral niceties of the situation. He was looking for dirt and he knew it.

"You're all in it together," Allison said with rising bitterness, his tongue heavier, his articulation difficult. "You can shit on anyone you choose to—or choose not to."

"Well, then why did you come to us?" Nick asked. He could feel the man's frustration.

"Because I wanted to shit on Henderson."

"That's obvious."

"Gunderstein believes me," Allison said thickly. "Don't you, Gunderstein?"

Gunderstein flushed, his pimples reddening. Nick became aware, at that moment, of the secret of Gunderstein's skill, the ability to inspire confidence in a source, a method beyond mere tenacity. There were no heroes, no villains, only people trapped in circumstances. Gunderstein began at that point. Everyone was credible. They had reasons for their actions. The lie was simply a tool for survival. Gunderstein took no moral positions. He was simply a vessel for their justifications.

"Yes, I do," Gunderstein answered.

"If you have that much confidence in his story, why couldn't you persuade him to be quoted?" he asked Gunderstein.

"They'll kill me," Allison said, terrified.

"The man's paranoid," Nick said.

"I know," Gunderstein said. "But that doesn't make the story any less valid." They were talking as if Allison didn't exist.

"At this point it's simply gossip. I admit its fascination, but that's all it is—gossip."

"It's the truth," Allison persisted. He got up unsteadily and poured more whiskey in his glass.

"I thought perhaps," Gunderstein said quietly to Nick, "that I would write the piece obliquely without using Henderson's name. There's got to be somebody out there who knows something."

"You want to go fishing?"

"In a way, yes. But we do that all the time."

Nick thought for a moment. Gunderstein was correct, of course. When they suspected a big fish they poked their lines into the water, carefully baited. It was hardly a subtle ploy since the fish, considering the scope of the line, could hardly fail to smell the bait. Once the *Chronicle* implied that it was out for a big fish, all the little fish and all the big fish's enemies would crowd the bait, waiting for the chance to get in a good chomp. This mask of self-righteousness was beginning to smother him. You are conspiring, you hypocrite, Nick chastised himself. He felt suddenly irritated, grabbed a glass from a shelf, and wiping out the dust with his hand, poured himself a drink.

"You realize," Nick said, addressing himself to Allison, now fading swiftly into a drunken stupor, "that

Henderson, if we are to believe your story, didn't actually do anything wrong in the sense that it was not part and parcel of American policy at the time. Obviously, he was following orders, doing what was considered an acceptable, though clandestine, act of American foreign policy." Nick felt that his explanation was convoluted, but even through his descending stupor Allison seemed to catch the subtlety.

"Who says different? Hesh a fuggin hypocrite, that's all. And he may be the fuggin President of the whole keboodle. That's wash wrong." He tried to stand up, then fell backward against the wall where he continued to find support, his head lolling on his shoulder.

"I better get him into a cab," Gunderstein said. He picked up the phone and asked the desk clerk to call a cab. When he had hung up, Gunderstein reached into an opened pretzel box that suddenly materialized from behind an end table and offered it to Nick, who declined.

"If there is any weight to the story, and I think there is," Gunderstein said, abstractedly biting into a pretzel, "it will surface sooner or later."

"Not necessarily, Harold," Nick said. It takes a visceral hatred, a commitment, he thought. If that element had been missing, they might never have gone after the President.

He had long ago assimilated his rationalization. It had ceased to nag him by then. It was a virtue that his life within the vortex of the storm, the press of the avalanche of events, could sublimate a galling episode with uncommon speed. But now it came rushing back to the front of his consciousness, and it was an indication of Gunderstein's sensitivity that he had deftly steered clear of the memory.

They had by then burrowed in, deeply, to the point where the *Chronicle*'s revelations were more than just an irritation to the White House. Other papers were beginning to join the fray, but Gunderstein's skill and singlemindedness kept him steps ahead of the so-called competition. They had spread the bait on the waters like oil and the bigger fish were making their first tentative forays toward the hook. When a week went by without a new revelation, both he and Myra had become edgy.

"We can't stop now," she had said. By then it had become a passion. "We owe it to the American people." It had added to the complexity that they were now responding to high-blown patriotic platitudes, and believing them. All except Gunderstein, whose pursuit, as always, was devoid of moral overtones. The story was all.

But for him and Myra there was added motivation, a visceral hatred that went far beyond the bounds of political opposition. Something in the man, then the sitting President, was able to inflame them, inspiring indignation and contempt. Perhaps it was his aloofness. A closed personality, he was difficult to know. There was also a transparency in his machinations. You could always see the works in motion, gears clicking, motors humming, and it was puzzling to understand how the bulk of the American people were so easily manipulated by them. Perhaps that was at the heart of it, since it had rendered them almost powerless in their influence, leaving them with the feeling that maybe they had been wrong all along—until Gunderstein had come to them with the idea of the cover-up and they had given him carte blanche to pursue it. Gunderstein had merely thrown the match on the already dry tinder.

"I've found the unimpeachable source," Gunderstein told him. He had come into the office, his hair plastered down by perspiration, circles reddening around his pimples.

"In the nick of time, Harold. There's gloom and doom on all fronts." Aside from the mere scent of blood, there were ancillary reasons for the story's further development. Circulation was rising swiftly now. Advertising lineage was up. And the editorial staff had been gripped by an infectious esprit de corps, a kind of David against Goliath syndrome, a rather endurable newspaperman's fantasy, easily stimulated.

"He's offered me two choices," Gunderstein said.

"The hard way and the easy way."

"Exactly."

"What's the trade-off?"

"In this case only two things. Anonymity and money."

"Mendacity is everywhere," Nick said, resisting the temptation to ask the man's name.

"What he means by anonymity is a total blackout. From everyone, including you and Mrs. Pell," Gunderstein said.

"And what did you tell him?"

"I said that money probably posed the lesser of the two problems."

"At least you've invested us with some morality, Harold."

Gunderstein ignored the sarcasm. "He's absolutely germinal to the story, knows the inside, dates, people, places."

"How can you be sure?"

"I'm sure."

"Sounds like it might be the President himself."

"In my opinion, he probably knows more than the President," Gunderstein said.

"And the money?"

"He wants a quarter of a million in cash."

Nick felt his throat tighten, stifling what might have been a hysterical laugh.

"Now that's what I call squeeze." In his mind, he had already rejected the offer outright. The *Chronicle* was, after all, a public company. As a practical matter, it would be difficult to bury that kind of money. Besides, to extend the knowledge beyond Gunderstein, Myra, himself, and the source, would create special dangers. You couldn't pass that kind of money without calling in the comptroller, the company money man.

"He thinks it's a bargain," Gunderstein said calmly. "He says that if we tried to get the story without his help it might cost four, five times more in time, personnel, running down false leads."

"A real businessman, this guy," Nick said. "Couldn't

you come up with someone else less crassly motivated? Revenge, jealousy, patriotism, ethics, morality, the need for expiation, confession, simple hatred?"

"A source is a source."

"Do me a favor, Gunderstein. Go home and take a cold shower. We'd blow our credibility sky high. I'd be putting the *Chronicle*'s image right on the line." He could think of a thousand reasons for rejection. "It's simply not the rules of the game," he said finally.

"Rules?"

"You can't become what you're trying to expose."

"Our business is to tell the story, Mr. Gold. That's our only reason for being."

"So you believe we should pay for it?"

"Yes."

"Get the information any way you can?"

"Yes."

"Torture. Blackmail. Are they also legitimate tactics?"

Gunderstein became thoughtful. He swallowed, his Adam's apple bobbing.

"Inflicting physical pain is not in my frame of reference," he said quietly. "I suppose, though, you might use some form of mental torture, and fear of exposure poses a kind of blackmail on a self-perceived victim."

He was exasperating.

"On second thought a shower might be hardly useful. What you need is to get laid, Gunderstein. Laid and parlayed."

But the idea had lingered. He remembered tossing around in his bed, sleepless, challenging Gunderstein in a nightmare of imagined conversations. Actually, they had always winked at the little bribe, the bought lunch or drink, or, on occasion, even women, a traditional inducement, although it was an offense of first-class proportions for anyone on the staff to accept any form of payola. Charlie had made it a religion, rigidly enforced, and he had carried it beyond the pale of human frailty. Not a lunch, not a drink, not the slightest hint of gratuity. Nick, too, was merciless in the enforcement;

rigid, unbending. It rankled him to know that the columnists were out of his reach, although he had some recourse, but hardly the same control as he could exercise over his own staff. Perhaps that was why his first reaction to Gunderstein's proposal was negative. And yet, he had paid for information in his career. It was a standard practice on the *News*. One simply put the payola on one's expense account, suitably buried but not without prior approval of McCarthy.

"Lay a few bucks on the bastard," McCarthy would howl when all else had failed.

But a quarter of a million! By morning, Nick had concluded that it wasn't ethics at all, purely the size of the money, that had prompted his irritation. It was, as Gunderstein had testified when confronted with torture, outside the realm of his experience. Myra's reaction was far more phlegmatic. He had been careful to outline the parameters without the injection of personal opinion, in content as well as nuance.

"What was your reaction, Nick?" she had asked coyly.

"I rejected it outright," he answered quickly, refusing to admit his second thoughts. They were sitting in her pleasant breakfast room with the sun shining through the high windows, throwing shimmering glints on the garden sculptures. She quietly sipped her coffee.

"It would be a shame if he gets away with it because of our timidity," she said.

"You have to weigh that against the possibility of our finding other sources and, of course, our own vulnerability."

"We've gone this far," she mused, "it seems a shame."

"And then there is the possibility that the information will be worthless, a case of entrapment. We've been assuming that Gunderstein is certain that the man is guilty, that a cover-up has indeed been perpetrated. He could be dead wrong."

"Do you think he is?"

"That's the hell of it, Myra. I believe in Gunderstein's

assessment. I believe that we'll get our money's worth."

It was, he knew, a Pandora's box of possibilities.

"If the man is guilty, the people have a right to know."

"I don't deny that."

"We can't allow this country to be raped, Nick," she said. He could see in her eyes the same firmness that had moved her father.

"Assuming his guilt."

"I believe he is guilty, absolutely."

There it was, he thought, the prejudgment so necessary for commitment. "It'll cost us a quarter of a million."

"That's the least of the problem," she said confidently. "I have private resources. It needn't be a company matter."

Once the mechanics of the payoff had been worked out, the story had begun to unfold swiftly, the bottleneck broken. Gunderstein had been right. The source provided the promised value and whatever guilt Nick might have felt became submerged in the euphoria of the victory, the greater good. It seemed poetic logic for the memory to surface at this moment.

But Gunderstein, ever the technician, saw only the story as an end in itself. He would hardly understand what was going on now, in Nick's mind, the wider implications, the hatching conspiracy, the rationalizations filtering through their prismatic screenings. What did Gunderstein understand about the duel under way between him and Myra, in which Henderson was merely a chess piece? What did he care about Henderson or moral right? It was absurd. Henderson was, like all the rest, a political prostitute. He would commit any crime if he felt it would get him one more vote, providing the moral stigma remained in the closet. There were no considerations of good and evil in this scenario, only power, raw and unrefined. Gunderstein got up and maneuvered Allison toward the door. The man looked at Nick as he passed, tried to speak, then shook his head and moved unsteadily on Gunderstein's arm.

When they had gone Nick settled onto the couch and sipped his drink. Despite its sloppiness, Gunderstein's living room had its own lived-in pattern, a mirror perhaps of the younger man's cluttered mind. It was not unlike his and Charlie's old bachelor apartment, a private stronghold, pugnacious in its maleness. It, too, was cluttered with books, although the bits and pieces of unfinished food never reached the level of being part of the decor. It seemed natural for Gunderstein's environment to stimulate recall, as if the ground had been gone over before in another life, which it had. The issue, like the others, was similar.

"It was like starting out at the finish line and retracing the track to make sure the race was rigged correctly," he had told Charlie during that time with Pelligrino.

"A good simile, Nick."

"Under those terms everyone is vulnerable."

"That's right."

"Somebody gets up in the morning. Throws a dart into a board imprinted with the name of some public figure, in this case the President of the City Council, and the game begins. Let's fuck Pelligrino."

"More or less correct."

"It's hideous."

"Do you give one shit about Pelligrino?"

"That's not the point."

McCarthy had gathered three reporters around his desk that morning, his heavy eyes a red network of veins, a map of yesterday's bout with barleycorn. "We're going to run this investigation on three levels. The political, the money angle, and the personal. The objective here is to get a well-rounded picture of this snake."

The question of Pelligrino's snakery was a prejudgment, not the concern of the reporters. It had simply been decreed. By McCarthy? By people above him in the hierarchy of the *News?* It was difficult to tell.

"I want this guinea's ass," he said, revealing the ferocity of ethnic contempt. The Irish and the Italians in New York were natural enemies, competing for protection of their own territorial imperatives. It was essentially a New York phenomenon; this fierce sense of belonging, chunks of unmelted fat in the myth of the melting pot.

Why did he want his ass? Nick wanted to ask, but held back, afraid of ridicule. Surely he was missing some important bit of information, some piece of knowledge that would explain why Pelligrino was a target now. His assignment was to learn about Pelligrino's personal life, to dig beyond the bland façade of political imagery. He had no illusions about what McCarthy wanted and, despite his own questioning, was determined to show his skills. It was from these ingredients that newspaper reputations were made.

Following the traditional journalistic starting points, he read and reread the old clips in the *News* library, piles of cardboard envelopes filled with the passing events of Pelligrino's political career. There was Pelligrino's public life cataloged in faded ink, an acre of strung-together words, descriptions, pronouncements, quotations. Only in the absorption of the mass could one get even a remote hint of the real character of Salvatore Pelligrino. A study of the clips gave him a mental picture of a small man, addicted in later life to well-cut, stylish clothes, a "dandy," smelling of heavy expensive cologne, with polished fingernails, scrupulously shined expensive shoes, a carefully trimmed moustache, with large brown sad heavy-lidded eyes and teeth still white and able to embellish a warm, broad, thick-lipped smile. But beyond the façade of the overdressed man of dignity, the clips hinted of poverty-inflicted early pain, the immigrant boy hustling for a buck on the streets, the parents who never learned English, propagating with Catholic fervor, creating their huge garlic-smelling brood, all with odd names like those of characters in the Italian movies then in vogue.

It might have been the first time that Nick had used old clips to sketch the picture of a man, an adversary, now, and all these bits and pieces put together by a crowd of indifferent reporters, all watching through their own private lenses, provided a fascinating and, he believed, accurate kaleidoscope of a man's character. He had not yet learned how the newspaper portrait of any public person fed on itself, was built on the gleanings of an army of observers, each embellishing what the other had observed before, preserved forever in these little cardboard envelopes, the bible of the rewrite desks. By the time he had read them all, he felt he had his quarry well focused, a cosmeticized little man, obsessed with the necessity to appear dignified, hiding behind a carefully constructed façade. And since it had been planted in his mind that the man was a snake, he had sought justification for the characterization. By the time he had read the clipping thoroughly, he imagined that he had found it and was quite ready to slice away at the man.

He knew in advance the object of his search. The reference to the personal side of Pelligrino's life was obvious. Nick's assignment was to come up with a record of philandering. It was not a question of whether or not Pelligrino was a philanderer—that was assumed —but to forestall any libel suit by proving the obvious. After all, didn't Italians in general like to fuck a lot and weren't Italians in positions of power certainly going to take advantage of the situation? He had already learned that confirming a stereotyped image was the best way to make a story believable. A rapist was always unshaven and beady-eyed; killers had slick black hair; blacks shuffled; girls who shook their fannies when they walked were great in bed.

By the time he reached Pelligrino's City Hall office he had the bit tightly clenched in his teeth. A man's office, like his home, often told more about the man than his own guarded speech. Pelligrino's outer office was filled, floor to ceiling, with pictures of Pelligrino; shifty eyes peering into the lens with Pelligrino the dominant constant. Nick spent a good deal of time looking at the pictures, stalling, as if he were waiting for someone, observing the comings and goings. There were three girls in the office, all carefully coiffured, with straight stocking seams and cool, efficient demeanors, reflective of Pelligrino's passion for dignity. One of the women was too matronly to be a possibility, but the other two could be considered prime suspects. After all, what was safer than fooling around with one's secretary? He fantasized about each of them, differentiated by their desk nameplates as Miss Simon and Miss Aquilino. Miss Simon was a big-breasted Jewish blonde with a well-girdled torso and long manicured nails that grew out of bony, thin white hands. Miss Aquilino was thin and dark, compact. Which one was he screwing? Both! Surely a man like Pelligrino would not deprive himself. A picture of Pelligrino and his family flashed before him, intruding on the image. He had six children. Nick had counted them with care since the caption had not given a figure. Noting the date of the clipping, he calculated that the children now ranged in age from six to twenty-five. The oldest would be older than both of the secretaries.

When he had finished his observations of Pelligrino's office, Nick walked down the City Hall corridors to the press room, a high-ceilinged pigpen of a place lined with small desks and old-fashioned, battered typewriters. He found Wiley Patton, the *News'* City Hall reporter, slumped over his typewriter in a deep snooze. Wiley was a man in his sixties, an old hand. Like all old-time reporters, he was conscious of his own legend and was treated with awesome respect by the younger reporters. The City Hall beat was his domain and the three reporters that McCarthy had assigned to the Pelligrino story were carefully briefed on how Patton was to be handled.

"Patton knows everything that goes on down there. They trust him. He'll buck like hell when he hears what we're doing. That'll be one big act for your benefit, for mine, for the politicians. Let him do his act. He knows what he's doing," McCarthy had lectured. It seemed to Nick a classic study in deviousness.

"He's got to appear to be on their side," McCarthy had continued. "A double agent." The old man smiled at the reference.

Nick shook Patton lightly, watching him stir as his eyes flickered open.

"Shit," he said, not recognizing Nick, although he had been introduced in the city room. Shaking himself awake, he reached for a half-smoked cigar in his over-filled ashtray and relit it. Nick introduced himself. Patton sneered. Nick explained what he was doing.

"The bastards," Patton said. "So the old man's got a hard-on for the wop."

"Surely it's not that simple."

"The hell it isn't."

"Why?"

Patton looked contemptuously at Nick, his lips already stained with the juice of the soggy cigar.

"Why does Carter make liver pills?" he said cryptically.

Other reporters began to straggle into the press room. Patton nodded at each greeting, indicating through contemptuous facial expressions his opinion of each reporter.

"That's Hillary of the fucking *Mirror*," Patton said, just loud enough to be heard over the sound of a single typewriter now being beaten in a corner of the room. Hillary, a tall, bloodless man, looked over his glasses and stuck up his middle finger.

"We outcirculate the son of a bitch," Patton said, returning Hillary's salute. Nick could sense the warm rivalry, perhaps friendship between the two.

"We better get out of here, Gold," Patton said suddenly in a whisper. "Too many ears around here."

Nick followed him through the high-ceilinged old corridors with their dusty light globes, through the ornate entrance of the archaic building. Remembering the sunlight and budded trees of the little park in front of the building, he could place the time in his mind as early spring. Patton walked quickly. He was a wiry man who moved with quick bursts of energy, despite a sallow complexion and a slightly stooped figure. Nick followed him into a dark, half-empty bar, oddly unmarked, ex-

cept for a weakly expiring neon sign which said "Bar."
The bartender greeted Patton with brotherly interest.

"How's the boy?"

"Another day, another dollar."

"Same old shit, eh?"

The place, the greeting, even Patton's frozen glare
of contempt seemed, by then, a repetitive syndrome of
the New York newspaper world, a romantic stereotype.
Cynicism and contemptuousness were the built-in props
of a newspaperman's self-esteem, a kind of inheritance
from more competitive rough-and-tumble newspaper
days, before respectability had somehow intruded on
the profession, along with the Newspaper Guild and a
master's degree from the Columbia School of Journalism. Patton, like McCarthy, was a relic of the spit-
toon and eyeshade days, now expiring under the
onslaught of technology. Even then, despite his nagging
feeling of intellectual superiority, Nick felt himself in
a historical presence, as if old Patton might be passing
him a relay stick.

The bartender poured whiskey into two shot glasses
placed on the battered bar. Apparently the assumption
of what a person drank was preordained when one was
drinking with Patton. He tossed off his drink with a
quick flick of his head, eyes tearing, loose jowls around
his neck pulsating.

"So they got a hard-on for Pelligrino," Patton said.
"That old WASP cocksucker just can't stand to see a
guinea get ahead in New York."

"WASP? I thought McCarthy was an Irishman."

"Not him," Patton said, "Beardsley calls the shots."

Beardsley was the publisher. He had seen him only
once, a shadowy figure who walked quickly through the
city room, an innocuous, smiling man with an easy
ingratiating manner.

"But I thought McCarthy . . ."

"That drunken flunkey." Patton unwrapped a cigar,
bit its tip off spat out a lump on the floor, and lit it.
"He was one hell of a newspaperman in his day, kid.

One helluva newspaperman." It seemed a genuine tribute, peer to peer.

"Are you saying the only reason that they'd like to see Pelligrino dumped is because he's Italian?"

Patton watched him, squinting through the fresh cloud of smoke. "That's part of it."

"I don't understand."

"It's the power of the press, kid. Muscle flexing is all. Nothing personal."

"Nothing personal. My God, we're about to ruin the man's political career."

"That's the way it goes. They're all the same anyway; a bunch of grafting bullshitters. One's as bad as another. The guinea's okay. Beardsley doesn't want him for mayor is all."

"You mean, just like that."

Patton looked at him. He seemed mystified. "Don't take it so hard, kid. Maybe Beardsley's wife got up on the wrong side of the bed one day. Maybe he couldn't get it up and she had a bad breakfast and couldn't shit and the first thing she sees on the crapper is this guinea's face in the paper. How do you think you'd feel if all those things had happened to you and the first face you saw was this guinea's cutting a tape, smiling for the cameras, looking to beat hell like he was having a good time, and all she could get off was one lousy little crampy fart?"

"That's ridiculous."

Patton sighed and pointed to his shot glass again, which the bartender quickly filled. "Not so ridiculous as it sounds, kid," he said. "It's all a whim. Beardsley can do anything he wants. All he's got to worry about is the laws of libel. He can chew up anyone he wants."

"We could refuse."

"What are you, a fucking Bolshevik? Don't cry over any of them. Pelligrino's a filthy little wop. He'd sell his soul to the devil for one more vote and you can buy him for the price of a piece of ass. What the hell?" Patton shrugged, drank off his whiskey, then looked at

Nick again and laughed. "Don't be so fucking self-righteous. Who the hell do you think's paying the bar bill?"

"Jesus," Nick said. He had just picked up the shot
glass to sip. He put it down again quickly, as if it suddenly had turned to a burning coal.

"You're kidding me," Nick said. It was more in the
nature of a question.

"I shit you not," Patton said, but it seemed incon-
clusive, tentative. It was beyond Nick's realm of
experience. Watching Patton, his face drained of color
in the dark bar, Nick tried to see beyond the patina of
cynicism that seemed to screen out all but the darker
side of human motivation. It frightened him. Was this
the way he would wind up after a lifetime of recording
human folly? He felt perspiration begin to roll down his
sides as he reached again for his drink and drank it off
with the same quick motion as Patton's. He could feel
the older man's eyes on him, cool and observing; perhaps, watching the drink downed, with renewed respect.

"As to Pelligrino," Patton said, his voice lowered,
"he's got a trail of droppings from here to Canarsie. Just
you tell McCarthy to call his buddies at the Police Department and pull a raid on Uptown Emma's. She's the
City Hall pimp. Got a Park Avenue place. You'll get all
the dirt you need on Pelligrino. He's one of the regulars."

"Just like that?"

"Just like that." Patton snapped his fingers.

Nick remembered the night at Shanley's, the big
beefy back of the Police Chief, McCarthy's heavy cough-
provoking laughter.

"It's disgusting," Nick said. "It makes a mockery of
the newspaper business, of the police, of government."

"Not a mockery, kid, a game. It's all a game. Either
play the game or get the hell out. What did Harry say?
If you can't stand the heat, get the hell out of the kitch-
en. Now there's your example, kid."

Standing there, watching Patton, Nick felt a sudden
tinge of nausea. Perhaps it was the whiskey or the heavy
acrid smell of the cigar smoke or the stink of human

mendacity and self-disgust, but Nick quickly left the bar and began to walk, at first through the park, then detouring, heading uptown on the sidewalk. Somehow his inner agitation and the physical exertion of the swift walk dispelled his nausea. His first impulse at rationalization was disbelief. These things only happened in movies, contrivances to further the plot, exaggerations to hold interest, broad strokes of the brush to make a point. Surely this was not the way it was in real life. He tried to imagine what Beardsley was like, the smiling face, hardly worthy of a second look. Was it possible for one man to wield such power? It was, he told himself, unjust, immoral, patently wrong. And yet, if one were to take Patton's analysis as gospel, what did it matter? Pelligrino, after all, was just a venal little bastard, a fraud. Or was it simply another prejudgment, inflamed further by Patton's cynicism? Perhaps Beardsley was acting out of outrage, decency, faith in the democratic process. Patton could be wrong, after all, wrong about Beardsley's motives, wrong about Pelligrino, wrong about life in general, the old mean drunk. People weren't all that bad. Besides, perhaps the Pelligrino story was all McCarthy's idea, an instinctive feel for the jugular of corruption. What did he care about Pelligrino? The people! The poor put-upon minions who lived in this pressure cooker of a city were entitled to honest government. That was their right, their heritage. Bits and pieces of speeches floated in his mind, bands playing, flags waving in the breeze on the public square of Warren, Ohio. Hell, he thought, he had nearly got his ass shot off fighting for that principle. Fuck Patton and all his posturing horseshit, all his meanness, all his sick twaddle. The issue was corruption. If Pelligrino was corrupt, he deserved his fate. Truth will out.

When, finally, Nick recovered his sense of place, he was crossing Third Avenue on Forty-second Street, passing the Horn and Hardart, chugging up the hill to the *News* building. When he arrived in the city room again, his feet ached. Sweat soaked into his clothes. He walked directly up to McCarthy and gave him the message about Uptown Emma's, watching as the older man reached for his private phone and dialed the number without hesitation, leering into the mouthpiece. "Good work, kid," he said.

When Gunderstein returned, Nick poured himself another Scotch and watched the younger man pace the room, his thin body taut, stooped, hands pushed deeply into his pants pockets.

"I believe him," Gunderstein said. Instinct again, Nick thought, observing him coolly, appraising the way Gunderstein's mind groped forward like a caterpillar on clusters of tiny feet.

"That's not enough," Nick said. He felt his own ambivalence. By now he had learned that there were no certainties, the prism of truth changed with the direction of the light source. It was all a question of will and interpretation, his will, his interpretation. To Gunderstein, the story was the story, impersonal, a brief photograph from many angles of a single subject.

"Frankly, Harold, without any attributable quotes the story has no weight, becomes pure speculation. The implication that the Diem assassination triggered the Kennedy killing is unsupportable, another mythmaker."

"That would depend on how I wrote the story."

"You'd still have to write it with Henderson somewhere up front. In today's climate even the allegation that he was part of the CIA action would be damning. The accusation that he was actually part of an assassination plot would kill his career off entirely."

"But it's the truth."

"You don't know that for sure."

"You heard Allison."

"I also saw him: a bitter, frustrated drunk."

"Would you run the story if I got him to allow himself to be quoted?"

Nick paused. It was time to be cautious. "I wouldn't want to commit myself." It's a lot different with palace favorites, he thought, ideological cousins. "Why is it that these informer types wait for years to surface?"

"They apparently fester until the boil breaks."

"And all we have to do is stand there with our cups out to catch the pus." He was revolted by his own image, finishing off the dregs of his drink.

"I know I could write the kind of story that could pass muster. Suppose I left out Henderson's name?" He would not give up.

"You're like a damned sea nettle, Harold."

"We should tell it," he said, with emphasis on the collective pronoun.

Nick rubbed his chin, the beard bristles rough against the heel of his hand. He felt his energy drained, looked at his wristwatch. It was after midnight. The liquor had hit him quickly, confirming his tiredness, his age, the fallibility of the human body. Rising, he felt the sluggish unlocking of his knees, a brief stiffness, more signals of time's encroachment.

"We'll talk about it tomorrow," Nick said, putting his empty glass on one of the Stonehenge piles, drawing his tie tighter, straightening his jacket. He let himself out, leaving the puzzled face of Gunderstein to its angular contemplation.

Outside, the air was chilling, although his head cleared and by prodding his legs along the pavement, he was able to loosen up a bit. For years he had been able to judge his energy by the use of his legs. In youth the early morning movement in the bright, clean, sunlit air always came as a shock, like cold water on a sweaty brow, cool and sweet and powerful. Later he could measure the progress of his life, the decline of the tissues, by this yardstick of remembered energy in his legs. Walking now, he could feel the slippage, and by the time he reached Foxhall, less than a quarter of a mile away, he was struggling to catch his breath and perspiring heavily. The security guard, alerted by his step, peeked out the door of the guardhouse and waved as he proceeded uphill to the entrance of the building, a glass palace built on one of Washington's highest points. When he had purchased the apartment a few years ago, the view with its unobstructed visibility of legendary landmarks seemed somehow a deserved gift to himself.

In his apartment, he moved from the foyer into the living room where floor-to-ceiling windows offered fantastic views of the city at his feet. He stood watching it for a long time, as he had often done, until a small clock chimed one and reminded him again that he was tired. It had been a long day, he thought, smiling to himself, remembering how it had begun. He removed his clothing in the bathroom, slipped into his pajamas which hung on a doorhook, brushed his teeth, then, clothes in hand, tiptoed into the bedroom where a big double bed stood on a raised pedestal. The bedspread was still pulled taut. Jennie had not come in yet.

If there was a brief flash of anxiety it was only, he told himself, based on the level of his expectation; he had assumed she was there. Lying down, he refused to allow his anxiety to proliferate. She had, he imagined, simply joined the party she was covering. Perhaps she had checked with the night desk, who told her that the story was spaced out for the late editions.

He could visualize her, without jealousy, flirting, being pursued, tantalizing, charming, in her special chic, with-it manner, always a delight, except when she groped for expression on the typewriter. There the charm and fluidity sickened and withered.

From his bed he watched the flickering lights on the nearby radio towers, feeling his muscles unstiffen in his legs. The residue of alcohol in his blood made his head swim at first, but soon he slipped into sleep. The jiggling of a key in the lock and the clock chiming three sounded in his mind simultaneously and he opened his eyes, listening for her step, fully alert.

She had taken her shoes off and was proceeding quietly through the apartment. He heard a bump.

"Shit," she cried.

"Jennie!"

"I woke you. I promised I wouldn't wake you, darling. And now I've done it." She sat on the side of the bed, the heavy sweetish scent of champagne mingled with her perfume.

She reached for his forehead, smoothed his hair. "Poor baby," she said. He looked upward, focusing on her face, the smooth cheekbones, large, carefully shadowed brown eyes, the frosted hair long and silky against the side of his face. "We danced and danced. It was quite a do. Then the ambassador invited us upstairs for scrambled eggs and champagne, which he made himself on a big skillet. It was so veddy British, so naughty, yet so proper."

"How cozy," he mumbled.

"Did you miss old Jennie?" she asked, pinching his side.

"*Old* is hardly the correct adjective."

"It was lovely, a charming party. I really don't think I'll be half bad on them. It all had a certain anglicized ambience that was refreshing. And the champagne was divine."

"I can smell it," he said.

"I'm gloriously smashed." She lay her head on his stomach over the blanket. He could feel the light pressure of her hand against his penis. The suggestion of sexuality recalled his feeling of tiredness.

"And it's so good to come home and find my man here." She put moist lips on his and kissed him deeply, her tongue flickering aggressively against his.

He felt her hand reach down under the covers and caress his testicles. She whispered into his ear. "I love my man," she said. "I love his balls."

"That's all you're interested in, just one thing." He smiled.

"You bet your sweet petunia."

He felt his tiredness again, becoming anxious when his response seemed slow.

He unhooked her dress, an expected reflex, and unzipped the top, feeling her small breasts fall free when he unhooked her brassiere strap. Willing himself to respond only made matters worse. Feeling his penis shrivel, he reached for her aggressively and pulled the dress over her head, watching the uptilt of her barely developed chest, so different from Margaret's huge breasts in which he could suckle and roam with tongue, hand, penis, an exploration of infinite variety. He moved over her, downward with his head, rolling down her panties, as his tongue sought her clitoris and she responded by caressing his head and ears, signaling her enjoyment. Pursuing her pleasure, he followed its rhythm with technical observation, hoping that he could induce a climax, perhaps end the need for further activity on his part. He felt empty and dead in his loins, ashamed of his tiredness, but still not daring to insult his maturity by a fear of impotence. It was a lurking beast that up to now he had kept at bay.

He worked his tongue around her organs, titillating, teasing, imagining some special rhythm, feeling her respond to a nerve-rending pleasure as his tongue, strained now and painful, played on this part of her body. He could feel her reaching for his penis, the tip of her tongue caressing its limpness as she sought the key to his own pleasure. He felt inadequate, his ego suddenly harassed. But she would not give up, as if it were necessary for her to validate his manhood, and soon she was concentrating the fury of her energy on the single-minded task of drawing forth his response. When erection finally came, she straddled him and inserted his tentatively erected organ, which she seemed to milk now as her lithe form swiveled on his pelvis. Willing himself to concentrate on the graphic stimulation of her swaying form, watching her lightly haired opening move upward and downward over him, he managed to spill his semen, a thankful release, giving him hardly more than a twinge of pleasure. He wondered if he had fulfilled her expectation, angered by the intimidation that the thought inspired.

"It was lovely," she said, snuggling against him. He wondered if she were lying.

"I'll be the wreck of the Hesperus in the morning."

"You'll be full of energy, alive. You'll see."

He lay with his eyes closed as she got up from the bed and went into the bathroom, feeling drowsiness begin again. Before he could doze off, she came back and began to move about the room.

"I spent a lot of time this evening with Burton Henderson," she said. Henderson again. His eyes opened.

"He's a very interesting man."

"Was his wife with him?" Nick asked. It was too impulsive a question, angering him.

"No. Apparently she's not much for parties, a home body." She turned toward him, started to speak, then checked herself.

"He's ubiquitous," Nick said.

"He does apparently get around."

"How did he latch onto you?"

"He didn't latch on. You know how these parties go. You sort of drift into things."

"And of course he was in the little egg-scrambling soirée in the chancery."

"Yes, as a matter of fact."

"And of course he was charming and attentive all evening, kissing your ass."

She turned and looked at him, puzzled. "It was innocent, Nick," she said.

"I'll bet he brought you home."

"Yes he did."

"You had him drop you off in front of your place, then walked across, right?"

"Of course. Knowing about us was no business of his."

"I'll bet he was what heated you up tonight."

"Christ, Nick," Jennie screeched, "cut it out. You're way off base and you know it."

"Am I?" he said bitterly.

"You're acting like an adolescent."

"I know about Henderson. I know what he's up to."

"So does everybody. He's running for President of the United States. He knows better than to go for my ass. Besides, he has them standing in line."

"What did you talk about?"

"Small talk. Trivia."

"To you, yes. To him, no."

"You couldn't expect me to ignore him," she said. "I am a reporter, you know."

"Allegedly."

"That's a crack."

He was too tired for combat. Besides, he was saturated with Henderson. His day had been choked with him.

"Go to sleep," he said. They lay quietly for a long time. He could feel her tossing restlessly.

"Why all the fuss about Henderson?" she whispered.

"He's Myra's boy."

"How do you mean that?"

"How do you think?"

Her hesitation seemed awkward, as if she had checked her reaction.

"From what I've observed," she said slowly, an edge of defensiveness in her tone, "I'd say the issue was sans flesh."

"Is that supposed to be intuitive?"

"Well, somebody has got to stick up for the sex. You guys look at all women from the eye of your cocks."

"I never even implied her interest was even remotely romantic." He paused. "Or sexual." Somehow Jennie's response seemed uncharacteristic. He let it pass.

"She wants me to kill the Gunderstein investigation," he said. "So far she's been subtle, but I can feel the pressure." He told her of his meeting with Allison in Gunderstein's apartment.

"So you're not sure about the story," she said when he had finished.

"That's what I told Gunderstein."

She remained silent for a time but he could feel her alertness. "But you'd really like to run it?" she prodded.

"Yes."

He was surprised at the swiftness of his response. Did he believe in the story or the use of it as a weapon against Myra? It annoyed him to know that he was afraid. "I'm afraid . . ." he began, then checked himself.

"Of what?"

"I'm afraid I'm just too tired," he said, hoping that
it had masked his sudden outburst. How could he tell
her he was afraid of his age, afraid of Myra's authority,
afraid of his own pride? Closing his eyes, he could feel
himself slipping into sleep.

He was having a carefully detailed dream, one he
knew he would remember later. The setting was the old
library in Warren, the high-ceilinged reading room with
the globes of light that hung downward from heavy
chains, throwing reflections on shiny wooden tables on
which he could see carved initials. He could smell the
musty odor of books and beneath it the sweetish scent
of some half-eaten apple that someone must have tossed
into a wastebin. The old clear-faced clock ticked in its
case showing 4:30, and as if confirming its accuracy, a
glow from the setting sun threw reddish spears of light
across the room. He was sitting at the table, turning the
pages of a newspaper, listening and watching for some
special aberration that would validate this imagery as
a dream. It did not occur to him at first, then he saw it:
the paper was the *Chronicle* and the stories that flashed
across its pages were contemporary events. Bonville's
editorial, uncut, the blue-penciled words glaring up at
him on the inked pages, filled him with rage. "How
dare they," he cried out, breaking the silence of the
room, tearing at the paper, throwing it in bits and
pieces to the floor, screaming with uncontrolled anger,
a tantrum that had never occurred in his waking life. He
heard footsteps, the sound of leather heels on wooden
floors, coming at him at full speed, from behind him,
then converging on him from all sides, terrifying as they
grew louder and louder. Then he saw that it was Henderson running, his blue eyes piercing, moving toward
him in the reddish haze. It was only a dream, he knew,
but the fact of no escape from the endless impending
onslaught of Henderson from all directions was a terrifying reality. The sound of the telephone brought back
his sense of time and he awoke, confused at first, then
thankful for being saved. He grasped at the phone,

then uncradling it, let it fall against his ear. "Hello" rattled in his throat, rasping and hoarse.

"Nick." It was Myra's voice, smooth and calm. "Did I wake you?"

"It's okay." He looked at the face of his clock. It was six A.M.

"Stop over at the house for breakfast," she said. He was suddenly alert, detecting a brief urgency quickly masked. "Could you make it by seven?"

He nodded into the phone, the fears of last night returning.

"Nick."

"Sure, Myra. Seven." She hung up.

He lay there for a while looking up at the white ceiling, his mind turning over possibilities, until the odd beeping sound of the telephone, lingering near his ear, recalled time. Jumping out of bed, he felt dizzy from the sudden movement. He waited for the feeling to pass, then padded into the bathroom. He felt tired, his energy drained.

But when he had showered and shaved he felt better, although his hand shook as he moved the razor on his foamed cheeks. He was at an age when things like that bothered him, a slight tremor in his hand, a brief passing pain in his chest, the intrusive stab of a headache pain, signals of the flesh's vulnerability. Hadn't he watched Charlie disintegrate and explode under the pressure? Dressing, he occasionally looked over to where Jennie's naked body snuggled in the warmth of the blanket. Before he left, he bent over her and kissed her forehead, breathing the scent of her young skin.

He waited in the chilled morning for a cab. Ordinarily he might have walked the half mile to Myra's house in the Kalorama area. It was just a stone's throw from her father's original mansion, which had been torn down years ago to make way for the Embassy of Venezuela. As he stepped into the cab, he felt his heart beat heavily, his anxiety uncontrolled. When he arrived at Myra's front door and pressed the buzzer, he was annoyed that his hands were sweating. He rubbed them against his coat, hoping to dry them before he had to submit to the ritual of touched flesh. He detested sweaty hands in others.

Myra's maid ushered him into the sun-drenched breakfast room, overlooking the neatly manicured lawn and the massive pre-Columbian sculptures that glistened in the chill morning. Myra was sitting at the table, on which stood a silver chafing dish that threw off the herbal scent of flavored eggs. Bowls of sectioned grapefruit gleamed in silvered settings. The man she was sitting with turned to greet him. The face was that of Scott Ambruster, director of the CIA.

"Well, Nick," he said, smiling, holding out his hand. "You've got the head spook for breakfast." Nick gave his hand reluctantly, knowing that the clammy feel of it put him at a disadvantage. Details like that were not lost on a man like Ambruster.

"I should have guessed," Nick said, joining them. He looked over the grapefruit to Ambruster's large brown eyes, set in a heavy face. He had the look of a kindly uncle, hardly the image one might have imagined, considering his job.

"It was Scottie's idea," Myra said, absolving herself. She was dressed in a bright green dressing gown with a trim of white fur. Could it be ermine? Her grey hair sparkled in the light. It was neatly combed and flipped jauntily on one side. The green gown brought out the green in her hazel eyes and fresh makeup masked the lines in her tight skin.

"The way we've been roasting the agency lately," Nick said, "you must feel a little like Daniel."

"Apt," Ambruster said, smiling at the reference. Nick had known him for years, meeting him first when he was Secretary of the Air Force. "That would make you the lions."

"Daniel survived," Myra said sweetly.

"I wonder if I will," Ambruster said, still smiling, charm exuding. They are good at that, Nick thought.

"We spooks are having a tough time of it these days," Ambruster said, as if soliciting their pity.

"More eggs, Scottie?" Myra asked, uncovering the silver dish.

"You're deliberately trying to ruin my image," Ambruster said, patting his large middle, ladling the eggs onto his plate.

"We're fattening you for the kill," Nick said. Myra laughed girlishly.

"They're marvelous," Ambruster said, a bit of yellow dripping on his lip. "And if I'm going to be the national heavyweight I might as well look the part."

Having been through these confrontations before, Nick waited for the moment for the trivia to be bridged. But Ambruster was not to be hurried. A man in his profession knew the value of patience. He looked about him.

"My, what a lovely room." It was as if they were all good friends. Being in an adversary relationship increased the bond which Ambruster himself surely felt. Nick knew Ambruster would also feel at home with the head of the KGB.

"You're a brave man, Scottie," Myra said, showing even teeth. "The way the *Chronicle*'s been beating on you, I'd think you'd be entitled to be suspicious about the eggs."

"He watched you eat them first," Nick said.

"Actually, I didn't," Ambruster said, smiling quietly and turning his head toward Nick. "Your observations are not infallible, my friend." There was a barely perceptible flicker of anger.

"As for the subject of fallibility . . ." Nick retorted, impatient with this fencing, his nerves frayed too thin for subtle thrusts and parries. Ambruster held up his hand.

"No need to go over that ground again," Ambruster said. "I've read it all in the *Chronicle*'s editorials. You can make a good case for the carelessness . . . no, pig-headedness, of my predecessors. Mistakes were made. Perhaps they were too overzealous. But then, it could happen to anyone without accountability." Nick looked at Myra. The reference was a well-aimed dart. "But at some point you've got to believe in change. After all, the premise of the CIA is still valid. We do still have enemies, you know. Or would you prefer that we stand naked?" Ambruster paused, buttering a biscuit.

"Surely, Scottie, you're not going to use that old wheeze," Nick said. "We just won't buy such scare tactics."

"We protect you as well. However undeserving." His sarcasm dripped with charm.

"It is amazing how parochial you people sound," Nick said, his annoyance showing now. "You've made the watchdog as tyrannical as the burglar. All the things we are opposed to in the enemy have become everyday tools of the CIA. Lies, domestic spying, covert mind bending, subterfuge beyond the pale, assassination squads."

"Now you've said it," Ambruster interrupted. "Assassination squads. Not just one man. Squads. Why not armies?"

"Diem, Trujillo, Tshombe, Allende," Nick said, counting off the names on his fingers.

"There's not a shred of evidence."

"You people are far too clever for that."

"Fairy tales," Ambruster said, washing down a biscuit with coffee.

"You mean it's never been an option?" Nick asked.

"It's always an option. We're not playing dominoes by the king's rules, old boy. I only said there's not a shred of evidence."

"Is that an admission?" Nick asked quietly.

"Of course not."

"Every investigation alludes to discussions of assassination conspiracies, ties to the Mafia, hit men," Nick pressed.

"We discuss these possibilities all the time," Ambruster said. "But that doesn't mean we do it. Like talking about sex when we were teen-agers. Besides, if you had the chance would you have planted a bullet in Mr. Hitler's brain? It might have been better for the world. Or Stalin's? We might have saved millions."

"Does that mean you're for its use?"

"I didn't say that."

"You implied." They were clever, Nick thought. Only a fool would expect such an option to remain unvoiced. Of course they would discuss it.

"The moral issue is one for the commander-in-chief to decide."

"Would you act if you were ordered to?" Nick pressed.

"Absolutely not," Ambruster said without hesitation.

"You'd resign?"

"Without question."

"On moral grounds?"

"How you people harp on morality! In the absence of war such an act could be interpreted . . . it would be interpreted as an act of murder, punishable by death or imprisonment, even though it might be an excellent, a cheap way to remove a tyrant."

Nick searched carefully for Myra's reaction. She was strangely silent. When they were going after the President she became livid whenever the CIA was mentioned. Now she seemed disinterested, docile.

"What's wrong with our way?" Nick asked, continuing to watch Myra.

"Yours is a particularly disgusting form of assassination, involving torture first under the guise of self-righteousness. After all, who made you the judge?"

"Without us, who would keep you all honest?"

"Gentlemen, please," Myra intervened. Ambruster held up his hand, like an opponent asking for time out.

"I admit our excesses," Ambruster continued, "but I truly believe we need this apparatus. True, it has gotten too big, too unwieldy, too all-encompassing, too spendy. All right. Let us accept that it's overgrown and clumsy. But, believe me, it is needed. We have got to keep our iron in the fire." His eyes drifted over them into the garden as if there were private mysteries to be seen there.

"And we've got to keep ours in," Nick said.

"You don't have to love us, just be tolerant. We're

on your side. All we ask is that you exercise some
sense of responsibility. Leave us room."

"In other words, screen out what you think damaging."

"Not at all."

"What then?"

He could see Ambruster's rising exasperation. Soon
the issue would be joined.

"This thing with Henderson, for example. It's preposterous. Your Gunderstein has been burrowing into
us like a sand crab."

"What's preposterous?" Nick asked, feeling for the
matter's pulse.

"The allegation, for one thing. As I've just told you,
there is no evidence to suggest that the CIA was ever
involved in overt assassination operations. Two congressional committees have tried; the Rockefeller Commission has tried. All they've come up with is hearsay,
circumstantial rot, innuendo, the typical politicized grab
bag. Frankly, they don't worry me as much as you,
the *Chronicle*." He paused again, his coffee cup descending on his saucer with a clatter. "My God, Nick,
isn't there any avenue of appeal? Can't you go on trust?
The implication of the allegation is that we just shoot
down any government leader who does not cooperate.
We do owe something to history, you know, and to the
generations that come after us; if they come after us.
Do you think we'd like future generations to know us as
cold-blooded killers?"

Nick contemplated the elements of Ambruster's
pleading: responsibility, sense of history, decency, national security. He had had them all before. There were
times when he could be persuaded, he thought. Perhaps Ambruster's point was not without value. Was it
Henderson who clouded the issue?

"It all boils down to the same thing, always the same
cry. You'd like us to hold the story, wouldn't you?"

"I'm asking you to be responsible."

"And you deny categorically that these operations
ever existed?"

Ambruster thought for a moment.

"Categorically," he said finally, "we do not assassinate people. We've been repeating it so many times we're hoarse."

Nick suspected that Ambruster was defining his position narrowly. Henderson was not being accused of pulling the trigger. He was alleged to be only the matchmaker, the puppeteer.

"Do you also deny that Henderson ever worked for you?" Nick asked.

"He's not in our personnel records," Ambruster said precisely.

"He admits being on detached service from NSA for special assignments."

"You'd have to check with NSA, then." It was the usual bureaucratic cop-out. "I suppose it's now a special crime to have worked for any intelligence agency. Talk about the arrogance of power." He looked at Myra, whose eyes narrowed. "You have become too powerful for your own good, you know." Ambruster sighed. He sipped his coffee silently. "I'm here," Ambruster continued, "because I truly believe that I can appeal to your sense of responsibility. Imagine the kind of power that you now wield in this country in the hands of less responsible people. It could happen. I've seen it happen elsewhere. You're in control of the most powerful instrument in the country. I'm sure I don't have to make that point. You've just toppled a President. I'm sitting here trying to use all my powers of persuasion to make you see that there are some matters that have to be carefully weighed against other factors. Our special problem is that we're absolutely powerless to defend ourselves and if you continue to discredit us we will ultimately be destroyed as an effective weapon of self-defense."

Ambruster was rolling out his big guns now. Was he succeeding? He looked at Myra for some clue to her reaction but her features revealed nothing. She was merely the affable hostess.

"Suppose, just suppose," Nick asked, "that we come

up with proof, witnesses, participants, who contradict your denials. What then? Is it responsible of us to still kill the story?"

Ambruster thought for a moment. "My appeal to you is to kill the story in any event. It can build. It can get out of hand. As for so-called witnesses, that too would be pure speculation since I assure you the story would not be true."

"But suppose they swore . . ."

"Look, Nick, the situation is academic. However you ran the story it would be damaging, witnesses or not. You'd be basing everything on half-truths. Impressions."

"Facts, Ambruster, not impressions," Nick shot back. "And we insist on confirmation from at least two sources."

"We in the intelligence business know that two sources do not necessarily a truth contain. We sometimes need twenty, thirty, and even then we still do not see the total picture. Ask thirty witnesses to describe an accident and you will get thirty different versions, all insisting upon the truth of their observations, yet somehow off the mark in terms of absolutes."

"Then you might as well challenge the whole concept of the news business. We do the best we can."

"Unfortunately, that's really not good enough."

"Better our way than yours."

"There will come a day when you'll be worse than we could ever have been."

"At least you have the ability to petition us." Nick looked around the room. "In these pleasant surroundings, everything so civilized. If the situation were reversed we'd be sitting on some wooden bench in some stark whitewashed room with knotted guts and sweaty palms." Nick felt the sweat of his own palms.

"You've been watching too many old movies."

He could see the unyielding stubbornness in the man, the abstracted superior high-mindedness. Surely Myra could detect his insufferable contempt. He watched her calmly sipping her coffee. He felt again the backwash of fatigue. The conversation seemed to be drifting. Perhaps sensing this, Ambruster made one more stab to refocus his plea.

"Let's just say that none of us is perfect. I'm here to try and convince you to think carefully before you leap on matters pertaining to us. I've tried to be candid."

"You couldn't be candid, even if you tried," Nick said. He noted the edge of sarcasm in his voice, his politeness worn thin. He turned toward Myra. Her control was infuriating. Why had she maneuvered him into this position?

"All I can do is appeal to your conscience," Ambruster said. It was the last arrow in his quiver. Looking into the garden, Nick blinked into the sunlight. If he were not a responsible man, he told himself, he would have run Gunderstein's piece as is and hang the human fallout.

Then Ambruster was standing up, a tall corpulent figure, as he moved toward Myra and took her hand. She stood up and took his arm, leading him past Nick.

"I'm not sure I made any impression," Ambruster said, holding out his hand. "At least I tried." Nick gave him a sweaty hand again, having forgotten to rub it dry against his trousers. Ambruster accepted it and smiled as he moved forward on Myra's arm.

When they had gone, Nick sat stiffly playing with a spoon, nervously banging it against the heel of his hand. Why couldn't he make it simple on himself, Nick thought. Why this personal flagellation? Was he determined to make a stand against Myra?

"Under it all, he's a rather sweet man," Myra said, flowing back into the room, sitting down, and pouring another cup of coffee.

"He's a viper," Nick said, pouting.

"I think we owed him the hearing, Nick. We've been murder on the Agency."

"The bastards deserved it," Nick said, lighting a cigarette and drowning the match in tepid coffee.

"He admitted that, Nick. He's inherited an awful bag of worms."

"They'll never change," Nick said. "The old-boy code. Protect the inside. Screw the outside. He would rat on his own mother if it meant protecting all the old boys. I don't trust him as far as I can spit."

"I don't know, Nick," she said. She was watching him, but, it seemed, not seeing, looking inward, reflecting on something within herself.

"Don't tell me you believed him, Myra?" He hoped he had broken into her thoughts.

"I felt his sincerity, Nick," she said, her attention regained. "At least on that single point."

"The Henderson issue?"

"Well, yes." She was trying to be casual.

He watched her cautiously, forcing alertness. Behind her tranquil air he could sense the determination, the iron will, assertive now. He knew he was not simply being persuaded. He was being assaulted. The meetings with Henderson and Ambruster were merely strategies. He felt himself grow tense, his vulnerability a heavy weight in his gut, his knowledge of her power over him galling. It was happening now, overtly. She was groping for total command.

"Maybe Gunderstein always presses too hard," Nick said. "It's part of his method." Hell, why was he going over this ground? Last year she had proclaimed Gunderstein a national hero.

"Henderson is our kind," she said quietly, the use of the collective pronoun a continuing offense. "He represents everything we stand for, Nick. We've spent hours talking about it. He's honest, liberal, decent, intelligent. Above all, he's a leader. And damn it, Nick, this country needs leadership. He's fair, balanced, objective, charismatic. If we allow him to get entangled in this mess, we'll destroy him, not as a man, Nick, but as a potential president. And that in my opinion would be a national tragedy."

He could not help but admire her calm eloquence, although his essential cynicism about the motives of politicians made her appeal ludicrous. Surely she couldn't believe what she was saying, not after a lifetime in Washington. He is your man, he wanted to say. Your possession. Your toy. She could, after all, order him to kill the story, he thought. But she was too smart for that. Why confront when you can outflank? Besides she might force him to resign, pressure him to react to some wellspring of pride buried inside of him. Without the *Chronicle,* what was his life?

"You know I'm giving it a hard look," he mumbled.

"I know, Nick."

Looking again into the sunlit garden, he noted that the glint of coldness on the sculptures softened as the sun changed its angle. The sense of age in the pre-Columbian conception seemed to calm him, draw him into a timeless orbit. He could feel her gaze lift, wash over him briefly, then retreat again.

"Let's examine it carefully," she sighed.

He was happy for the respite, impotence clinging to him like sweat.

Standing up, he felt a slight nausea as the overdose of coffee sloshed in his stomach. He looked at his watch.

"I'll talk to Gunderstein," he said.

She followed him into the hallway. From a table in the foyer he reached for a copy of the *Chronicle* which lay there on a pile.

"Trust me on this, Nick," she said.

"You've never given me reason to do otherwise," he answered. Not until now, he told himself, bitterly, feeling the cutting edge of her growing obsession. He wanted to say more, but turned instead and let himself out into the chilled air. Once outside, his nausea dissipated as he breathed deeply.

In the back of the cab, Nick watched the stately embassies of Massachusetts Avenue flow past, sensing his smallness, a bit of flotsam churning in the whirlpool of the epicenter. Even as he swirled in the agitation, he marveled at the manner in which power flowed, seemingly with no logical design, pursuing an obscure continuity.

It could happen with equal force at breakfast overlooking a sunlit garden dotted with pre-Columbian sculptures or beside a urinal. Decisions affecting millions could turn on a minor affliction like acid in the stomach or a father's long-remembered affront or a mother's withholding of natural protection. Because Hitler as a boy had observed his parents in a sexual encounter, whole armies could be laid to waste on the frozen steppes of Russia. And Johnson, his macho exploding as the cells in his afflicted body aged, could send 50,000 boys to their death and another 400,000 to the crucible for ritualized maiming. We are all trapped by our own genetic code and how we observe experience, Nick thought, wondering about his own lonely vulnerability in this minuscule gasp of time. He felt his exhaustion and fought against it. The *Chronicle* needed his strength. After all, life ebbed and flowed; victory and defeat were simply other sides of the same coin, quivering like a leaning horseshoe at the edge of the rounded stake.

It had been the primary lesson of Election Eve, 1948, the odd, maddening duel between the man on the wedding cake, Thomas E. Dewey, and bumbling, bespectacled, hickish Harry S Truman. It was before the use of computers for election vote counting and the *News* brought in all the bodies it could muster, including its entire Washington staff, and rearranged its city room to calculate and process election results swiftly. Newspapers were still obsessed, in those days, with the idea of scooping the competition. An army of copy boys were enlisted to rip the copy off the banks of Associated Press, United Press, and International News Service tickers and feed it to people, ranged in desks, representing the complicated geography of states, districts, and precincts.

A few blocks away, the floors of two major hotels had been booked for the brass of the two opposing political armies. The Democrats were ensconced in the Roosevelt Hotel and the Republicans in the Commodore. The Democrats were enveloped in the heavy gloom of impending disaster, all except old Harry who had gone to sleep in the family bed in Independence,

Missouri, while the Dewey team waited for its certain victory.

Aside from the excitement generated simply by the break in routine, Nick looked forward to seeing Charlie again. They'd been in touch by telephone since Nick's visit to the Parker place in September, although Nick had noted that their calls were diminishing in frequency.

By then, his involvement with Margaret had reached pinnacles of possession and passion, and although she officially resided in Brooklyn, she had moved part of her clothes to Nick's apartment. By going home on most nights, Margaret was able to somewhat placate her father, whose simplistic moral code was beyond breaching, and more important, she could still maintain the hopeless charade that she was "uninvolved." As for Nick, Margaret had become the quintessence of his existence, the gift of herself an unbearable joy, a delight so excruciatingly ecstatic that he passed through moments away from her suspended between afterglow and expectation. Seeing her walk through the city room, her large wonderful breasts jiggling in their supports, turning the lecherous eyes of his co-workers, gave him a special selfish pride.

It was not uncommon for them to slip away to the apartment in the middle of the day, after a few hours' respite, and, like beasts in season, clutch each other, transferring their body heat into an awe-inspiring sexuality. Even now he recalled the memory of the passion in great detail. The tremulous hands unhooking her brassiere strap, the falling free of the great white globes with their perfect adornments of large red nipples, the gentle hands unzipping him and pressing together those marvels around the urgent swelling of his manhood. Nothing that occurred later could ever erase the joy of that brief time of his life.

During that time, too, his by-lines were appearing regularly and he was building a reputation as a zealous reporter, enjoying the admiration of his peers. Dutifully, he would cut clippings of his stories and send them to his mother.

Margaret, too, was moving into a new orbit and her name was frequently seen on movie posters, proclaiming carefully contrived praise.

Only occasionally, usually around the onset of her period, did the old demon of feminine insecurity assail the idyllic nature of their relationship. "I will never marry you, Nick," she would say, the thought articulated at incongruous moments, as if she had suddenly been compelled to eject it. It was always near the surface of her consciousness.

"I didn't ask you," he would respond testily.

"Well, then, don't."

"I won't."

"Promise me you won't."

"I promise."

She would pause then, her eyes glazed, moistening. "That doesn't mean that I don't love you."

"I know."

"We're just good chums, Nick."

"Good chums."

In its way, the return of Charlie to New York became an uncommon intrusion, a break in the rhythm of their harmony. They were both assigned to cover Dewey headquarters. Charlie had arranged it with McCarthy.

"It'll get us the hell out of the office," Charlie said into the telephone.

"Great," Nick had answered, calculating the time frame in connection with Margaret's assignment, which was to assist in the city room vote count. He assumed then that Dewey would win early and they would all be finished working by midnight.

"I'm bringing Myra up," Charlie announced. "We'll have a helluva time."

By six the city room was a mass of activity. Desks had been moved into a huge circular chain manned by everybody the paper could muster. The first brief returns began to be ripped off the ticker machines by the copy boys and passed around to the appropriate desks. McCarthy's face was already beet red with booze and excitement.

"Keep in close touch," he said, watching them both. "We want to be the first out on the street with the victory story, so keep the copy moving." He looked about him cautiously, opened a desk drawer from which he removed a front-page press proof.

"Dewey Wins," it read.

"Used old wooden 108-point type for this. Couldn't do it for Truman. We're missing a *T*. The bastard doesn't have a chance anyway."

"I wouldn't be too sure about that headline," Charlie said coolly. McCarthy turned bloodshot eyes upward.

"What have we here? Another Washington pundit. What the hell happens to you guys in that burg?"

"You can't fool the people. Dewey is a stiff-necked phony."

"The people? Oh, shit. What have you been smoking?"

"I'll lay you ten bucks even money."

"Even money? Are you nuts?" He paused. "I wouldn't say it so loud. They're laying eight to five around here."

"Even money," Charlie repeated.

"Make it a hundred," McCarthy said, sneering. "Why don't you take some too, Gold?"

"You're on," Charlie said, turning to Nick in expectation.

"I'll go for the ten," Nick said.

"He was the best goddamned District Attorney this town ever had. Kicked the mob right in the ass. Those cocky sons of bitches. They tried everything to buy him. That man's got it."

"Well, you've got your money where your mouth is boss," Charlie said.

"You bet your sweet ass," McCarthy said, turning to answer the phone, an indication that they were dismissed.

"How can you be so damned sure?" he asked Charlie later as they walked toward the hotel.

"I feel it, Nick. Besides, I talked to old Harry. He's

got balls. I like a man with balls and I think the American people do too."

"I think you're getting naïve in your old age."

"Maybe," he said, a frown wrinkling his brow. Stopping, he bought a warm pretzel from a vendor. Tearing it apart, he offered it to Nick, who refused, and then stuffed a large piece into his mouth. "I miss these damned pretzels," he said, chewing heavily, as if the taste were nostalgia itself. They walked silently now, Charlie continuing to chew on the heavy pretzel as they made their way through the crowds.

Nick followed Charlie as he elbowed into the lobby of the Commodore, awash with Dewey-Warren buttons, banners hanging from the baroque ceiling. American flags were everywhere. People overflowed from the public bar, crowding together in the lobby, waiting expectantly for the first returns. Flashing their press cards, they passed through a cordon of policemen and took the elevator to the fourteenth floor, which had been set aside for the candidate and his party, and the press. A bar had been set up in a large suite adjacent to one occupied by the Dewey people.

A crowd of reporters was busy chewing on chicken legs, taken from a silver chafing dish, which they washed down with booze. The large suite was a mess. A bank of typewriters filled one end of the room and clusters of telephones stood ready to pass the word to the world.

"Dewey's napping," a reporter said.

"They've already got his victory speech ready," a woman reporter squealed, her face flushed with drink.

"Why don't they just make it and let us all go home?" another reporter said.

"Am I glad this is nearly over," someone else said.

A man wearing a badge which said "Official" came in and tapped a spoon on a glass. He was dressed in a pinstripe suit and wore round horn-rimmed spectacles. They could tell by his attitude and demeanor that he was the Press Secretary.

"The candidate is resting." He looked at his watch.

"He'll be down in one hour and we'll allow ten minutes for picture taking in the main suite. No more than ten minutes." A group of scruffy photographers groaned in the corner.

"Any returns yet?" someone said.

"Just sporadic," the Press Secretary responded. "You'll be informed."

"Could we get an advance of the victory statement?" a reporter asked.

"When the time is appropriate," the Press Secretary said confidently. "We'll try to wrap things up as fast as possible. As soon as we learn we've won, the candidate will make his victory speech from the podium of the Grand Ballroom. We'll make arrangements to get you all down there on time."

"And if he loses . . ." Charlie said loudly. The Press Secretary turned to him bristling with indignation. The question had a distinctly quieting effect on the other reporters in the room.

"We have contingent plans," he said, lifting his nose, a caricature.

"Just asking," Charlie said, smiling.

"Of course," the Press Secretary said with an effort at politeness.

"I'd like to stick a pin up their ass," Charlie whispered, moving to the bar and grabbing a bottle of beer from a silver tub. As he opened it he looked at Nick. "I can handle it, kid. Never touch the hard stuff anymore. It doesn't seem to like me much."

"So I've noticed."

Charlie drank the beer quickly, smacking his lips. He looked around the room. "They're all a bunch of lazy sheep," he said. "Look at them, hungry lambs waiting to sip the milk from the waiting teat. I tell you, Nick, newspapering is changing. It's strictly news by handout now, spoon-fed, manipulated. They manage us. It really pisses me off." He looked ahead in silence, his eyes turning inward, glazed.

"We're just twenty years too late," he sighed.

Unwilling to penetrate his brooding silence, Nick

picked up one of the phones and dialed the city desk. He described the scene to the rewrite man.

"The bastards are pretty cocksure, eh," the rewrite man commented.

"Dead certain," Nick answered.

"The early returns here indicate that Dewey is beginning to build up a big lead."

"You might as well get the victory story written. The old man wants to be the first on the street."

When he returned he noted that Charlie was already sipping a second beer. "Where's Myra?" Nick asked.

"Oh, Christ," he answered, "I was supposed to call her. She's up at the Democratic headquarters with the wheels. Old Myra is always with the wheels. She's probably sitting quietly beside the campaign manager, holding his hand." Nick noted a barely perceptible edge of envy. "Besides, she hates the fucking Republicans more than her father, and that's going some." He picked up the phone and, after some exasperation, got through to her.

"Gloom and doom, you say." He turned toward Nick. "All is gloom and doom up there. Here?" He looked about the room. "The usual slobs and, as they say, the feel of victory in the air."

He listened to her voice for a while. "Of course I do," he said. "I'll call you later." He hung up. "She's quite a woman," Charlie said. "Quite a woman." Knowing Charlie, Nick could sense an impending revelation. It came quickly, a gust of heavy air expelled in his face.

"She's giving me a fit. They want me to quit the *News* right now and work for the *Chronicle*."

"I thought that's what you wanted."

"I'm not so sure anymore." Charlie mused. "I'd be the damned Son-in-Law."

"So what?"

"It's more complicated than that." He finished his beer and looked at Nick. "It's an odd arrangement," he continued. "The old man won't put Myra in the business but he's fixed it so that the *Chronicle*'s ownership stays in Myra's hands after his death." He shook his head.

"Apparently he believes in bloodlines and property, but not in women," Nick said.

"Which makes me a kind of surrogate for Myra, a stand-in. What the hell happens when the old man dies?"

"You'll be working for your wife," Nick responded.

Charlie shrugged. A nerve palpitated in his jaw. "I'm not afraid of the responsibility," he said suddenly ignoring the response. "I've got a lot of ideas for that paper, but it requires absolute control, no democratic bullshit, one man at the helm. You can't run a newspaper by committee."

Apparently he had given the matter a great deal of thought. Nick sensed he was merely debating with himself now. He remained silent as Charlie moved to the bar and found another beer.

The Press Secretary darted back into the suite. Dewey was sufficiently rested to make his appearance, he told them. Photographers ran for their Speed Graphics. Then, on signal, they rushed into the corridors, jostling the Press Secretary as he attempted unsuccessfully to discipline their movements.

Pushed from behind, Nick and Charlie moved with the crowd. Charlie held his beer bottle up over the heads of the mob as it came to a halt in front of the elevator banks.

"What's the latest results?" someone asked.

"Dewey's winning."

The elevator door opened. Cameras popped and a short smiling man with a heavy squared moustache and a shiny face walked into the center of the group, like a trained monkey about to perform. Questions burst from the crowd.

"How do you feel?"

"Confident."

"Where's your wife?"

"She's still in the suite."

"What did you have for dinner?"

"A piece of pie. I wasn't very hungry."

"Are you glad the campaign is over?"

"Are you kidding?"

"Will you vacation after your victory?"

"I haven't won yet."

"Who will be your Secretary of State?"

"That's being presumptuous."

"Are the returns going as expected?"

"Exactly."

"When can we expect a victory statement?"

"When victory comes."

"And suppose defeat comes?" It was Charlie's question. Dewey squinted into the crowd, lights bouncing over his glistening forehead. Nick suddenly caught the anxiety in the man, the greediness for success. He seemed frightened, trapped. He stood in the midst of the crowd, small and vulnerable, a lonely figure. Charlie's question was never answered as Dewey pressed on down the corridor in a trail of popping flashbulbs, beefy policemen making a path through the newspaper crowd. Then the group made a rush for the telephones. Charlie made the call this time, embellishing the story out of his own specially tinted observations. When he hung up the phone, he stopped again at the bar for a beer.

"What did you tell them?"

"I said he looked worried."

"Christ, Charlie," Nick said. "That could change the focus of the story. One simple observation like that."

"I know."

"It didn't seem that way to me."

"He *is* worried, Nick," Charlie said. "They tell me at the *News* that the returns are beginning to show slippage."

The other reporters were getting the same information, prompting a nervous reaction in the crowded room. Newspapermen were always catching things from each other: enthusiasm, depression, cynicism. The tone of the group began to change. The Press Secretary came in carrying notes. He was sweating, his arrogance dissipating. He read a statement.

"We have every reason to believe that the results

are still favoring Mr. Dewey. The Western returns, just coming in, indicate the strength of our thrust."

"What the hell does that mean?" Charlie shouted. The beer was beginning to have some effect.

"It means," the Press Secretary said, with an effort to regain his former aplomb, "that the final Western returns will assure our victory."

"Baloney," Charlie said. "You're starting to lose and you're scared as hell."

"That is simply not true," the Press Secretary responded, glaring, the sweat beading on his forehead.

"How is Mr. Dewey taking it?" someone asked. The dam had burst. The tide of the press optimism had turned.

"Mr. Dewey is confident."

"Has he got a concession statement ready?" Charlie asked. The question rattled the Press Secretary. "We intend to win this election," he said, his voice breaking.

"Answer the question," someone shouted.

The Press Secretary seemed to deflate entirely, a pricked balloon. "We will prepare any statement that is appropriate," he said disdainfully.

"Why the hell can't he tell the goddamned truth?" Charlie hissed. "Why can't he just say that he's scared, that Dewey is scared, that it's not at all going as they expected? Why do they all have to be such a bunch of liars?"

Finally the Press Secretary retreated. Nick phoned the paper. The rewrite man put him through to McCarthy.

"What do they think up there?" McCarthy asked. He seemed depressed.

"They say that they're hopeful about the Western returns, although they're not as cocky as they were earlier."

"Shit!"

"Worried about your bet?"

"I just took a chance on getting a victory edition on the street. Hell, the Chicago *Tribune* is out with a victory extra saying that Dewey has won. What a goddamned donnybrook!" He had never observed such confusion in McCarthy. "One edition is already on the street with O'Donnell's column congratulating Dewey as the new President-elect."

Nick looked around the room. The crowd of reporters was thinning out. "Where the hell is everybody going?" Nick asked the waning group.

"To Democratic headquarters," someone answered. "That's where the action is now."

"I think you better hold that edition, boss," Nick said. "There's a mass exodus here."

"I need a drink," McCarthy said suddenly.

"Apparently," Nick said, holding a bulletin of the latest returns that someone had brought from Dewey's suite, "California will decide. It looks like a long night."

"Yeah," McCarthy said, hanging up abruptly. Nick went to the bar and poured himself a shot of Scotch, gulping it quickly, feeling it burn as it dropped downward. Charlie had sprawled on a couch in the now quiet room. A tipsy reporter stood in the door.

"I just came from the Ballroom. It's now a wake. Even the band has stopped playing."

"The fortunes of war," Charlie said. "The *Chronicle* was one of the few papers that supported Truman. The old man was right."

"Stubborn, I'd say. He was a tiny minority."

"The power of the lone voice." Charlie became silent, staring into space. "It would be one helluva challenge, Nick," he said after a while. "If only . . ."

Nick remembered Margaret. He looked at his watch. It was getting late, nearly two A.M.

"If only what?" he said abstractedly.

"You think I could handle it, kid?" Charlie asked. It was an appeal. "I want it so badly I can taste it, but I'm scared shitless."

"Of what?"

"Of myself. Of Myra. Of the kind of commitment required."

"I can't tell you what to do, Charlie," Nick said.

"Do you think I can handle it?"

"I think you could fuck an elephant if you put your mind to it, Charlie."

"You're a blind boob, kid. Did anyone ever tell you that?"

"Yeah, you."

After a while Myra appeared at the door of the press room, squinting through the stale smoke. She looked neat and cool and bending over Charlie's sprawled form, she kissed him on the forehead.

"Come to kick the carcass of the Republicans," Charlie said, sitting up.

"I thought I might get you to come up to the other place. They'll be having a victory celebration."

"It won't be definite until California comes in," Nick said after he greeted Myra with a kiss on her cheek. Her flesh felt cool on his lips.

Charlie looked at his wristwatch and got up. "What's the latest?" he asked.

The Press Secretary came in again and stood before the thinned-out group of reporters. "We are confident that the returns from California will assure our victory," he said, tight-lipped, like a little boy whistling in the cemetery. A wave of chuckles greeted his statement.

"How is Dewey taking it?"

"Mr. Dewey is confident," the Press Secretary said.

"Bullshit," Charlie hissed. The Press Secretary turned to him. "There's no need for profanity," he said.

"Why don't you just tell us the truth?" Charlie said.

"I have."

"Bullshit again," Charlie said.

"I don't have to stand here and take this."

"Well then, don't."

The Press Secretary's humiliation hung in the air.

"Why don't you just say that Dewey is concerned?"

"Because he isn't."

"Then let him come out here and tell us so."

The Press Secretary shook his head and flushed, then turned angrily and walked back to the candidate's suite.

"They've probably got him tied down so he won't jump out the window," a reporter said. Charlie went to the bank of telephones and called the office. Nick felt a pressure on his elbow as Myra edged him into a corner of the room.

"Can I ask you a favor, Nick?" she asked quietly, coolly, with deliberate articulation. Her hair was short, bobbed then, almost mannish, the green in her hazel eyes accentuated by a kelly green kerchief she wore tied around her neck.

"Sure, Myra." Even then, Nick thought, she had the ability to radiate humility.

"We've been trying to get Charlie to quit the *News* and come to Dad's paper," she whispered.

"You mean there is some question about it?" Nick lied, trying to sidestep the responsibility.

"He vacillates like a pendulum. He's afraid of something."

"Maybe he doesn't want to be the Son-in-Law."

She looked at him coldly. "That's part of it." Then she smiled. "Nick, I think you can help him decide."

He could sense her urgency.

"We're offering him a brilliant future," she said. "It'll all go down the drain if he decides against it. My father will sell it before he lets me have it," she said bitterly. "Please, Nick, I'll never forget it as long as I live."

"You're exaggerating my influence," Nick said.

"There's a bond between you two, a kind of male bond that we females can't penetrate."

"We're friends," Nick protested, as if that might explain things, "but that doesn't mean ..."

"Please, Nick," Myra persisted.

Charlie hung up the phone and came toward them. "Please," she repeated. Nick was moved by the ferocity of her plea. It occurred to him that she might be over-killing her cause, since Charlie was already half-convinced to make the move in his own mind.

"I'll do what I can," Nick said as Charlie moved toward them in long strides, a beer bottle in his hand again.

"Bless you," Myra said. He felt her sincerity. Often, later, he remembered the single-mindedness of her appeal, its strength. Nature had tricked her. The wrong sex in the wrong time.

"Well, that's that," Charlie said smiling. "Old Mc-Carthy's in a real stew. They're still calling it a cliff-hanger, although as I see it, Dewey's dead and Harry's going to get up in the morning and find that he's still the top banana."

"Gold," a reporter called out, holding out a phone. Nick knew at once it was Margaret.

"What the hell is going on?" Margaret's voice was angry.

"Dewey's losing."

"I don't mean that. How come you haven't called? I thought we were going to meet."

"We are."

"Thanks for informing me."

"What are you so mad about?"

"You said you would call."

"I was working. I was busy. So were you."

"I expected you to call."

"Come on, Maggie. Let it go."

"Every time you get involved with Charlie . . ."

"We're on assignment."

She paused, perhaps ashamed to show her insecurity. Was Charlie now an issue between them? Could she be jealous of Charlie?

"I'm sorry, Nick. I'm tired. I think I'll go straight home."

She clicked off the phone. He felt an unbearable sense of loss. This is ridiculous, he told himself. Why was Charlie disrupting his life? Who needed Charlie and all his problems?

When Dewey finally emerged it was nearly six A.M. They had dozed, eaten sandwiches, waiting for the finality of events. Nick had already lost interest. He was tired and he missed Margaret. Charlie had fallen asleep on the couch. Myra quietly read a magazine.

Walking into the sporadic clicking of flashbulbs, a sputter now, Dewey proceeded down the corridor toward the elevator, a ravaged man, his eyes glazed, his skin puffy, a smile embedded incongruously under his moustache. He held onto his wife's arm, two lonely, defeated figures. The reporters remained silent, perhaps out of respect for the terrible finality of defeat. Nick watched as the couple backed into the elevator, small figures dwarfed by the large, beefy, red-faced policeman. As the elevator door closed, Dewey's eyes flickered behind a beginning mist.

"There goes one busted bag of dreams," Charlie said.

"Life is full of missed opportunities," Myra whispered; she looked at Charlie and grasped his arm. "Now let's go over to the winning side," she said, smiling sweetly.

12

Nick opened the late morning edition of the *Chronicle* he had taken from the pile in Myra's foyer and turned to the editorial section, rereading Bonville's editorial to assure himself that his remembered dream had not, somehow, breached reality.

Arriving at the *Chronicle*'s offices, he walked through the half-empty city room, looking for Gunderstein, who apparently hadn't yet arrived. Then he proceeded toward his glass cage.

Miss Baumgartner followed him in, balancing a cup of steaming coffee. Sitting down at his desk, he felt the weight of his body falling, a hint of his fatigue. Through the glass he watched Madison's beefy back slowly turn as the man's clairvoyance responded to Nick's glance.

"Martha Gates wants to see you," Miss Baumgartner said.

"Not again," he said, remembering yesterday's episode with irritation.

"I think you'd better," Miss Baumgartner said, in-

vesting the matter with rare importance. He nodded and
began thumbing through the New York *Times,* reading
the headlines and making mental notes of stories of
mutual interest that needed follow-up. The *Times* gave
only two paragraphs, buried in obscurity, to Henderson's
speech. Such comparison was unworthy of the *Chronicle,* or so he had lectured his staff. After all, it was
expected that the *Chronicle* had always had the beat
on the *Times,* especially in terms of Washington news.

Surely some editor, like himself, had had to make the
decision to treat the Henderson speech routinely. At the
Times, too, decisions had to be made on assignments,
layout, pictures, relationships of stories to one another,
the myriad of daily details. He could almost sense the
exact pitch of Sulzberger's temper by the way in which
the stories were treated. Objectivity! He snickered at
the word, recalling old Mr. Parker's obsession.

Looking up, he saw Henry Landau wave, then
squinted to observe the time on the large clock in the
city room. The editorial conference would soon con-
vene. He dreaded facing Bonville and his pouting bitterness, surely primed by a night of brooding. When he
turned, Martha Gates was already seated, her long
blonde hair unruly and lustreless. Her eyes were puffy
and she sucked nervously on a cigarette.

"What's with you?" he asked impatiently, deliberately
indifferent, keeping her at a distance.

He watched her hands shake as she handed him some
copy. It was badly typed, he noted. He read it quickly.

"Christ," Nick exclaimed, "her husband has blown
his brains out." He had not heard the story, which he
might have picked up on the radio while he was shaving
if he had followed his normal habits that morning.

"Look, Mr. Gold," Martha Gates said, her voice
cracking, holding back hysteria. "I followed careful
procedures. I made the inquiries. I spoke to Mrs. Ryan.
She was very indignant. I could see the trail of denial.
I spoke to Mr. Kee and his girl friend. I spoke to the
hotel in Puerto Rico. I spoke to the White House Chief
of Staff." He watched her thin throat constrict.

"Take it easy, Martha," Nick urged. He handed her his coffee which she held in her shaking hands. She lifted it to her lips, spilling a few drops on her dress.

"I even talked to Mr. Ryan. He sounded very calm. As you can see he's an associate professor of history at American University. He sounded calm, very pleasant actually. He said he had reimbursed Mr. Kee for the tickets and the hotel bill for himself and his wife. He told me it had never meant to be paid for them, that it was merely an easy way to handle the bookkeeping. He said there was absolutely no conflict of interest and, after all, his wife was only a personal assistant to the First Lady, not a career person, and wouldn't we please not use the story since it was all a misunderstanding." She paused, emptied the coffee cup, and relit her cigarette, her fingers shaking, barely able to find the cylinder's tip. "Then I got a call from a psychiatrist, a Dr. Petersen, who said that Professor Ryan could simply not take the kind of pressure he was being submitted to and would I please not run the story. I told him that wasn't my decision; I was merely tracking down a lead. He asked me where I got the lead and I told him I couldn't tell him. Then I asked the doctor what Professor Ryan was suffering from and he wouldn't tell me. Before he hung up he said to me that I would have to face the responsibility for the consequences if the story ran." Her shoulders began to shake. "I feel responsible, Mr. Gold. I feel it was my hand on the trigger."

Nick felt his stomach knot as he looked at the emotionally decimated girl. Quickly walking around his desk, he lifted her to her feet, leading her unsteady body into the inner conference room, shielding her from the city room eyes. He could see Miss Baumgartner watching them. In the conference room, Martha collapsed in uncontrolled tears. Miss Baumgartner knocked lightly and brought in a box of Kleenex. Looking up at the harlequined face, the girl smiled briefly through her tears and reached into the tissue box. Nick hated watching women cry. It seemed such a biological contradiction to those who pushed the myth of sexual equality. Because he did not cry, he always felt stronger, superior, in the presence of hysteria. After a while the girl tried to speak, but convulsive sobs clogged her windpipe.

"Calm down," he said firmly. The Ryan suicide was hardly uncommon, easy to fathom. Fear of exposure, the cracked façade, the unmasked guilt. You could never tell where the mud would splatter, where the bullets would ricochet. Like a doctor to whom death was commonplace, he had long ago steeled himself against such pain. He had helped many a young reporter pass this Rubicon.

"How was I to know he was a sick man?" she said finally, her convulsions ebbing.

"Would it have mattered if you had known?" Nick asked gently.

She looked momentarily confused, her eyes darting about the room. Finally they settled on Nick again. "I guess not," she said.

"Are you responsible for the man's illness?"

"No."

"Is it not a clear-cut violation of the code of ethics at the White House to accept gifts from anyone who has a political motive?"

"Of course."

"And is it not true that if Mr. Kee had ingratiated himself in the White House circle it would have meant some political profit for him, however subtle?"

"That was the premise of the story."

"All you were asking for was confirmation. If you hadn't found it, do you think we would have run the story?"

"I feel certain that you wouldn't have."

"That is an absolute discipline of this newspaper," Nick said. He sensed his own pomposity. "We do not go about destroying people for the joy of it." He thought of Henderson, saw a brief flicker in his blue eyes, felt an errant pang of guilt. Would she see through his self-righteousness? "You did not destroy this man. You are not responsible. When people accept public roles, they become public property. They no longer belong to themselves. They are our employees. Who do you think pays their salaries?" He did not wait for her to answer, his impatience accelerating. "Do we pay them to receive gifts from foreign lobbyists with special interests? The ball is in their court, not ours. There should never be anything personal in it."

"Maybe I'm not hard enough," she said. "Maybe this isn't the job for a woman after all. Yesterday I felt so confident." She blew her nose, its tip reddened, then she wiped away the moisture under her eyes. "The man had a record of depression," she said. "I called the psychiatrist again when I heard the news. He really laced into me. Said we were all callous, unfeeling rats. He really knew how to stimulate my guilt."

"Psychiatry's a lot like the newspaper business. An art, not a science."

He watched her repair her makeup. She was under control now as she peeked into the mirror of her compact. "Now you go back and rewrite the story."

"It's pretty botched up, isn't it?"

"Yes it is."

She looked up from the mirror. "You would have run it, wouldn't you, Mr. Gold?" she asked.

"If it was confirmed."

"And now?"

"Now the story of the suicide makes the confirmation moot. It would seem to me that the premise of the story is the newspaper investigation triggering the suicide. Only be careful that you don't go overboard on the original accusation. Let the dead man have his denial."

"But the wrongdoing is there by implication."

"Yes, it is. And if the poor devil hadn't pulled the trigger, it would hardly have made a really important story. Now it has page one possibilities." She stood up and held out her hand. He took it, feeling a squeeze of gratefulness.

"Thanks, Mr. Gold." Her narrow cold hands felt fragile. Before she left the room she turned, "I'm afraid

I still feel like a shit," she said. "Hell, I wouldn't like to have someone poking around with my secrets."

"Come now, Martha. Surely a pretty girl like you has no dark secrets," he said stupidly.

She looked puzzled. "Everybody has secrets," she said as she left the room.

He sat for a moment, looking down at the yellow pad on which he had been doodling. He had been making penmanship swirls, in the prescribed way of the schools of the thirties. Perhaps he was secretly yearning to go back in time again to childhood. That would be one way to escape the present. Professor Ryan had chosen another.

Before he could stand up, Henry Landau came in followed by Bonville, Peterson, and Milton Palmer, the editorial cartoonist. They took their accustomed places around the table, all except Bonville, in whose place Nick had inadvertently sat during his meeting with Martha Gates. He refused to move, conscious of having set up some further imbalance. It was odd the way people staked out territory. Bonville sat on the unaccustomed chair at the other side of the table, looking different from that angle, as if he were experiencing some metabolic change.

"Hear about the Ryan thing?" Landau asked.

"Hear about it? I was just bathed in it," Nick answered.

"Terrible thing," Peterson said. "A real tragedy."

"Might be an idea for an editorial in there somewhere."

"It would sound self-serving. I don't think we have to beat our chests," Bonville said. In his present position at the table, he looked even more hunched, the paleness taking on a yellow cast.

"You're right, Bonville," Nick said. He was conscious of smiling broadly, an attempt at placation. He could see that Bonville was still fuming over the emasculation of this morning's editorial.

"I've been reading the Henderson speech," Bonville said suddenly. Both Peterson and Landau reacted swiftly, their eyes turning toward Nick's, then downward to their yellow pads.

"Oh, shit," Nick said. He drew long X marks over his penmanship swirls.

With his usual insensitivity, Bonville continued. "He's come up with a lot of interesting statistics. I think it deserves another push. The program could be lost unless we give it massive backing."

"We just gave it a big push," Landau said flatly, obviously taking sides with Nick. So Henry's in line again, Nick thought, grateful.

"Yes, but you see, the timing is essential. There are attempts on the Hill to keep it pigeonholed, prevent it from reaching the floor, making it a political football," Bonville argued.

"Henderson's identification with it makes it implicit. He's wrapped himself in it like an American flag," Landau pressed.

"True. But it must be taken out of the political context. We need the kind of universal medical plan that the bill provides. The costs of medical care are going beyond the pale, actually beyond the reach of most people. I know it could have great political benefit to Henderson. But that's not for us to judge. The bill stands by itself as a monumental piece of legislation and deserves our strongest support."

Nick felt trapped by Bonville's logic. His palms began to sweat again. He wondered if Bonville had been approached by Henderson or his people in the last twenty-four hours. "It's too close on the heels of the last editorial," Nick said lamely.

"It gives me a hell of an idea for a cartoon," Milt Palmer said. Since his heart attack, his ears perked up at the subject of health and medicine. He started sketching on his pad.

"But," Bonville continued, "it's a subject that we're apparently all agreed on."

"I think we should hold fire for a while," Nick said softly, his voice losing timbre. He could feel the precariousness of his position, not wanting to appear arbitrary. Where was his strength today? "I want to keep the *Chronicle* politically neutral on the question of Henderson's political future," Nick said.

"Why do that?" Palmer said, still sketching. "He's a hell of a guy."

"That's beside the point."

"That *is* the point, Nick," Palmer said, ripping the cartoon off his pad. It showed Henderson in traction on a hospital bed. Beside him stood a doctor with his pockets filled with dollars. The caption read: "And for Another Thousand We'll Take You Out of Traction."

Peterson chuckled. "Not bad, Milt."

"Not bad? It's great. You guys and your fucking understatements."

"Let's move it up for next week," Nick said.

"I'd rather see it run now," Bonville said. "It would have more impact, more logic, coming on the heels of Henderson's speech."

"No," Nick said, "next week."

"Why, Nick?" Palmer asked, his moon face benign and innocent, his good nature infectious.

"Gunderstein's tracking down a story that could be damaging to Henderson." He was trying to be casual, almost indifferent. He wondered if they could sense his agitation.

"I know," Bonville said flatly.

"Christ, this place leaks like a sieve," Nick said petulantly.

"I thought there was nothing to it," Bonville said.

"Who told you that?" Nick asked sharply.

"Actually, I forget," Bonville said, squirming.

"You forget?" Nick pressed.

Bonville looked around the room, seeking support, unable to comprehend his sudden defensiveness on a subject that had never been controversial. Only Palmer came to his rescue.

"What the hell difference does it make? We're all in the same family." He laughed, then choked it off, apparently confused by the lack of camaraderie, the strange feeling of rising tension.

"Actually it must have been Henderson," Bonville said, his color becoming greenish as the rising blood mixed with his yellowed complexion. "I spoke to him this morning to get some additional material on the speech." Pete Peterson coughed nervously. Henry Landau lowered his head as he scribbled on his yellow pad.

Nick became conscious of his fists tightening, the tips of his fingers digging into his palms. If only he could unzip himself from his skin and spend some time in long contemplation of the scene around the table, suspending the minutes in a frozen frame, surveying the image in an unhurried investigation of all the tiny bits of revealed information. Surely there was something here he was missing, some link malformed in the chain of his own understanding of events. Finally, when he had remained silent too long, certain that the others were becoming discomforted, he spoke, a cracked mumble. "Henderson is ubiquitous," he said, remembering he had used the phrase last night with Jennie. He cleared his throat. "Henderson is ubiquitous," he said again, sensing the relief in the men around the table that he had not pressed Bonville, who had in his innocence blundered into the minefield.

"Look, let's shelve this one for sometime next week," Henry Landau said, jumping to the rescue, leaving Bonville shattered and confused, a shade more shrunken than usual, puffing furiously on his cigarette. Nick felt compassion for the man, clumsily tangled in unseen wires, knowing that he could never explain it to his satisfaction. Surely he must have faith in his own instincts, he told himself, only half convinced that he wasn't imagining the whole thing. Hadn't Myra herself urged him to kill the Henderson story? Wasn't that an obvious enough clue? Yet despite her revealed position, the real question was whether or not she had inspired an orchestration, was deliberately involved in a conspiracy to manipulate him. If he accepted that premise, then he was surrounded by traitors and informers, a concept too difficult to comprehend.

Hearing the voices around him, he roused his concentration, determined to pick up their thread, to re-capture a measure of his authority in their eyes. Landau was suggesting a position on the use of energy, a strong warning to the Administration on their neglect in not pressing for a more comprehensive energy policy.

"I'd suggest, too, that Congress be equally roasted," Nick said, satisfied that his voice had regained its res-onance. "The stopgap measures have proven of little value."

"The motivating force has still got to be the Admin-istration," Peterson said, as Palmer began again to stroke his pad. They debated the premise until a firm line had been established. Nick was disappointed that Bonville could not be roused to participate. Surely they all sensed his depression, his despair. When they had finished the meeting, they filed out silently. Bonville hung back a moment longer, paused briefly as he passed through the door, then pressed on.

Back in his glass cage, Nick picked desultorily at the heavy pile of hate mail. It had little interest for him that morning, the barbs blunted. He cursed his visibility, wondering if his mental state could be perceived by those in the city room. It had never occurred to him be-fore that his visibility might provide a kind of feedback of influence, projecting his own mood on the people working in the big room, an invisible radiation of him-self, of his own agitated psyche. He was being absurd, he told himself, an amateur metaphysician, definitely out of character for him, usually a pragmatist. Maybe he needed a rest, a vacation. Peripherally he noted that Gunderstein had come into the city room and was sit-ting at his desk staring into space, chewing his toasted English muffin, washing it down with black coffee. Henry Landau tapped on the glass and Nick waved him in.

"Can I ask you a question?" Henry's tanned face seemed calm though the lines were deeper, showing his worry.

"I knew you would, Henry."

"Why is this Henderson thing getting under your skin?"

"Is it that obvious?"

"Is the Pope Catholic?"

"I'm not sure, Henry," he sighed.

"Is there some antagonism you have for him?"

"You're wide of the mark, Henry."

"Well, for crying out loud, Nick, what then?"

He was asking himself whether Henry could be trusted, an obscene suspicion. Nevertheless he held back the confidence.

"I think we're losing our objectivity, Henry," he lied. "And I'm afraid this CIA thing is going to blow up."

"But I understand that it can't be adequately confirmed."

"I'm not as certain this morning as I was yesterday."

"It would be a damned shame, a damned shame," Henry said, shaking his head. "Henderson would make a helluva President." Nick watched him coolly. No, he was definitely not ready to confide in him.

"Are you suggesting that we leave the story alone?" Nick snapped.

"You know better than that, Nick." He got up, pouting.

"Easy, Henry. Don't get your balls in an uproar. Why is everybody so damned sensitive on the subject?"

Henry Landau sat down again. He pulled a pipe out of his side pocket, filled it from a leather tobacco pouch, and lit it with care.

"I'll tell you what I think, Nick. Maybe it's this suicide that's bugging me. Maybe it's a reaction from the Watergate thing. We're becoming too destructive, always chipping away. Too much of a watchdog syndrome. On my vacation I thought about it often. It's really bothering me. As if we go out of our way looking for rocks to hurl. Maybe it's guilt! We're too damned powerful. They can't fight back. Once we get a fix on someone, we dog him till he dies from exhaustion."

"Let he who is without sin cast the first stone, eh, Henry?"

"Yes." Landau's face brightened. "That's it."

"Why is it"—Nick paused, choosing his words—"that we suddenly become chicken-livered and guilty when we are attacking someone we essentially agree with? Why all this selective guilt? When we were after the President, you were all for turning the knife in the wound. How come you weren't being philosophical and guilt-stricken then?"

"He deserved what he got," Landau said. "In the end we proved he was guilty as hell."

"In other words, we went by gut feeling."

"And facts."

"But would we have made the commitment if we didn't hate the man to begin with?"

Nick could tell by the accelerating clouds of smoke being puffed out of his pipe that Henry was becoming agitated.

"The truth is, Henry," Nick continued, "that you would hate like hell to see us bomb the darling Henderson, because Henderson's supposedly like us, or so it is believed."

"You've misunderstood me, Nick," Henry said, becoming defensive.

"You really believe that?"

"Yes, Nick, I do," he said with conviction.

"As long as I'm in this chair the chips will fall where they may."

"I liked the other one better . . . the business about casting the first stone."

"If we did it that way, we'd run nothing but social announcements and garden news."

"I really don't think I'm getting through, Nick." He got up and tapped the half-smoked pipe into Nick's ashtray before he went out.

When he had gone, Nick felt oddly refreshed, as if the conversation had somehow refocused his thoughts, cleared his mind of the uncertainties. The lines of demarcation were becoming more defined now. The perception of it dispelled his fatigue, raised the adrenaline.

He picked up the phone and dialed Margaret. The familiar voice responded strongly.

"Maggie. What pictures do you intend to use on the British Embassy do?"

"I've just been looking them over. We've got a good shot of the Ambassador and a group."

"Is Henderson in any of them?"

"As a matter of fact, he is."

"Kill the ones with Henderson."

"You're kidding, Nick. He's always good copy."

"Just kill it, Maggie, okay?"

"Sure, Nick. I'll kill it. What about the story?"

"I'll work that out."

"You're the boss," she said, sarcastically.

"You just remember that, Maggie."

"How can I forget it?" She slammed the phone down angrily. He made a mental note to call Jennie. Searching the city room, he waited to catch Gunderstein's eye. When he did, he waved Gunderstein toward him. Madison, too, back turned, caught the movement, and strained his neck to watch.

"Okay, kid," Nick said as Gunderstein fell into a chair, like a puppet whose strings were suddenly released. "I want to give you a little back-up on this story." Gunderstein straightened in his chair. "Who the hell of our people was in Nam in late 1963?"

"Robert Phelps," Gunderstein said. "I've talked to him. He feels the same way I do, but here again he could produce no basic confirmation."

Phelps was now their West Coast man.

"Suppose I put him on temporary assignment?"

"That would be helpful. He could find a lot of old Nam hands that he might be able to pump. Yes, that would be helpful."

"What else do you think you need?"

"Someone to chase down leads. Someone I could work with."

"How about Martha Gates?" She had remained somehow on the surface of his consciousness.

"Martha would be fine."

"She's got the bit in her mouth, although she suffered a setback today."

"I know," Gunderstein said. "It happens." Gunderstein, as always, betrayed no emotion, hidden as he was behind the cerebral myopic glazed look, his eyes in their perpetual squint-through contact lenses.

"Have you heard from Allison this morning?" Nick asked.

"I tried calling him. No answer. He must be sleeping it off. I'll try later."

Nick felt a brief pang of worry, mirrored as a barely seen frown on Gunderstein's brow, a minuscule betrayal of some inner uncertainty. Nick turned from Gunderstein, his attention deflected by the arrival of a news aide who laid a pile of copy on his desk. He could feel Gunderstein suddenly standing over him, rocking on his feet, waiting for some sign of dismissal.

"All right, Harold, get going," Nick said without looking up, his eye traveling down the typewritten columns.

"I just wanted to say, Mr. Gold," Gunderstein stammered, his articulation difficult, a sure sign of his inner agitation, incongruous in his impassive face, "I think you're doing the right thing. The story is crying to be told."

Without looking up, he waved Gunderstein away. It annoyed him to be the object of Gunderstein's judgment. Or was it simply a comment? It was one of the observed aberrations of Gunderstein's mind that the only judgments he made were of story values, a kind of perpetually set steel trap that snapped shut only on the flesh and bone of story tissue. Perhaps his own affinity for Gunderstein was based on the same set of values. Where did humanness end and the idea of story begin?

He watched Gunderstein move toward his desk, then rang Madison and filled him in.

"Now you're talking, Nick." Madison could barely restrain his enthusiasm.

"Keep an eye on them, Ben. And be careful with Martha. She's still shaky from the Ryan thing." Madison's bias was almost refreshing, an unabashed conservative in this den of bleeding hearts, Nick thought, chuckling. For the first time that day he felt in command of himself, strength surging back into him, the defined battle lines dispelling his own previous uncertainty. It was good to see the path through the jungle again.

He continued to read through the overseas dispatches, a cacophony of discordant notes from distant places, details of the world in ferment, shifting balances in the superpower chess game, the lives of millions ransomed for power. As he read, he was conscious of his own screening process, the filtering through of the word, as he read with the habit of years, a copy pencil stuck between knobbed fingers ready to stab at an errant phrase. There was always some pedantry in his action, as if it were necessary to mask a changed word in the cloak of the grammarian and the stylist. Besides, he felt he had an unfailing sense for spotting the preachiness of the moralist or the propaganda of the ideologue among the reporters and correspondents. He had his private jokes too, since he knew he had mastered the art of defusing a biased thought by the mere elimination of a word or two, a word surgeon's deft stroke. He worked swiftly, filtering the information through his mind punctuated by occasional jabs with his copy pencil. He felt strength returning, his purpose defined. He was resisting, he told himself joyfully, his eye searching for hidden meaning among the words.

His eyes scanned Gordon Stock's column. Stock was a syndicated black columnist, a former speech writer for Kennedy, who had come to terms with his blackness at the very moment it became fashionable and profitable to flaunt it. Nick had decided to carry the column a few years ago, knowing that the *Chronicle* would be the flagship, the showcase of the Stock syndication. He had, he knew, made the decision on the basis of race, bowing to the not-so-subtle pressure of the times. Perhaps it was, after all, his own feeling of guilt, then a national affliction, or the remembered caveat against the reporting of Harlem murders in New York. Lately he had begun to regret his decision as Stock's columns grew more strident with the growth of the black political voice, and he found himself repeatedly berating Stock for his racial muckraking. The premise of the column was setting up a straw enemy—a traditional ploy—then taking the offensive against the imaginary windmills.

Worse still, Stock had developed a penchant for buck chasing. He was picking up large lecture fees, and it was obvious in his columns that he was on the take for causes that could meet his price.

It was one of the problems of the business that the syndicated columnist, unlike the employee of a newspaper, had the freedom to choose his subject matter and, therefore, the freedom to espouse, to favor, to condemn at will. Many, like Stock, maintained life-styles that matched their bloated self-image. Unfortunately, in the context of today's world Stock's black face gave him a measure of protection, vested him with arrogance. One could not forget that Washington was a black city.

From the moment his eye caught the name "Henderson" in Stock's first paragraph, the message was telescoped. Stock had been recruited for Henderson's counterattack, an obedient soldier, doing his bit for money or favor. There was a massive conspiracy afoot, he was alleging, to discredit Henderson, here cast as the blacks' friend, which was, of course, politically accurate. Henderson had at one time courted black affirmation, was anointed by King and, when it was fashionable, was in the forefront of the civil rights movement. Of late, however, he had been backing off; there was even the somber hint of an anti-busing stance as he tried to move rightward over the thin ice. Nevertheless, the Stock column, Nick saw, was a clever weapon to select at this moment, and few would see through it.

Although he worked in a building next door to the *Chronicle,* Stock was hooked in by extension. Nick looked for his number in the *Chronicle* telephone book, began to dial, hesitated, then hung up. He wanted to be sure that he held no anger, that he was cool inside. He wanted his reactions to be pointed, unemotional, steady. Was the evidence of Stock's column conclusive? Why was he so trusting of his judgment today? He picked up the phone and dialed Stock's extension. The arrogant coolness of a receptionist's voice responded. Without having ever seen her he could picture the woman, good-looking, sexually enticing, and white, a kind of intimidating symbol of black mastery.

"Whom shall I say is calling?" the cool voice asked. He was tempted to say something sarcastic but held back, answering traditionally. Stock's voice came on resonant, carefully modulated in the phone's speaker.

"I think your column's full of shit, Gordon," Nick said.

"It wouldn't be the first time, Nickie baby," Gordon said good-naturedly. Obviously he thought Nick was joking. It seemed a clue to his lack of knowledge of any counterattack, as if he had been merely a pawn himself. After all, Henderson was a *Chronicle* favorite. Who could suspect that such a column would not pass muster?

"And I'm not going to run it." There was a long pause.

"Are you serious?"

"Deadly."

"You can't do that."

"Yes, I can." There was a clause in the contract with the syndicate allowing the paper to reject whole columns at its own option.

"I don't understand."

"It's a Henderson plant, transparently self-serving, a piece of pure puffery. More than that, it's patently dishonest."

"That's a crock."

"It may be. But I'm not going to run it."

"I think you've flipped, Nick." He could hear the snicker of bravado. "It's the Israel thing. I knew it. You're too damned frightened to call me on that one, so you rap me on this." Nick let the shot pass. He could almost smell the Arab oil money through the telephone and he'd heard about the poker games with the Arab ambassadors in which Stock had won huge sums of money.

"I know all about the poker games, Gordon."

"What's that supposed to mean?" Stock spluttered, his temper rising.

"I wouldn't go to the barn on that one."

"You're out to get me," Stock said, "and I know why."

"Why, Gordon?"

"I can tell every time I shave."

"Don't push it, Gordon."

He could feel Gordon's retreat. Losing the Washington *Chronicle* exposure would be a serious blow to Stock's prestige. Nick knew he had him by the short hairs and enjoyed the exercise of his power, the release of his timidity.

"You're making a mistake, Nick."

"I make them every day." He hung up, feeling good. There was a partial truth in what Stock had said, he knew, and yet he could honestly tell himself that it was no challenge to his objectivity. He had never killed a Stock column before and was fully prepared to accept the pressure that he knew would come. He wondered whether Stock, in his first flush of anger, would cry censorship by the *Chronicle* in a future column. He knew that Stock was too smart to challenge him, although he would fight back. The strategy was predictable: a call to Henderson, who would call Myra, and the battle would be joined, wide open now, steel on steel.

"You'd really be proud of me, Charlie," he caught himself whispering, remembering the exact moment when he had said it before.

He had just been appointed Assistant City Editor of the New York *News* and had, almost at once, after McCarthy had broken the news as a barked decree, sat down at the typewriter and dashed off a letter to Charlie. It did not occur to him that there was any illogic in his reaction, feeling that, after all, Charlie had first claim on the outpouring of joy on his good fortune. Hadn't it been Charlie who had planted the seed at the beginning? The Kerryman thing had somehow stuck in Mc-Carthy's brain, a first unerasable impression that had provided a bizarre kinship, however inaccurate. Mysteriously, doors had opened and Nick and McCarthy had found the magic denominator that cuts across the demarcation of age.

When the letter had been posted, Nick called Margaret, now at home with Chums, who had arrived, both unexpected and unwanted, viewed by Margaret as a vicious attack on her person. It had been an intrusion of traumatic proportions more like an accident during a vacation, the sudden drop of a ski lift on the way to the summit, the capsizing of a sailboat on calm waters. She had gotten the results of the rabbit test while they were both in the office. He could see the answer in her drawn paleness as she had walked toward his desk in the city room, a beaten figure on the verge of hysteria. Seeing her coming, he had risen and walked toward her, then led her quickly to the elevator and the late-afternoon coolness of Shanley's.

"I can't understand it," he had whispered, after bringing two Scotches from the bar and urging her to sip one. She tried taking a big gulp, then spat it back into the glass, gagging.

"I'd like to curl up and die," she said, wiping the edges of her moist lips. "I knew this would happen. I knew it."

"We took precautions," Nick said.

She looked at him with unmistakable contempt.

"You can't play around with biology," she said. "We've been taken."

"I hadn't meant it to happen," he said awkwardly, feeling stupid and platitudinous. The predicament seemed a cliché. Why does she not feel joyous? he remembered himself thinking, feeling both love and compassion for her and a yearning for this thing that they had created.

"You talk of it as if it's the end of the world," he said. "I do love you, remember, and being married wouldn't be exactly a tragedy. You see, you can't fight

City Hall." He put a hand over hers and squeezed it. Talk of love seemed to soften her.

"And I love you, Nick. It's just that I'm not prepared for this. It comes as a shock."

"For both of us. You know I'm part of this deal."

"You're a man," she said helplessly. He knew what she meant.

"We could get married and hell, you could work up to six months, maybe more. Then take leave and come right back to work. Women have been doing that for years."

"You just don't understand, do you?" she said. "It's a setback, an illness, a biological curse. The men who hand out promotions, who decide who shall rise and who shall fall, equate having babies with housewifery and motherhood. Actually it's a black mark against me on the record."

"I don't believe it," he lied, searching his mind fruitlessly for examples.

She tried sipping the Scotch again, sucking it in through clenched teeth. Turning, she searched the deserted bar. The big bartender was polishing glasses.

"I want an abortion, Nick."

He watched her flickering eyes, misted now, the look of a trapped animal.

"I think I have something to say about that," he said. From the moment of their suspicion, when her period had not come, it had been alluded to, and he had laughed it off. But it had set off an inner turmoil, as if they were discussing the murder of someone they loved. He wondered if it were the ego inside of him crying out to be validated. Certainly, he knew, it was not a moral position. In the end, he had pushed it from his consciousness, unable to find two sides to debate. Now that he was confronted with the reality, he could only summon indignation, annoyance at her callousness.

"I won't hear of it," he said, envisioning going up sleazy corridors in foul-smelling tenements, having her soft white body abused by an unshaven doctor with trembling fingers. It was not an uncommon image for the times, he remembered later, feeling, long after Chums had been born, that he, too, had been trapped by chronology. Perhaps, after all, Chums in her embryonic state was listening, had heard the discussion of her possible execution.

"It's my body and my life," Margaret had said, her throat tightening, her voice sharply raised. He could see the bartender turn briefly, then look away.

"You sound as if marrying me would be a stretch in purgatory," he said.

Later, he had relived the moment again when abortion emerged as a national issue, feeling the pain of it. He could never approach his pro-abortion position without a nagging sense of guilt. Suppose they had killed Chums?

Margaret had actually searched for an abortionist. He was on the extension during the initial contact, the discussion revolving around the details of money and place. Perhaps it was the voice on the other end, furtive, gruff, cautious, that dissuaded them, or the screen of guilt which clung to them like chewing gum, but the idea was ultimately rejected. Emerging through tears and anxieties, sleepless nights, tender couplings, passionate ecstasies, they finally decided on marriage. It took place in a simple ceremony at City Hall, attended by Margaret's mother and father, awkward and bumbling, holding back their anger. Later he had taken her to visit his mother in Warren, Ohio, and it seemed better in the glow of familiar faces, piecrusts, and the nostalgic odors of his old room, where he had insisted on their sleeping, although his mother was willing to give up her double bed.

Chums, Charmagne, arrived with Charlie as absent godfather. By then his involvement at the *Chronicle* was keeping him busy and his telephone calls and letters were growing scarcer. They moved to Brooklyn after Chums was born to be near Margaret's mother, who they assumed might be a built-in baby-sitter, when Margaret was ready to tackle work again. Unfortunately her mother developed phlebitis, which made it difficult for her to maneuver an infant, and Margaret was forced to postpone the end of her sabbatical. That, and the unaccustomed longish subway trip to Borough Park, once taken with such delight, became a plague, compounded by Margaret's nagging and continuing feeling of regret and entrapment. As if in compensation, Nick took to spending more and more time in Shanley's where McCarthy's boozy Irish eloquence could calm the troubled soul.

"She's my whore," McCarthy would say, pointing to the building across the street. "Her ink was her perfume, and when it wafted past my nose, my goose was cooked. No home, no children, no warm fireside. Only her whoring ways." He'd shake a fist in the whore's direction. "I'll beat her yet, the fickle, devious, black-hearted, faithless adultress." Toward morning, as the bartender made his last pourings, he would begin to rave and thrash his arms about. "Was this the face that launched a thousand ships and burned the topless towers of Ilium? Come, Helen, suck forth my soul with a kiss."

Despite the thickness of his tongue, the lines always came out crystal clear, an invocation of irreversible fate, as if it were the ultimate explanation of McCarthy's hopeless entanglement. While others would politely excuse themselves from McCarthy in his nightly cups, Nick felt drawn toward him, fascinated by the never-ending articulation of his imagined burden, as if the editorship of the country's most circulated newspaper were a disease to be endured, its terminality ordained by supernatural forces.

"If you don't keep her petted, adored, indulged, she'll turn on you like a viper. The bitch is never satisfied, a bottomless pit of satiation. Throw whatever meat you can find in her maw and it leaves her perpetually open for more. Her appetite never ends. She goes on, never sleeping, always greedy, hungry for whatever garbage you can dredge up. And the bitch has got no conscience, no conscience whatsoever. Give her half a chance and she'll swallow you up and regurgitate the bones."

Years later, a mirror image had cascaded out of

Charlie's drunken mouth, the same allusions, linked, it seemed, by a love-hate relationship with the same dissatisfied whore. And now him.

In the silent listening, the receptive ear, McCarthy had apparently sensed some succor for his loneliness and perhaps it was appreciation for this that prompted his promotion. Nick was actually embarrassed by the quick change in his fortunes, since his befriending of McCarthy was not rooted in his own ambition. He was, after all, content to be a reporter, an observer, having achieved a pinnacle that was even then beyond his dreams.

"You're Assistant City Editor, Gold," McCarthy had barked without looking up from a sheaf of copy paper. He had not even known that the post was open, learning only later that the opening of the newspaper's television station was thinning out the deskmen's ranks.

Is he serious? Nick wondered.

"Boy," McCarthy shouted, looking up, seeing that Nick was still standing around.

"Don't just stand there with a finger up your ass, Gold," McCarthy shouted. "Get to work."

"I can't believe it," he had told Margaret on the phone.

"Why not?"

"It's just hard to believe."

He had dreaded the call, knowing how she related his success to her own failed hopes. She had been writing with a by-line before he had been hired.

"You deserve it, Nick. You're a professional." He could feel her voice crack, then the click, as if further conversation would have prompted tears. He had meant to tell her that a raise came with the new job, enough to be able to afford a competent nurse and let Margaret return to work. Forgoing a night at Shanley's, he had traveled home, the joy of the promotion erasing the pain of the last few months, determined to make a fresh start with their marriage. He was barely in the door of the apartment when Margaret announced that she would return to work whatever the practicalities of their financial situation. He ate his dinner in silence, feeling the closeness of the walls. Later, Chums began to cry.

Even in his memory, those first years with Margaret and Chums' babyhood seemed blocked out by remoteness, as if they had happened to other people, the impact of recall as muted as the insipid actuality. Both he and Margaret threw themselves into the rhythm of the *News,* tools of the great maw, losing all sense of outside involvement. On the level of work, the incidents and technique, the kaleidoscope of journalistic events, the gossip, were absorptions that could compete with marriage, which had become poisoned long before the beginning, which Chums victimized by the evidence of herself.

Neither he nor Margaret tortured themselves over what was, in retrospect, only neglect of Chums. She was, after all, only a baby, a cocoon in a narrow world, a toy to be fussed over and played with on Sunday mornings and then only until she grew moist or smelly or cranky. They went to movies and sat in the dark, unspeaking, relieved to lose themselves in the lives of the giants on the screen. Margaret continued to be the assistant movie reviewer and it was apparent that it was a slot reserved, an heir apparency waiting for death of the queen reviewer, a frail tiny lady who had already held the job for nearly twenty years. Who could tell what guilt her wished-for end inspired in Margaret, whose sense of entrapment grew with every third-rate movie reviewed. Not that she didn't try to get out of the well-worn rut, once so promising a stepping stone.

"Please, Nick, get me out of there."

"I'll try." But it was always awkward, since he had no power of trade-off. The city editor took all the prerogatives of his fiefdom and, although there was power in certain decisions of coverage, he was forever the lieutenant, with little clout in getting Margaret promoted to feature writer. It became another bone of contention, an irritation, poisoning their bed still more.

"Nick, I'm going nuts, you've got to try."

"I did."

"Well, try harder, damn it."

"You overestimate what I can do."

"Just try. Please."

"I'll try again." But it was too formidable an obstacle and he could sense stiffening resistance in the features editor, a peppery redhead who ceased trying to be polite.

"Get off my back, Gold. The answer is no."

As if in direct proportion to her lack of advancement, Margaret's sexuality began to expire, implanting a new contentiousness. As it was, her sexual appetite moved in an odd rhythm, running a course from craving to indifference. This was natural enough, except that craving might come in the middle of bitter silent pouting anger, an abrupt energy, disturbing sleep as she prodded his body to the quick intensity of her own need, repetitively urging him on until inevitable exhaustion. Then it was he who was pushing and she who dutifully submitted, a receptacle of orifice and breasts, available but unmoved by all his stirrings.

"I can do better with masturbation," he said to her after an episode of frozen response.

"Please do," she said sleepily, turning over as if his flesh inspired only disgust. Then he would vow to stay away from her, testing his own will and her sexual starvation, the latter proving far more durable than the former.

In his loneliness, he felt the need for Charlie's friendship. But Charlie was remote now, an apparition. There had been a wedding, only relatives, and Charlie had written him a short humorous note. As a wedding gift, he and Margaret had sent them a cut-glass vase with some sweetish poetic sentimentality about a perpetually flowering future. They had taken great care in the choice, which cost them nearly fifty dollars, outrageously high for them.

They had received only a printed acknowledgment, not even a handwritten word scrawled beside the neat engraving. It gave Margaret new opportunities to inflict pain, fresh ammunition.

"A fair-weather friend, your Charlie."

"He's found another life."

"Now that he's up there, why should he have anything to do with the peons, like you?"

"You're being unfair."

"You mean to say you're not a trifle upset?"

"No, I don't mean to say that."

"Not just a trifle bitter?"

"Charlie and I owe each other nothing."

They did get Christmas cards from Charlie, usually oversized pictures of the Parker mansion, bathed in snow, and a neatly written "personal" note in what might have been Myra's handwriting, telling them how much Charlie and she had been thinking about them during the past year.

If Margaret hadn't made the one-sided estrangement an issue, Nick might have accepted things with better humor. He did not need any special symbols of Charlie's friendship and it was with some smugness that he showed her a note he had received from Myra inviting them to their suite in the Waldorf "between five and seven," a few weeks off.

"It's a crumb," Margaret had responded, looking contemptuously at the card.

"You don't have to go," he sneered.

"I won't."

But he had gone in spite of himself, oddly tortured by a loss of pride. Feeling like a poor relation answering the summons of a rich uncle, he arrived at Charlie's tower suite, pushing into a large crowd that spilled out into the corridor. Almost immediately he had wanted to leave, feeling obscure. But he pressed relentlessly into the throng. They were a collection of politicians, actors and actresses, celebrities who, as he later learned, always answered the call of a media mogul. Not that the *Chronicle* had yet arrived at any plateau of power, but apparently it was making inroads, one measure of which was its steadily rising advertising lineage which he followed carefully in the weekly editions of *Editor and*

Publisher. Under Charlie's command, the *Chronicle* was unquestionably on the move.

Nick moved through the crush toward the bar. Ordering a Scotch and soda, he reached through arms and over shoulders to receive the comfort of the chilled glass and perhaps the courage of the drink itself, before he would let his eyes search the room for the face of his old friend. Awkwardly he lit a cigarette, inhaling deeply, forcing himself to find strength. Then he heard the boom of Charlie's voice rising clearly through the din.

"Nick." It seemed a gift. "There you are." Turning, he saw a flushed, filled-out Charlie descending on him, pinstriped and vested, taller, it seemed, than when he had last seen him. He crooked his arm around Nick's neck and squeezed hard.

"How the hell are you, kid?"

"Terrific, Charlie."

"Christ, kid, we never get to see you anymore." His eyes flitted past him as he greeted others with a nod and smile. "Harry, Joe, Scotty. How the hell are you?"

"So how come we never see you anymore, kid?" he repeated to Nick, then deflected again. "Hey, Mark, meet Nick Gold, my old New York roomy." Nick shook limp hands as Charlie introduced him. Myra lifted her head from conversation and waved to him from the other end of the room.

"How the hell are you, kid?" Charlie repeated, lifting a glass of champagne to his lips.

"Terrific, Charlie."

"You old son of a bitch. How come we never see you?"

"We're busy as hell."

"Hey, where's . . ." apparently he was stumbling over the memory of Margaret's name.

"Margaret's fine. The baby's great too."

"Jesus, that's terrific, kid. Did you say hello to Myra?"

"Yes," he said. "I understand the *Chronicle*'s doing pretty well."

"You wouldn't believe it, kid."

"And how's Mr. Parker?"

"Getting on. Doesn't come in too much now." He kept glancing past Nick, calling out names, shaking hands. It was definitely a different Charlie. Or was he, Nick, different, outclassed, perhaps? He wanted to cry, knowing that he could not.

"So how come we don't see much of you anymore?" he heard Charlie say, wondering if the words had been directed at him, watching Charlie moving away into the crowd, a stranger. When finally Charlie's back was turned, he edged his way into the corridor and putting down his glass near the wall, pressed the elevator button.

In the street, he stood for a long time in a deserted store front, feeling for the first time the end of his youth.

Coincidentally with the deterioration of his personal life, the *News* experienced its first major circulation setback. Not considered cataclysmic, it produced just enough shock waves for management to demand remedial steps. The cause of this visible interruption in the rising graph was not a mystery. Television had come. Out of its infancy now, the bouncy baby was growing too fast for comfort, a gawky, squawky pre-adolescent, knocking down all competing media in its path.

Reactions to the new phenomenon spawned overreaction and decisions were made emphasizing areas where the *News* and television were not competitive. One of these was the province of sex. Television news, inhibited by the watchdog FCC, dominated by a basic provincialism and fear of government reprisal, was both cautious and circumspect in its coverage. But the *News,* which had built itself as a maverick, had always set aside columns for titillation, reporting in gossipy terms the couplings of movie stars and the peccadillos of the rich and powerful. Stories about these juicy tidbits of scandal were concentrated on page 3, whose operation fell to Nick, the junior deskman.

Each day, Nick would confer with Al Pinelli, fat and perpetually breathless, who was on permanent assignment to the area of adulterous divorce scandals. It was a role he played with great seriousness, believing that he was actually the legal reporter for the *News*. Pinelli had built a vast network of informants—divorce lawyers, judges, court clerks, private detectives, prostitutes, policemen—most of whom would, for pin money or spite, tattle on those who made the best grist for the page 3 mill.

To Nick it had become a game, the high point of the day, as he gleefully picked over the catalog of dying marriages that Pinelli, with an air of self-importance, would provide. The objective was to find a divorce involving some well-known figure. Heirs and heiresses, particularly if they could be traced to well-known products, were particularly good material.

At first it had seemed to Nick a harmless, almost trivial pursuit. Many times, according to Pinelli, the adultery account was merely trumped-up legal maneuvers, a collusion of both parties. Besides, as long as the human aspect remained locked in ink and pulp, legitimized by public acceptance, the stories seemed fictional, unrelated to real people. It was only when the human wreckage came in over the transom that Nick learned the full extent of editorial power, the power to torture and destroy, as it did one day in the guise of Mrs. Brett Carter.

It had seemed a routine story. A Mrs. Carter was being sued for divorce on the ground of multiple adulteries by her husband, Brett Carter of the pharmaceutical Carters, the company that made a well-known brand of prophylactic. What could have been better grist? Pinelli wrote and Nick edited the stories which had developed into a big city-room joke, replete with scores of imaginary headlines alluding to the Condom King and his "royal screwing." The euphemisms used to describe the product provided pinnacles of challenge for both Nick and Pinelli that sent waves of laughter down the copy chain.

Mrs. Carter, according to the legal briefs obtained by Pinelli, had been diligently traced by private detectives. They had documented a pattern of incipient nymphomania. All of the better East Side hotels were cited as scenes of her trysts, promoting an avalanche of calls from desk clerks, upset that their hotels had been omitted. Nick had let Pinelli write beyond the allotted words. It was, after all, the quintessential phenomenon of its genre.

To Nick, Mrs. Carter had the same reality as a character in fiction. She was real only in his mind. He suspected that the stories were inflicting pain on a real person but he could not visualize its depth except as it related to him. And since he was uninvolved emotionally, he could understand only the comic overtones, not the human considerations. Later, he would actually seek such a state of uninvolvement, deliberately avoiding the human subjects of a story. Humanness destroyed objectivity, he was to learn.

But curiosity was a strong temptation. When Pinelli told him he had set up a meeting, Nick had wondered about his motives.

"What good is the work, if you can't see the results?" Pinelli had explained.

"Like a criminal returning to the scene of the crime," Nick had observed.

Pinelli looked at him curiously. "Wanna come?"

Nick shrugged indifferently. His courage had faltered.

"Afraid?" Pinelli leered.

It had been a challenge. Nick reluctantly accepted.

Mrs. Carter had agreed to meet at Volks, a German restaurant on the corner of Third Avenue and Forty-second Street, under the still existent El. Arriving first, Pinelli chose a booth in the rear which provided a measure of privacy. They ordered beers, and watched the door for Mrs. Carter's arrival. She came deliberately late, it seemed, a slim, hesitant figure, holding herself straight as she moved toward them.

Deep circles rimmed her eyes, and even her careful makeup could not obscure the relentlessness of time and humiliation. She slid in beside them, ordered a martini, lit a cigarette, and delicately picked a crumb of tobacco from her lip. Confronting her at this distance, with the pain of her affliction so apparent, Nick wanted to run, his courage drained. Pinelli, in contrast, seemed impervious, perhaps by his own convoluted logic having attributed to the woman an evil intent, deserving of punishment. Smugly sipping his beer, a fat avenging angel, he had suddenly become detestable. "It's too late to plead for myself," she said, taking a deep puff on her cigarette. It was obvious that the ordered martini was not the first drink of the day.

"There was nothing personal in it, Mrs. Carter," Pinelli said. "We were just doing our job."

The woman looked at him with contempt, her lip trembling. "Your job? Is it your job to destroy my life?"

"We just reported facts."

"Facts?" She held back anger, seeming to search for the reasons she had come. Was she, too, curious?

"It was all carefully documented," Pinelli said. Nick remained silent, watching the woman's eyes lower as she sipped deeply on the martini.

"I kept saying to myself: Why are they doing this? What is the reason for my punishment? I could understand my husband's vindictiveness—he, at least, was entitled to his pound of flesh. But you? Surely you can't be that devoid of compassion."

"It has nothing to do with compassion," Pinelli said.

"No. No, I guess it doesn't," Mrs. Carter corrected after a long pause. "That seems too much to ask." Nick watched her, searching for the clue to her motives, the beer congealing in his stomach. It had been a mistake for him to come.

"You said on the telephone you had something to add to your story," Pinelli said. "We thought perhaps you had something to say in your own defense. Really, Mrs. Carter, we'd be happy to print your side of it." He winked at Nick.

"My side of it?" She finished her martini and looked

around helplessly for the waiter. Pinelli caught his eye and pointed to her empty glass.

"I have no defense," she said. "I have lost my children, my security, my self-respect, my dignity. I don't even know if I have the strength to pick up the pieces of my life. I doubt very much if I can ever recover." Self-pity was rising out of her like steam.

"People forget," Nick said, compelled to offer solace, feeling stupid in her presence.

"Forget?" Her persistent questioning exclamations were grating, as if she were helplessly trying to communicate in a foreign language. The waiter brought another martini. She picked up the glass and sipped deeply.

"Who are you to judge me?" she said, trying to resummon pride.

"We didn't judge you, Mrs. Carter," Pinelli said in mock frustration. "We simply report what interests people."

"Oh," she said bitterly. "Is that what you do?"

"That's our job," Pinelli said, as if he were addressing a child. "We didn't create the situation. We merely told it. Right, Nick?"

But Nick persisted in his silence. He felt the woman's wretchedness. Why have we done this? he asked himself. He wondered why Pinelli could not feel the same guilt.

"Why did you come?" he asked the woman gently.

The woman, perhaps feeling his softness, dissolved into tears. They ran down her cheeks. She made no effort to wipe them away.

"I thought," she began, swallowing to clear her throat. She paused, fighting for composure. "I thought I would like to see those who are punishing me, judging me. What do you know about me that you must hurt me, hold up my life as a public entertainment? I've done nothing to hurt you."

"Well, now you've seen us," Pinelli said with contempt.

"Yes," she replied.

"Disappointed?" Pinelli sneered.

"No," she said, looking into Pinelli's pouchy face. "You're exactly as I pictured you. Monstrous. Crude. Indifferent." Her voice rose.

"You cunt," Pinelli exploded.

The words hit her like a hammer blow. She seemed to collapse within herself. Tears cascaded down her cheeks.

"This is ridiculous," Pinelli said. "When they can't do anything else, they cry."

"You callous bastard," Nick hissed, his voice rising. Pinelli, taken aback, clenched his fat fists.

"You fall for this fucking whore's line?" he said, pointing to her as if she were inanimate. The woman reached for her bag and began to fumble with the clasp. Her fingers shook. Nick wanted to reach out to help her but she quickly stood up, and without turning, ran from the restaurant.

"Don't bleed for that scum," Pinelli said. Nick turned and faced the fat Italian face, a thin film of sweat forming on his forehead. Pinelli looked back at him with contempt and spite.

"You're too goddamned lily-livered for this business, Nick."

It was all so antiseptic to view Mrs. Carter's fate from the vantage of the city desk, surrounded by familiar faces, bathed in the sounds of typewriters and telephones. Surely there could be no real Mrs. Carter, tissues and cells that breathed, that suffered ecstasy and despair. She was only words. Until now!

"You shouldn't have come," Pinelli said. "They'll try almost anything to gain your pity."

"And it doesn't bother you at all?"

"Me? Why should it bother me? It's a story."

He remembered feeling the backwash of his own disgust, wondering what he would be like years from now, frightened that he might become like Pinelli. I'll quit before that happens, he told himself.

The years that followed seemed beyond recall, a time of stagnation. What he could recall of it was only the shape of his paralysis, the curve of the well-worn rut as he performed his life by rote.

He did not dwell much on Charlie in that time, a fading memory of his diminishing youth. Life with Margaret and Chums seemed without movement, repetitive. Perhaps a time bomb had been ticking, for suddenly Charlie exploded again into his life.

It came as a telephone ring in the middle of the night in midsummer. "Nick?" his voice said urgently.

"Charlie?"

"Yeah, kid."

"My God."

"It's a hell of a thing to lay on you, kid. But can you meet me at the airport? I'm taking the first plane out. Should be there around eight-fifteen." There was a long pause. Nick could hear Charlie's heavy breathing at the other end.

"What's happening?"

"It's my mother. She's dead. My father just called."

"Sorry, Charlie." He could feel the effort to reply, then a kind of muffled gasp. "Eight-fifteen."

"Okay, kid." He heard the phone click at the other end.

"Jumping through the old hoop." It was Margaret, still turned toward the wall. He steeled himself for the acid comment, perhaps a mirror of his own thoughts. "You haven't seen the son of a bitch for nearly five years, then he calls in the middle of the night and old dumb Nick jumps to attention."

"He sounded pretty bad. I couldn't turn him down."

"Is he drunk?"

"No," he shot back, resentful. "It's his mother. She died."

"The loony from Hempstead?"

He ignored the retort, feeling her alertness, not wishing to precipitate an argument. Ignoring her, he got out of bed and began to dress.

"Call the office for me," he said, when he had finished a hasty shave.

"You're a damned fool, Nick," she hissed. "A god-damned patsy."

"He's my friend."

"Some friend."

He was, in fact, joyful. Charlie had invoked the bond of friendship, had never lost his faith in its strength.

He circled the LaGuardia entrance a dozen times in his aging second-hand Chevrolet before Charlie appeared. Watching him approach, Nick noted changes in his friend's appearance. He had gotten stouter and his hair had begun to grow grey.

"Thanks, Nick," Charlie said, flashing the remembered smile as he slid in beside him. Nick maneuvered the car into Grand Central Parkway. For a long time Charlie remained silent. Then the loosening process began with trivia. How's this? How's that? How are things going? How about McCarthy?

"And you, Charlie?" Nick asked, cautious in the timing.

"On the plane coming up I thought about how I might answer that question, kid. Since I got the call, I've been doing a lot of thinking. You know I haven't been to see them since our last visit. Oh, I call occasionally, and listen to the old man. It absolutely tears me up. The damned waste. I just couldn't face it alone, kid."

"So here is good old Nick."

He caught the sarcasm and grabbed Nick's arm.

"You're damned right, kid," he said. Then, after a pause, "I suppose you think I'm a bastard."

"I figured you'd call me when you needed me."

"You're fucking A." It was an anachronism, from the war.

"Fucking A," Nick repeated. He was conscious of unintended sarcasm.

"You know how it is, kid," Charlie said. "I have no life now beyond the *Chronicle*."

"I understand it's going great guns."

"Beyond anyone's wildest dreams. We're about to

buy out our principal morning competition. Imagine, we'll be the only morning paper in the capital."

"Sounds like you're on top of the world."

There was a long silence as they watched the landscape recede. There were more houses visible now along the highway. In some spots they could see endless lines of exactly replicated homes.

"It's draining me, Nick," Charlie said suddenly. "It's crushing me to death." There was a long pause. "You can't imagine the responsibility. You can't know what it's like. It's the kind of thing that eats you alive."

Nick remained silent. There seemed no adequate response.

"All those words," Charlie sighed. "I should be there now."

"It'll be there when you get back," Nick said.

"What will?"

"The *Chronicle,*" Nick said.

"I am the *Chronicle,*" Charlie responded. Nick shrugged, not comprehending.

They turned off at a sign marked Hempstead. The edges of the town had expanded. New stores had sprung up. The streets were crowded now. Traffic choked the town's center.

"Progress," Charlie sighed.

They pulled into Charlie's parents' street. The white house seemed small and faded now. The front lawn had been carefully trimmed but the paint on the front of the house was chipped and fading. Walking toward the house, they could see the irreversible signs of wood decay and the warp of the door, gone awry on its jamb.

The bent, yellowed man who opened the door was gnarled like a petrified tree. Despite the years of absence, nothing seemed to have changed in the placid way father and son greeted each other.

"The Princess is gone," the older man said, tears welling in the deep sockets of his eyes. They followed him through the hallway to the living room, now musty, the furniture worn and shabby. The old man stood for a moment blinking as he looked at his wife's chair.

"It's all over now, Pop," Charlie said quietly.

"We'll have a nice cup of tea," his father said, "then we'll visit her at the funeral parlor. I wouldn't like to leave her alone too long."

They drank tea in silence from cups Mr. Pell had assembled on the low table in front of the worn couch.

"Did she suffer, Dad?" Charlie asked, his voice suddenly hoarse.

"The Princess never suffered," Mr. Pell said. "Not for one minute." He looked at his son, squinting in the yellow light of a single lit lamp. The shades were drawn.

"What are you going to do now, Dad?" Charlie asked. Nick watched him trying to hold back tears.

"I haven't thought about it," Mr. Pell said quietly.

"I'm glad it's over," Charlie said.

"Glad?"

"At this point, it's hard to tell who was crazier. You or her." He seemed deliberately cruel. Mr. Pell ignored the reference. It had long been a source of irritation and estrangement. They drank their tea silently. When Mr. Pell had cleared the cups, they went out again. The air had heated up, although the house, the windows shaded from the rising sun, had been cool.

Mrs. Pell was laid out in a small room of the funeral parlor in an elaborate coffin lined with red velvet. She was painted in the manner in which they had last seen her, a hideous white mask over a shrunken face. It was a caricature of humanness, the face of a doll with a fixed horrible expression of concealed misery. Charlie turned his face away in disgust.

"Doesn't she look beautiful?" Mr. Pell asked.

"Why don't you close the lid?" Charlie asked. He made no motion to reach for the coffin's lid.

"She loved you," Mr. Pell said.

"It's all over, Dad," Charlie whispered, almost as if he were afraid the dead woman would hear. "You don't have to pretend."

Mr. Pell looked up from his contemplation of the face of the madwoman and shook his head.

"I never pretended."

"Christ, I can't stand this," Charlie exploded.

"Easy," Nick said, gripping his arm. Charlie turned from the coffin and walked out into the corridor.

"I can't stand it," he said, pacing the thick-carpeted floor. A man in a pinstripe suit poked his head out of the office.

"Dr. Hansen is waiting for you. First office off the right." He pointed showing the way.

"Dr. Hansen?" Charlie seemed puzzled.

"Yes," the main said. "He asked me to inform him when you arrived."

Charlie glanced at Nick, mystified, then followed the man's directions, finding what was presumably Dr. Hansen in the little office. Nick had followed him. The doctor was red-haired, sweating, pools of perspiration staining the armpits of his seersucker suit.

"I would like to see you alone, Mr. Pell," he said.

"This is Nick Gold. My closest friend."

"Please, Mr. Pell. Alone."

"I'll wait outside," Nick said, stepping out of the room and closing the door discreetly behind him. He walked outside and lit a cigarette. It felt good to hear Charlie refer to him as his closest friend. When he finished his cigarette, he punched the butt out in the box of sand near the door. The doctor, still sweating, rushed past him and walked quickly down the street.

In the corridor, Charlie, his face chalky, leaned against the wall. Nick noted that his hands were shaking.

"What the hell happened?" Nick asked. He wondered if Charlie were about to faint. It took him a while to get himself under control.

"He killed her, Nick, the old man killed her," he said hoarsely.

"You're not serious?"

"There's good evidence. The doctor took a blood sample and analyzed it himself. Definitely an overdose and knowing the condition of my mother, he knew that she would not administer it herself. He saw the empty pill bottle."

"My God."

"He didn't confront the old man. He was waiting for me. I told him I appreciated that. The son of a bitch."

"I don't understand."

"I gave him a check for five thousand dollars."

It was a burden not easily shared, Nick thought, confused by the knowledge, since it also made him a conspirator in a crime. This is the ultimate test of friendship, he thought, feeling a sense of his own selfishness. Charlie had given him another piece of his private hell. And Nick accepted it proudly.

"Will that be the end of it?" Nick asked as if to verbally validate his participation.

"For the doctor, perhaps," Charlie whispered. "For me, never."

The funeral had been arranged for the next morning, making it necessary for Charlie to stay over, a step to be feared since it meant bedding down in his old room in that tainted house.

"You don't have to stay," Charlie protested. "It's not your problem."

"Of course I'll stay." What is friendship for? he wanted to add, but checked himself.

Nick called the office. Margaret's voice on the other end was cold.

"Who gives a shit?" she said.

"He needs me," he said lamely.

"Who gives a shit?" she repeated, slamming the phone. It had not disturbed him, an expected response. With almost a whole day and night to get through while waiting for the burial, Charlie and he walked through the town in the hot sun. Charlie talked about his life.

His mother had apparently cracked early, since his life as a child and later as a teen-ager was tied to the subterfuge of keeping her condition hidden from neighbors and friends. Early on, his father had made him a reluctant partner in his martyrdom.

"You can't believe what living with that was." He shook his head. "It's left me injured, Nick, and scared to death that her condition was congenital."

"That's ridiculous," Nick argued.

"I've studied it. It runs in families."

"I doubt that," Nick protested.

"I have less doubt as time goes on. The inclination does run in families, although experts can't agree on whether it's prompted by the fear of the propensity or the propensity itself."

"If you think you're going to be sick, you'll get sick," Nick scolded.

"Exactly. Myra buys it. She won't have kids. Had her tubes tied. I can't really blame her, although it galls the shit out of me." He shrugged. "Who the hell wants kids, anyway?" He spat on the curb. "That would give the old man a laugh."

"Doesn't he know?" Nick asked.

"No."

Later they had eaten silently in a restaurant. Charlie's father looked haggard, lost. When he had gone to bed, Charlie and Nick sat together on the back stoop watching the fireflies. The noise of the crickets was soothing, stirring memories for Nick of quiet times in the yard of his father's house. His own childhood was a happy time. Having emptied himself of a measure of his pain, Charlie began to dwell on his life in Washington.

"Washington is like the head of a pin. Everyone crowding to get on it. People slide on and off. The place stinks with ambition and intrigue. When I first went down there, I thought: Gee, I'll stand back and observe this crazy play and tell people about it. Actually it's not that simple. You wind up being a player, the playwright and the audience all at the same time. I hadn't realized it until I took over the *Chronicle*. At first I thought I was watching and listening to them. Then I discovered that they're all watching and listening to us, the media. We're where it's happening. It's frightening. I keep thinking that someday I'll wake up and find the *Chronicle* the only newspaper left in Washington, the fucking capital of the U.S.A. The handwriting is on the wall, Nick. We've just bought out our only morning competition and the unions will eventually squeeze out the afternoon papers. And then"—he paused and lit a cigarette—"and then they'll all be listening to me, watching me."

"I'd say that makes you a pretty important fellow," Nick joshed.

"I'm not without ambition, kid. But I never aspired to be God."

"It's everybody's fantasy," Nick said. "Think of all those people kissing your ass."

"I'll admit that at first I used to revel in the obeisance. Everybody throwing their guts at you, pawing you for favors."

Nick saw flashes of his friend's face in the brief light of the fireflies.

"But when it finally occurs to you that you really have a kind of superhuman hold over these people, the ass-kissing becomes offensive, ugly. You begin to develop a kind of moral armor. Everything you do gets measured against this standard that you've set for yourself. The power of it becomes a hot potato. If you don't hold it in just the right way for just the right amount of time, it begins to burn your fingers."

"You have to learn to handle it, I guess," Nick said, feeling compelled to say something. "Otherwise you'll bleed to death."

"You've got no one to learn from, Nick. You're playing God, remember? You make the rules. Who lives? Who dies? Who gets theirs today? Who gets smiled upon? Who gets pissed upon? Who are the good guys and who are the bad guys?"

"Do you always know?"

"You never know. You can only guess, trust your instincts, your judgments. Whip your people to gather facts. Then you begin to question your motives. Am I being fair? Am I being honest? Am I doing good? At that point you're feeling like a goddamned hypocrite because you know that inside, deep inside, you're asking yourself: Is this a story? How will it play? Will people read it? Will it get attention?"

"At least it keeps you from being too self-righteous."

"It also keeps you on your toes. I swear, Nick, I never sleep. I'm always guarding the damned gate. I'm scared to death to let a single wayward word creep in without my knowledge. Right now I'm going out of my skull wondering what's happening."

"You make it sound as if the *Chronicle* were printing the Gospel, that every word were coming directly from Mount Sinai."

"I used to be skeptical too, Nick. What the hell? We were just one paper in one city. But America is the center of the world and Washington is the center of America and in this dead center the words of the *Chronicle* are, in a way, a kind of Gospel. And who sits in the eye of the storm, right in the deadest of the dead center, deciding the information that goes into the minds of the people who move America, which is the center of the world?"

The sound of crickets grew louder, the air heavier, the fireflies more intense. The question hung in the air.

Nick searched the darkness for the outlines of Charlie's face, envisioning its anguish.

"You actually begin to think of yourself as the keeper of the Holy Grail, an avenging angel with the power to decide who shall live and who shall die." Charlie's voice cracked briefly, then recovered. "It's a monster and no single man can control it, Nick. I'm frightened to death at what it could become. And I'm not sure if I can hack it myself."

Charlie's words came rushing through the heavy air like gas escaping from a fallen balloon. Was it self-pity? Nick wondered.

"Why me?" Charlie said. He seemed angry now. "That bitch." He appeared to be having a dialogue with himself. "It was pure random selection."

"You've lost me," Nick said.

"Myra. She's made me the sacrificial lamb." His voice rose.

"I'll never let her get her teeth in it, never." It was suddenly beyond Nick's comprehension, this sudden attack on Myra. It was the measure of his friendship that he accepted this view without question. Later it had become somewhat of an affliction, seeing Myra through Charlie's eyes.

Charlie remained silent for a long time, then Nick felt a grip on his arm, tight and urgent.

"There's got to be someone I can trust, kid. I need you with me, Nick."

"I'm here, pal." Nick laid his hand over his friend's. "Old Nick is here." What was there left to say?

In the morning, Charlie's mother was buried in a grassy knoll of a small cemetery at the edge of town. Mr. Pell, a yellowing apparition in the bright morning light, stood beside the open grave, his head bowed. Dry-eyed, Charlie watched the coffin descend into the ground, the quiet of the morning shattered by the hollow sound of the first clumps of earth hitting its lid.

13

A disaster intruded in mid-morning, refocusing the routine of the entire paper. A crazed gunman had sprayed bullets indiscriminately in a crowded bus, killing or maiming nearly twenty people, all black.

Despite the horror of the event, Nick welcomed the intrusion. The Henderson matter was becoming corrosive to his concentration.

Ben Madison, as animated as a fledgling reporter, had sprinted into the glass office, the bulletin clutched in his large fist.

"It's a donnybrook," he cried, the term itself a casualty of chronology. Nick looked at the bulletin, envisioning at once the layout of the front page.

"Get photographers down there pronto," Nick said, rising from his chair, the new excitement a mounting release.

"I've got the bases covered, Nick."

Nick nodded. There was no need to be redundant. Madison was a professional; covering the bases meant reporters at the scene, the death list, the eyewitness ac-

counts, the visits to relatives, the inevitable story of
fate intervening, lives saved or lost by a whim of fortune. There was little to tax the ethical sense, no moral
mountains to traverse. Just the facts embellished with
irony, fleshed out by details, a buffet of horror to
fascinate the greediest palate. It was the kind of disaster
story that newspapermen cut their eyeteeth on. He had
covered stories like it at the *News:* subway wrecks,
fires, explosions, airplanes colliding with skyscrapers.
It was the measure of a newspaperman's maturity, this
recording of life's major horrors, brutal memories to be
relived over drinks in the coolness of a paneled tap-
room on a lazy summer afternoon.

Ben Madison had come in again, flushed from the release of his inner spring, which had catapulted him to
rare physical action. He showed Nick the yellow UPI
bulletin.

"It's like a war," Nick said. Madison rubbed his large
hands in mock glee.

"Now we can stop bullshitting around," Madison said.
Nick, feeling his elation, slapped him on the back.

"Now you can do some newspapering for a change,"
Nick said sarcastically.

Activity in the city room accelerated. People moved
quickly like characters in a stepped-up movie film.
Sounds of voices and typewriters rose in decibels. The
budget meeting would be greatly curtailed, the available
space gobbled up by the tragedy.

He saw Myra hurrying toward him, her face tight.
She advanced stiff-legged, the perpetual sweater neatly
arranged like a cape on her shoulders.

"My God, it's horrible," she said, sitting primly in a
chair. It was a revelation of her lack of journalistic
poise. She was merely a spectator now, hopelessly inex-
perienced.

"We've put a lot of staff to work. May cost us some
overtime."

"I'm sure you'll do what's best."

He watched her light a cigarette, using his Lucite
lighter.

"You really don't get the feel of a newspaper except from here," she said, looking out into the busy, crowded room.

"Yes," he said, riffling papers on his desk, hoping she would feel her redundancy.

She remained silent for a while, puffing deeply, blowing smoke through her nostrils. "Have you thought over what we talked about this morning?" she said quietly. He knew she was searching for relevancy.

"This morning seems an age," he said. "As you can see, we've suddenly got other fish to fry."

"I know, Nick," she said. Her presence in the room was an annoyance. Busying himself with a pencil, he made notes on a piece of copy paper.

"Stock called me," she said suddenly.

"That son of a bitch." He refused to look up from his papers.

"Are you really planning to kill his column?"

"Yes."

"Do you think that's wise?"

"What do you mean, wise?"

"Well, you know, he's black."

"That's his problem."

"He could be irritating."

"Not to me."

She puffed again. Feeling her eyes watching him, he looked up. Surely she could sense his annoyance.

"I'm sorry, Myra. These stories have made the day somewhat less than routine."

"I know, Nick. I'm sorry." She punched out her cigarette, then, almost as if it were an afterthought, she said, "Come up later. We'll have a drink and talk it over."

"I'll try, Myra."

"Do try, Nick," she said emphatically. There was no mistaking her message. It was an order. She turned and walked out of his office, through the bustling city room, a stranger. Hardly anyone took notice.

The budget meeting had an air of excitement as the editors quickly reeled off the plans for their space allocation. He listened, fighting for concentration. Myra had unnerved him again.

"Let me see the British party story," he asked Margaret pointedly.

"Yes, Jennie will bring it up." He felt the edge of her sarcasm.

"Good."

"Have they identified the race of the bus killer?" he asked Madison.

"White," Madison replied.

"Oh my God," someone said.

"Do you think there will be riots?"

"We've got three men covering Police Headquarters," Madison said. "It's still too early to tell."

The meeting passed quickly. There were too many variables to make fixed decisions possible. When he returned to his office, Miss Baumgartner followed him in, her face pinched.

"The Mayor called. He seemed anxious."

"Get him for me."

Thoughts of Henderson were crowded out by new anxieties. The possibility of riot was a real fear in this city, balanced tremulously on the brink of ghetto frustration. The intercom buzzed. He nodded to Miss Baumgartner and punched the blinking hold button.

"It's a bitch, Nick," the Mayor said. Nick could picture his black face and the fringe of white hair that gave him a sagelike dignity.

"How does it look?"

"It's quiet now. But I'm worried about the way the TV boys may play it. I've already alerted the police who are watching for any signs of agitation. Treat it gently, Nick. You know this city; the slightest inflammation . . ." His voice trailed off.

"We'll watch it, Howard," Nick said.

"Do you know anything about the killer yet?" the Mayor probed.

"Not a thing. The reporters are out. What's your information?"

"White. About thirty-eight. Dressed in work clothes.

Carried a shotgun, which he calmly reloaded time after time, spraying the shot into the passengers. It was horrible, Nick. Horrible."

"Let's stay in touch, Howard," Nick said, feeling the rising hysteria in the Mayor's voice. He knew what the man was pleading. Go easy! Pull the punch! Was the motivation of the killer racially based? Would the emotion of learning feed the emotion of hatred in the reporter, inflame his words? Would the anger of the photographer embellish the horror? He must keep himself steady, alert to all nuances, cool, analytical, objective. In his mind, he sorted images of the front page, rejecting each in turn, waiting for the results to be in. He pushed the buttons of Madison's extension, seeing him turn almost at the moment of the ring, watching him through the glass.

"Let me see everything that comes in. Tell Nichols to show me all the pictures on both stories."

Within himself, he could feel the elation of command again, the challenge of his carefully honed skills, the meaning of his editorship. This was the part he loved best, he knew, quintessential newspapering. He felt released, relaxed. Looking up, seeing Jennie, he felt a smile form, hardly remembering what she might have come about.

"You wanted to see my copy," she said, anger bubbling, her lips pressed tightly together. He could tell by the way she held herself, taut, stiff, that she might have lashed out in temper if they were alone.

"What the hell is eating you?"

"She said you wanted to see my copy. Did you have to make a point of it like that? We could have handled it as always. She seemed to enjoy making a special point of telling me that she hadn't the authority to edit the British party copy."

"That's what I told her, Jennie. I made a special point."

"It was a shitty thing to do."

"Don't tell me how to run my business," he said, edginess returning.

"You know what you can do with your copy?" Jennie began, her reserves starting to go. He lifted both hands, palms outward, and stood up, annoyed that the others could see this angry gesture. He could see her eyes move toward the glass into the city room, the sight quieting her, stifling the hysteria that seemed on the verge of bursting through.

"Just hold on, Jennie. I'll explain it later." He knew she was not placated and would certainly be difficult, pouting, aloof. "I'll explain later," he said again. "At the moment we've got two big stories running and I have no time for this shit."

She flung the copy on the desk and turned, her shoulders pulled back, a contrived symbol of her hurt pride, as she walked swiftly out the door and through the city room. He looked dumbly at the sheets of copy that had floated carelessly over his Lucite desk, hiding the snapshots of his past, him and Charlie, him and Chums, him and his mother, his father, faces of his history. It seemed suddenly comforting to be reminded that he had not simply dropped into this glass cage, an egg hatched in limbo.

He pushed Jennie's copy aside, too busy to cope with such trivia. Perhaps later, he thought, automatically judging the available time until deadline. He buzzed Madison again.

"Anything new on the killer?"

"Pratt just called in. He lived in Prince Georges County. Had three kids, wife, worked for GSA. Apparently one of his kids was recently knifed in school."

"Motive?"

"I'd say it would be a good bet."

He knew Madison's prejudices, the conservative mind. Would objective judgment hold? It never did. He'd have to be watchful.

"Who's writing?"

"Downes."

He thought a moment, recalling Downes. He knew the styles, the subtleties and nuances, the points of view, the coloration of the lenses, the extent of vision, the tools of vocabulary and speed of each writer. Downes was a good choice, a master of the clipped sentence, the short paragraph, the absence of ideology. A classical journalist, hewing to the textbook line.

"Any casualty lists?"

"Not yet. They're waiting for next-of-kin notification."

Henry Landau came in, his tan fading swiftly.

"It's like covering a war zone," he said, shaking his head. Nick liked Henry, felt his softness.

"I hope you're not upset with me, Henry."

"I'm used to you, Nick. You take too much on yourself."

"Inertia, Henry."

"You can trust me, Nick. Let me inside that complicated head."

"Sure, Henry."

Landau had been carrying a ticker clip, which he put in front of Nick, holding it up as if it were a sign. Nick read it quickly. It was the Harris poll, another syndicated feature that the *Chronicle* had bought. Reporting a trial heat among Democrats, it indicated that Henderson was leading the pack. Henderson again!

"So?" Nick said.

"You're the Henderson maven, Nick. Do we run it or don't we?"

"You've heard about Stock?"

"Who hasn't?"

"Of course we'll run it," Nick said calmly. "Did you have any doubts?"

"No, Nick. Frankly, I'm fishing for answers. I just don't understand your sudden passion for downplaying Henderson. I need some answers for myself, for my own . . ."

"Self-esteem." Nick chuckled.

"You might put it that way."

"You'll get them," Nick said, knowing that it would hardly be that simple, truth seen through distorted mirrors. How can you articulate gut feelings, little private clues? He determined to keep his own counsel.

Henry Landau stood over him for a few more moments, shrugged, then stepped out of the office.

Actually, he knew he had been gratuitous. There was no way that he could not carry the Harris poll. The *Times* would have it. It would be splashed over every television screen in the country.

It was far beyond the province of his own control. Not like Stock at all. He remembered Jennie's copy, took a pencil in hand, and began to read. Today he had little patience with her awkward phrases, her heavy quips. Henderson was embedded in the story, woven through it like a glistening thread, "the rugged Redford looks in brunette," and "the incredibly blue eyes, still piercing, as others reddened." He sliced with ruthlessness, enjoying the surgery, telling himself that he was restoring objectivity. When he had finished he motioned through the window for a news aide, who would return the copy to the Lifestyle department. Now Margaret would know for sure. Why this sudden delight in Jennie's humiliation? he thought.

The phone buzzed. He picked it up. It was Madison.

"There's been a fire-bombing," he said. "The police moved in fast."

"Does it look like the beginning?"

"The police think it's merely a test. I think they're right."

When he hung up, Miss Baumgartner came in, harlequined, wearing a puzzled look.

"A Mrs. Henderson called. Said she was Senator Henderson's wife. I told her you were in a meeting." It was part of their silent understanding to take no calls without giving him preparation. He told himself that he had expected it. The counterattack. By now Henderson had established command posts, was sifting intelligence, calling in reserves, going over options. He knew the game, although the new tactic, coming in the midst of this new excitement, had taken him off guard. Perhaps they had done it deliberately. He wondered again who Henderson's spies were in the *Chronicle*. Other than Myra.

Political wives, he thought contemptuously, searching for some excuse not to call her back. Her face was familiar to him from pictures and he had met her once or twice a few years back, when he was traveling the Washington cocktail circuit, before he had deliberately hermitized himself. He dreaded making the call, as if the conversation would somehow personalize his judgment. Thankfully Nichols intervened. He laid a group of pictures on Nick's desk. Incredibly graphic, they depicted unrelenting brutality and gore.

"Beauties," Nichols said. Nick studied them. The photographer had concentrated on mutilation.

"They're pretty raw," Nick said.

"They're good, Nick. The boys got turned on to it."

"The poor bastards." He weighed the emphasis he would give them, remembering the Mayor's words. He set aside those where the faces were clearly visible, showing expressions of pain, horror, impending death.

"That would have been my choice, too, Nick."

"I'm rejecting them."

"You're kidding."

"Too inflammatory," he said, bracing himself for an argument.

"These are one in a million, Nick. Better than a thousand words, as the saying goes."

"That depends on the message we're trying to convey."

"I thought we were just reporting the facts. These pictures tell the facts." He paused. "Accurately!"

Nick knew Nichols was sneering at the wordsmiths, part of the natural competition.

He put an arm around Nichols' shoulder. "The buck stops here, kid," Nick said, an echo of Charlie. God, he missed Charlie.

"I think you're wrong, Nick."

He moved the pictures about on his desk, picking a group in which the faces were hidden, although the puddles of blood were quite visible.

"You've killed the best of the lot, Nick."

"I want them laid out on five columns on the front

page." He handed Nichols the chosen pictures. Nichols gathered up the rejects and tucked them solemnly under his arm, walking out of the office, crestfallen.

As the deadline for the street edition neared, the copy rolled over his desk like an avalanche. Reading every word, black pencil in hand, he cut and refashioned, correcting even the most inconsequential typo. Was it a measure of his word greed, he wondered? He would brook no philosophical intrusion from himself, the years of training assuring his discipline.

Madison's gruff voice and his heavy form standing over him destroyed his concentration.

"I've sent her back to the well twice," Madison said, dropping a sheaf of copy paper on Nick's desk. "She's getting pissed off at me." He looked at the name of the writer, the slug on the upper left-hand corner, Atkins. He visualized a black face, chocolate-toned, fierce Afro cut, belligerent expression, dark soft eyes.

"Carried away, eh, Ben?" he asked, his eyes beginning to read the copy. The girl's emotion spilled out, an avalanche of white-hatred. "Jesus," Nick whistled. "She's really pushed it. 'He had found his own personal solution to relieving the white man's burden.' My God. 'His lily-white fingers pressed the instrument of death.' We can't print this."

"I know, Nick. I think you better handle it. She thinks I'm nothing more than a prejudiced honky bastard."

When she came in, he could feel her outrage. A tall woman, with delicate long fingers, the knuckles wrinkled in the special way of black hands, she refused his offer to sit down, as if her full stature was needed to fend off intimidation. Nick consciously sought to choose his words carefully. But time was pressing.

"This story is inflammatory, Virginia."

"I can't write it any other way."

"You're a professional, Virginia. You've taken the racial thing and spread it over the story like butter. The man was unbalanced."

"His motives were quite clear."

"You're being superficial, making assumptions based on your own fixed attitudes."

"I can't forget that I'm black."

"You asked us to forget it when we hired you. We don't use racial references, nor do we identify reporters by race."

"I was hired because you were forced to do so." Even beyond her anger, he felt that she knew she had overstepped. She blinked away a mist from her eyes.

"I'll let that pass, Virginia," he said gently, knowing that she was partially correct.

She stood, awkwardly erect, facing him. Was she taunting him?

"You're a professional, Virginia," he repeated. "We haven't got time to fool around. Either you take out the inflammatory racial references or I kill the piece. If you make the white race responsible, you'll have to accept the blame for any consequences. Am I making myself clear?"

"Perfectly." She was not going to compromise.

"You're putting pride and emotionalism before your sense of duty, your professionalism. Don't you see that?"

She stared at him, the hatred burning beyond reason.

"I wish you would see me as a person, not a delegate," Nick said. He picked up her copy and tore it in two, flinging it in the wastebasket.

"Sorry, kid," he said, watching her turn to hide her tears. She rushed from the room, past his window, sweeping through the city room. Angrily he pushed the buttons on Madison's extension.

"I saw," Madison said.

"Put someone else on that piece, Ben. We'll use it in the next edition."

When the front-page proof came in, he looked it over carefully, satisfied that it was a reasonable facsimile of what he had suggested to his editors. His eye roved over the headlines, the pictures, the captions. The report of the disaster seemed balanced, honest but restrained. He was rather proud of himself. Not that they had achieved perfection. There was never enough time for that. But pride quickly dissipated when he saw the lower-right story on the results of the Harris poll. Had Henry Landau sneaked it in on the front page, a deliberate confrontation? His fingers started for the phone, then stopped, caressing its coldness instead.

He let himself calm down. After all, he had approved the insertion. But the front page? Perhaps Henry had seen it as an act of protection, a sop to the Henderson troops who, by now, were spreading into the tissue of the *Chronicle,* probing for soft spots. Moving his hand from the telephone, he completed the front-page proofing, then he called for a news aide. As the young man left the room, he stopped him.

"Bring me another copy," he said. The young man looked awkwardly at the sheet in his hand, then hurried off, coming back quickly with another copy of the front page which Nick shoved into the inside pocket of his jacket, hanging on its hook on the clothes tree.

"Shall I get Mrs. Henderson?" Miss Baumgartner asked, seeing him stir toward his coat.

"No," he answered sharply, then softening, "not yet."

Watching the still frenetic activity in the city room, Nick saw Gunderstein come into the room, walking quickly, his jacket thrown over his shoulder, held there by a single finger in the hanger loop. He walked to his desk, looked over a sheaf of messages, then, perhaps feeling Nick's eyes on him, looked up. Nick waved him in. As he waited a news aide came in with additional copy on the bus murders. He looked them over. No recognizable names. Random victims, he sighed, feeling the horror of the act. Five of the victims were children, their single-digit ages glaring beside the neatly typed names. His fists tightened in anger. Please, no emotion, he begged himself, remembering Virginia Atkins. It was then that he felt the vibrations of the big presses seeping through the floors and walls. He put his hands flat on his Lucite desk, feeling the coolness and the vibrations through his fingers. The feel of it gave him comfort.

"Well?" he said, as Gunderstein came closer, searching his face.

"Phelps is flying in. He'll be at my apartment tonight."

"What was his reaction?"

"Odd," Gunderstein said. "He said he had waited thirteen years for my call."

"What the hell does that mean?"

"That's what I asked him. He said he'd talk about it when he got here."

"And Martha?"

"She says she's also onto something. She said she'll call if she can pin it down."

Gunderstein stood over him awkwardly, picking at his face.

"Henderson's wife called," Nick said.

"She's a mess. Insecure. Maybe even unstable."

"Do you think she wants to blow the whistle on her husband?"

"I doubt it."

"What could she tell me?" Nick asked. "Defend her husband. Make an emotional appeal. Try to work herself back in her husband's good graces."

"She's been avoiding me," Gunderstein shrugged. His concentration seemed elsewhere. "I've been down more blind alleys on this story than anything I've ever tackled. That's why I know I'm right. It's something you can feel."

"We've had quite enough feeling around here for one day," Nick said, remembering Virginia Atkins. Gunderstein looked tired, edgy. He moved toward the door.

"Let me know," Nick said. Was he suddenly pressing? Were their roles being answered? What was this new compulsion to know? The reporter's sixth sense in operation? The telephone jingled on his desk. He looked up, saw Miss Baumgartner forming words with her lips: "Mrs. Pell." He picked up the phone.

"Are you coming up, Nick?"

"Yes, Myra. I'm on my way."

"All right, Nick." She hung up, her tone urgent.

As he came into her office, Myra got up from behind her big desk and moved toward the bar, where she fixed martinis, a ritual she had mastered. Nick noted that her fingers shook as she lifted the cocktail glass and passed it to him. Sipping, he smacked his lips, the expected compliment dutifully proffered.

Raising her glass, she began to say something, then, stopping, sipped her drink instead and walked toward the sofa. Primly she sat down and placed her glass on the cocktail table. Nick knew she was winding up, feeling the temperature, toes in the water. He kept silent, refusing to make it easy for her with small talk.

"I feel I'm handling this Henderson thing badly," she said. "You may think I'm trying to shove things down your throat." He had to hand it to her. She had struck right to the heart of the matter, the frills gone. He shrugged, determining to prolong his silence.

"I want to make my position clear," she continued, her voice constricting, betraying emotion. She seemed to try to cover the weakness with a cough, as if she had swallowed badly.

"What I mean to say, Nick, is that I don't want you to react as though I'm telling you what to do." He persisted in his silence, knowing it was a growing annoyance. "This man does not deserve to be destroyed." He continued to watch her, waiting for her to unwind. "Henderson is a good man," she said softly. "He stands for those things that we believe in. I've talked to him. I've watched him. This is the kind of leader that we have got to have. He stands head and shoulders above any other candidate on the horizon. Really, Nick. Burt Henderson is our kind."

"A news source has made serious allegations about him that deserve to be checked out," he said firmly.

"Since when do we run down every flimsy allegation?" she asked.

"We did it when we went after the President."

"That was different."

"How so?"

"He was an enemy. We knew what he was: a liar, a cheat, and a fraud. He deserved what we gave him." She flushed. Her upper lip quivered.

"Myra. We committed ourselves. We put everything we had behind it. We made it happen."

"He deserved it."

"We hung him right here, Myra. Long before the end."

"We were right, Nick."

"But we didn't know it in advance."

"We were sure."

". . . and he deserved it. In our view. From the beginning. Right, Myra?"

"Right." She paused. "Surely, Nick, you're not having second thoughts?"

"Not at all," he replied. "I'm merely comparing."

"There is no comparison."

"We're dealing here with the same basic ideas. The credibility of a public figure."

Her eyes narrowed as she pulled herself straight. "Well, it's about time we drew the line, then."

"Where?" he pressed. He knew he was baiting her now.

"Damn it, Nick. On our friends!" The words had been hissed through clenched teeth, her jaw jutting defiantly. Watching her, he knew he had goaded her to her outer limits. A confrontation now, he was sure, would impel an action for which he was totally unprepared. Forcing himself to smile, he held up his hands.

"Myra," he said, disgusted at his fawning, "I haven't advocated that we go after Henderson." He hesitated. "I merely want to be certain. He could be a liability if we go too far."

"I'm prepared to take that chance."

"And there's always the problem of credibility among our own people. Gunderstein, for example. We can't just

shut off the tap without adequate, rational explanations."
Would she see that he was stalling?

"It appeared strange, Nick. As if you were moving
backward." She made two more martinis and poured
them out, handing him a fresh glass. "You've got three
reporters on it. You've killed Stock's column. You've
shut Henderson out from the editorial pages. Even a
lousy Lifestyle story. Really, Nick."

"You've got one helluva spy system, Myra," Nick
said, feeling the anger rise. "You're worse than the
CIA."

"I don't need a spy system, Nick. It's going through
the paper like a disease. Henderson's extremely upset.
Frankly, I can't blame him."

"I think you're making a mistake, Myra," Nick said,
conscious of his caution. "Suppose there is an involvement?"

"I don't think I'm making myself clear."

"On the contrary."

"Come on, Nick. If you look hard enough you're
bound to find something."

"I assume you think he's clean as a pin."

"Probably."

"I don't understand."

"Yes you do, Nick. Every public figure has something, some skeleton that we can dredge up." She
paused. "We all have."

"We're not fishing. Merely investigating."

"Even Charlie knew when to stop," she said suddenly. She could always invoke Charlie. "He was no
saint either. He could look the other way when he
wanted to." What is she trying to say? he wondered.

"He was privy to all sorts of things he never used.
Toward the end, before the crack-up, he was being compromised all over the place."

He didn't want to hear, he told himself, suddenly
panicked, his own anger rising.

"He and Kennedy were buddies."

"That's no secret."

"He knew things."

"I'm sure he did."

"Things that he never told you."

Nick doubted that. Was it possible? She was heading into fertile ground.

"You look skeptical," Myra said. "I'm convinced he knew all sorts of backdoor things, especially during the Kennedy years. No, he didn't confide in me. But there were bits and pieces that only the years have put together. I'm sure, for example, that he knew about the Bay of Pigs in advance and he was privy to all sorts of CIA things that he deliberately kept out of the *Chronicle*."

"That's just supposition, Myra. I was around, too." He was trying to remember. "We've always been asked to shut things out on the grounds of national security. They're still trying. What about this morning? It's all a crock of shit, Myra. And you know it."

"Charlie kept it all to himself." She looked at him. "He adored Kennedy. He would do anything he asked."

"Maybe," Nick said. "In those years you could still believe the national security ploy. Maybe. I didn't have to know everything." But he did know, or thought he knew, all about Charlie. Indeed, he and Charlie shared unbearable burdens, he thought, remembering that time in the funeral parlor. Even in the Kennedy days when Charlie would slip out to the White House or meet the young President in his place in Virginia, or Cape Cod, or Palm Beach, he always felt that Charlie had told him everything. It wasn't the keeping out of things that bothered him. Rather, it was not knowing, the knowledge that Charlie had done it without his knowledge. That was Myra's point, the wedge inserted between the living and the dead.

"Even if Burt were involved," she said, embarking on another tack, catching a wisp of wind from another direction, "which I don't believe, would it matter now? It's all over. 1963. That's an age away. Even if, by some strange fluke, you could dredge something up, what would it prove? That he was acting on the orders of the President, that he was doing something to help the country, even if it was patently immoral. In those days it was perfectly acceptable to excuse the immorality..."

"On the grounds of national security."

"Nick. You know how I feel about the CIA. All the lies and sham. All the horrors that were done in our name. I'm against it. I don't need any special credentials. It's just that there were people in those days who did these things and were victimized, just as we were, as Charlie was."

Charlie again, he thought, watching her method of pleading with growing interest, glimpsing the stubborn passion beneath the façade of calm.

"If he *was* involved," Nick said, feeling the morning's weariness return, "then it deserves to be told. Now! Before the man becomes president." He felt the paper folded in his pocket and pulled it out. "See," he said, holding it up in front of her. "Look on the lower right." He waited for her to read it. "I'm not exactly out of control on this." He felt stupid justifying himself, wondering why she did not merely fire him, since she had the power and he had been taunting her to use it. Or was he simply testing the limits of his own power over her?

He watched her stand up and walk to the bar where she mixed another beaker of martinis, pouring the liquid into fresh glasses. He emptied the dregs in his own glass and took another from her.

"We've worked together so well these last few years, Nick," she said.

"Yes, we have, Myra." He tried to read her implication. Was it a warning? Or was this a sign of her narrowing vision, the consequences of too much power, too many victories? Or was she merely validating her ownership, asserting her right to possession? That, he knew, was the heart of the problem, his problem. He had become what he could never own. The *Chronicle* had seeped into his brain, his tissues, his cells. He was its living embodiment. He was the *Chronicle*. His blood had turned to ink. The drinks must be getting to him, he thought, shivering.

A news aide brought in the first street editions and laid them on the edge of her desk. Reaching for the top copy, he opened it and began to study the words, the habit drowning his agitation.

"How terrible!" she sighed, looking at the pictures on the front page. Suddenly he longed to be in the city room again, the comfort of his own domain. He started toward the door.

"Do we have an understanding, Nick?" she asked gently. He had resolved to act as if he hadn't heard, but her tone was compelling.

"Haven't we always, Myra?" he answered, feeling the full measure of his helplessness.

14

Seeing Charlie in the environment of the *Chronicle* for the first time came as a shock, as if his friend had remolded himself into a totally different shape. They were still in the old building then, and Charlie's office, glass-enclosed, looked out over a crowded city room which, compared to that of the *News,* seemed a hodge-podge of misdesign. Desks were crowded together, people bunched against each other.

"I've reworked things a bit," Charlie had said, noting his confusion.

It was an unfamiliar format. The traditional desk system had been scrapped.

"It looks funny. But it works better," he had said. It was an odd sensation seeing Charlie in the center of the storm, in full command, totally absorbed, barking orders.

That first day, Nick had felt clumsy, an appendage, the center of a vacuum, with activity swirling about him as he floated rudderless. Charlie paid little attention to him, working nonstop at fever pitch.

It was only when the street edition had finally been delivered to Charlie's desk that he saw his friend unbend, lean back, put his feet on the desk and his arms behind his head.

"Another day, another dollar," he said, watching Nick. "What do you think, kid?"

"I think you're working your ass off."

"Yeah, ain't it loverly?"

It seemed in retrospect to have been a Thursday, since the paper piled on Charlie's desk was unusually thick.

"It looks prosperous as hell," Nick had said, thumbing through the pages.

"Food day. We've really had to scratch to fill it up."

Later, Charlie had taken him on a tour. He remembered that it seemed endless and that Charlie seemed to know everyone who worked for him by first name, and that all who greeted him seemed to take pride in the operation.

"We're building the best goddamned paper in the United States," Charlie had said, repeating the phrase over and over again as they roamed through the building.

"It seems awesome," Nick had commented.

"Nothing to it," Charlie had responded proudly. "And we're well in the black."

Nick was content, in those early days, to stand in Charlie's shadow, follow him, learn the rudiments of his special brand of personal editorship.

The move to Washington had brought other benefits. Charlie had given Margaret a job as feature writer on the woman's pages, which had for the moment brought a respite from their bickering. Even Chums had settled into their new life with contentment.

"You see, Charlie came through for us," he taunted Margaret, who was silent now.

But mainly those first months at the *Chronicle* served as indoctrination into the mysteries of the Charlie he had not known before. He had given Nick the title

Assistant to the Managing Editor, much to the displeasure of the rest of the staff. It was, after all, an intrusion, the insertion of a total stranger into what had been a tight family group. He could feel their mistrust and aloofness.

It was not unnatural, he thought. He was, he knew, a contrivance of Charlie's friendship, pure nepotism. If Charlie saw the staff's reaction, he said nothing, having endured his own sticky journey as the Son-in-Law.

To complicate the adjustment, Charlie gave Nick no specific duties in the chain of command. As he saw it then, Nick's role was to watch Charlie, to observe carefully. Charlie pursued his editorship frenetically, with consuming concentration. Hardly a moment of his day was given to any activity other than to feed the *Chronicle*'s greedy hunger for information.

Only when the building began to vibrate with the workings of the presses did he allow the old wisecracking Charlie to emerge. But even that was a brief respite. The delivery of the street edition would set him off again and he would bury his eyes in the inked pulp, flipping each page swiftly, commenting often into the telephone, as he continued to refine and reshape the day's offering.

Sometimes Charlie was hard to follow. It was as if he had calibrated his mind only to the special rhythm of the *Chronicle*. Every word, every phrase, every sentence seemed to carry a special meaning, an important note in a full orchestration, the complete conception of which was carried only in Charlie's mind. And when a single note was off-key, Charlie could catch it instantly. Like the incident with Lighter.

Charlie had spotted it first as a buried paragraph in a New York *Times* story under the by-line of a Pentagon reporter. It referred to a new missile delivery system now under active consideration by the military, soon to be submitted for congressional approval.

"Goddamned son of a bitch," Charlie muttered under his breath.

"What is it?" Nick had asked.

"It's Lighter." He was referring to Martin Lighter, the *Chronicle*'s Pentagon reporter.

"You'll see," Charlie said, relishing the mystery. He picked up the phone. Through the glass, Nick could see Lighter stir in his desk in the rear of the city room. Looking up at Charlie's glass office, he rose and began the long trek toward them. Charlie waited, absorbed, his eyes narrowed, gathering the threads of the planned confrontation.

"What's up, Charlie?" Lighter said, confused by his editor's somber mood.

"Have you seen the *Times?*"

"Of course." Lighter exuded a sense of pedantic superiority. He was the *Chronicle*'s military affairs reporter and in Washington that carried with it all the geegaws of rank and prestige, which he bore with appropriate arrogance.

"There isn't a single reference to it in any of your copy. Obviously, it's one of the most important military stories percolating."

"Yes, it is."

Charlie looked at him, his frown deepening as Lighter's veneer seemed to harden. He was a thin, balding man, with glasses perched low on the bridge of his nose and thin lips which curled with indignation. There was also the air of the old-timer about him and the usual contempt for the youngish hotshot editor, the Son-in-Law.

"Then why are you sitting on it?" Charlie asked.

"I gave my word," Lighter said. Charlie's anger began to seep through his studied control.

"Your word?"

"My word," Lighter repeated. "You don't think that anything goes on around there without me knowing about it, do you? It's my beat, remember?" He had said these words with no attempt to hide his contempt for Charlie's questioning. "Obviously the *Times* man broke his word."

"Or never gave it."

"Of course he did. I know Jack O'Brien quite well. He probably used it because Senator Bowker of New York is head of the Armed Services Committee of the Senate and it was conceived as a kind of trial balloon, to test the local waters."

Charlie watched him, his anger rising. "Around here," Charlie said slowly, "you give your word only to me. You are responsible only to me."

"I gave my word to the Secretary of Defense."

"You have no authority from me to give your word to anybody. As editor of this newspaper that is my option. Not yours."

"Don't you think that's a bit dictatorial?" Lighter asked, his contempt rising fearlessly. "My success is built on these confidences. I'm a responsible reporter. If I violated their confidences they would shut us out of a wide range of legitimate information. After all, they're in the business of guarding our security. Frankly, Charlie, I should think you'd be more mature about this."

"That makes you an accomplice in their shenanigans."

"I think that's a rather strong word. I can't be a good authoritative reporter if I am not in their confidence. You can't expect me to reveal all my knowledge."

"I certainly can. How am I supposed to make editorial judgments if you keep me in the dark?"

"You have to trust my judgment," Lighter said, lured somehow into feeling he was getting the upper hand.

"Are you telling me that if I asked you this minute to empty your mind of all your little so-called confidences as to new weapons systems, manpower plans, planned base shutdowns, and all the other intriguing bits of information, you would refuse to give them to me?"

"Probably."

"In other words, I buy what you give me on copy paper. Take it or leave it."

"You have the option to reject my copy."

"But how can I make an intelligent judgment if I'm not privy to the background information?"

"You've got to play it as it lays."

Charlie stood up to his full height. He towered over Lighter, who still faced him bravely.

"Listen, you turd," Charlie said. "You've become nothing but a damned flack for them, a goddamned conduit for anything they want to do. You've been bought, you dummy, by their insufferable deference to your egomania. I won't run my paper like that. We're adversaries, not cohorts in league against the public's right to know."

"You're being naïve," Lighter said, swallowing his words, betraying the first signs of fear.

"I decide," Charlie said. "You either accept that or you can't work for the kind of newspaper I run."

"If you were around Washington as long as I've been you'd understand," Lighter said, trying to recover his flagging courage.

"Thank God I haven't been. Lighter, you're working on the wrong team. You should be a damned government flack, intriguing with them on how to perpetuate the bureaucracy."

Lighter swallowed now, his thin lips tightly pursed, feeling at last the weight of his defeat.

"You're too fucking big for us, Lighter," Charlie pressed, turning the knife. "You don't seem to understand what we've been trying to do here. Kick open a few windows. Let in some fresh air."

"Muckracking," Lighter said, obdurate now, having reached the outer edge of his courage, his last line of defense. Despite Charlie's power over him, he was not bending easily, not accepting graceful defeat. Nick had to admire his last-ditch effort to vindicate himself.

"There is room on this paper for only one final arbiter, one editor." Lighter stood silently, obviously taking refuge in a stubborn pride. Nick felt compassion for the older man, staring bravely into the mirror of his defeat.

"I'm sorry, Lighter. You're being reassigned as of now."

"Obviously I couldn't accept that," Lighter said, his voice cracking. But Charlie betrayed no mercy.

"You know where the door is."

The words hit Lighter now with almost physical velocity, his body bending briefly to absorb the blow.

"If that's the line you're establishing you'll have to fire half the staff."

"If that's what it takes to follow the disciplines of this newspaper, then so be it."

Lighter's eyes moved from side to side, as if searching for a clear exit. But before his body could move, he held out his hand. Almost as a reflex, Charlie took it.

"I'm sorry, Lighter," he said.

"You're in command," Lighter said, making an effort to remain rigid, to keep intact all symbols of his pride.

When he had gone, a forlorn figure despite his attempts to preserve a sense of dignity, Charlie fell into a chair.

"That was tough, kid," he said.

It was a flash of compassion, quickly dissipated. Charlie stood up again and paced his glassed-in office in agitation.

"You see what I mean, kid. It's not like newspapering in any city in the world. They're always out to use us, subvert us. I've got to be on my guard all the time." He looked at Nick. "You see why I need someone around that I can trust. Wheels within wheels. I'll root it out of this place if it's the last thing I do."

The incident with Lighter did begin a kind of ideological purge within the *Chronicle,* bloodlessly achieved, since not all the offenders were as stubborn in their views as Lighter. Charlie had wisely chosen to undertake it without formalization, encouraging a kind of philosophical exchange of views on how the bureaucracy would be covered without undermining the delicate balance that could block their already established conduits. It was Nick's first major assignment. Ironically, it had never ended, since the natural consequences of human contact made the idea of being a true adversary workable only in the abstract. Human confidences persisted, would always persist. As Charlie might have learned, it was impossible to be God.

15

The downward movement of the elevator accelerated the feeling of alcoholic haze that the uncommon intake of three martinis had produced. It was not, as he soon realized, a happy high. It made his mood heavier, more somber. As he moved through the city room, unusually busy for that hour, Ben Madison turned and waved him toward his desk.

"Look who's in your outer office."

"Christ." He had recognized Mrs. Henderson. "They're letting out all the stops," he said, conscious of the tightness on his tongue. Had Madison detected the astringent smell of gin?

"And there's this note from Gunderstein." Madison handed him a sealed envelope, which he opened.

"Could you meet me later in my apartment?" the note read. "Phelps is staying with me. I think it would be important."

Nick showed the note to Madison, who shrugged.

"A bloodhound like Gunderstein deserves to be

heard," he said, his eyes nodding approval of the way events were going.

He patted Ben Madison on the back and pressed on to where Mrs. Henderson was sitting. As he approached he could see the faint stirrings of a smile begin from the tight corners of her lips. She had retained the remnants of girlish grace, despite the cruel crenulations that age was painting on her skin. From her pictures, and from brief observations in past social contacts, she seemed one-dimensional, wafer thin, without substance.

"I hope you will forgive the intrusion," she said, standing up, a hand outstretched. Her dominant characteristic was her fading traditional good looks, as if in her younger days Henderson had pulled her off the rack, like a good suit to be worn for political occasions.

"I guess it must be my week for the Hendersons," Nick said, feeling the faint thickness on his tongue. "I had lunch with your husband yesterday."

"Yes," she answered, following him into his office. He motioned her to a seat and stepped behind his desk, resentful that she had robbed him of his time to scan the street edition.

"I hope this isn't an awkward time," she said. "I deliberately waited until the paper was"—she paused— "I think the expression is 'put to bed.' "

"Actually it's a misnomer," Nick said, looking at the unopened front page, his mind trying to absorb the inked pages. "She may get put to bed, but she never really sleeps."

"You must consider this visit unusual, Mr. Gold," she said. Her cloying humility was beginning to grate on him. Why didn't she say it and get the hell out? He willed himself to remain silent, wanting her to feel unwelcome, intrusive.

"I know what's happening, Mr. Gold, and frankly it's beginning to wear us both down. First your Mr. Gunderstein and now another person, a young lady, Miss Gates, I believe."

"Martha Gates," he said.

"Yes, that was her name."

He noticed for the first time that she was twisting a handkerchief in her fingers.

"It's wrong," she said, her composure cracking. He vowed that he would walk out of the office at the first tear.

"What's wrong?"

"What you're trying to do," she said hesitantly, her voice recovering, gathering strength. He felt himself losing patience, sensing her weakness, feeling his power over her. He felt totally without compassion.

"Does Burt know you're here?"

"No," she said emphatically. "This is my own idea."

"You realize that it's stupid?" he asked, feeling his own malevolence.

"My husband is innocent," she said. It was the kind of melodramatic delivery hardly worthy of a bad high school play. Whatever possessed this woman? he asked himself. Did she really believe that her presence would make a difference?

"You might characterize him in a hundred different ways, Mrs. Henderson. But innocent. Really now. There isn't a politician in this town who would consider that quality as part of his baggage."

"I mean of your accusations." Her façade of humility was also corroding before his eyes.

"You don't know anything about our accusations. As I told your husband yesterday, we haven't come up with any conclusions."

"You could take his word for it."

He felt his annoyance growing as the pressure of time became more apparent. If only Miss Baumgartner had stayed to shield him. Looking at the woman, he felt he could see her motivation, a wild gamble that she might inject a note of compassion, an appeal to emotion that might regain for her a place in her husband's life. To Nick she seemed a ludicrous cliché, the abandoned wife, helplessly adrift in the stink of her husband's leavings, cast off, humiliated, searching for ways to find a path back to him.

"I'm making a fool of myself," she said, fishing for some word of approval.

"I appreciate your sense of concern," he answered, sidestepping the opportunity she might have suggested. He watched her, wondering how she would react to suddenly being thrust into the White House, the First Lady. Would it salvage her life?

"It doesn't matter to you at all," she said bitterly, standing up. "You don't care a bit about what you do to people. My husband is a fine, wonderful man. This country needs a man like him. And you're willing to destroy him. It's so damned unfair, so damned unfair."

"I'm really sorry he's not here to see your performance," Nick said. The woman was getting tiresome, her sincerity suspect. Surely Henderson had not been stupid enough to put her up to this inept display. But then, he had been through it all before, the appeal of distraught women, acting out of misguided impulses.

"You are a bastard, Mr. Gold."

"From where you sit, perhaps," he agreed, feeling the alcoholic effect begin to dissipate as his impatience and anger grew.

"You and that bitch upstairs." She had hissed the words, like air escaping from a punctured tire.

So there was more here than met the eye, he considered calmly.

"What has Myra Pell got to do with it?" he asked, gently now, his newspaperman's mind dissimulating, searching for information, his head finally clearing. The woman continued to twist the handkerchief, her knuckles white with tension. His abrupt change in attitude confused her. She might have mistaken it for compassion.

"I shouldn't have mentioned her," Mrs. Henderson said, contrite now, her weakness blatantly exposed.

"She is your husband's greatest defender," Nick pressed, conscious of his maliciousness.

"Sure," Mrs. Henderson said angrily, her bitterness showing.

"Frankly, I don't understand your implication."

She looked at him, startled. "I suppose you don't," she said.

"What are you trying to tell me, Mrs. Henderson?" he asked pointedly. Her eyes flitted helplessly about the room.

"I should never have come," she said, getting up.

"Then why did you?"

"I thought I could help my husband," she said weakly. He watched her, annoyed that he had to witness her pain.

"Are you trying to tell me that your husband and Myra Pell are lovers?" The accusation seemed so incongruous to his nature, gossipy, unworthy of his sophistication. "Is that the message you're trying to bring me?"

She seemed a study in conflicting emotions: indignation, shock, confusion. The blood drained from her face. He wondered if she would faint.

"Are you all right?" he asked.

She nodded.

"He spends more time with her than with me," she whined. She carefully avoided answering his question. Could it be true?

"Then why didn't you go to her?" From her look, he could see she had debated the point.

"Because I know what she's trying to do." She threw her head back, stifling a forced laugh. "She wants to make him beholden, to swallow him up. She wants to own him."

"And you think we're merely gathering blackmail on your husband?" Nick stood up.

"Yes," she said, her face actually brightening, thankful, perhaps, for the gift of the words. He could see that she was guessing at motives, hoping that Nick might confirm her suspicions about her husband and Myra Pell.

"You're wrong," he said. "Just as wrong as you are about the other."

She appeared totally confused now. Standing up, her face flushed, she seemed a tragic, humiliated figure, her looks ravaged by time, her self-confidence shattered.

"I should never have come," she said again, turning and leaving his office without a glance back.

He looked after her and shrugged. It was the humor of it that finally struck him and a giggle erupted, growing in intensity. Did it all boil down to the stupid blindness of a woman's love? Emotions, he thought, destroyer of objectivity. If only their readers knew. Was the fate of Henderson to turn on such emotional garbage? He had better not be so contemptuous, he told himself, recalling his entanglement with Jennie. He shook his head, trying to crowd out the interview with Mrs. Henderson as he reached for the front page again, gathering his concentration.

But he could not find its threads. Unintelligible type stared back at him as he tried to find meaning in the neat slugs which carried his conception of the day's picture. It was only when a news aide came into his office with a sheaf of wire copy that he felt the authority of his mind return. Glancing through the short pica paragraphs he again came across the casualty lists from the bus shooting. Studying the names carefully, he was annoyed that he could recognize no familiarity, feeling briefly the guilt of the survivor.

The gloomy thoughts triggered in him a peculiar state of anxiety and loneliness. God, how he missed Charlie. He felt himself being crushed by the weight of decisions, like heavy rocks cascading over him in an avalanche. Yet all he had to do was sidestep and the rocks would fall harmlessly to the valley floor. Was it a death wish that haunted him, a desire, perhaps, to be with Charlie? Or was it lofty motives of truthfulness that goaded him to taunt Myra, challenging her power, testing its limits? Did he long for such a termination at last, the final stoppage of the presses in his brain, the end of continuous pressure to feed the greedy maw of the machine? Henderson as an issue seemed remote. After all, what did Henderson mean to him? Another hollow politician, an opportunist, a mere reflection. He felt suddenly unsure, lonely. He picked up the phone and dialed Jennie's extension, the ring persistent and unanswered. Finally a voice, annoyed and distracted, answered perfunctorily. It wasn't Jennie. He hung up. Jennie must still be mad over his earlier display of authority, he thought. Ego-centricity! At this moment, she surely was contriving for him a kind of massive punishment.

He put aside the street edition, knowing that in the morning, when his lucidity returned, he would find a vast array of mistakes and misinterpretations of his implied directions. Who but he would know? he thought.

He lit a cigarette, puffing deeply, feeling again the urgency of his need for Jennie. Dialing his apartment, he let the rings persist until the desk operator's voice came on. Then he hung up and dialed Jennie's place. At the impersonal voice of her answering service, he hung up. Feeling ridiculous, like a schoolboy, he tried to shake the feeling of anxiety, as if the sudden dependence were somehow obscene. When he found himself finally dialing Margaret's extension, he cursed his weakness, girding for his impending humiliation, hoping she would have left for the day.

"Margaret?" He paused.

"Nick."

Searching his mind for some casual question, he drew blanks, felt awkward.

"Nick," Margaret repeated.

"I was thinking about Chums," he lied. But it was, after all, the bridge between them.

"Should we call her, Nick? It's been a long time." He detected a hesitancy, a softness.

"Are you worried?"

"Of course. Not a day goes by that I don't get a flash of worry."

He looked at his watch, calculating what the time would be on the West Coast.

"I suppose we should call," he said, dreading the confrontation, the family friction. He hadn't meant to stir that up. Pausing, he cursed his silence, knowing she would see through it.

"Jennie's left, Nick," she sighed, sensing his priorities.

"On assignment?" he asked, hoping that he might sound casual.

"No. Not tonight." Had she caught his panic?

"Perhaps we'll call Chums tomorrow," Nick said, distracted. Later he knew he would feel fatherly guilt, having used Chums once again. He hung up.

There is no fool like an aging fool involved with a woman half his age. The thought gave him the strength to stir and walk swiftly out of the city room, avoiding the upturned eyes seeking recognition. Outside, falling heavily into the seat of a taxi, he closed his eyes and let his fatigue take over. The taxi moved quickly up Connecticut Avenue, around Dupont Circle to the entrance of Gunderstein's apartment house. He got out and proceeded through the ritual of announcement.

Gunderstein's apartment seemed even fouler than the night before, although the smells were more exotic and definable. A half-eaten pizza lay in its pan in the center of the battered coffee table, surrounded by a forest of beer cans. Martha Gates sat on the floor, cross-legged in tight jeans and, Nick noticed, braless in a tight Mickey Mouse T-shirt, with a shorthand pad poised on her flat stomach.

Standing near her, neatly vested and pinstriped, smoke billowing aromatically from a large pipe, Robert Phelps nodded a friendly greeting and extended his hand. Gunderstein lay slumped back on the sofa, his shoes off, revealing a big hole in his sock, near the big toe of his left foot.

Phelps was a compact man, pale with thin greying hair, the self-consciousness of his dress indicating that he took himself too seriously, as if he were making a statement of his esthetic and intellectual superiority. Nick hadn't seen him for two years. Ten years ago he might have been described as a kind of gentlemanly Gunderstein. The two were a study in contrasts, a sign of changing mores in the newspaper business.

"That was some quick hop over the land," Nick said, feeling the warm pump of his hand.

"I took the first plane," Phelps replied.

Nick looked at the half-eaten pizza, felt a fleeting pang of hunger, then revulsion, as he reached for a beer instead. Sitting down on an upholstered chair, he put his feet up on the cocktail table and stole a glance at Martha's nipples pressing arrogantly against the big ears of Mickey Mouse.

"We've been busy people today, Mr. Gold," she said, her seriousness incongruous with her dress. He could detect the intensity of their newspaperman's curiosity, the impending excitement of revelations to come.

"It's like playing hot potato, Mr. Gold," Gunderstein said. "We've been passing it around among each other. Finally it got so hot we had to put it down until you got here."

"Stop the hard sell, Harold," Nick snapped. "It doesn't become you." He drank his beer, swallowing deeply. He caught a glimpse of Martha looking fearfully at him, as if his presence were an intrusion, intimidating.

"Robert has been most helpful, Mr. Gold," Gunderstein said calmly, oblivious to Nick's outburst.

"Let Robert tell it, Harold," Martha said. Gunderstein nodded, picking at his pimples. Nick watched as Phelps paced the room, smoke pouring from his mouth and nose, then he stopped and removed his pipe.

"It wasn't meant to be bottled up this long," he began. "You can't imagine how debilitating it is to keep these so-called secrets." He paused to be sure he was commanding attention. "Covering South Viet Nam in those days was like covering any third-world country. You had to know where the CIA bodies were buried or you simply wouldn't be able to interpret events. You see, it's the CIA that really carries the ball out in the boonies. The straight diplomats are merely pawns in the game. The real power is held by the CIA, deriving it directly from the President. Actually it's no mystery. I'm sure you've all read the Pentagon Papers which describe in detail events concerning Diem's downfall. They're very accurate—up to a point. The CIA was, we know, the conduit between the generals who effected the coup and the President who engineered it. Actually, they were quite efficient. The Ngu brothers were boxed in before they knew it and it was all over quickly, almost a routine CIA activity."

"You knew all this at the time?" Nick asked.

"Of course."

"If I recall, it wasn't even implied in your stories."

"Even if I wrote what I knew we wouldn't have printed it."

"Why not?"

"Because Pell had given Kennedy his word."

Nick felt himself grow tense. Why had he not known?

"How did you know?"

"He called me and told me. It was as simple as that."

"The overseas lines were tapped. Charlie wouldn't have been that stupid."

"He was cryptic. I knew what he meant. I'll never forget the way he put it. He said the company had asked that I omit the golf balls from my next shipment. I knew exactly what he meant. So I filed the acceptable version of what I knew as a bunch of bullshit."

"It never troubled you?" Nick asked calmly. He had begun to reach back into time, remembering Charlie during those last Kennedy months.

"Trouble me? Hell, I ate my heart out about it. But what was I to do? What would you do? I wasn't prepared to blow my job."

Nick listened, contempt building inside of him, not only for Phelps, but for himself. "And you sat on it for all those years?"

"What was the point? Besides, it was over, squirreled away. You'd be surprised how efficient the human mind is in rationalization."

"And why now?"

"Because you're asking. You really want it." He paused. "How hard was I expected to fight?" he said quietly. "I had gotten the word. I knew the ground rules."

He looked into Nick's face.

"It's safe now," he continued. "For people like me, that is. Safe."

Phelps watched Nick's face for a reaction. When none came, he proceeded. "Hell, we all felt we were instruments of American policy in those days, regardless of how it went against our newspaperman's morality. All that First Amendment stuff gets pretty gooey when they start leaning on you like that. Besides, I was a Depression baby. I had two kids." He relit his pipe and puffed deeply, revealing his agitation.

"But the Pentagon Papers made no reference to the assassination of Diem as a CIA intrigue. It said that the deed was perpetrated by old enemies, old rivals."

"Yes, I read it. It simply didn't go far enough."

"Why?"

"Because the evidence wasn't conclusive. There were no documents showing that Diem's assassination was engineered by the CIA."

"Back to square one," Nick said, finishing his beer. He felt his belly bloat.

"Not quite. Even back then, I was convinced that Henderson was the man personally sent to prepare the logistics for the assassination."

"Supposition," Nick said, goading him.

"The scenario went something like this. Henderson was an NSA man. He had been responsible for setting up the original South Vietnamese coding when he was in the army after World War II. That was his basic expertise, that and the language. He was literally one of the handful of men in the States who knew the language. He was deliberately sent across to manipulate the assassination. I saw him only once. He steered clear of the embassy, but since I knew what seemed to be afoot I kept my eyes on the CIA man. I followed him everywhere, a shadow."

"Deduction, Robert. That's all. Not proof."

"I remember Allison. He was actually merely a go-between, a courier. He was the one who brought the message of how Diem was to be transported to his enemies. Henderson was the one who set him up."

"That's what Allison told us," Nick said. "The ravings of a drunk. Besides, he won't let himself be quoted."

"Quote me, then," Phelps said. "I'll be glad, in fact, to put my by-line on it. Let them deny it."

"If he gets up front on it, so will Allison," Gunderstein said. "I'm convinced of that."

"Look, Nick," Phelps continued, "the way those birds operated they always built in what they call plausible denial. He really can't deny he was there. He can't deny he was with NSA. He can't deny his intelligence connections and once the ball is in the air, others will step forward."

"And that will be the end of Henderson's carefully built political career, the end of his dream of the presidency."

"So what?" Phelps said. "What kind of twisted morality could let a guy like that become President of the United States? In a pig's ass, I say."

"Don't invoke morality, Phelps. Not now."

"I'd like to make amends. It's Christian, you know. Black sheep and all that. I was never in a position to argue the point. I had no choice. Like the Germans, I obeyed orders."

"We've suddenly become a bunch of self-righteous purists," Nick said lamely. Surely, in the light of more than a decade ago, it could not have seemed to Charlie a betrayal of principle. But why had he not told him? Could he have been ashamed?

"And the Bay of Pigs?" It came out as a cryptic retch.

"Pell knew about that, too. That's the way they censor, Nick. We both know that. They con you by letting you in on the inside. You feel important, in the know. Then you lie for the bastards."

"For America," Nick said. His throat felt dry. He reached for another beer.

"Bullshit," Phelps said.

"We've got to have legitimate secrets."

"That's what got us into all this trouble. You can't run morality on two tracks."

Nick could feel Martha Gates unwinding, the sense

of her presence rising in the room as her body moved, her breasts jiggling in the warmth of her tight T-shirt. He knew, as he might have believed in his younger days, that it was the idea of morality, the very fiber of good motives, that was making her move, had made her move toward this idea of what journalism meant. She was still young enough not to have drunk too deeply of futility; a part of her innocence was still intact. He felt it odd that this silent youthful figure should suddenly dominate the room, making him somehow ashamed. He felt his eyes magnetize toward her, forcing her to respond.

"It's wrong," she said simply. "Soon you won't be able to tell the difference between the idea you're protecting and the idea you're against."

He felt admiration for her special sense of purity and the private inner glow of her conviction. Of course, in the abstract, she was correct, given that all humankind were saints. Yet it was insufferable of these young people to condemn the motives and instincts of others in another time, another environment. Nick felt a sudden need to defend Henderson or, at the very least, to give him a chance. He owed that to his conscience. As for Phelps, his contrition, his need for salvation, didn't become his age.

"You're making judgments years after the fact, distorting the motives. Let's face it, a few years ago the world looked a hell of a lot different. We had just learned what Stalin had done to millions of people. It reinforced our fear of what those people were capable of doing to us. They had built the Berlin Wall. There was a Geneva Treaty to protect. People believed in our word. You could justify such activities. Diem was known to be corrupt. We hadn't yet sent many boys to Viet Nam. Look at it from Kennedy's point of view. The Geneva Treaty was made between governments. Was it our fault that their leadership was sick? It wasn't as simple as divorce. There could be no divorce. We had signed for life, or so we thought."

He felt energized by his argument, wondering about

his conviction. The human mind, he thought, could rationalize almost anything.

"It's not his motives that we're questioning," Gunderstein said, trying to refocus their concentration. "That's not our business. Only the story."

"It's an apologia," Phelps said contemptuously. "It was wrong then. It's wrong now."

"I agree," Martha said, obviously finding courage in the alliance with Phelps.

"The point is that it has story value," Gunderstein said, his pimples reddening, revealing an uncommon display of emotion that his flat, matter-of-fact way of speaking concealed. "Our only concern must be his involvement. Was Henderson involved in an official attempt at assassination? It's not a question of our right to tell the story, or even make moral judgments on it. The question is: is the story correct, accurate to the best of our knowledge?"

"It's still too circumstantial," Nick persisted.

"We're not a court of law," Gunderstein said. "Responsible allegations are worth printing. You didn't push for that kind of proof when we went after the President."

He had said the words without passion, but their implications seemed an accusation.

"The man has denied the allegation," Nick said hoarsely. "To my face."

"And do you believe him, Nick?" Phelps asked.

He hesitated, not wanting to see his own malice. "No," he admitted, daring not to dissimulate in this group, but adding quickly, "purely a gut reaction and, as we all know, that's no way to run a railroad."

"You're splitting hairs, Nick," Phelps said, relighting his pipe.

"There are other factors to consider," Nick said. He felt the beginnings of compulsiveness. His fatigue was beginning to betray him. What could they know of the isolation of command? If he bent over backward any more, he'd lose himself up his own asshole.

"Like what?" Gunderstein asked.

"Like the destruction of a man's political career," Nick said.

"I've heard that before," Phelps said. "It sounds to me as if you want to protect him." Nick watched Phelps' eyes move toward Martha's. She nodded assent, reinforcing his courage. "It's almost as if we were as bad as they are, protecting our constituency, being selectively self-righteous." Phelps' neck muscles visibly tightened. Nick hoped he wouldn't choose this moment to make a stand. Not now!

"I had hoped that you'd be more perceptive, Robert," Nick said gently, trying to head him off.

"If I'm overreacting, Nick," Phelps said, "forgive me. That comes from eating one's heart out all those years."

"It doesn't necessarily follow that you'll be destroying the man's career," Gunderstein said, taking a new tack. "Not that it should be any of our business. He can make a defense. We're not all that omnipotent. After all, we're digging back a few years. He's a pretty resourceful guy."

"He'll pursue a strategy of denial," Phelps interjected. "But I agree with Nick. It will make him suspect before his basic constituency. It will haunt him."

"I suppose," Gunderstein conceded. "But if we thought in those terms we would print nothing but social events, sports, and the comics."

"You'll have to forgive my humanity, guys," Nick exploded sarcastically. He reached for another beer, pulled off the tab, and drank greedily.

"Case in point: Mrs. Henderson was in to see me today," Nick said, watching their reaction.

"I expected that, Mr. Gold," Martha said. "I pressed her very hard."

"So she tells me."

"Poor thing," Martha Gates said. "She became very incensed with me, very indignant."

"They're good at that," Phelps said. "Hiding behind their indignation."

"A futile act by a futile woman," Nick said.

He wondered if he should tell them more. Then he felt his tiredness return, his energy flatten.

"Shall we write the story, Mr. Gold?" Gunderstein persisted.

"I'll let you know tomorrow," Nick said. He was too exhausted for decisions.

Watching Martha Gates, he remembered Jennie again, his anxieties returning, loneliness descending. He stood up, feeling a rush of dizziness at the sudden rising.

"I'll let you know tomorrow," he repeated.

"Really, Nick," Phelps said. His pipe had gone out again. "It should be told." He planted himself directly in front of Nick. "Hell, it might even restore my faith in editors."

"I hope not, Robert," Nick said. "We'll think we're doing something wrong."

He noted a look of disappointment on Martha's face. Did he really need the night to sleep on it? Or was he afraid to show them too much flexibility? To them it was an important story, to him a gauntlet to be thrown, a move, perhaps, to change his life. He walked toward the door, turning to nod a farewell, ignoring the intimidating innocent face of Martha Gates. Gunderstein remained impassive. The red circles around his pimples, the measure of his contained anger, were gone now, but he continued to pick at them, contemplatively. Phelps followed him out the door, waiting with him for the elevator.

"I hope you don't think I was out of line," he said. "I know you might think that it's a little late in the game to get religion. But I've begun to think like those kids. Nick, we've got no right to employ selective censorship."

"We do it every day," Nick said wearily. "We're only people, Phelps. Only people."

"But we have an obligation, Nick."

"To whom?"

"To our readers. To the truth."

He looked at the compact man, the pipe held high

near his chin with delicate fingers, effeminate in their grace. "You're about to make me sick, Phelps," Nick said, thankful that the elevator arrived. He stepped into it and turned in time to see Phelps' face, pale and confused. He deserved it, Nick thought to himself. Why was he showing off, flaunting his suddenly discovered sense of ethics in front of these intense, beady-eyed young people, this tribe of avenging angels?

In the street a breeze was rising. Cold air whipped his heated cheeks as he walked homeward on the deserted sidewalks. His mind, like his head, felt heavy, sluggish. It's the male menopause, he told himself, finding humor in it, remembering the column on health that was the *Chronicle*'s regular feature. He had remembered the symptoms: depression, temporary loss of virility, insecurity, loneliness, anxiety, the feeling of unfulfillment, indecisiveness, the haunting specter of life's ending just around the corner. He must be in its terminal stage, he thought.

Shivering, he tucked his chin in his upturned collar, searching for warmth. He was drowning in self-pity, missing Charlie. How could Charlie have kept things from him? He, Nick, who had tucked away the most damning secret of Charlie's life. Unless Phelps was lying. But even Myra had alluded to it. Had Charlie confided in Myra, whom he supposedly despised?

He had missed something and only now he felt its loss bitterly. Retracing the memory, he looked for clues among the ashes. He had by then become the acknowledged honcho, Charlie's man, number two in the hierarchy of what the *Chronicle* had become. The competing paper had been humbled badly and was in decline, its vaunted number one position finally surrendered as the *Chronicle* surged ahead. Power, like an old whore, had been passed along to new hands, new faces, new lusts.

He was not surprised when the young President made a beeline for Charlie, whose acquaintance had been casual up to the nomination. Then after the Inauguration they had become buddies and Charlie hopped around to the White House and all those vacation places, a regular member of the club that followed the President around the world in those days.

Not that Charlie had been totally captured. From time to time the *Chronicle* would deliberately mount a critical attack.

"Just to keep the mick honest," Charlie had said. Nick had seen him pick up the phone and actually preview an editorial in advance, enjoying the banter and posturing as Nick had cringed. He had heard only one end of the conversation. Later he was regretful that they had never been taped, but that was in the days when wit was in vogue. It was the time of Camelot, and Charlie had his special rights as one of the Knights of the Round Table.

The bantering was sometimes an embarrassment. After all, the man at the other end of the phone was the President of the United States and the language used was definitely inappropriate to the station. But it was sop to one's vanity to tell the President to take a flying fuck for himself, which Nick had heard with his own ears.

"You're the Prez, kid. I'm only an ink-stained, free-loading, drunken newspaperman, which outpisses by two yards any thickheaded Boston Irishman with a roll of lace curtain up his gazoo."

With the relationship, the importance of the *Chronicle* soared. After all, if Charlie and the President were such close buddies, what appeared in the *Chronicle* was now the bellwether of American policy. What Nick did not know until later was what Charlie had screened out—or how it had affected him.

The news of the Dallas bullet came to them while they munched sandwiches in Charlie's office. The ring of the telephone, its special urgent timbre suggestive of intruding pain, was still a terrifying memory. The blood drained from Charlie's face.

"My God," he had finally uttered, swallowing with difficulty. "My God." A kind of paralysis seemed to grip him. Nick took the telephone from the desk where it had fallen. "My God," Charlie kept repeating.

"The President has been shot." It was Ben Madison's voice. He had been a White House reporter then, in the President's party.

Nick could remember in detail his own reaction, his mind crowding out the horror of it, working toward the practicalities of covering what was certainly the biggest story of his lifetime. He was already cataloging assignments, watching through the glass as the city room stirred with the first news rattling over the wires.

"He'll never make it," Ben said. "They blew his head off."

"Who?"

"God knows."

He saw Charlie, still pale, remove the remains of the mashed sandwich from his mouth, his eyes misting with tears.

"The bastards," he shouted. It came as a primal scream, the anguish of his own life spilling out.

"Who do you think did it, Ben?" Nick asked.

"We'll probably never really know," Ben answered. Nick pressed for more details, holding the telephone up for them to see, signaling the desperate need for a rewrite man. Then the call was rerouted, while the editors gathered quickly in the old conference room where the budget meetings were held and Nick mapped out the coverage, assigning a troop of reporters to the story. Later, when he had come back to his office, Charlie had regained his composure with the help of a brandy bottle. They called for a television set and helplessly watched the details of succession, the trip home, the bloodied widow watching the passing of power on the airplane.

"He knew they would get him," Charlie said, his tongue thickening with booze and grief. "He told me they would get him. They would take their revenge. Retribution! He was clairvoyant. He knew it. He said no protection would matter. They would find a way, no matter what."

"Who?" Nick said, distracted, listening with half an ear, humoring his friend.

"They," Charlie answered cryptically.

He seemed on the border of hysteria, but late into the evening, with the presses grinding relentlessly and most of the exhausted staff in heavy pursuit of information, Charlie dozed off on the couch in the conference room.

At one point, well into the early morning hours, Nick looked up from Charlie's desk, where he had been working, into Myra's pale face. It was odd to see her in the city room at all. Seeing her reminded him how effectively she had been cut out of the life of the *Chronicle*.

Nick sensed her annoyance at seeing him at Charlie's desk and felt compelled to offer apologies.

"He took it very badly, Myra," he said, standing up. "He's resting." He pointed in the direction of the conference room.

He was sure she was holding back her anger, having expected to be offering solace to a grief-stricken husband in this rare moment of potential reconciliation. It was no secret that their marriage had become a nightmare. But she was protective of her dignity, as always, and sitting on a chair, reached into her purse for a cigarette. She lit it carefully, ceremoniously.

"I'll wait," she said quietly, looking off into the city room. He could feel her envy.

She was, after all, a victim of Mr. Parker's medieval view of the world, the right of blood to property succession, the role of woman as helper to man, the paternalism of ownership. When his will had been probated, it was revealed that he had given one-third of the paper to his employees, in proportion to their service and responsibility within the newspaper hierarchy. Charlie had not been included. In the old man's mind he controlled the paper through marriage, and marriage was inviolate, ending only in death. It did, however, produce progeny, and progeny inherited property. Blood succeeded. He had taken his genetic snobbery to the grave.

Ironically, it was Charlie who made the announcement to the employees, an occasion of solemn thankfulness, appropriately ending in prayer and a moment of silence for Mr. Parker. Nick, too, had received his share and was grateful, although he could feel his friend's anguish. It was a terrible legacy. Myra owned what she could not have and Charlie had what he could not own.

"She can fire me, you know," Charlie told him. "She has the power to do that." He paused. "But the old boy was pretty shrewd. If she does that the stock reverts to a trust. And the trust can only be abolished when my children reach their majority."

"But you have no children."

"Sticky, don't you think?"

"Incredible."

"She does, however, retain full control over the stock in the event of my death. The old boy couldn't hedge all his bets. He assumed that we would have kids, sons."

"But you said that Myra had had her tubes tied."

"He didn't know that and we wouldn't dare tell him. But he kept his secret well, too. When the will was finally read, she made a mad dash to the gynecologist to see if she could get him to untie the goddamned things. He said it wouldn't help."

"You could always adopt."

"No. Only blood. And she thought only my side of the family had a screw loose."

"What if you divorced?"

"He didn't miss a trick. In the event of divorce it's back to the trust. It's rather obscene when you think about it. I really loved the old boy. I also understand what he was trying to do. The *Chronicle* had become a kind of extension of himself, just as I had, and he wanted it to be protected as much as possible. Actually, even in death, he still holds the strings."

"Could she take legal action?"

"I'm sure she considered it. But he had it written by the best legal brains in the country. Even she knows that it would be too traumatic for the *Chronicle.* No, kid, she has only one real alternative."

"What's that?"

"Read Agatha Christie. There are hundreds of variations of doing away with the old body."

He had chuckled over that. Watching Myra now, waiting stiffly, Nick could sense her alienation and her bitterness, as her eyes swept the city room.

"They were very close," she said suddenly, meaning the assassinated President and Charlie. He had grunted some answer, feeling her intrusion like a weight. Then, as if her voice in that environment had thundered an alarm, Charlie was standing in the doorway of the adjoining conference room, his hair disheveled, eyes glazed, still heavy with torpor.

"What the hell are you doing here?" he asked. His tongue's heaviness had cleared.

"I thought perhaps you might have needed me," she said meekly. Nick, embarrassed, started to leave, but the ring of a telephone held him. He picked it up thankfully, but could not blot out their conversation.

"Well, I don't," Charlie said. "Go on home. We're busy."

"Let me help, Charlie," she pleaded.

"You hated him," Charlie said venomously, showing a cruelty Nick had not seen before.

"That's absurd."

"You jealous bitch," he said, his voice hissing through clenched teeth.

"There's no reason for this, Charlie. No reason. I'm your wife. We can help each other."

"I don't need your help."

"Everybody needs help."

"I don't need yours."

Nick could tell by the cadence that this was a well-trodden path, an endless routine.

"Charlie. Please. Let me in on something. Please." Nick could see her hands clasped helplessly together, the cigarette burning precariously low on her fingers. The voice at the other end of the phone clicked off and he was forced to hang up. A copy boy came in with a remake of one of their editions. They had been replating through the night, as new aspects of the story became available. Interrupted by the aide's arrival, Charlie picked up the paper and looked it over, his mind apparently cleared now, his sense of command returning.

"So they caught the bastard," he said, ignoring Myra's presence.

He had missed a good portion of the breaking story while he was asleep. Now he read greedily.

"I don't believe it," he said. "There's more to this. Put more people on it. How many people have we got in Dallas?"

"Just Ben. But others are already on their way."

"Good. I want everything you can get on this guy. There's more here than what we're getting." He picked up a telephone, began to dial, then looked at Myra.

"Go home," he hissed.

"I belong here," she said defiantly.

Charlie shrugged, continued to talk on the telephone while Myra turned, her eyes misted, and peered into the city room. She sat down, a curious apparition, silently watching the turmoil.

"It's been a blow, Myra," Nick whispered, as Charlie turned his back. "He's not himself." I'm sorry, he wanted to say.

"I don't know what his real self is anymore, Nick," she said, her lips trembling.

He reached out his hand and touched her shoulder, feeling the shudder in her body.

"It'll pass."

"Sure," she said, shaking her head in contradiction.

16

In front of him the concrete circular monument of Fox-hall loomed like the prow of a ship slipping through the fog. He wondered if Jennie might be in his apartment after all and, suddenly hopeful, he increased his speed.

"Good evening, Mr. Gold," the doorman said, tipping his hat. The pleasantness of his greeting raised his optimism. Letting himself into his apartment, he made deliberate noises with his key. The apartment was still, its deadness nerve-racking to ears used to a world of noise. He walked around the silent apartment, poking into each room as if expecting to find her playfully hiding.

Opening a bedroom closet, he saw her clothes hanging limply. He fell heavily on the bed, his shoes on the bedspread, ignoring a compulsion for neatness taught by his mother. Lifting the bedside phone, he punched Jennie's apartment number, letting the cold instrument lie against his ear as it rang. The long series of rings gave him hope that she had returned. But the harried

voice of the answering service intruded. He let it inquire repetitively, almost a welcome sound in the dead
silence. Leaving the phone beside him on the bed, he
heard the click of the broken connection, then the frenetic bleeps that the telephone company used to indicate
a receiver off the hook. He replaced the receiver and
lay back on the bed again, staring at the ceiling.

He had known from the beginning that Jennie had
zeroed in on him, a pinpointed target carefully recon-
noitered, the attack preceded by a barrage and culminat-
ing in a final assault. Perhaps he thought of it in that
way because her father had been a general. He had
been moderately successful as a logistics expert, which
planted two stars on his epaulets. But his real calling
had been that of a social lion, a companion in demand,
handsome, witty, charming. He had been divorced early
and Jennie had spent her childhood in a series of girls'
boarding schools, growing into attractive womanhood,
a tall thin high-cheekboned articulate woman, who
moved with an exaggerated model's grace, an air of
cool self-possession.

By the time Jennie was ready to stake out her own
territory, General Lynn was an important social fixture
in town, a gallant dashing figure, living in the aura of
past conquests, an old roué. He doted on his daughter
and, in retrospect, had manipulated his maze of Washington connections in a burst of activity aimed at getting her on the staff of the *Chronicle*.

"You must meet my daughter," he had said to Nick
one evening at a dinner party at the Argentine Embassy.
Later he realized that the old man must have put the
pressure on his friends to insist that he come. As a
single man, he had been placed next to Jennie at the
dinner table. His first brief assessment was that she was
too thin, much too thin, far too flat-chested to remotely
tantalize his libido. She told him that she had free-
lanced articles for the two years she had been out of
college.

"Your coverage of most Washington social events is
a dreadful bore," she said, smiling broadly under her

polished cheekbones and whipping her long eyelashes together. She spoke in an anachronistic, Noel Coward cadence with a slight British accent. He recalled trying to frame an answer, but before he could, she attacked again.

"You portray all of these people"—a thin arm swept the assemblage in the ballroom of the embassy—"as pieces of cardboard, razor thin, as if the mere mention of their names is enough to give them character."

"We're newspaper people, not novelists," he had protested, struggling to stick his spoon into an unripe melon.

"There is a lot of subtlety here. Your reporters completely miss it."

"Oh," he had said politely, amused at her method of gaining his attention.

"Absolutely," she insisted. "This is actually a den of wolves. That old Senator there, for example, is an alcoholic and has been having an affair with that woman there, the wife of our esteemed Ambassador from Morocco, for years. That's why he's never been transferred. And that lovely lady there is a professional freeloader. I'll bet you thought she was loaded herself. And if your taste runs to sexual aberrations, Congressman Geegaw there"—she actually pointed and smiled—"is a transvestite. As for our host, he's big on little girls. And see that haughty grande dame in the corner? She's a compulsive masturbator."

He gave up trying to negotiate his melon and, putting his spoon down, turned to face the girl.

"You sound as if you spent a great deal of time at keyholes." Assuming that she had engaged his interest, she proceeded to press her advantage.

"And that fellow next to you is a necrophiliac."

"Good God!"

"Common knowledge."

"I won't ask you how you know that."

"Not unless you have a strong stomach."

"Are you for real?" he said finally. She patted his hand.

"I'm just trying to illustrate how second-rate your coverage is. You need someone to crawl beneath the surface."

"Like who?" Nick asked.

She stretched her hands outward, palms up, and bowed her head.

"We'd burn out a hundred blue pencils a night."

"Not if you're subtle enough. You could be cleverly euphemistic, like the Li'l Abner strip, dirty as hell. But then you'd have something. The real people would know."

"How would you work in that necrophiliac business?"

She thought for a moment, then laughed.

"I'd describe what he put on his buffet plate in lascivious terms."

"And the masturbator?"

"She'd be playing with her earring."

"And the freeloader."

"Second helpings."

Despite himself, he had become intrigued.

"It would all seem very civilized," she had said.

He had danced with her, but had not asked to take her home. That was his womanizer period and, since she was not to his sexual taste, he hadn't been inspired to make any moves.

When he began to receive letters from prominent figures, urging him to hire her, extolling her talents, he knew that there was a campaign afoot and he was determined to resist. It was Myra who revealed how far the campaign had progressed.

"You know our social stuff is getting to be a bore," she told him.

"So they've got to you, too."

"Who?" she asked innocently in her usual oblique way. "I met the kid at a dinner party. A charming girl."

"Did she point out the necrophiliac?"

"And more. Lots more. She's actually quite amusing."

"If she had her way, she'd turn us into a gossip rag."

"Maybe we need some of that," Myra said. They had been over this ground before. "You know we have been getting a lot of flack from the women's movement to change the concept of our so-called social pages. They've got a good point, Nick."

"Are you saying that I'm a male chauvinist pig?"

"Yes, as a matter of fact." She smiled. What had evolved was their Lifestyle section. He had invited some of the top guns in the women's movement to lunch and they had convinced him that his present coverage was an anachronism. It was one time he welcomed the pressure, convinced that they were right, and one day they simply changed the masthead of the section. Margaret was, of course, ecstatic when he announced his decision to her over drinks in Myra's office.

"Finally," she said, her eyes misting. "As the cigarette ads say, 'We've come a long way, baby.'"

"It'll mean a restaffing," Nick said. "We're going to need to put some bite into it."

"I'll do my best."

"You were always pretty good when it came to bite," Nick said. It had been meant only as a wisecrack, but the remembered pain of their marriage rushed back.

"She'll do a great job," Myra said, kissing Margaret lightly on the cheek.

After the first week of the new Lifestyle, he got a call from Jennie, preceded, of course, by additional letters of recommendation.

"See, I was right," she said, her voice crisp and seductive.

"I never said you weren't."

"So hire me."

Perhaps it was her voice, her method of articulation, with its beautifully pitched snottiness and carefully timed little shocks that began to attract him. He asked her to lunch with him at the Sans Souci. She was waiting for him at a table against the wall, champagne glass raised to her lips. Paul, the maître d', moved the table to enable him to get beside her, pouring champagne into his waiting glass. He could see she was determined to make a final assault. Despite his previous impression, he found himself expectant. She seemed beautiful suddenly.

Even her flat chest in her tight bodice appeared mysteriously attractive. And she was deliciously young.

"I've been sitting here composing a story in my head about all the people in this place." She clinked her glass with his and sipped champagne.

"A potpourri of aberrations."

"You see that man in the corner . . ."

"Enough," Nick said.

"You don't want to hear about his proclivities?"

"Not at all."

"Then how about mine?" She reached for his hand under the table, enmeshing her fingers, squeezing his.

"I'm sure it would be interesting," he said, warmed by the champagne, feeling her sexuality emerging. She held his hand until their lunch arrived, releasing it, finally, to slice her veal.

"You really should hire me," she said, lighting a cigarette, lifting her coffee cup. "I've got all the requirements, a powerful sense of observation, great contacts. I know everybody. At least my father does. I'm not bad-looking, although I am missing a bit in some departments." She dropped her eyes to her chest. "But then I have compensating characteristics. You, Mr. Big Shot Editor, actually need me."

"Can you write?"

She puffed deeply on her cigarette, a first sign of some agitation.

"I'm workmanlike," she said, as if it were an admission. "I'm no Anaïs Nin, but then again, I'll have you."

"Me?"

"You're an editor, aren't you?"

He wasn't interested in being a Pygmalion, he told himself. Later when she excused herself to go to the ladies', he watched her cross the room. Observing her tight, rounded rear, he remembered her reference to compensating characteristics. Somehow it seemed tied to the decision to give her a free-lance assignment. What the hell, he thought, he was not above trading his position for flesh. It was, after all, one of the fringe benefits of influence. Was it really a form of rape? He snickered at the reference. I am a male chauvinist pig, he thought.

For obvious reasons, Henry Landau was the go-between with Margaret, who immediately saw through the ploy.

"I thought I was going to pick my own staff," she had complained to Nick. "Henry has ordered me, literally ordered me, to give this kid an assignment."

"I'll check," he said innocently, calling her back later.

"She might be exactly what you're looking for. You make your own judgment after you see her copy." He chuckled over the conspiracy.

"I wasn't born yesterday," Margaret fumed.

"You're a goddamned whoremonger," Henry had also observed, smiling.

"She's really not my speed," he had responded, flushing.

Her assignment was to cover a Kennedy Center event, a social, artsy affair, in connection with the opening night of a British play starring Rex Harrison.

Arranging to meet her for breakfast in his apartment the next morning, he had prepared an elaborate seduction breakfast: orange juice and champagne, scrambled eggs, croissants, and coffee all laid out on a table near the terrace with a single yellow flower as a centerpiece. He felt giddy with his foolishness, silly. He also put on a velvet smoking jacket which he had found hanging in the closet and topped it off with an ascot.

"You look like Little Lord Fauntleroy," she said, breezing into the apartment, taking in the scene knowingly. "You little devil."

But under the patina of chic sophistication, she was nervous, her fingers wrinkling the copy paper as she pulled it out of her pocketbook.

"The moment of truth," she said. "I was up all night, trying to get it right. As you'll see, Nick, I talk a good game."

He opened the copy, thankful for the opportunity for professionalism, and began to read. Without a pencil at the ready, he felt frustrated. She must have sensed it, since she pulled a ballpoint pen out of her bag.

"It stinks, right?" she said.

"It's not all that bad," he lied. "It needs a little work." He walked to a desk in the corner and began to refashion it with the pen, while she stood over him, sipping the champagne and orange juice. He worked swiftly, carefully, jabbing the pen as he sliced and rewrote, fitting together the pieces with swirls and curlicues. Feeling her breath near his ear, he spurred himself on to refashion the story with special care, showing off. He was, after all, doing his thing.

"Shorten your sentences. Use the omnipotent point of view. Take a position as superior observer. You should write the way you talk."

"Believe me, Nick, I try."

He turned his face upward to her, watching her coolness evaporate as she read the changes in her copy.

"You must think I'm full of shit," she said.

"Just young. You can learn it, Jennie." He stood up, watching her, sensing the vulnerability beneath the coolness.

"I want to learn," she said, putting her champagne glass on the desk and leaning her body against his. He kissed her deeply, his hands roaming to her hard, curved buttocks, pressing her pelvis toward his already erected organ. She reached down and felt it.

"I want that," she said, leading him to the couch in the corner, kneeling between his legs, unzipping his pants with a feathery experienced touch.

"I'm told I do this beautifully, far better than I write," she said, lightly moving her tongue up and down the shaft of his erected penis, moaning lightly. He reached out, curious about her breasts, which were tiny mounds. He unbuttoned the back of her dress, feeling her boniness. He noted from the beginning that she was sexually aggressive, a challenge he felt, at least on that first morning, that he could meet, and did, as he held back waiting for the moment when he would tell her to stop so that he could plunge himself into her. But she would not desist, increasing her oral activity, caressing him with marvelous experience, goading until he could not find the will to move, feeling his body explode, his semen pouring into her mouth.

When she had completed the act, decelerating with gentle zeal, she lay with her head against his thigh, her eyes closed, her long lashes resting it seemed against her high cheekbones.

"I'm good for something," she said, as if she were hinting at some inner sense of self-abasement. He had detected from the beginning something curious in her sexual nature, as if the least important point of pleasure was the most natural.

He had, of course, engineered her hiring. She had retyped the copy, handed it in to Margaret, whose objectivity prevailed.

"Her stuff's terrific," she said at the budget meeting that day.

"Let me take a peek."

Later he had called her. "You're right. I think you might have something there."

Jennie came over that night. She was jubilant.

"You've got to have patience with me," she pleaded, as they lay in the afterglow, windows open to the lights of the city, clearly seen as they lay on his raised bed.

"I won't let you down, Nick," she said. "You teach me. And I'll teach you."

He had not imagined such sexual propensities, eagerly pursued by her, imbibed to surfeit by him. A man not careless in his relationships, his affair with Jennie engulfed him, not only in a sexual sense, although that part of it was powerful enough, but also in another, more complex way. He was flattered by what he assumed was his attraction, his allure, which in a man who was heading swiftly toward his middle fifties, provoked all sorts of danger signals. For this reason, he was never completely secure, always on the thin edge of disquiet.

"I think I love you," he told her one night, months after they had become involved. They were sitting quietly in his living room reading, oblivious to communication. He remembered he was reading a biography of Woodrow Wilson.

"You are romantic, Nick," she had answered. "Be careful, you'll exaggerate your expectations." The cool, quick, almost flippant answer seemed to strike right into the heart of the matter. Of course, that was his problem, he thought, remembering Charlie.

But the remark had made him cautious and he was not above increasing his hold of dependence.

"You've made me a success, Nick."

"Isn't that what you wanted?"

"I wanted to do it on my own."

"You did."

It became a kind of duel as she would try to increase his dependence on her, through sexuality, which drove him to unimagined ecstasies. At times he flagged, which caused her to find other ways. When she discovered he could be anxious about her, manifested by jealousy or fits of controlled rage, she could be cruel. Although she lived with him, she had moved across the street from his place, but withheld from him the key to her apartment.

"I won't let you have it," she had said, joking, then taunting.

"I've given you mine."

"You've got to leave me something of my own, Nick," she had replied, dead serious.

Sometime later she had actually disappeared for forty-eight hours, her two days off, driving him crazy with anxiety.

"Where the hell were you?"

"My place."

"I called."

"I didn't answer. I left the service on."

"So I found out."

It reached a point where, if he watched closely, he could sense the onset of these withdrawals and he tried, emotionally, to prepare for them. When she would finally return, he would sometimes greet her with contrived indifference. Her reaction never quite fulfilled his expectations. Not that he would ever reveal to her the real extent of his anxieties. He was too cautious for that. He imagined that the difference in their ages had something to do with it. Was that the real reason he had opted to keep the relationship secret? A fear of failure. His! He was conscious of using his power over her, pressing his advantage, not without a twinge of guilt. After all, wasn't she using him as well?

He was, of course, aware of his self-deception. Jennie was ambitious, greedy for recognition, and since he was certain it was her most obsessive drive, he was ruthless in his manipulation of it. But he also knew that someday, somehow, he would lose his hold. C'est la guerre, he thought. When his power faltered, that would be that. He allowed himself no illusions on that score and understood her need to keep some part of herself free of him, an escape hatch, a bailout door.

But tonight he felt a special need for her closeness. His tolerance was strained. Lying on his bed, watching the lights, he felt washed out, fatigued beyond sleep, unable to calm himself.

He got up, went to the bathroom, dipped his face in handfuls of cool water, then left the apartment again. Outside, he crossed the street to her building. Waving to the guard at the desk as if he were a tenant, he reached the elevator before the man's curiosity could be aroused. When he reached the door of Jennie's apartment, he put his ear to it and knocked lightly. Inside nothing stirred. He banged harder, recklessly, he thought, knowing that he was being watched on the security television monitor, feeling the humiliation. There was still no answer.

"Jennie," he called, "it's Nick. Open up." No sound came from within. He could hear only the surge of his own blood. He felt an urge to kick the door in, but resisted, concluding that she was probably not home. But where? he wondered, a pang of jealousy tightening his gut. Where are you, Jennie? he screamed within himself.

"I thought you lived here," the guard said as he passed. He paid no attention and moved into the empty street again, walking swiftly, heading toward Wisconsin Avenue. He felt his fists tighten as if he were preparing to fight off a mugger. Let them come, he taunted the night, feeling himself an exposed target, imagining his own violent reaction to an attack. Why don't they come? he wondered with disappointment and he reached the well-lighted main artery of Wisconsin Avenue and headed south toward Georgetown.

He looked at his watch. It was past two. In Georgetown the streets were still lively. Students turned out from bars, lounged in doorways. Why did he see them as arrogant? he wondered, thinking about Chums. They seemed to be withholding some secret knowledge, some mystery known only to youth. He felt his age, his aloneness, the full lash of his anxieties, his fears. His mind picked over minute details, bits and pieces, revelations. It was the familiar gnawing sense of betrayal, the feeling of furniture out of place, of unspecified anguish.

He recalled the scene in Gunderstein's apartment, Phelps' accusation concerning Charlie. There were too many secrets, too many rationalizations of dark deeds. If only he could discourage his preposterous need to know everything. It was only when he found himself at the doorstep of his old Georgetown house that he knew where his subconscious had been leading him. He had not been as disoriented as he imagined. As a reflex, he reached into his pocket for a key, then remembered it had been years since he had owned one. Ringing the doorbell, he waited. Then rang again. A light went on in the second floor. Margaret peeked out from behind a curtain. Stepping back, he showed himself. She parted the curtain and lifted a finger.

Letting him in, she watched him pass through the foyer into the living room, following him as he slumped into a chair.

"You want a drink?" she asked, rubbing the sleep from her eyes. He noticed that her figure was heavy beneath her nightgown, her huge breasts sagging with their large circles of nipples showing pinkly through sheer material. Before she got close enough, handing him a glass of Scotch, he imagined he could smell her special night odor, her scent. She sat opposite him on the couch, cross-legged, her belly ballooning against her thighs. He drank deeply, and placed the glass on the cocktail table.

"I'm slightly discombobulated tonight, Maggie." She watched him silently. "Something's going wrong," he said.

"Personal or business?" she asked.

"A little of both."

"Jennie?"

They had never discussed her before, nor had Nick ever confided his relationship. Yet he pressed on, as if there were no gaps in Margaret's knowledge.

"She's on one of her toots. I think she's pissed off at me about that Henderson piece."

"To put it mildly."

"You noticed?"

"I've got eyes."

"I'll bet they all think I'm acting pretty strangely on the Henderson thing." He was hardly conscious of his shift of focus. The *Chronicle* was more common ground.

"As a matter of fact."

"What are they saying?"

"They're only surmising. Nobody knows for sure, including me. Some say it's an old grudge. Others give it a political tinge. Everybody knows that you and Myra and Henderson had lunch together the other day."

"Everybody's a yenta."

"That's what the newspaper business is all about, Nick. We're all yentas."

"And that sums up our problem. We know too god-damned much about other people's lives."

"Shades of Miss Lonelyhearts."

"West was right, you know. Right on the money."

Nick lifted the glass from the cocktail table, sipped

again, and replaced it, watching Margaret, her hair, even for bed, still in its upsweep. She lifted her fingers to pat it, perhaps feeling the pressure of his stare. In a way, he envied her. She was so complete, so self-contained; she had reached—what did they call it?—a philosophic calm. He felt compelled to articulate the compliment.

"I've got to hand it to you, Margaret."

"Oh," she responded coyly, perhaps suspecting his evaluation.

"The dream just never died. You really look fulfilled, you know, a happy woman."

"I don't know about happiness, Nick," she said. "But I do feel I've achieved something. You can't imagine how satisfying that is." She paused, her eyes narrowing. "Oh, I do have regrets about the pain I've caused others. You and Chums. But you know, Nick, I don't feel guilty, only regrets. I'm where I've always wanted to be, the top of my profession. I owe a lot to you, Nick. I'm thankful and I'm grateful. But I do know one thing. You wouldn't keep me there if you didn't think I could hack it."

He wondered if that were really true, but sensing the importance of this conclusion to herself, he allowed her to think it. He envied her feeling of accomplishment, her security. She, at least, had won her battle.

"Yes," he said, "I guess that's true." He saw a brief frown, as if she might have read his thoughts, causing him to add quickly, "You're good, Margaret. No question about that. You can be proud of yourself." Her frown disappeared. But his thoughts were already racing in another direction. Henderson! If only the lines were clearly drawn, as in the case of the departed President. They were all allies on that one, eager participants, enjoying the systematic destruction, the steady methodical bulldozing through the façade. Why had the victory soured so swiftly? They had been so self-righteous, so puffed with their own evangelism, so euphoric in the final days as the façade splintered. Not a tear of compassion was shed as they toasted victory in Myra's office and after, at all the victory dinners and cocktail parties.

Was it exhilaration or merely smugness? Like zealots they had cleansed the nation, and the shock waves still rumbled throughout the world. Old Mr. Parker was surely reveling in heaven, perhaps pontificating to his fellow angels on the ultimate wonders of the objective truth. Selective truth, he told himself, with contempt. He reached for his glass and drank down the contents in one gulp, as if it were needed immediately to increase his powers of insight. But it wasn't really necessary. He knew the root cause of his disorientation. Myra was crossing the Rubicon at last. The other shoe had dropped. She wanted a president of her own, like Charlie, and nothing would stop her, nothing at all. He shivered at the thought of his own vulnerability in the face of her passion and knew he was doomed if he resisted. She was asking him to submit to his own castration. The Scotch curdled in his stomach, inducing a slight nausea.

Margaret got up, moved to the liquor cabinet, and bringing the bottle, poured another drink into his glass, filling it. He noticed the heaviness of her breasts as she bent over, as if they were separate from her body, living a life of their own.

"I'm damned if I do and damned if I don't," he said, knowing that it would be cryptic.

"I don't understand," she said.

"She would never stand for us bombing Henderson. He's her handpicked boy. If I buck her on this, I think she'd toss me away like a stale loaf."

"Myra?"

He nodded.

"After all you've done," she said, drinking deeply, perhaps worrying about her own mortality. "There would be a revolution on the paper. You're a goddamned shrine. We're all your people. I doubt if she would risk it."

"There's more here than meets the eye. Mrs. Henderson came to see me today. She insists that Myra and Henderson are lovers. I can't believe it, but the woman seemed quite sure." Margaret smirked and shook her head.

"It's quite obvious that the woman doesn't know Myra," she said, moving her body for emphasis, her drink spilling on her nightgown. "Myra carries her own balls around with her."

"It's quite possible," he said quickly, almost with a touch of pedantry as if his experience with Jennifer had a quality of universality. "Don't write it off so fast. Emotions have a way of betraying reason."

It occurred to him then that it might be simpler for him if Myra and Henderson had been lovers. At least he could understand that, could find a way to cope with that. But this other, this sudden quantum leap for more and more control, that implied a far more difficult confrontation, and for him, a denser minefield.

"I know, Nick," Margaret said, taking a deep sip of her drink. "And I really don't want to invoke that silly wheeze of woman's intuition. A male must have concocted that, as if women couldn't really think except intuitively, a mystical gift. But goddammit, Nick, from what I know about Myra, and myself, I'd say she's put all that behind her and was more tantalized by her role, the thrill of achievement, the sense of being boss."

He watched her huge ballooning breasts as she spoke. It had always been a distraction, was one even now.

"The titular head," he said. She understood the implication and flushed slightly, looking down at her ravaged glory. He knew she was concocting some kind of a put-down, drawing again from the well of old hates, ancient angers.

"Your problem, Nick," she said with deliberation—her eyes told him that she was softening the blow—"is that you don't understand the mind of a woman. You look at her too much from the crotch."

"Goddammit, Maggie," he exploded. "Not now. Don't lay that superior sister shit on me now, not now."

She hesitated, watching him, nervously lapping at her drink as he finished his off. She rose, moved her heavy body toward the Scotch bottle, and repoured their drinks.

"I'm just trying to get you to understand a woman's mind. To take the blinders off."

"You and your damned female generalizations," he said, more tranquil now as he felt the alcohol move into his blood, soothing him. "Believe me, Maggie, what Myra has in her mind is not as mysterious as you allow."

"Not mysterious at all, not to me."

"Or me."

"But you can understand her only if you look at it from the vantage of her femaleness. And the way that being a woman has shaped her."

His mind groped back to that first dinner at Mr. Parker's house. He could almost smell the steaming vegetables and hear the clink of the crystal wineglasses. "I understand her perfectly," he said. "That's exactly the point."

He wondered how far he could go with Margaret, who he knew must be relishing the idea of this conversation and its implications. But could he really trust her? Surely, half a lifetime shared counted for something. He caught himself looking at her breasts again, feeling perhaps the beginnings of an urge to bury his face in those warm pillows of flesh. He imagined his head lying there, an embryo in the safety of the womb, hearing only the heartbeat of life.

"I'm frightened," he said, aware that the words had been mumbled, as if he had not wished himself to be understood. But Margaret's hearing was alert.

"You are down," she said, surveying him suddenly like some prized butterfly pinned to a specimen card.

"But not out," he said quickly, shivering as he finished the Scotch which she quickly rose to repour. Could he really trust her? he wondered. Was the paranoia seeping into his marrow? He felt his mind racing in different directions at once. His eyes searched around the still familiar room, alighting on a picture of Chums. It had been taken at her fifth birthday. The innocent child's eyes stared back at him, large eyes, like his, always questioning, never able to hide a hurt. Margaret followed the direction of his concentration.

"Remember how pretty she looked then?"

"I had forgotten," he said honestly, although he had the same picture in his apartment. Odd, he thought, that he had never really looked at it for years.

"We botched that one up rather badly," he said, recalling the memories of the painful parts of their marriage.

"Someday she'll simply have to stop using it as an excuse for self-destruction," Margaret mused aloud. Perhaps she had repeated it silently to herself and was testing its effect as a spoken thought. "And I don't intend to feel guilty about it forever." Like him, she was still fighting her guilt about Chums.

"She'll find herself, Maggie," he said gently, but without conviction. It was the one element of sharing still left. They drifted into silence. Nick sipped his drink and placed the glass on the cocktail table. Talk of Chums rekindled his sense of home, and he untied his shoes and stretched his legs.

"More?" she said, holding out the bottle.

"Just a drop." It would be futile to get drunk, he thought.

Finding his concentration again, he felt the tension had begun to ease. He felt his guard slipping, more secure somehow.

"I can't shake this sense of being surrounded," he said. "And I can't seem to find my way out, the path out. The fact is, Maggie, that Myra's got me by the short hairs."

"Nothing lasts forever," Margaret said, forcing an attempt at cheerfulness.

"You're a great help."

"Please don't misunderstand, Nick," she said. "Let's face it. You couldn't expect her to remain passive little Myra forever. It wasn't in the cards."

His antenna caught an odd vibration. His defenses rose. Again he had the feeling of something amiss, the furniture awry. She finished her drink, an action perhaps to cover a sudden discomfort. She knew him well enough to tread cautiously.

"Sounds like you've seen some of the hands."

"I have, Nick," she said emphatically. He remembered her odd frown, the joining together of lines on her forehead, her unconscious signal of determination.

"You're not going to lay this intuition shit on me?"

"No. We were close once."

"You and Myra?"

"Perhaps I'm exaggerating. Let's say I had her confidence once."

"The sister thing?"

"As a matter of fact."

"I hadn't realized."

"You wouldn't have known what to look for at the time."

His mind groped back over the years. There had never appeared to be any real closeness between Myra and Margaret.

"It was just after Charlie died." She took a deep breath, sipped her drink again. "She was frantic with guilt and despair."

"Guilt."

"She needed someone then," she said evasively. "Someone who might understand. She took a stab at me and I was there. She was lucky. I did understand."

"Understand what?"

"Well, for one thing," she paused. "What it means to suffer the humiliation of male domination . . ."

"Christ," he interrupted. "That was just ass-kissing. Charlie was dead. You saw in it a good opportunity to short-circuit me." He had not wanted to say it just that way, to reveal his vulnerability. But his training had taught him the smell of a half-told story.

"Don't, Nick," she said gently. "I'll tell it." Watching him, her eyes misted. She wasn't prone to tears and quickly recovered, finding control. "Myra needed someone," she continued, her hands folded as if to restrain nervous fingers. He could see the whiteness of the pressure around the knuckles.

"She was glad that Charlie had blown his brains out," she said quickly, an ejaculation. She paused again and refilled her glass, ignoring his, drinking swiftly, as if to drown the words that she must have known were coming. "It was unbearable for her to endure his madness, his hate. He was detestable, disgusting. He beat her, abused her."

"I know all that," he said bitterly. "But Charlie was already institutionalized. She had the power to keep him there."

"She thought he was getting better. She felt she owed him that last chance."

"I saw him there," he said, remembering that last visit, the flights from lucidity. It had puzzled him when he was released. "He was still sick. He was beyond hope."

"She owed him that last chance," Margaret said flatly. "She told me that herself."

"And you believed her?"

"Yes."

"And the guns. Her father's guns. They were in a gun case in their old house on Massachusetts Avenue. The case was kept locked. And how come the guns were in such perfect working order? Charlie never hunted."

"What are you implying?" Her mouth remained open, the circles under her eyes seemed to deepen.

"Come on, Maggie. She didn't have to pull the trigger. He was sick, crazy. All she had to do was give him the opportunity."

"She wouldn't," Margaret whispered, on the edge of panic. "Not Myra."

"That was the only way she could get control. She must have tried to break the trust agreement on grounds of non compos mentis. I'll bet she consulted lawyers."

He could see that she was reacting now out of some wisp of memory, confirming what he had suspected, although he had kept it hidden, even from himself. Was it merely Charlie talking through him? Did he need a justification for Charlie's death?

"No matter what you say, I'll never believe it." She

paused, watching him. "And even if I did, she had good cause." He remembered the day at the funeral parlor in Hempstead, the memory clear. The secret was buried, never to emerge again in Charlie's lifetime, except in his anguished brain. He might have seen his suicide as an act of retribution.

"You've always been in league with him," she said, the panic receding as she found her strength again. "That relationship was a real aberration," she hissed. He could feel her anger now.

"I'll bet it was quite a coffee klatch, all that damned confiding. She found the right person, all right. Someone with whom to share hatred of Charlie. Sick old Charlie, who wore out his substance trying to make the *Chronicle* something. Where the hell would any of us be without Charlie?" He stood up, pacing the room in his stocking feet. "You ungrateful bastards. Charlie made us . . . even Myra." He paced silently, feeling her eyes watching him.

"There are limits, Nick."

"To gratitude?"

"Even that." She paused. "Also to pain."

"He was sick. He didn't know what he was doing."

"That didn't make the pain any less."

He sat down again.

"The two of you must have had a field day. It's a wonder I'm still around."

"She had planned to fire you," Margaret said, softly now. The words stabbed into him. "She was determined to get rid of any last vestige of Charlie. I convinced her to keep you, Nick. I did. I invoked the power of our relationship and her manipulated vulnerability. I did it."

He felt the beginnings of a retch, an exploding glob in the pit of his stomach. Fighting it back, he stammered, "The *Chronicle* would have fallen on its ass. She had no experience, no training. She would have blown it."

"She was willing to take that chance," she said smugly. "It wasn't easy to convince her." But he was protesting within himself, without conviction. He be-

lieved her, refusing to be grateful. It was her only logical move. "As it turned out, I was right. Years later
she admitted it. Thanked me."

"So you're still sharing confidences."

"I'm afraid not. I said Myra had changed. She's more
protective of herself these days. Considering her responsibilities, I can't blame her. Besides, I'm a little
wary myself. And, you may not believe this, but I
don't want you to think I've gone over your head."

"That doesn't seem to bother some people."

"Like who?"

"I'm not sure," he admitted.

"Ambition does strange things, Nick."

"So they tell me."

Despite her outward look of confidence, he knew she
was concerned with his reaction. He believed her. He
felt her trust and loyalty.

"I'm not ready to give it up, Maggie," he said. "Not
yet."

"I know that, Nick."

"But I'm in a damned jackpot, and I haven't been
able to figure a way out."

"Are you asking for advice?"

"Let's say I'm open to it."

She hesitated, perhaps carefully going over her response.

"I'd say she is determined. If it came to a showdown
she'd expect you to bend. She's strong now, probably
sure of herself. It's obvious to me just from the little
bit you've told me that she's come to some understanding with Henderson. She was always intimidated by
Charlie's talents. Beyond her hate. She wants herself a
president, Nick. Wants to surpass Charlie. She wants
to be on the inside."

"That's what's frightening, Maggie."

"She's entitled," Margaret said.

"Entitled?"

"It's her ball game. She owns us, all of us, even you."

"Delusions of grandeur," Nick shrugged. "Only
they're not delusions. We can tell people what to think.

It's not ordinary property rights she has, Margaret. She owns one of the most important information monopolies in the country. Getting a president to resign might only be a beginning."

"You're exaggerating," Margaret said. "Besides, Nick, you've had that power all along. And before you, Charlie. She has a right to clip your wings."

"The full extent of our power was only a myth, until we proved we were stronger than the presidency, stronger than our most powerful institution. It's like putting an atomic bomb in the hands of a child."

"That's so typical of you men," Margaret sneered. "Since when are you the sole repository of all wisdom? As soon as a woman gets ascendant you buck like hell." She threw her head back and laughed, the deep well of some secret malevolence revealed. "She's cutting your balls off, Nick, and there's not a goddamned thing you can do about it."

His mind groped for a reply. But he was too stunned to respond. He could only look at her empty-eyed.

"You seem almost joyful about it," he said after a long pause, recovering himself.

"Not joyful. Oddly proud to see her make the move. But damned upset about you."

"And the thing with Henderson?"

"The prerogative of power."

"You've missed the point."

"You asked me for advice."

"You're advising capitulation."

"I'm facing reality."

He searched her face for some softness, a sense of yielding. But he could find no solace there, only the harshness of her own fixation, the warped vision of generations of trapped females. But the fact that she was torn, teetering between the poles of her inner life, invalidated her advice.

He stood up, felt shakiness in his knees, as he looked down at her seated figure, bloated by time, the big breasts no longer objects of desire, merely appendages.

He put on his shoes and staggered, letting himself

out, not looking back. It was quite enough for one night. Perhaps he was only dreaming after all, a nightmare induced by a late snack of heavy cheese, and he was really lying on his bed, fully dressed, still waiting for Jennie. But once outside, his sense of place returned. He breathed deeply, felt better as gulps of fresh air recharged him.

There were no cabs to be found, and after he had stood in the chill for some time, he began to walk again, feeling now the drag of his exhaustion as he willed himself forward. Tiredness, he knew, had always left him vulnerable.

Each of them, Margaret and Myra,. had good reason to detest her femaleness, had always detested it. He felt compassion for them. But what did it matter to him? If that was the issue then he was doomed. There were simply no defenses against it. Like his marriage. Destroyed before it began.

In his bedroom again, he undressed. Even the aching absence of Jennie seemed trivial. It was nearly five. He lay on the bed, and felt his pores open, the juice of his sweat emptying over his skin. It was, he knew, a time to search deep within himself.

He was suffering, he suspected, from brutalizing self-analysis, from an offensively programmed Semitic reaction which insisted on sweeping into all the inner corners, overturning all the psychic furniture to get at every wisp of offending dust. This thing that he had discovered, lurking under the carpet's edge, hard as rock, was his own fear. It had him scared out of his wits. The ends of his hair ached. He was frightened, terror-stricken, frozen with petrification at the prospect of catastrophic events rushing down at him like a great tidal wave.

Without the *Chronicle* what would his life be? Without the *Chronicle,* he was certain his mind would explode, his tissues clog, his cells atrophy. What did he care about Henderson and his insufferable blue eyes, his ambition, his aspirations? What mattered was the

Chronicle and he was the *Chronicle*. The paper was a mirror of his soul, his prejudices, tastes, hopes, ideas, passions. When he changed a comma, the subtle rearrangement sent shocks through an army of analysts who probed, ingested, and regurgitated the words he had let through the screen. It was not the illusion of power that he held in his fingers, the kind of negative veto power that Myra, up to now, had been content with, could play with, like a form of masturbation. It was real, raw, uncut, creative power, the kind that counted, that could move men's minds. He had always been modest in his own evaluation of the extent of this power, but now, with fear splashing all around him, he could tell himself exactly what was at stake. The prospect of handing this kind of control to Myra was preposterous, stultifying, patently sinful. It was one thing to have a disembodied idea of how the world might be refashioned, to maintain a posture of political ideology, to control the sword of Damocles that hung over all public figures, but quite another to exercise the balance that kept the credibility of the machinery intact.

Was it his ego or his fear? The *Chronicle* gave meaning to his life. To lose it might prompt him to the gun case, like Charlie, to whom the recently oiled guns and the clearly visible keys were unmistakable road signs to oblivion. Even avenging angels could not be perfect, he told himself finally, the fear beginning to recede, like a flood seeking the level of gravity.

He could imagine Henderson and Myra spending long hours in contemplation of their envisioned world, mulling over the abstractions of political promise, the details of the impending joint rule outlined, expanded. Between them they could control America. He could imagine Henderson posing as the zealot, fresh-faced, craggy, high-cheeked, the blue eyes blazing with contrived sincerity as he pandered, persuaded, flattered, assured her that he, Henderson, was her kind. Little did he know that he was ransoming his manhood.

Let her have her goddamned president, he agreed

finally, feeling drowsiness descend. It was giving him too much pain to resist. Nothing was forever.

The sound of the alarm found him, like a beam of light in a dark pit. He felt surprisingly refreshed, although he had only slept for two hours. At first he had reached out, feeling for Jennie, her warm flesh. He felt ridiculous. That was another thing, he vowed. He would untangle himself from these debilitating emotional distractions, these unnecessary anxieties that drained energy. Not that he would abdicate sexual adventures, and Jennie was a great comfort in that way, but to step over the brink of emotional chaos, was, he felt now, adolescent stupidity.

He showered, found himself whistling, and dressed, picking out his newest suit, blue pinstriped, vested, and choosing a gay tie that Jennie had bought him. There's life in the old carcass yet, he told himself, patting his greying hair, and rearranging it over the crown to hide the growing bald spot.

Outside it was a bright morning, although a chill persisted. He hailed a cab. There was luck in the swift response, he agreed, a kind of harbinger of good tidings. Saturdays at the *Chronicle* were mainly reflective days, since most of the huge Sunday edition had been locked in, a great mass of trivia, filler for the gobs of advertising that hungered for their mass Sunday circulation, which was more than fifty percent that of the daily and double that of their nearest competitor. It was good to be thinking about the technical details of newspapering again, although contemplation of the Sunday paper always elicited a kind of professional despair. It was a formless monster, a mass of treacle, with inserts upon inserts falling over each other like snowflakes. As a work of newspaper art, it was a mess, although financially it was a fantastic success, which inhibited motivation for change. But he was ashamed of it, another symbol of compromise that he somehow managed to live with. After all, he could tell himself and those among his staff who found the courage to protest, the

Chronicle was not an eleemosynary institution—a cop-
out that would send some of them scratching in panic
for their dictionaries. He resolved now to renew his
efforts at rethinking its structure, which meant gearing
for the inevitable clash with Delaney and the rest of
the advertising department. He chuckled at the prospect. It was good, reassuring, to think about.

Myra's house came into view on his right. He signaled the driver to pull into her driveway. What the
hell, he thought. It was time to reduce the tensions, remove the anxieties. He'd tell her he'd drop the Henderson story, although he foresaw problems with Gunderstein and now Martha Gates and Robert Phelps. He
should have let it die aborning. Besides, he could always
hide behind the veil of inconclusiveness, the absence
of an airtight second source.

In every war there is an appropriate, even honorable
time to retreat. Nothing should ever be measured in
absolutes, he told himself. Let Myra have her little victory. There were a thousand subtle ways to scuttle the
machinery, gum up the works. A new tactic was called
for now. Let it appear as surrender. He would simply
call off the confrontation . . . for the moment.

Standing in her doorway, he felt light-headed, suffused with warmth. Wasn't he taking things far too
seriously? Hell, he chuckled to himself, he'd make her
a buddy, one of the boys. They'd cement their new
friendship by pissing side by side in the urinals.

The maid seemed hesitant, but let him in, leading
him to the den, paneled, filled with floor-to-ceiling
bookcases which he recognized as part of Mr. Parker's
extensive library. Two wing chairs faced a large fireplace. Between them, on the floor, was a thick animal
skin. He sat down on one of the chairs and crossed his
legs, looking about the room, enjoying the smell of recently burnt wood, stirring old boyhood memories of
forests and mysterious nights around the fire.

He noted two brandy snifters near the legs of the
opposite chair, indicating a cozy night spent peering
into the fire. On the floor above him, he heard hurried

movements, voices, then the sound of footsteps on the stairs. It was an intrusion on his part, he agreed, but necessary. Better to clear the air immediately.

Myra breezed into the room, her dressing gown rustling. Her hair looked freshly combed but her makeup was incomplete, still shiny, as if she had been interrupted while applying the finishing touches. She wore a thin smile and her eyes seemed nervous.

"Nick," she said, forcing a lightness, betrayed by the way she held her arms, hands buried in the pockets of her dressing gown, tight to her body, the bulges in the shiny material indicating fists.

"It's a lousy trick, Myra. A compulsion," he said, smiling at her confusion. He noted that she had refused to sit down, as if by standing she would emphasize the transitory nature of this visit, hasten his departure. He sensed her discomfort, but was not deterred. The news he brought, he thought, would be well worth the visit.

"I've been thinking over the Henderson thing, Myra," he began, deliberately leisurely. She watched him woodenly. "I believe Henderson, despite what he says, was mixed up in this Diem thing." He felt compelled to say that, to give her further evidence of his sacrifice. Could she find a measure of her own guilt? He hoped so. "But I've decided to drop it."

He watched her face brighten, the smile, held tightly, loosen and broaden, although the hands remained fisted in her dressing gown. Did he detect a deep sigh, tension giving way?

"Thank goodness, Nick," she said.

"You're the boss." She was, indeed.

"It's never been that way with us, Nick." In a way that was true. She seemed to be clipping her sentences, urging his departure. He was disappointed at her reaction, expecting more gratitude. Surely she could see the immensity of his decision?

"I'll have to do some fancy stepping as far as Gunderstein is concerned."

"You can handle it, Nick."

"I'm sure you don't want us to go overboard the

other way, Myra. You wouldn't want us to overkill him with kindness."

"No, I was only concerned about a kind of reverse bias. I just didn't want you to lose your objectivity about him."

He heard the echo of Mr. Parker, although that old gentleman would also have seen through the narrow, quite inaccurate definition of the word.

"I never intended to."

"He's our kind of folks, Nick," she said as if compelled to justify herself. "His is the kind of leadership we need. He stands for the same things as we do. I've talked to him. He's a warm, compassionate man and I'd hate to see us ruin him just on the verge of his greatest triumph. Nick, he deserves the chance. I'm convinced of that."

"I'll grant you that he's got great political acumen."

"More important, Nick, he knows what this country needs."

"You understand, Myra, that our dropping the story doesn't mean that it's dead by a long shot."

"We've calculated that." It was the first time she had used the collective pronoun, a portent of her complicity. "If the conservative press breaks it, it will backfire in their faces. Imagine throwing stones at their darling CIA. Actually it would raise his stock with their readers. We'd only worry about the *Times*, but their approach might be far more cautious, as it was in the last go-round." She checked herself, as if she hadn't expected to say so much.

"It's not important now, Myra. You sound as if you're planning his campaign strategy."

"Does it?" She smiled. "I'd better be more circumspect."

"It definitely wouldn't do to flaunt your bias, Myra. Now that we've made this decision, you should be cooler about it."

"If I can't be honest with you, Nick, then with whom?"

Remembering Margaret's conversation, he wondered if she really believed that. Her ability to slip into a skin of self-righteousness was maddening. Finally, he stood up. Her reaction seemed mechanical, distant, as if she had expected it all along. Once again, he had exaggerated his expectations. He noticed that her eyes were staring nervously at the two brandy snifters on the floor. He imagined that she wanted to bend down and pick them up, her passion for neatness offended.

"You've made the right decision, Nick," she said, lifting her eyes, for the first time removing her hands from her pockets, the fists gone. She thrust an arm through his and moved with him out of the den. "It's a great relief to me. It proves that we're not all that cold-blooded, are we, Nick?"

"That was never the issue, Myra," he protested lamely, conscious that he was trying to avoid any hint that he was pandering to her.

"We do have a responsibility to this country, Nick."

"And to the truth," he said.

"Absolutely."

He let himself be led through the hallway, toward the front door. Stopping for a moment, he pulled a paper from the pile on the table near the door. As he did so, he felt a brief tug, almost a physical magnetism, that channeled his vision toward a familiar leather purse lying beside the papers as if it belonged there, was comfortable being there. Its initials, that odd eccentricity, the J and the L in antiquated script flourishes, encapsulated the story, the cause of Myra's nervousness, the mute evidence of his betrayal. So Jennie was the conduit! He covered his sudden shock by a kind of stage business with the newspaper, as if he might be surprised by a story on the front page.

"What is it?" she asked, unsuspecting.

"I thought I saw something amiss here." He folded the paper and put it under his arm, turning toward her, feeling his upper lip quiver. She held out her hand, a farewell gesture. He took it mechanically in his, which had started to sweat. He cursed his own impotence, feeling the cutting edge of the castrator's knife.

"You'll have no regrets, Nick," he heard her say sweetly as the door closed behind him.

17

The heavy blow to the side of her head had sent her spinning across the main living room of the old Parker house. She fell in a heap, her hair awry, her stocking torn. Charlie stood over her, remorseless, glass in hand, his eyes dancing with drunken rage and madness. Then he had sent the glass where she had fallen.

He had run toward the telephone, lifted the receiver as she screamed to him: "Please, no, Nick."

But Charlie had by then grabbed a whiskey bottle by the neck, removing the cap with his teeth as he up-ended it between his lips, sucking it, like a baby with a bottle, the liquor pouring over his chin. He rushed into the den, wobbling, his shoulders banging against the jambs as he slid the heavy doors shut. They heard the click as he locked himself in.

Nick rushed to help her off the floor. She stood unsteadily, rubbing the side of her head where the blow had fallen, brushing her dress, uncomfortable at the indignity of her condition.

"You took him out too soon, Myra," he admonished.

He had been surprised when she told him only the day before that she was bringing him home.

"He seems better, Nick," she had said cheerfully on the phone. It was an uncommon call. "And I feel so damned guilty about leaving him there."

"What do the doctors say?"

"Doctors," she said with undisguised contempt.

"I hope you know what you're doing."

"We'll see," she said.

An unholy alliance, he and Myra. By then it had stretched over two years, this descent into the pit, as Myra would characterize it in hurried whispers each time Nick carted Charlie back home to the Parker house. Because his condition was masked by drunkenness it was hard to tell how lucid he would be once the effects of the alcohol wore off. At first he was contrite, ashamed. Then nothing mattered. One simply stood aside and watched. To be a watchdog was futile. Charlie was simply descending into a private hell, his own mind. Sometimes Nick would be in at the beginning. It might start as an allegedly innocent drink at Matt Kane's self-named authentic Irish pub, a noisy contrivance, beer-soaked, screamingly ethnic, where the American Irish might imagine that outside the door was the old sod. It had, though, the same odd ambience of Shanley's, the same reddening Irish faces, the same startling eloquence and self-pity.

Quickly, Charlie became a celebrity in the netherworld of Matt Kane regulars. They were a motley assortment: tired waitresses, their big butts perched ominously on the bar chairs, loquacious government intellectuals whose obnoxiousness increased in proportion to their intake, the failed and lonely, some, like Charlie, worldly successful, others merely worldly. The bartender's name was Murray, wildly incongruous, he remembered, since there couldn't have been a single Murray in all of Ireland. For five bucks, he would keep an eye on Charlie while Nick walked the two blocks back to the *Chronicle,* picking up the reins of leadership that Charlie had by then cast aside. At first he had tried euphemisms, little evasions, white lies, to hide Charlie's condition from the *Chronicle* staff. But the stragglers at Matt Kane's soon spread the word, and what people had thought was merely an indisposition on the part of their executive editor was now specifically diagnosed.

At first he had tried to be a loyal friend and companion, dutifully spending the time at Charlie's side until the wee hours of the morning, then steering his friend to the car and planting him at his doorstep. But that soon proved debilitating. He had not yet learned to exist on four hours' sleep and Margaret was using the evidence to increase the pressure for separation.

"I think you're carrying this too far, Nick," she would say, turning in her sleep, heavy-lidded and annoyed because she had been awakened.

"I owe it to him."

"I suppose," she would grunt, rolling heavily from side to side to find her comfort again. "But I think you're a damned fool." She might have thought he was joining in the drinking. There was always a slight odor of alcohol, a brief dab since he rarely let himself have more than three drinks a night while Charlie guzzled to insensibility.

Charlie did make valiant attempts to return to work each morning, a white hulk, hands out of sight to hide the shakes, beads of sweat on his forehead as he struggled for concentration, a pot of coffee at his side.

"You're killing yourself, old friend," Nick would say, feigning light-hearted disinterest.

"I'll get over it, Nick."

"Not unless you break this cycle."

"I will."

"Why don't you get away, Charlie?" he would sometimes plead. "You and Myra. Take a trip somewhere."

He would look up, eyes blazing with hatred.

"With that bitch? Are you crazy?" It was the focal point of his rage, an obsession. Soon he gave up the pretense of working, hardly able to survive through the first editorial conference and he was off to Matt Kane's, usually arriving before the barstools had been taken off the bar.

Because it had happened by degrees, there was always the hope that Charlie might snap out of it, as from a periodic bender. He had learned from his experience at the *News* that there was a rhythm to these episodes. At the *News,* when a man called in sick, his colleagues would nod knowingly, calculating that the absent peer would emerge in a few days physically ravaged but psychically refreshed. But Charlie, although he tried, could not emerge. Not that he was without courage. Sometimes he would make it almost to the point of the budget meeting, then shamefacedly mumble some excuse and disappear out of the city room, trailing his jacket as he walked heavy-stepped toward the elevators.

After months of this behavior, Nick had expected Myra to call, to consult. But she remained aloof. And yet he sensed that he could feel her eyes staring down at him from one of the upstairs windows of the house as he led Charlie to the front door, putting the key into the lock and turning it quietly, pushing the door aside for Charlie to stumble through. Perhaps she was too ashamed, humiliated, although it seemed a measure of her confidence that she assumed he was handling Charlie's editorial duties with some skill. Apparently she always had confidence in that.

Finally she had come into the office. Nick had found her there sitting at Charlie's desk, looking vaguely confused, trying desperately to wear a pose of authority. She was sitting stiff and prim in Charlie's chair, staring at an opened copy of the morning paper. He had seen her first through the glass, a pitiful figure, paralyzed with fear, immobilized by the sudden reality of being in Charlie's place.

He would always remember his own resentment at seeing her, wondering if Charlie had finally been unable to get out of bed. He looked at his watch, calculating that Charlie's driver might be just hauling him awake and throwing him into the shower. It had come to that by then. He went into Charlie's office, feeling vaguely annoyed.

"Myra," he said, feigning surprise, masking his real feelings. She looked up at him, her helplessness undisguised.

"I feel I owe it to my father," she said apologetically, "to be here." She was hesitant, confused. He watched her without pity.

"Is he very bad this morning?" he said, forcing himself to be gentle.

"It's hard to tell," she said. "He's beyond communication." She lit a cigarette and Nick noted that the ashtray was already filled with half-smoked lipstick-tipped cigarettes. "I'm determined that my father's work shall not go down the drain," she said, her voice strained. Then, turning to face him, "I need your help, Nick."

He nodded. There was not much else he could do. Suddenly the telephone rang on Charlie's desk, startling her. She looked at it dumbly, her resolve fading swiftly as she watched it without reaching for it. He could see her panic, and made no move to rescue her. It rang again. She stamped out her cigarette and stood, stepping back from the desk, as if the telephone were something threatening, evil. It rang again, persistent, urgent. Was he being cruel not to pick up the receiver, end its ringing? It had become one of those frozen moments of regret and years later he had wondered if it might have been a cause for secret contempt. And yet it was the very first time that he could sense the feel of her power over him, despite her hesitancy, her helplessness.

He could never recall whether the telephone had stopped of its own accord, for Charlie's voice had intruded, crackling with anger, startling them both, as he emerged through the office door, a shaky pale figure, dapples of red flush painted on either cheek.

"What the hell are you doing here?" he shouted at her. Faces in the half-filled city room looked up, embarrassed. Some turned away, perhaps sensing some future retribution for being a witness to the event.

"I will not let you destroy this paper," she said, the strength in her voice ebbing. He was beginning to feel some compassion for her.

"You get the fuck out of here," Charlie shouted.

"Charlie," Nick said, the words sticking in his throat as he made a move toward him. But Charlie moved, as if his very survival had been challenged.

"You keep out of this, Nick." He turned again toward Myra, now cowering, a cornered helpless animal. "I want you the fuck out of here," he shouted again, his arm outstretched, shaking a finger, pointing to the door.

"You've no right."

"You get out of here."

"I will not," she said, summoning every ounce of her defiance.

"You get out of here or I'll kill you. I swear I'll kill you, you miserable bitch." His hand reached for some object on the desk, a small paperweight, which fell from his hand as it left the support of his desk. Nick jumped toward him, reaching to restrain him. But he managed to shake himself free and swing out at her, as she covered herself with her arms, expecting a blow to fall.

"I think you better go," Nick shouted, struggling to keep Charlie's arms pinned to his sides.

"I will not go," she said, recovering some determination. "I belong here. I have every right."

Charlie became slack in his arms, a ruse, Nick discovered, for as soon as he relaxed his hold, Charlie stiffened, managing to loosen an arm which he swung in Myra's direction, catching her in the upper arm, the force of the blow pushing her against the wall.

"If you don't stop, Charlie, I'll have to call someone." Nick's threat seemed to calm him.

"I just want her out of here," he said quietly, almost pleading.

"Please, Myra," Nick begged.

"Let him go," she said, rubbing her arm, glancing toward the city room, watching the tense faces. Charlie seemed suddenly spent as Nick released him. Sitting down on a chair, he slumped over and put his hands over his face. Myra came forward and put a hand on his head.

"It's all right, Charlie," she said, tears misting her eyes, as she raised them and looked helplessly at Nick. He was sorry for her now, sorry for them both.

"I'll go now," she said, looking at Nick, who could sense the beginning of their alliance. Or was it a conspiracy?

Apparently the realization that he could be violent had some effect and Charlie quickly submitted himself to treatment, allowing himself to be registered in a local sanitorium. There they attempted to dry him out while a battery of doctors poked around in his head for some hint of his malady. Even Myra could appear hopeful on the telephone, reporting to Nick as part of their new relationship, although she obediently refrained from setting foot in the city room.

"He's improving, Nick. Really improving. And he looks marvelous. He's even beginning to talk to me." She laughed gaily, like a young girl.

"Great," he would comment, then reassuringly, "Everything is under control up here. Tell Charlie we're not letting him down."

"I know that, Nick. I'm very grateful." He felt her sincerity and he threw himself into his work with passion.

It was the first of many cures. Charlie always returned well rested, tanned, filled with enthusiasm, and with vials of pills, which he lined in his desk drawer, but quickly refused to take.

"They're trying to poison me," he assured Nick, and soon he was back at Matt Kane's, caught in the mist of his confusion, now complicated by an odd sexuality, as if booze could no longer be an efficient escape.

He had befriended a huge, big-buttocked woman named Mary Lou. Coarse-featured, with hair dyed a reddish mouse color. She drank great quantities of beer and possessed a howling laugh that could splinter the air, an abrasive, nerve-racking sound.

By then, Nick was paying Murray regularly to make sure he got home in one piece. Even his driver had quit and Nick had refused to play watchdog again. One couldn't possibly keep up with Charlie's pace, losing sleep, then be expected to put in a grueling day at the *Chronicle.* This did not prevent shattering intrusions of telephone calls in the night, when Charlie could not be placated.

"You better come over, Mr. Gold. I can't be responsible," Murray would hiss urgently into the phone. On the first occasion of the complication with Mary Lou, he had rushed into his pants with a sweater thrown over his pajama top and jumped into his car for a wild ride to Matt Kane's. When he banged on the now closed door Murray opened it swiftly, his face oddly calm with a broad smile breaking on his face, irritating to Nick, whose heart had not yet stopped beating in anxiety. Without a word, Murray's head indicated the direction in which Charlie could be found.

Charlie and Mary Lou half lay, half stood, in an amorphous mass, totally senseless, knotted together it seemed, obviously too much for one man to extricate.

"I just couldn't lift them." Murray shrugged as he looked at the ceiling. "What the hell was I supposed to do?"

"They're gone," Nick said.

"Gone," Murray agreed.

Between him and Murray they managed to get Charlie and Mary Lou separated. It was ludicrous, Nick thought, sadly seeing his friend's deterioration, the sympathy waning, since Charlie was a burden now, beyond rationality. Seeing them, the blank mooning paralyzed faces, the rubbery limbs, the deadweight immobility, he could not resist the humor the scene invoked.

"The lovers," Murray said.

"A beautiful couple," Nick replied with disgust.

Black humor, it seemed in retrospect, for Charlie and

Mary Lou became in the next few weeks a weird kind of Bonnie and Clyde duo.

To make matters worse there were moments of lucidity, or apparent lucidity, since the words were clear but the logic faulty, in which he was forced to witness his friend's further debasement. One afternoon Charlie called him at the *Chronicle,* urging him to rush over to his house, an invitation he would just as soon have declined, especially in the middle of the day with the endless pressures of the *Chronicle* building to their peak.

Charlie apparently had shaved and cleaned himself up, dressed himself in a silk robe, and seemed unaccountably steady after his usual night's revelries. He rarely showed up at the *Chronicle* anymore. He and Myra sat facing each other on the matching wing chairs, the ones that later had been used to front the fireplace of her cozy den. There was a strange air of calm in the room. Myra looked at him briefly as he came in, lowering her eyes. It was apparent she had been humoring him. Charlie sat stiffly in the chair, pale, the first traces of his future gauntness beginning, since his diet was now erratic, as if the act of eating were offensive.

"We've agreed to separate, Nick," Charlie said. Myra nodded, shrugging.

"I told him I wouldn't stand in the way of his happiness," Myra said. She seemed to be playing a role.

"I love Mary Lou, Nick," Charlie said. He had half expected him to wink. Nick summoned up the memory of the woman, a glob of flab in Matt Kane's bar. They had since been checking into various Washington hotels from which he had finally been called upon to extract them. It was becoming a public embarrassment to both Myra and himself, not to mention the *Chronicle,* although one could depend on the discreet Washington hotel managers to keep the matter quiet. Besides, he controlled what went into the *Chronicle* and there was, after all, a gentlemen's agreement between competitive editors. It was quite rare, almost nonexistent, to find media competition spilling over into the denigration of editorial personalities. Myra knew they were quite safe on that score.

"You should follow your loving instincts, Charlie," Myra responded, as if she were speaking to a small child.

"I know I've been acting strange these last few months, but I'm convinced now that Mary Lou is what I need."

"Whatever you say, Charlie," Myra said. "Don't try to talk him out of it, Nick," she said, winking.

"I don't intend to."

Charlie stood up.

"You can't know how it feels to be in love," he said. Nick wondered why he had been called, then realized that Myra had persuaded Charlie to call, to witness this new aberration, a kind of final validation of his madness, which indeed it was. She, too, had seen Mary Lou. Keeping an eye on them had been a full-time job and she had been reluctant to recommit him, but this meeting was apparently an attempt to convince herself that there was no longer any choice. The evidence was compelling. Myra looked at him, her eyes indicating that she was about at the end of the rope.

"I know when I'm licked," Myra said to Charlie, who took the remark in a totally different context.

"You're very understanding, Myra," Charlie said. "Considering the way I've treated you, that's very understanding. Don't you think so, Nick?"

"Yes, Charlie, very understanding."

"But I do think you should check yourself into the hospital. Get yourself together. You'll see how wonderful you'll feel." She winked again. "Even Mary Lou will think so."

Reacting like a wind-bent tree snapping back after a heavy gust, Charlie stood up, his face contorting.

"Never," he said. "See, Nick. See, she wants me out of the way. I'll never go back there."

"It was just a suggestion," Myra said quickly.

"All I need is Mary Lou."

"Sure, Charlie, sure," Nick responded. Charlie sat down again, briefly placated.

"You'll see," he said, then looked ominously at Myra. "She'll never put me away again." Charlie's hands began to shake and sweat started to show on his forehead. Nick watched him, glazed, lucidity fading, lips twisting as if he couldn't make up his mind whether to laugh or smile. Suddenly he got up and walked out of the room.

"I'm scared to death, Nick."

"You've got good reason," he conceded.

"This thing with Mary Lou. It's beyond belief. It's a wonder he hasn't come down with a physical disease." She stood up, walked the length of the large room, then back again. He noted that her fingers clutched a handkerchief. "I've got to put him away, Nick. I think we've both got to face the fact that he's almost beyond hope." Nick didn't answer. He couldn't bring himself to echo her sentiment, to articulate the truth of it, legitimize it. Myra was no Mr. Pell, no dedicated saint ready to sacrifice her life to someone else's madness. As if reading his thoughts, she said, "He could do something crazy at the *Chronicle*. Undermine all that has been built up."

"That he built up," Nick corrected, annoyed at his compulsion. What good did it do to defend Charlie now? It seemed a lost cause.

"I know, Nick. Believe me, I'm grateful." It was a clue to the way she thought, that Charlie had built up the *Chronicle* for them, her and her father, always the son-in-law. She looked at her watch.

"I told them to come at four," she said, looking at the grandfather clock in the corner. "I don't think I have a choice."

He still refused to agree. He knew he was being selfish, insuring himself against future regrets. When Charlie came back into the room, he held a glass of whiskey in his hand. He sat down cross-legged in the wing chair.

"My father hid my bicycle," he said, suddenly giggling. Something tugged at Nick's memory, the neat house, the clean snow, the painted face of his mother, the talk of bicycles. It was almost as though he had willed himself to madness. Myra looked at him and sighed. See, she seemed to say, there is no hope.

It was not easy for them to remove him from the living room. Two big burly men held him down on the floor while they strapped him into an ugly khaki-colored straitjacket. He writhed and fought them, finally in his helplessness reverting to spitting, screaming like some abandoned animal. Myra gripped Nick's arm, digging her fingernails into his biceps as she watched them lift Charlie between them and carry him to the waiting ambulance.

"What could I have done?" she said, turning to Nick as they heard the ambulance leave the driveway. "I had no choice." Still he refused to respond, feeling that to do so would be a betrayal of his doomed friend.

"I didn't want this to happen, Nick."

But he only half-believed it, not that it was the first time that Charlie had been committed. "What choice did I have?"

Remembering that scene, he had secretly agreed with her decision, although he could not, would not give her the satisfaction of affirming it. She had, indeed, been abused by Charlie in the last months, physically, mentally, cruelly used. He, Nick, had also been driven to despair. But why couldn't he trust her, with the same warm openness that he imagined had existed between him and Charlie? Had Charlie ruined that possibility forever?

Perhaps that was why he was confused when she had called him that day and told him that Charlie was coming home again, that he had made great progress, that he was ready for a return to meaningful living. It had been a placid time at the paper. He was careful not to make major changes, as if to tamper with the existent chemistry would somehow be an act of disloyalty. Besides, the *Chronicle* seemed to be moving relentlessly forward, powered by Charlie's early decisions, creating the inertia of success. Even Myra held back, although

they met occasionally with advisors, the various business types, whom he detested.

He wondered if he, too, had been actually expecting
to hear the shotgun blast, a single sound-searing explosion that shook the windows in the room and
twinkled the bric-a-brac. Neither he nor Myra had
moved quickly, rooted. He had wondered why Myra
had turned her face from his, as he finally roused himself and opened the sliding doors. The room was a
mess, the ceiling and walls slopped with bloody pulp.
Even at the initial horror of the sight, he remembered
Charlie's sloppiness when they lived together in New
York. With his usual disdain for neatness, he had put
the shotgun in his mouth, pointed upward. Even in
death, his features showed no calm, distorted by the
blast, as if he had exited cursing. Stepping backward, he
slid the doors closed and turned to Myra, shaking
helplessly now in a far corner of the room. He would
save the questions for later, he decided, the matter of
the oiled guns, the access to the case, the availability
of ammunition.

18

Saturday was a day when Washington motors were revved down and those workaholics who insisted on attending to the bureaucracy's business, or their own, could be seen in their offices blue-jeaned and sport-shirted, assuaging loneliness, persuading themselves that they were involved with their highest priorities.

In the city room of the *Chronicle,* the difference of the day could be detected in subtle ways. The sound of the reporters' typewriters, more thoughtful and labored. The murmur of conversation among the staff, leisurely, expansive. For the staff of the *Chronicle,* Saturday was distinctively make-work, a time of suspended hopefulness.

In his office, the coffee steaming beside him, its pungent odor deliciously tranquilizing, he could feel again the mastery of himself, the agitation dissipating as his mind picked up the rhythm of his work. He assured himself that he would not let emotions rule his judgment, that he would preserve this oasis within himself, this place of purity, where there would be no ruffling breezes, no changes in temperature, or seasons, or time, or even light. Let people victimize others or themselves by betrayal and mendacity. He would simply lock himself in that pure place, that chamber of weighted judgments, through which the information would have to pass, through him, the screen. He would become the disembodied brain, all mysterious inner systems alert and ready for decision. No amount of outside interference would deflect his concentration.

From where he sat he could see Gunderstein, Phelps, and Martha Gates, a triumvirate of conspirators, he thought, glancing at him in turn, waiting for the word. It would not be the first time he had dashed golden hopes. What did it matter? It was all a pinprick on the ass of time, he told himself. He had made his decision. His resolution was clear. It must not be deflected by what he had just learned about Jennie and Myra. One thing had absolutely nothing to do with the other. He was surprised, too, that he could not sustain the anger, or the humiliation of having been deceived. To have illusions about Jennie's sense of faithfulness would have been the epitome of self-deception. Her ambitions were suspect from the beginning and he had just been a simple rock across the stream, the stepping-stone. A fair trade, he had concluded. He had gotten his money's worth.

He looked at his watch. The editorial meeting was scheduled for nine-thirty, a half hour away. Lifting his head again, he watched the unholy three waiting for their chance, animals anticipating raw meat. He could sense the tension transmitted between them, as his mind sought logical explanations, credible rationalizations. He might say, for example: "Look, kids. If we run that piece, yours truly will be wasted." It was a good word for honesty, a military word incongruously hatched in connection with Viet Nam. "You wouldn't want to see the old boy canned, would you now? Truth? Responsibility? Come on now, kids. He who fights and runs away, lives to fight another day. Besides, there is no absolute, positive, conclusive, undeniable proof." He could always use that as the final cop-out, the ultimate ploy. "You must understand that nothing is all black or all white. We're newspaper people, not judges."

Better face them now, he told himself, feeling the inadequacy of his hypothetical explanations. Perhaps in the give and take he would think of something more convincing. Maybe he would find some clue in them, in their reaction. Lifting his arm, he hailed them.

Watching their faces as they came in, he could feel their anticipation. Martha Gates, her blond hair glistening and fresh, like golden thread, her eyes dancing, smiled as she entered. He could actually read what the others must have felt in the young girl's face, the clean, satisfied look of dedication. Apparently there was an agreement between them that the older man would provide the opening gambit. Phelps was clean-shaven, clear-eyed, the pipe jaunty in his teeth, the grey hair neatly combed.

"We've written the story, Nick," he said, putting a sheaf of copy paper on the desk. "Spent half the night at it." Gunderstein, who surely had guided the typewriter keys, sat impassively picking his pimples. Nick had not expected this complication. He looked down at the offering with revulsion, resisting the impulse to read it.

"We've concluded," Phelps said, "that there can only be one decision you can make. The issue demands presentation. It goes to the very heart of the system, not only of ethics in the intelligence community, but the moral obligation of our national leadership. It simply can't be ignored."

"And you're absolutely convinced," Nick said, stupidly, he felt.

"There is not a shadow of a doubt that this was standard practice for the CIA, on direct orders of the President—all presidents since Eisenhower. There is enough evidence to cast suspicion."

"And Henderson?"

"He's going to have to pay the piper."

"In 1963, it would have been concluded that it was an act of patriotism." He felt he was going over old ground, stalling. He knew they could detect his hesitation.

"Patriotic or not, it was still immoral."

"Absolutely," Martha Gates chirped. She seemed certain that he would give them a complete go-ahead. "It's not the moral question alone, Mr. Gold. It's . . ."

"But it is," Phelps interrupted. "In the end it boils down to a moral question."

"We run a newspaper, Robert," Nick said, thankful for the issues being raised, "not a church."

"You can't deny we have a moral point of view," Phelps persisted, looking at Martha, who was watching him with admiration. Had Phelps made love to her, Nick wondered, prancing like a cock in a barnyard, preening his feathers?

"You can't take it lightly, Nick," Phelps said, flushing. "How can you preach a kind of national morality and deny this story? It's wrong. Patently wrong."

"I agree," Martha Gates said. Gunderstein kept his eyes on Nick, searching for a reaction.

"I think if you'll just read the story, Mr. Gold," Gunderstein said, "it will speak for itself."

Peripherally, Nick could see Henry Landau's tanned face peering through the glass. Welcoming the intrusion, he felt the emergence of a new idea.

"We're going to have an editorial meeting in a few minutes. Let's submit the story to them."

They seemed caught unawares by his new tack. Phelps exchanged a knowing glance with Martha. He knew the two of them would be easily persuaded, led into the trap like sheep. After all, how could they possibly believe that other fair-minded men could not see the compelling moral position?

"No," Gunderstein said quietly, his pimples reddening, the Adam's apple bobbing in his thin neck. Phelps and Martha turned to him in confusion.

"No," Gunderstein repeated, "that wouldn't be right at all."

"Why not?" Phelps asked as Martha's eyes flitted between them.

Gunderstein ignored them and looked at Nick, who could see the glisten of his contact lenses as they caught the light.

"You know why, Mr. Gold," he said. Of course, Gunderstein knew his motive. The men around the editorial table were too ideological, oriented to the Left, protective of the liberal view. It wouldn't do to have them sit in judgment on one of their darlings.

"I don't understand," Nick lied. "These are people of great independent spirit and judgment."

"That's not the point," Gunderstein said.

"Then what is?" Nick snapped. He couldn't understand why he could not simply will the story out of existence. He had the power to do so and he had accepted his surrender. Why did they complicate matters with their insufferable principles? He felt himself losing patience, knew that Gunderstein's view of him was diminishing. If he were Gunderstein he might feel the same way. What would Gunderstein do in his place? He knew that too. Gunderstein would have walked, turned his back and simply walked away. What would Charlie have done?

"The decision is yours to make, Mr. Gold. You're our editor."

"If the story has integrity, it should stand up before these men."

"That's not their job," Gunderstein said with conviction.

"I don't see why you're so wary, Harold," Phelps said.

"The story stands by itself. It has nothing to do with moral principles or your own feelings of guilt."

"That's absurd," Phelps said. "My feelings are not involved."

"I really don't believe that, Robert," Gunderstein said quietly. Nick knew he was right. "It's not meant to be insulting. You've been very helpful to the story, Robert. You've been a corroborative source and a great help in shaping the story. In fact, your knowledge of events in Viet Nam in 1963 has been crucial, the missing link.

"But this moral stuff is not relevant," Gunderstein said, ignoring the attempt to be insulting. "The story is quite simple. Henderson is quite obviously running for President. He has something in his past that bears on the question of his future leadership. Many might condone his action or even the suspicion of his action. Others will detest it. Who are we to ascribe constituencies? Make prejudgments on the political impact of the story? That's all irrelevant. You mustn't let that inhibit your judgment, Mr. Gold."

"I'm afraid it does, Harold," Nick said gently, feeling Gunderstein's confusion.

"It shouldn't be submitted to the editorial conference. They also deal in moral postures. It's not their job. I'd rather you reject the story yourself than submit it to them."

"Well, it wouldn't frighten me," Phelps said, pouting.

"Nor me," Martha said.

"It was just a suggestion," Nick said sheepishly. "I wanted to be fair since my inclination is to reject it."

"I can't believe it," Phelps said.

"On what grounds, Mr. Gold?" Martha Gates asked.

He felt cornered, unable to come up with an adequate explanation.

"I really feel put upon, Nick," Phelps said. "You send for me from across the country. I feel misled. Used badly. Really, Nick. It wasn't fair." It seemed odd to hear protestations of unfairness from one his age. Coming from Martha Gates, who obviously agreed with Phelps' assessment, it might not have seemed so out of character.

"You'll just have to live with your disillusionment, Robert. After all, you managed it for more than a decade. You've had lots of practice swallowing your sense of morality." He paused, feeling rotten. "I'm sorry," he said, tasting the backwash of his own cowardice.

"Ours not to reason why," Phelps said sadly. He seemed spent now, the optimism of his arrival gone.

"I don't see why you don't let him submit it to the others," Martha said.

"Gunderstein is right," Nick said. It was, after all, only a self-serving bureaucratic ploy, as Gunderstein knew.

"The story should be run," Gunderstein said.

Nick fingered the copy on his desk.

"I'll read it," he said. "I'll continue to keep an open mind."

"That's doubtful," Phelps said bitterly. Nick let it pass. Leave him something, he thought.

Gunderstein stood up, an action obviously protective of Phelps. He knew now why he admired Gunderstein.

Gunderstein was truly the man in the hermetic room, untouched by the river of emotion that threaded its way through a personal life, the unencumbered observer, the true journalist. During the heady days when they were pulling down the President, Gunderstein had been the centerpiece of the drama, the man who shook the trunk of the tree itself, rattling the coconuts to the ground. And yet he had never, like them, been ideologically committed. Gunderstein had taken only the slice of the glory that was his, while he and Myra glutted themselves on the moral niceties.

He would have liked to view the Henderson story from Gunderstein's viewpoint. But he was hopelessly trapped, compromised by position, by power, by age, by fear.

"I'll read it. That's the most I can promise," he said.

"I want you all to know," Phelps began—one could easily see he was headed for personal martyrdom.

"Don't, Robert," Nick warned, "it wouldn't be any use."

"It's contemptible, an outrage," Phelps said.

"Restrain it," Nick pleaded.

Phelps sputtered, a fleck of saliva on his lip. His eyes misted. "It's wrong, Nick, wrong." Martha Gates gripped Phelps' arm and moved him out of the office.

Let them think what they wanted, he decided. Somewhere along the line he would square it with Gunderstein. He watched them move from his office, not at all graceful in their defeat. Martha Gates turned back and watched him with unmistakable contempt.

"I'm sorry," he said, then seeing Gunderstein hesitate, he waved him back.

"There are wheels within wheels, Harold," he said, knowing that such a ridiculous explanation would hardly be adequate.

"Read the story, Mr. Gold."

"I will, Harold," he said, hoping that he could explain his position without revealing his infamy. He could find no other word to describe it, annoyed that Gunderstein could still find hope in the possibility of publication. It is as dead as Kelsy's nuts, he wanted to say and might have whispered it if Gunderstein had lingered a moment more.

Lighting a cigarette, he proceeded into the editorial conference, where the men were waiting. Things went smoothly, the sourness of their last two sessions muted with Bonville still pouting, nodding with eyes fixed on his yellow pad, as they agreed on the positions of the next day's editorials, bland subjects, it seemed.

"We could do something on gun control," Peterson suggested.

"Shotguns will never be regulated," Henry Landau said.

"Then how are these matters preventable?" Peterson retorted.

"They're not," Henry replied.

Nick could not focus his concentration and the meeting broke up earlier than usual.

Back in his office, he sat down heavily in his chair and looked again at the front page of the morning's *Chronicle,* studying the pictures of the bus massacre. Feeling someone staring at him, he looked up at the chocolate brown face of Virginia Atkins, who stood in the doorway, tall, defiant still, although he could detect a touch of contrition in her dark eyes.

"Can I see you a moment, Mr. Gold?"

"Sure," he said. Her voice was soothing, without a

trace of the stereotyped Southern caricature of the black man's tongue. She looked at him without fear.

"I want to apologize," she said.

"For what?"

"For that outburst of mine yesterday."

He remembered.

"In the heat of battle passions run high."

"Mine went through the roof. I wasn't professional. I let my blackness smother my objectivity."

That word again, he thought. "So you see it's not that easy to achieve." He felt he might be lecturing himself. He did not want to appear patronizing. Searching for a posture of grace, he wanted to match her dignity.

"I hope it won't affect your judgment of me, Mr. Gold. I've already talked to Mr. Madison."

"Did you square it with him?"

"Frankly, I wouldn't blame him if he screens my assignments."

"He'll come around," Nick said, knowing that Ben would bear his grudge.

"I'm prepared for the penance," she said, then pausing, "I want you to understand that it's not just wanting to protect my job. I know how lucky I am to be here. I just feel as if I let you all down somehow. I had no right to get carried away, to have lost my objectivity."

"You're not alone, Atkins." She nodded, then moved away, her dignity intact.

The city room was beginning to fill up again, although it would never reach the pitch of midweek. Luckily there was enough follow-up from yesterday's disaster to keep the reporters busy. The telephone rang.

"Nick?" It was a vaguely familiar voice. "This is Burt." Henderson again. His heart sank. What now?

"I've just talked to Myra. You can't imagine how much your decision means to me."

It was the insufferable ego of politicians to feel the need to offer thanks, as if the utterance of gratitude carried with it some sense of giving a kind of trophy. So she had called him immediately to be the harbinger of the good news.

"I really feel so damned grateful. Could you join me for lunch? I've got to be downtown and, frankly, Nick, I'd like to talk."

His first inclination was to refuse. There was nothing he had to say to Henderson, whose point had been won, who had found the key to press protection, an important commodity at this moment in his political career. He felt himself mumbling a half-hearted excuse.

"I'll meet you at Duke's at twelve-thirty," Henderson persisted, not hearing, or ignoring the refusal. Instantly he felt the sense of possession, the invocation of the rights of property. So they think they've wrapped me up, he thought, irritated.

"Sure, Burt," he said, repeating the place and time. The phone clicked off, leaving him to contemplate this subtle change in his role. He had given the inch and she had taken the mile. And yet, as he looked about the city room from his special perch, nothing had really changed. He could still pick up the telephone and order a total remake of the front page or the removal of a single offending word, a misplaced comma, the emasculation of a semicolon, the obliteration of a dangling participle. More important, he could deflect an offending idea at will, choke off an errant opinion, crush an incompatible ideology, and with the stiletto surety of his pencil weapon, he could exile a budding politician to obscurity at the flick of the lead. All but Henderson. The change, he felt in his panic, could hardly be termed subtle. Myra had made her move. He had given her veto power. He knew it was just the beginning.

He felt the need to validate his power, his sense of command. Picking up the phone, he asked the operator for Atkins' number, dialed it, watched her pick up the phone languidly from a desk in a spot along the far wall in the corner of the room.

"Come in here, Atkins," he commanded, watching her stiffen to alertness, rise quickly, and stride across the room, her long legs moving her gracefully toward him.

"I want you to put together a reflective piece on the bus killer," he said. "Really probe. Look inside the man. Give us an in-depth profile. I want motive, the things that prompted him to violence."

"You want me to do that?"

"Why not?"

"You know how I feel."

"I don't care how you feel."

She seemed confused, torn between dignity and despair.

"You said you were a professional. Now here's your chance to prove it." Was he making her a victim simply to prove something to himself? he wondered. Perhaps. But he had the right, the authority to order her to take the assignment, to direct its point of view, to dictate its conclusions. It was the perfect yardstick of his power. It was too bad she had chosen the wrong moment for apology. He had needed to throw something and she had become the handy rock at his elbow.

"I'll try, Mr. Gold," she said, fearful now, surely regretting her apology.

"You'll do more than try, Atkins. You'll perform." He watched her leave, picked up the phone, and dictated a note to the pool steno for Madison. Madison was off, he saw on the scheduling sheet. Weekends off were a prized possession at the *Chronicle,* the option of the privileged few.

Thumbing through the pile of wire copy, he noted that it would be a light news day. The world was strangely quiet; it would require deeper penetration to find the "hot" news stories. The pressure to fill pages was relentless and finding material that would measure up to front-page story value was difficult on doldrum days like these. The events of recent years had made them jaded. Wars, assassinations, corruption in the highest places in the land. The public was callous now, demanding more than it was in their capacity to purvey. Gone were the days when a simple killing could be thought of as an event. Murder had become too commonplace. Now only a mass murder like yesterday's could have enough impact to titillate the masses. Looking down the road, years from now, he wondered what the level of horror would have to be to create the kind of sensation that warranted a front-page headline. He could envision parameters requiring deaths by the score as even worthy of consideration. As for corruption, after a president, all else was anticlimax. Even war, after the horror of Viet Nam, would require weaponry of massive killing power, body counts in the millions, to bring the interest up to snuff. His eye roamed through the wire copy looking for news of India. Perhaps that was why his interest in India was becoming acute, the guerrilla warfare beginning, the impending deaths multiplying, the possibilities tantalizing in that sweaty, crowded, starving subcontinent on the verge of explosion. Would there be a story there?

It was no wonder that groups espousing causes sought ever greater levels of horror, staged events that by their sheer disgust could magnetize the media. Blow the head off a baby and it was a certainty that you could squeeze a few paragraphs into the story that would hawk your case in the crowded arena. Punch nails into the skull of an old lady and you might even get a picture out of it. He could envision the day when such horrors would require massive duplication to be worthy of mention, a world in which the gas chambers of Auschwitz could hardly merit a paragraph or two, when one might have to choose between that and say, the total obliteration of an island, like Ireland, for example, by atomic disintegration or nerve gas. A big kill of the whole population in one swoop. It was coming. The IRA might say: "If we can't have her, no one will." Given the state of destructive weaponry, it was quite possible. Now there would be a story! Against all that, he thought, what was Henderson, a mere annoyance, a pimple on the head of an erected penis, irritating, but not able to prevent one's using it. He found it pleasant to contemplate the situation in terms of sexual symbols. Somehow it took the sting out of the humiliation, assuaged the feeling of helplessness, as if the remembered pleasure of orgasm were more potent than the purely mental anguish of a bruised ego. It was like that Italian game of hands, where paper, the outstretched hand, covered rock, the tight fist. The telephone rang. He picked up the receiver. It was Jennie.

"You pissed off, Nick?" She was making an effort to emulate a little girl's voice, always a refuge, a weapon in her repertoire that had its effect in the past. He mocked her silently.

"Hell no, Jennie. Are you over your pout?"

"Completely. I was mad as hell at you, Nick."

"Maybe I was too damned heavy after all. I've got to leave you some pride."

"You mean all is forgiven?"

"Hell yes."

"You must have been worried. I was even too mad to leave a note."

"Forget it."

He was sure now how little he felt for her, and he found it liberating to know it. In a way he was grateful for the discovery of her—how could he characterize it?—peccadillo, disloyalty, brown-nosing the boss. The last was a potent image; she did have an infallible nose for power. Now Myra would have to protect her.

"Where are you?" he asked, hardly interested.

"Back at the grindstone."

He shrugged, saying nothing.

"It's good to hear your voice again, Nick. And it's good to know you're not mad at me." Perhaps Myra, too, had noticed the pocketbook on the table and had urged Jennie to test him, probe for suspicions. He wondered, too, if Myra had developed an emotional attachment for her, a natural identification with a younger woman whose ambitions would not be stifled by the prejudices of her own father. Sad for Myra, he thought. Without it they could have bounced her between them, he for flesh, she for solace. Now that he had severed the cord, what did it all matter?

"I'll see you back at the apartment later, Nick. Okay?"

"Sure," he said. "Why not?"

"You sure you're not angry?" She had detected the slight sarcasm.

"Not at all," he said, feeling a tug at his crotch, a hint of sexual delights to come. He chuckled to himself, knowing that he would no longer be rewriting her copy. Let Myra try, he thought, or Margaret.

He noted as he hung up that he had been fingering Gunderstein's copy, his attention caught by the compelling lead paragraph, drawing him into the story.

"On the day that Diem and his brother were assassinated, Senator Burton Henderson, then a young intelligence colonel in the army, was on special assignment in Saigon," the story began. It was written as all Gunderstein's stories were written, in flat prose, short sentences, unemotional, with the complete absence of both adjectives and interpretive adverbs, which could be so devastating in the hands of devious writers. A person could be described as doing something slowly, feeling something keenly, acting swiftly, and the meaning of the observation could be focused toward a desired response. Gunderstein was careful to avoid any hint of bias, any faint echo of prejudgment. His method was the simple juxtaposition of facts, piled one on another, a relentless parade, almost monotonous, like a bill of particulars being read in a monotone. There was no accusatory tone, no attempt at moral interpretation, no use of abstract subtle nuances. The story emerged just as it had been discovered: Allison's tip, his name appropriately omitted, and Phelps' observations, with copious quotes. Here interpretation was allowed since it was scrupulously ascribed to Phelps. Doubts and lack of corroboration were carefully annotated, not woven into the story but stated straight out, leaving the door open to denial. There were quotes from the Pentagon Papers, which outlined in detail the last days of Diem, Kennedy's motivation in having him removed by encouraging the coup of the generals, even the vague references to Diem's assassination as having been carried out by "rivals." And of course there were denials by the heads of the CIA, the State Department, and past officials of the Kennedy and Johnson administrations.

As a piece of journalism, Nick gave it high marks, although he was upset with himself for having read it, since at this stage it could only be an exercise in self-flagellation. Of one thing he was certain, the story would certainly turn off a large segment of Henderson's constituency. All the denials in the world would be powerless against the pregnant possibilities implied in the story. Henderson could cry foul from here to doomsday, but the voice would be drowned in the swamp of accusation. And he could hardly blame it on a conservative conspiracy. Its very appearance on the pages of the *Chronicle* would negate that. He was tempted to pick up the phone and compliment Gunderstein on his story, but felt his inhibition keenly, cursing Myra and his own inability to stand firm against her. Instead, he could only utter a weak profanity, and push the copy aside to the farthest corner of his desk, as if it were unclean, coated with deadly bacteria.

He was late getting to Duke's, having left the *Chronicle* building later than he had expected. The story had kept him absorbed, perhaps a subconscious sign that he should not be going to lunch with Henderson at all, knowing that somehow it would make him a party to the cover-up—an odd word to be dredging up, considering the events of the past.

Duke, his bald pate shining in the sunlight that streamed through the curtained windows, greeted him with a wisecrack and a heavy handshake. The restaurant was a hangout for politicians and athletes, a logical combination that gave the place a macho air, a den of masculine arrogance, clubby, with its front room kept carefully elite by its owner host. Huge cartoons showing the corpulent Duke as a paunchy athlete graced the walls while the smell of garlic in the ubiquitous pickles on each table set the gastronomic scene as distinctively

New Yorky. Saturdays were strictly slacks and sport shirts, the front room filled with Washington high and mighty. He caught sight of Henderson, placed by Duke for prominent display in the center of the room. In the corner he saw Swopes, owner of the Redskins, who would be their host at tomorrow's game. He waved a greeting. To be seen with Henderson, the act in itself, was a kind of bonding. Certainly, as Henderson and he both knew, it was a clue to relationship. In strictly Washington terms it dripped with special meaning. Enemies did not break bread in Duke's, certainly not on Saturdays.

Henderson stood up to greet him with a strong, pumping handshake, embellished by a squeeze to the biceps, as if to underline to those present that theirs was a tight friendship, not a casual encounter. Nick noticed that Henderson was nursing a half-finished straight-up martini, served with a little pile of olives in an adjoining shot glass.

"Drink?" he asked politely, his blue eyes glistening as they encountered a shaft of sunlight. Nick nodded, pointing to the glass.

"Benny, bring us a round," Henderson said, turning to the middle-aged waiter. Nick sliced a pickle into small pieces as they waited for the drinks which arrived quickly. Duke's was noted for its swift service and the independence of its waiters, who might have been rushing their service chores so that they could get back to handicapping, their notorious group affliction.

"You can't imagine how it's taken a great weight off me to know your decision, Nick. I'm really grateful." He finished off the dregs of his first martini and carefully sipped the second.

"Apparently your future means a lot to Myra," Nick said.

"She's quite a wonderful person, Nick. Politically quite mature."

"You've apparently become good friends," Nick said, careful to appear bland, disarming. Let him appear to be winning my confidence, he told himself smugly.

"Right in front she said that all editorial decisions were yours to make, that she didn't interfere with that aspect of the paper. She said you were your own man, Nick. That's quite a compliment."

"I suppose it is," he said cautiously.

"But apparently both you and she think alike politically. There are those that think you're too damned liberal. Like me. What they don't understand is that the old labels are fading. Oh, there are still knee-jerk liberals around, but they're no longer a factor. Today you've got to be eclectic in your ideology to make any sense at all."

"I quite agree," Nick said, sipping his martini, watching Henderson, noting the deep blue in his checked shirt, chosen with meticulous care to match the incredible blue of his eyes.

"Many of our friends in town think of the *Chronicle* as arrogant, too powerful."

"And you?"

"It depends on whose ox is gored. I'm one of your fans. That's why I felt so put out by your investigation. It was like being stabbed in the back by your best friend. Frankly, I felt a bit victimized. The staff beat it around for weeks. We felt that you were reacting from this thing with the ex-President, the resignation. There were those that thought you might hit me simply to show your nonpartisanship, your objectivity. You can't imagine how helpless you can feel against that kind of action."

"I can imagine."

"A politician is made or broken by the way he appears to the public, through the media. It's a damnable way to live. It's a curse." He paused. "But that's the name of the game. Harry Truman said it all when he talked about the heat in the kitchen."

"The polls seem to be quite favorable for you," Nick said.

"I'm grateful," Henderson agreed. His gratitude suddenly seemed cloying, his humility stultifying.

"With the right breaks you might actually be moving

around the corner. They say the facilities are quite good. They even have a swimming pool again."

Henderson smiled broadly. He sipped his drink, then shook his head. "I'm really sorry about that little visit you had yesterday," he said. "The one from my wife."

"You knew?"

"After the fact. I'd never put her up to that. It was her own idea. I can assure you she felt like a damned fool." He tossed down an olive. "Hell, she meant well."

"I'm sure she did."

"It's a tough row to hoe to be a wife of a politician. She has me in bed with every broad in town. Bet she told you that Myra and I were playing around." He said it casually, as if fishing for an answer.

Nick's caution increased. "Not at all," he lied. "Besides, I wouldn't have believed it."

"I'm glad," Henderson said, as if he were intending to swallow the lie. "We have a fine relationship, Myra and I, purely platonic. She has a remarkable grasp of events. Her interest in me is purely political. We see eye to eye on the future."

"I'm sure you do."

"If I didn't feel that I can make a contribution, I wouldn't spend another minute in this business." It was the routine plaint of all ambitious politicians, a common refrain. "And if I thought I had something in my past that would make my candidacy questionable, I can assure you that I would never have submitted myself to the grueling possibilities of the campaign."

"Of course," Nick said. If Henderson had bothered to probe beneath the surface, get to know him better, he would have understood how platitudinous he was sounding.

"I mean raking up what might have happened years ago, at a different time, a different climate, a wholly changed environment, would have been meaningless, a useless bit of information."

"Frankly," Nick said, "that's exactly what I concluded. What would be the point?"

"Myra understood immediately," Henderson said,

growing expansive, unsuspecting. "To her credit, she said it was your decision to make. Obviously, Gunderstein must be getting too big for his breeches. How is he taking it?"

"I don't think he's too happy about it."

"Do you think he might leave and take the story elsewhere?" Nick could feel his anxiety.

"I doubt it," Nick said. "But let's face it. You've made enemies. The intelligence community is under fire. Don't expect this to be the end of it."

"I don't," he said. "But the appearance in the *Chronicle* would have given it credence at exactly the wrong time. Later, its impact would not be as formidable, as the campaign jells."

"As we have learned. Besides, it wouldn't be such an easy story to run down. Your intelligence boys have a tight club working. They don't crack so easily."

"Thank goodness for that," Henderson said quickly. Nick could see a brief chink in the protective wall. Was he beginning to open up?

"Anyway," Nick said, cutting another pickle, "the Diem business hardly made a difference. The Viet Nam debacle was inevitable. Besides, Diem had already lost power. It wasn't as if he were assassinated while still in power. Although they probably perceived it as insurance. Dead is dead."

"It was overkill. In the final analysis, sheer stupidity."

"You sound bitter," Nick probed, deliberately averting his gaze.

"The whole business was regrettable. I wished it had never happened." He motioned the waiter to bring them another round. "The whole idea of it is obnoxious. To have to suffer for it so many years later, for such a stupid act . . ." His voice trailed off. Looking up, Nick saw in Henderson a distracted, regretful look, eyes glazed as if they were searching inward.

"What's done is done," Nick said quietly, his voice modulating, not wishing to interrupt Henderson, obviously on the verge of revelation.

"The fact that the whole sordid mess was official

business—it's hard to comprehend. The blind fools. As if the elimination of a man would eliminate the problem."

Nick could feel the man's discomfort, a personal thing, tightly walled in. Suddenly he had no desire to know, since knowing would somehow make him a party to the conspiracy, forcing his confidence. It was the curse of his business, this knowledge surreptitiously received, as a tendered gift, humanizing the information. He could feel his heart beating heavily, his palms begin to sweat. He wanted no special rights to the knowledge. He would rather accept the man's denials, the empty protestations, the self-serving protective machinations. Don't trust me! he wanted to scream out, but the dikes were already opened.

"How can you be so sure you'd make the moral decision if you were president? Considering the times, Kennedy may have considered his act as moral. The coup, I mean. The assassination would have required a different view of morality. The ends justifying the means."

"When you see it from the underside as I did, you can understand what it means. There is never any justification. By engaging in an immoral act, you become immoral. You can't fling mud without getting some of it on your hands."

He wondered who was the cleverer of the two. There was an absolute ring of sincerity in Henderson's tone, in his distracted manner, in the whole aspect of concealed pain. He could see how Myra might have been seduced; mind-fucked, as the younger generation might put it. It was a heavy-gauged appeal. You could be easily suckered in, as he was now, almost. He searched the man's face for some validation of his own cynicism. Was it possible that this politician could exercise a great sense of moral responsibility? The test of a good leader was his conduct in office, Myra had said. He cursed the obvious fact that he had become what he had feared he would become, a judge. That was the one role he must avoid at all costs.

"You know, Senator," Nick said, "I would have preferred that you let sleeping dogs lie."

Henderson looked up from the contemplation of his drink, frowning. "We're family now," he said simply.

"How can you be so sure?"

"I have great faith in Myra's judgment."

"Don't."

He seemed quizzical, suddenly unsure. He drank deeply, threw his head back, and smiled. "Look, Nick. I'm laying myself bare. If I didn't feel I could trust you, I wouldn't have said a word."

Nick shrugged. At least he wasn't denying anything. He felt the man's vulnerability, the offering of his head to the chopping block. As much as he wanted not to hear any more, his curiosity was piqued.

"How was it done?"

"Are you asking professionally?"

"You said I was family."

Henderson hesitated, rubbing his chin. "What the hell," he said, "that's the fucking trouble with this business. Who can you trust?"

"I know what you mean."

Henderson's eyes looked around the restaurant furtively, his head coming closer to Nick's, his voice modulated to a barely audible whisper.

"Actually it was quite simple. The brothers had enemies who were easy to flush out. It was purely a question of logistics. Getting the lambs to the slaughter. The release of the brothers was timed so that their enemies could arrive on the scene at exactly the right moment. We handpicked the people, although even they never realized it. The motive was revenge. You'd be surprised how potent it can be. Actually, all I did was serve as the matchmaker."

"As simple as that?"

"Frankly, I felt quite proud of myself at the time. Real professional."

"No compunctions?"

"Not one. They were butchers. The jails were filled with their enemies. They were corrupt, greedy, disgusting men. I felt that I was on the side of the angels. Besides, I loved that man."

"Who?"

"Kennedy," he said, swallowing, perhaps tamping down the bile of regret.

"You mean you got direct orders?"

"Not direct in the sense that it was from the horse's mouth. But I believed the orders came direct from him, through a third party."

"Who?"

"His brother Bobby. I believed it. I could feel their agony. It was not an easy decision. They foresaw what might happen, what did happen. It was a long shot. And it lost. It only drew them in deeper."

"The President was assassinated three weeks later."

It was like a lion unleashed in a herd of antelope.

"I've thought about that. You can't imagine the endless nights of wondering if the killings were connected. They keep talking about the relationship between a plot on Castro and the Dallas horror. But I can't get it out of my mind that somehow it was the Diem thing."

He could understand now why Henderson's compulsion was so overwhelming, the terrible sense of guilt.

"We could still believe we were invincible in those days," Henderson sighed. "It was inconceivable that anyone could mount a counterattack against us. We were on the right side, the side of freedom. History might mark the Dallas shot as the beginning of the end of America."

It was more than the stink of ambition he had scented, Nick thought. Henderson had revealed a far more powerful obsession, a kind of fanaticism. But surely the pursuit of the presidency demanded that brand of single-mindedness, the sense of mission, a searing bolt of lightning that could strike down anything in its path. He felt like one of the victims now, as if he had stood in the path of the spear of fire.

"So you see, I would not have been the only casualty," Henderson said, almost smugly, as if he had won a victory and was now searching for magnanimity.

The waiter, who had been watching them, came over to take their order. Henderson put a hand over his glass to signify that he had had enough liquor.

"And Myra knows all this?" Nick asked, remembering Charlie.

"Of course."

He felt a sudden feeling of giddiness as the image of Gunderstein floated into his mind, the infallible Gunderstein and his remarkable nose for the big story.

"That's the basic problem with the newspaper business," Henderson said, as if he had been leading up to this. "It only considers a single dimension. Nothing is ever that simple."

"How would you make us better?" Nick asked, annoyed at his sudden hostility.

"I'd begin by loosening the trigger."

"We have to move fast."

"I'm aware of that. But if you took just a bit more time to reflect instead of rushing to fire, you'd be surprised how more effective you might be."

"You might have the same criticism for politicians."

"Oh, I do, Nick. I do. You put the pressure on us. We react. Our perceived interests aren't necessarily compatible. After all, we both have constituencies. You have to sell papers. We have to get votes."

"It's hardly that simple," Nick said, as the waiter put their food in front of them. He had ordered a salad.

"That's my own special dressing," Duke said from behind him, insisting on cataloging the ingredients.

It was all so casual, the big comfortable room, the light smell of garlic that rose delicately from the shiny green pickles, the talk and laughter of easy male companionship, the taste of pleasantly prepared American food. To contemplate Henderson against this backdrop, while the words registered their persuasive logic, seemed beyond comprehension, like a sudden hailstorm on a summer's night.

"You see," Henderson said, as if in the phrase he had set up an imaginary mind to debate, "you begin to wonder who your constituency really is, who you are really accountable to. If you say the people it becomes an abstraction, because reaching them, truly communicating, is done through third persons. People like yourself. Editors of media. So you see, I'm actually playing to you. And it is you—I'm speaking generically—who determine what my constituency really knows."

The words seemed strained, cautious. But the sense was clear.

"You exaggerate our power," Nick said, half believing the well-worn phrase.

"You can make or break any one of us," Henderson said.

"I suppose if you had your druthers you'd legislate us out of business."

"As a matter of fact . . ." Henderson smiled, relegating the response to humor.

"You see," Nick responded in the same vein.

"It boils down to who knows best."

"Somebody has got to keep you fellows honest."

"Who keeps you honest?" It was an accusation.

"Answer that question yourself and you get some appreciation of what it means to be an editor."

"So you police yourselves."

"Yes we do." Nick knew he was being defensive. "And if we goof, there are still the laws of libel."

"Political careers rise and fall on misplaced adverbs. What good are damages to a damaged man? A kind of Pyrrhic victory at best." He put his fork down and sipped the remains of his drink. "We're at your mercy, Nick. That's the long and short of it. And it's not what you say about us editorially. People understand when you clearly label things 'opinion.' It's the other ways you express yourself. The subtleties of story placement. What you choose to run and not to run. The pictures you print or don't print. There are a thousand myriad ways to jab a guy."

"And build him."

"And build him."

"The sword cuts both ways."

"It's awesome. You've got too damned much control."

"Power is always dangerous in the hands of the wrong people," Nick said, conscious of the weakness of his argument. He wanted to confront Henderson with his own cynicism, throw it back at him like a live grenade. Here he was, he thought, America's most promising politician, with his tongue literally stuck up Myra's ass. How he must have sickened at the notion! And yet, who was he, Nick Gold, to challenge Henderson's image of his own sense of goodwill? Evil, like love and beauty, could also lie in the eyes of the beholder.

"What makes you so sure you know what's best for this country?" Nick challenged. He knew he was playing to Henderson's strength. But he wanted to see it displayed, needed to see it, as if to validate his own helplessness, searching for a rationale for his surrender.

"See? You've phrased the question so that anything I say could be suspect. 'When did you stop beating your wife?' You've invested me with having some sort of magic potion, forcing me to acknowledge its possession. The answer is that I'm not sure, not sure at all. I only know that I am essentially a man of goodwill with the ability to attain office, to put me in a position to exercise my goodwill."

"In other words, you're saying that your principal expertise lies in getting yourself elected?"

"More or less. Any politician who speaks differently is a damned liar."

"Are you saying you have no programs, no panaceas, no real solutions?"

"I have a posture. I'd like to see a contented, prosperous, creative America at peace with itself and the world. With every man a king, every woman a queen, every one of us with a fine feeling about his own self-worth."

"And how would you achieve that?"

"How the hell should I know?"

"You're applying for the job, not me."

"I couldn't possibly do much worse than my predecessors."

"That's hardly a qualification."

"Then what is?"

Despite his preconditioning, Nick found himself enjoying the exchange, the wonderful candor of the man, or so it seemed. Was it merely a performance for his own titillation, this self-effacement, this light-hearted humility?

"I'd say that if you were to drive my car, I'd first find out if you drove well enough."

"Ask anyone who knows anything about traffic safety and he'll tell you that a previous record of good driving is no insurance against accident."

"You've got an answer for everything."

"That's my business, the word business. Like yours."

"Only we don't have our fingers on atomic buttons."

"Except by proxy."

"Again you exaggerate."

"I don't think so."

They had by now reached the abyss, the who-struck-John stage. In a way it was comforting to know that Henderson was just as unsure as himself, just as tentative, with the same fears and anxieties, the same cursed humanness, the same realization of infallibility. He could see how easily it must have been for Henderson to manipulate Myra. How blandly he had lied, denied his involvement in the Diem thing. It was as if he believed in some higher set of values, a chosen one, like himself perhaps, with the power to decide what the people were entitled to know for their own good. Democracy is dying, he thought. After all, did the people really have to know everything? Every little thing?

When they had finished eating Henderson paid the check, indicating a subtle change in their relationship, as if his confidence had been bought for the price of a lunch. He had actually wanted to reach for his credit card, raise a protest, make a stand. But Henderson had been deft, signing the check swiftly. Nick noted that he had left the waiter an oversized tip. Stopping at each table Henderson shook hands all around, while Nick merely waved, avoiding the touch of flesh.

"See you at the game tomorrow?" Swopes called.

"Sure," Nick answered.

"I'll be there, too. Freeloading as usual." Henderson laughed. "I hope they beat the shit out of the Skins."

"I'll convey the message. That could lose you twenty-two votes. Not to mention mine."

"Hell, I've seen your ballot. You voted for Goldwater and McGovern."

"The ridiculous and the sublime."

It was warm, heavy male banter. It was odd the way Henderson suddenly reminded Nick of Charlie. He wondered if Myra could detect the resemblance. It would be poetic justice, he thought, if someday Henderson were to find himself dumped suddenly, unsuspecting, in midstream, never knowing why. They said good-bye in the chilly sun-brightened street, Henderson's blue eyes glistening in the cold, his hand strong as it gripped Nick's, not an ordinary politician's handshake, but a symbol of brotherhood.

"Well, I've given you my balls," Henderson said, smiling. It was a strange reference, disturbing. He had no right, Nick thought. He watched as Henderson waved, a cab drawing up immediately as if it had materialized at Henderson's command.

He walked back to the *Chronicle,* his hands shoved deep into his pockets, annoyed at Henderson's carefully planted image. It was, to him, an obscenity to sense the feel of another man's testicles in his hands. He shivered and rolled his head, as if trying to shake the terrible obscenity from his mind.

19

Walking through the city room, he found he could not keep his eyes from seeking out Gunderstein, not without guilt now. He could not deny his sense of shame, although he made ritual attempts to rationalize his position. After all, he could not empty the knowledge from his mind, could not will himself to upend his repository of secrets and spill them into some special cesspool. Charlie, too, must have agonized over the secrets handed to him, like IOUs from the young President, which he never had a chance to collect.

When he had seated himself at his desk, the telephone rang. It was the girl at the message desk reporting his calls. On Saturday there was no Miss Baumgartner to screen them, remove the wheat from the chaff. He listened with little interest, except to note that Margaret had called, the mention of her name recalling last night's conversation. He had hardly dismissed the idea of calling her back, when he saw that Henry Landau had followed him into the office.

"Hot potato," he said, sitting down in the chair in

front of Nick's desk. Nick noted that his tan was fading fast, having lost some hue even in the last few hours.

"I had Flanders do a piece on crimes of violence, a sidebar to yesterday's mass murder. It started out as purely statistical. You know how many murders were committed in the District last year?" Nick shrugged, uninterested.

"You know how many were committed by blacks?"

When he did not answer, Henry responded: "Ninety-five percent."

"So? It's a black city."

"Precisely why I'm here, Nick. I'm kind of torn. On the one hand, my sense of journalism ethics screams out at me to run the story, while on the other hand, considering the environment, our posture, where we are, I think to run it would be inflammatory, an attempt to balance the fact that the mass murderer was white. It'll look as if the honkies on board cooked up a rebuttal."

Nick listened, feeling Landau's dilemma, knowing the taste of it, the feel of it. He felt again the sense of his own exhaustion. Was it the walk that had tired him? Weights seemed to press down on his mind. Wasn't there anyone with whom he could share responsibility? What would Charlie have said? But even that contest was no longer valid. The world had changed considerably since Charlie's death, metamorphosed, like altered genes.

"What do you think?" he asked quietly.

"That's why I'm here, Nick."

"Put the shit on my stoop, eh?"

"That's the only place I know where to throw it."

"It's the system."

"In a way," Landau said, fidgeting, perhaps feeling slightly diminished, "I don't want to make your life any more difficult than it is."

"Then why didn't you kill the story?"

"Because"—Landau hesitated—"I probably really want it to be told."

"And you distrust your gut feeling."

"Only because of the consequences."

"Run the fucking thing, Henry," Nick said, feeling the heavy bile of anger again rise in his gorge. "We're not sociologists. We've got to stop feeling so damned guilty."

Landau smiled.

"Funny, Nick, I had expected a different reaction."

"Shows you how unpredictable I am." Landau continued to sit on the chair, rubbing his chin, eyeing Nick.

"I just don't feel comfortable about it," he said finally, after a long silence, during which Nick had deliberately looked at his watch. It was nearly time for the budget meeting.

"It's the knee-jerk thing, Henry. You've got to learn to control it."

"But . . ."

Buts, buts. Nick felt his patience erode as anger seeped upward, bubbling, pressed by mysterious inner gases. "Isn't it about time we stopped pandering to all these sacred cows? Let's erase the labels we've branded on their butts. Blacks are people, not a cause. Women are people, not a cause. All those goddamned causes. What the hell ever happened to our objectivity?"

He wondered if he were making any sense, feeling his palms sweat again, watching Landau's surprise mature into confusion. Could Landau ever fill his shoes, he wondered? Had he filled Charlie's?

"You look tired, Nick," Landau said, getting up.

"I am tired," he said.

The words came as a double echo, voices bouncing in the cavern of his memory. McCarthy had said the same thing one night in Shanley's, as he sat at the bar, hunched over his shot glass.

"I'm a burnt-out case," he had said, his articulation pristine, although the hour was four in the morning and the bartender had already begun to upend the barstools to leave room for his sweeping.

"It's simply too much for one man," he had said. Nick had thought it was only the plaint of momentary self-pity. "I'm tired of being the keeper of their bloated souls."

And Charlie had said it, although somewhat differently, as the twilight was descending. He could barely remember the scene, although the words could not be erased.

"We count too much. We're the keepers of the word," he had said.

"We count too much," Nick said, aloud, watching Landau, who had frowned, not understanding. He was too tired to offer explanations. "I am tired," he confessed again.

"Why don't you take off and get some rest?"

He nodded, lit a cigarette, puffed deeply. Landau sighed, stood up, and left. Watching him go, Nick wondered how he might be observed, felt himself observed by himself. It was an odd sensation, himself watching himself. He simply knew too much to be objective. Surely it would be highly unlikely that an ignorant, dispassionate observer could really understand what was happening in his mind, since the tendency would always be to generalize, simplify. When people talked of the media, the press, they meant "them," a faceless band of insidious, immoral, effete elite, as Spiro Agnew might have said. As dispassionate observer, Nick chuckled to himself. There was some truth to it after all, he agreed. With a handful of replicated minds, like his, they could control the country, the world. And maybe they did. But he doesn't look like much, the dispassionate observer observed. He's just a tired, frightened, overworked, betrayed, unsure, anxiety-ridden, menopausal, middle-aged man. He shivered slightly, returning to the unobserved isolation of his mind, cursing the loneliness, the absence of viable competition. What if he were the only editor left in America, the last screen? At least there were checks and balances on the president, while he was reasonably free to work his will. And if he were gone, there would be only Myra. He picked up the phone and dialed Gunderstein.

"Get the hell in here," he hissed, hanging up, leaning

back in his chair as he puffed deeply, down to the darkest corner of his lungs. Was he being mildly suicidal?

"I read your damned story, Gunderstein," he said, knowing that Gunderstein could hardly understand the source of his anger.

"The budget meeting," Landau said in pantomime, tapping on the glass wall.

"You go," Nick mimed. "Then report back here." It was the reflex of control. Landau's eyes opened wide, as he turned and started toward the meeting room. Nick could see the editors gathering. He spotted Margaret's upsweep as she moved along the well-traveled route, between the rows of desks with typewriters, now being furiously pounded, as the deadline moments sped on.

"What makes you so damned sure?" he said, turning to Gunderstein.

"It's really no mystery, just logical deduction based on fact."

"A regular Sherlock Holmes."

"In a way."

"Nothing will ever be safe with you around, Gunderstein. No one will have any more secrets. You're like the grim reaper."

"It's hardly that esoteric," Gunderstein said, confused, not smiling.

"Do you think we should print everything we know?" he asked, watching Gunderstein registering the question in his mind.

"I don't know."

"What kind of a dumb answer is that?"

"It's too broad a hypothesis, Mr. Gold. My focus is much narrower than yours. If you asked me if we should print everything about Henderson that we know, I'd say yes. Just as I said we should print everything about the President, the former President, that we would find out."

"Regardless of the consequences."

"You see," Gunderstein said gently, "that's where we just miss any contact. I'm a journalist. I don't think in terms of consequences, only in reporting the story."

"You're a great help."

"I'm sorry, Mr. Gold."

There was a long pause in which Nick contemplated the younger man. "You're just a guardian of the truth, Harold," he sighed.

"I'm just a reporter, Mr. Gold. No more. No less. What about my story?"

"I'll bet your two colleagues are pissed at me."

"That doesn't matter," Gunderstein answered. Nick could see his pimples flushing.

"Then what the hell matters?" Nick hissed.

"The story, Mr. Gold."

"The story. The story." Nick stood up and paced the floor. "If it were only that."

"It is only that, Mr. Gold," Gunderstein said, refusing to be intimidated, Nick observed, unbending, obsessed.

"Don't you give a shit about what this will do to Henderson?"

"That's not the issue," Gunderstein persisted.

"You're so fucking above it all. So damned superior."

"I'm not," Gunderstein responded quietly.

A sense of intimidation rolled over him, like a wave of thick molasses. He felt like an animal with his paw caught irrevocably in a trap. "Well, I'm not going to run your damned story, Gunderstein." He was shouting now. Heads turned in the city room.

"May I ask why?" Nick could see a slight tremor in his lip, the flushes around his pimples expanding.

"I don't have to tell you why," he said, surprised at his belligerence. If only he could summon some justifying response, some caustic argument, a raw human response of antagonism. "This power tripping has got to stop." He half hoped Gunderstein would see it as unworthy of him, a measure of his ignorance. Was he giving a good enough performance? he thought. Judging from the reaction of his one-man audience, he was failing abysmally.

"You're insufferable, Gunderstein," Nick said, sitting

down again behind the desk. "Why don't you even argue for it?" he said, his voice weakening.

"Because it speaks for itself."

"Yes. Yes. I suppose it does." He could feel the bile of his own resignation. He paused again. It was difficult to do this without conviction. "I suppose you could walk," he said quietly.

"Walk?"

"Quit. Hell, Harold, you don't need the money. Besides, half the newspapers in the country would grab you."

"Who said anything about quitting?"

"Harold, I'm rubbing your nose in it. Where the fuck is your self-respect?"

By then, he knew that he had gone too far, although he could not find in himself the power to stop. He would not have been in this fix in the first place, he told himself, if it weren't for Gunderstein and his infuriating ability to ferret out a good story.

"All right," he said, "it was a dumb remark."

"Sooner or later we'll have to carry the story," Gunderstein said. He got up and stood for a moment watching him. Then he turned and walked away. Nick reached for printed copies of the Sunday sections for review. But the words swam before his eyes. He wanted to call Gunderstein back, to plead his forgiveness.

Unable to concentrate, he turned again to the wire-service copy, its large pica type clearly spelling out the day's events in tight flat sentences. It was a light news days and the wire-service people were stretching their news sense, seeking ways to keep the words flowing, to satisfy the never-ending appetite of the member papers.

He was interrupted by the sight of the budget session disbanding, the editors or their weekend substitutes beginning to walk back to their departments. He could see Margaret coming toward his office. He wanted to run, to hide in the adjoining small conference room. He had seen quite enough of Margaret.

"Are you okay, Nick?" she asked, hovering over him, as he played at looking over the wire-service copy.

"Of course," he mumbled.

She said nothing for a few moments, her eyes continuing to stare.

"I'm genuinely sorry about last night, Nick. I hadn't meant to ever say anything about that time with Myra. I made it sound as if you owed your job to me."

"Forget it."

"I just hope there'll be no recriminations."

"Recriminations?" he asked, looking at her for the first time. She looked tired, aged, sagging. "Still worrying about your job, eh?"

"I just want to be sure everything is kept on a professional level."

"Isn't that the way it's always been, Margaret? Very professional."

"Yes, Nick. But . . ."

"But what?"

"It shouldn't make any difference."

"It doesn't."

He could feel her struggling with herself, obviously searching for some lever to bond their understanding. For his part, he enjoyed her discomfort.

"I've given Jennie the White House assignment tonight. There's a big state dinner." He felt a compulsion to laugh. Who did she think she was kidding? Surely she must know about Jennie, Jennie the ambitious asskisser, the betrayer, the spy. Was she thinking of him with such contempt that she assumed he could not know about Jennie? But then, he hadn't known about Margaret.

"That's terrific," he said with blatant sarcasm, the kind that couldn't be missed. He knew she wanted to speak further, but he had already reached for the telephone, dialing Landau's number. He could feel the responding ring through the adjoining wall, as Margaret turned. He noted that her upsweep was not so carefully arranged as usual, as if her toilette that morning had been somewhat distracted.

"I'll keep it all professional," he shouted after her.

"Professional as hell." She moved quickly, her walk accelerating, as she passed out of his vision.

"All right," he said as Landau came in, dummy sheets in hand to show him how he had arranged the front page.

"It's a bullshit day," Landau said.

"So I see."

He looked over Landau's news selections with mock attention, searching for changes, some one thing over which he could be assertive, simply for its own sake. Landau had apparently given special prominence to a story about the collapse of another Italian government.

"Let's pull that one inside, Henry."

"It's the fall of a foreign government. Against today's crop it's relatively important."

"Just pull it off, Henry. Who cares about another Italian government falling?" He knew he was right. Landau shrugged. It was hardly worth making a stand, he had surely surmised.

"What's this?" Nick asked, looking over the budget sheets. His pencil pointed to a statement about aerosol cans.

"More testimony about the dangers of aerosol cans, the gas in them. This scientist has told a congressional committee that the ionosphere, I think that's what they call it, is deteriorating at a rapid rate. He says that at its present pace we'll have no viable atmosphere in about two hundred years. Nothing particularly new in it, just another dire prediction about the end of the world."

"Put it on the front page," Nick said.

"You're not serious?"

"Give it a snappy, scary head. A three-column banner. Make it look important. If the lead's dead, rework it to give it more urgency."

"I'm not saying it's not a serious business, Nick."

"That's a double negative, Henry."

"Really, Nick. There's nothing really new in it. I can show you piles of clips on it."

"Has anything been done about these aerosol cans?

Has there been any legislation introduced to stop us from choking to death in two hundred years?"

"Probably so. There's been legislation introduced on everything. But it's of no consequence."

"That's just the point. Put it there, Henry."

Landau nodded. Tomorrow a whole industry would quake, a huge tidal wave of fear would cascade throughout the world. All those aerosol cans that dispensed their ridiculous wares. All that useless shit floating on a sea of gas that would destroy the world in less than two hundred years. He smiled to himself and searched the budget sheets again.

"Here's one," he said, pointing again to a story slug that proclaimed "New York bankrupt."

"That's another one we've done a hundred times before. So what's new about Fun City going down the drain?"

"You've become jaded, Henry. What ever happened to your sense of outrage?" He knew he was baiting him, but couldn't stop.

"I'm not jaded."

"New York City has always been the symbol of America's innocence, all the exaggerations of the American dream, supersuccess and supermisery. Now it's the symbol of America's decadence and decline. It's choking to death on its own indigestible dung. Make it urgent, Henry. Here, I'll write the head." He thought for a moment, ignoring Landau's confusion, then started to print out penciled letters on a clean sheet of copy paper. Working quickly, he crossed out words and recounted letters.

"New York Sinking in Quicksand," he wrote, showing the scribbled head to Landau.

"Who said anything about quicksand?"

"Have someone get a quote to match the head."

"Are you all right, Nick?"

"Come on, Henry, don't be so self-righteous."

"I think it's irresponsible."

"Please, Henry. No arguments. I'm just trying to hype

up the front page on a bullshit day. Didn't you call it that yourself? It's a question of judgment."

"And degree."

He was in no mood for abstract moral arguments. He continued to ponder the budget sheets and look over the front-page dummy, now penciled over almost beyond recognition. It was enough, he thought.

"That ought to do it," he said, putting down the pencil, his weapon. Landau looked dejected, but said nothing, getting up and walking out of the office.

When he had gone, Nick stood up, felt a slight quiver in his legs as he braced himself against the glass wall. In the city room the typewriters were still sounding out their staccato rhythm in ever-descending decibels, like small arms fire after a savage battle, a residue of anger. Pacing his glass cage, he could not seem to shake a vague sense of loss, and soon, his strength spent, he sat down again.

When a news aide brought him the proof of the front page, he pored over it greedily, like a starving man taking his first sustenance. Landau had followed his directions to the letter, had used his head with the quicksand reference with quotes suitably documented to underpin the headline's integrity. He deliberately kept the use of his editorial pencil harnessed. He had, after all, asserted his authority. He would only correct that which was blatantly offensive, which he proceeded to do, a series of changed words, mostly in headlines, and a quick rewriting of an awkward lead. When they brought him a proof of the editorial page, he felt less mercy, changed words vigorously, and passed it back to the composing room with his ubiquitous initials boldly imprinted on the upper right-hand corner. The sight of the proofs restored his energy, certainly his equilibrium, and he felt able to leave the city room without the tug of guilt that would assail him when he had missed seeing a final proof, a rare occurrence.

Back at his apartment, he noted that Jennie had been there, had dressed and left him a note.

"Off to 1600. See you later, darling. Love, Jennie."

It was scrawled carelessly, in keeping with the obvious hollowness of the words. Detesting the thought of her return, he threw himself on the couch in the living room, watching the bleak November night. It had begun to rain. The streets were glossy, reflecting the headlights of the traffic in the last gasp of the tepid Saturday rush hour.

He could not have determined how long he had been asleep, only that his dreams seemed disjointed, the memory of them fading as the telephone bell sounded in the still room, a jangling intrusion.

"A Miss Gates," the downstairs receptionist said.

"Who?" He had a momentary lapse, ascending as he had from a troubled sleep. It took him some time to remember who Miss Gates was. The scrap of recognition emerged as a quick image of a young braless girl in a tight T-shirt at Gunderstein's place. Of course, Martha Gates.

"Tell her I can't see her." He was treasuring his seclusion now. Looking at his watch, he realized that he must have slept for three hours. He felt oddly refreshed. Remembering his weakness earlier, he admired his recuperative powers.

"No," he corrected, "tell her to come up."

If it had been a simple memory of the Martha Gates at the office, the teary-eyed, helpless, long-haired blonde, he might not have changed his mind. In the bathroom, he doused his face with cold water, stuck his tongue out for inspection, and patted down his hair. His mouth felt furry, the backwash of the garlic from Duke's pickles lingering. Sucking mouthwash from the bottle, he gargled and spat. Why all this precaution? he wondered.

She stood in the doorway, her face indicating agitation, hesitating on the threshold.

"I'm terribly sorry, Mr. Gold," she said, taking one tentative step in the hallway, then standing there, as if rooted.

"It's all right, Martha." He turned toward the living

room, felt her following behind. She looked out the window.

"What a marvelous view," she said, watching the lights.

"Yes."

She unbuttoned her coat, leaving it on, as she searched, then found a chair to her choosing, straight-backed. He went to the bar.

"Drink?"

"If you have white wine."

He opened the little bar refrigerator and uncorked a bottle of Chablis, pouring it into a large wineglass and handing it to her. He noted that her fingers shook. Sipping lightly, she smiled.

"Wonderful," she said.

Sitting down on the couch, he asked, "Well?"

"It's about the Henderson piece," she said.

"Now that was no mystery, Martha."

She sat with her knees together, shoulders stiff. The glass shook lightly. He felt embarrassed for her nervousness, knew what was sure to be forthcoming, explosions of disillusion, the expiring gasp of idealism.

"Robert's gone back, thoroughly discouraged."

"You seem to have struck up a fast acquaintance," he said, wondering if he were being cruel.

"Yes, we have," she said, a hint of pride in her voice. "Harold is more complacent. That's because he doesn't show his feelings." She sipped the wine, then looked out the window again. "It's wrong, Mr. Gold. It's absolutely unconscionable. That story has got to be published."

"Why?" he asked, conveying innocence, he hoped.

"You know why, Mr. Gold. The carrying-out of as-sassinations in the name of national policy by a man who could very well be our next president. What does America mean if we allow such things to happen? Don't you see? It's simply wrong, unjust. We have a responsi-bility."

"You'll have to admit we've got a pretty good track record," he said, the reference obvious.

"But why stop now, Mr. Gold? We're supposed to be vigilant, moral." She took a long sip from the wine, half emptying the glass. Did he have to defend his position now to little Martha Gates, he thought, wide-eyed, young, unfinished, blond, tight-assed Martha Gates? Despite his attempt to see her as a little ninny he admired her stubbornness. Why can't a woman be like a man? he sang silently, smiling inwardly.

"I needed an adequate explanation," she said. "I took Robert to the airport. We both looked at each other like dummies. We couldn't explain any of it to ourselves. I walked around the rest of the day like a nervous cat. That's why I had to come. I know it's simply not the thing to do. But I'm troubled, Mr. Gold. Maybe I'm still suffering from the effects of that man that committed suicide. But you see, I just can't get it together."

"I'm afraid, Martha, I'm not going to be of much help." Could he tell her of his own problems, his own sense of personal crisis, his own doubts and anxieties? He could see his own helplessness mirrored in hers.

"I know you think it's foolish of me to come here," she said, flushed now. Gracefully, she slid her arms out of her coat sleeves, her breasts straining in her blouse as she pushed outward.

It was then, perhaps, that the idea stirred within him, his own sense of being the instrument, the sculptor, and she the malleable clay. There was perverseness in it, he knew, since he could create the dialogue of her protestations from rote, dredged out of his own small preserve of innocence, isolated somewhere within.

"Maybe I have an exaggerated sense of fairness," she continued, the words coming swiftly now as she had found her course. He got up and filled her glass again, as if it might stress his solicitude and interest. He hoped that she would perceive his concentration, would feel her role on center stage, the principal actor. He kept his eyes staring into hers as if plumbing limitless depths.

"It's the badge of your generation," he said, knowing that the flattery would swell her pride. "Yours was the generation that dared to challenge the established order. You tore down the ramparts and taught us something about our destiny. In a way we've got a lot in common. We both toppled a President."

"That's exactly the point," she said, perhaps surprised at the ease with which she had broken down the first line of his defenses. "What's wrong is wrong. Period. You can't excuse flaws in one set of leaders that you condemn in others. The point is that it shouldn't matter if Henderson's career is destroyed because of the truth. The truth should uplift, teach, enhance, not destroy."

"What makes you think that's the reason that the Henderson story won't see the light of day?" After all, he had to put up some sort of a mock fight, he thought.

"What else could it be?" She seemed suddenly confused, sipping deeply of the wine. He watched the glass tip, the fingers held delicately around the shiny bowl.

"I still am not convinced the evidence is conclusive," he said, setting her up for a rebuttal.

She finished the wine and set the glass down on the ledge of the chair, precariously, it turned out. A hand gesture toppled it to the floor. He got up quickly, picked it up, went back to the bar, and filled another glass, which he returned to her hand.

"We've been through all that, Mr. Gold. Surely there is enough to set in motion a chance for a fair appraisal, even a denial. Once the allegation is printed, he would have a right to make the denial. Or, on the other hand, he might confess. Frankly, he'd rise a notch in my own appraisal of him if he chose that route."

"You sound as if you were convinced of his guilt."

"I am." She said it with a wave of her blond head, a kind of imperiousness, as if his attention were titillating her. He was, he hoped, a lofty figure in her eyes, especially since he did, indeed, control her destiny, her job. Certainly she must be flattered by his interest, he thought, testing the assumption by placing his hand on hers. She might think it a fatherly act.

"You haven't a single doubt?" he asked gently, stroking the back of her free hand. She felt no agitation, he decided, his hand caressing her flesh. She drank another deep draft of the wine.

"Of course I have doubts," she said. "But the point is that there is enough here worthy of being told."

"That's Gunderstein's argument. He's right."

"Then why not print the story?"

"Because there are no absolutes in this business. Everybody perceives the truth differently." He squeezed her hand, waiting for a return movement, but it remained limp in his. How could she know that it was not in his power to decide? She would find that out soon enough. He must now give her some hope of victory, some sense of his own hesitation, as if there were any.

"I haven't completely made my decision," he said simply, hoping she would jump to the bait.

"Well, you haven't satisfied me as to why you're not going to run it. Perhaps I can make you see that we have got to run this story."

"I hope you don't see me as pigheaded."

"Not at all, Mr. Gold." He felt the return of her pressure on his hand, knowing then that he had touched her compassion, feeling no remorse or guilt, forcing himself now to see only the abstraction of her young body, her attractiveness to his senses.

"Being the commander isn't easy, Martha. This power over the word is a ridiculous burden. You can't imagine how difficult it is. It requires a great respect for moral value."

"Yes, that's exactly the point. It is, after all, a moral question." She finished the glass of wine. He moved closer to her now, seeing the flush begin on her cheekbones, a gentle film of goose pimples on her arm. He felt his sexuality stir, dispelling the fear of potential fulfillment. It was a special joy to feel his manhood harden in his pants.

"Do you really understand?" she asked, letting him frame her face in his hands.

"I understand," he said, which he did, her sense of outrage, her exquisite belief in fairness and honesty.

This is strictly a peccadillo, a lark, he told himself. He had no desire to be mentally intimate, felt unable to abide the thought of afterplay, the intellectualizing of the act, the need for her to unburden. It was an unhappy prospect and for a brief moment he hesitated. There was no way she could make the remotest dent in his resolve to keep the Henderson story out of the *Chronicle*. He had already made his surrender, had tasted the bile of defeat, and Henderson with his unwelcome confession had put the finishing touch on the decision.

She might be giving the experience a mystical frame, hallucinatory, as if it were necessary to offer herself to the cause of truth. Lifting her from the chair by the pressure of his hands on her face, he touched her body with his, feeling the softness of her flesh beneath the incredibly thin film of her clothes. He pressed his pelvis toward her so that she could feel the urgency of his hardness. He felt himself shiver, giddy with the desire to humiliate her, create some violation on her body. Perhaps he would strangle her, he thought, as his hands slipped from her cheeks to her throat. Instead, he lifted her chin and brought her lips to his, kissing her, tonguing her deeply, until her response was sure.

Who is this stranger? he asked himself, lifting her dress, his fingers groping between the cheeks of her buttocks. He was hoping she might resist now, challenge his manhood, force his brutality. Am I feeling Charlie's madness now? he wondered. Must I feel Charlie's madness to find myself? But she did not struggle, perhaps feeling his need for this violation, as if it might seal a bond between them. I am being ludicrous, he told himself, as he tugged downward on the elastic of her panty hose, pinching each cheek of her buttocks, urging her to cry out in pain. Stepping back suddenly, he removed his trousers, watching her, feeling the hard length of his erection as she watched it, her eyes revealing confusion, fear. Not a sound passed between them as he pulled her downward to her knees, feeling her resistance, then surrender. Her hands groped on the carpet for support, perhaps knowing what must happen, expecting it to happen. Did she suspect his mendacity, his need to abuse? He kneeled behind her as he sought a swift, brutal entrance in the attitude of pursuit, the way of dogs. She was dry, tight, but despite his own pain, he pushed on relentlessly, feeling the strength of his brutality and her humiliation as her body fought silently to reject him. She cried out, a wailing sound of agony, as she accepted his thrust, his abuse. The wail was drowned in the air, as he plunged forward, gripping her hips, forcing her movement as she whimpered in pain. There was no pleasure in it for him, only compulsion, which whetted the fury of his movements, made him see the shape of his own helpless animality. He could not will himself to stop as he moved her body back and forth, feeling the harsh envelope of her flesh as it fell back on his erection which spitted her without mercy, until he felt his own pain turn to numbness.

"Please come," she shouted at him through her agony, reaching a hand behind her to caress his testicles, but he knew that was impossible, since it was hardly the culmination he could induce as he gripped her body, holding her buttocks close as she tried desperately to disengage. He could feel the sweat pour from him through his exposed flesh, the pores of his hands, his belly making sticking sounds as he plunged relentlessly. He did not know how long it went on, except that he finally became conscious of a sudden sag in her body. Disengaging, he turned her over. She had fainted, her features frozen in pain. He lifted her limp body to the couch and ran to the bathroom where he soaked a towel in cold water, then returned and bathed her face, watching her regain consciousness. Her eyes looked up at him, terror-stricken, helpless.

"You fainted," he said. Even at that moment he could not find any gentleness.

"You hurt me," she whispered, the color returning to her cheeks. He seemed to be goading her to hate him. She pushed his hands from her body and sat up, the towel still pressed to her forehead. It was only after she had stood up, balancing herself against the couch as she winced in pain, that he could summon any compassion. He watched her walk unsteadily into the bathroom, her buttocks still exposed, her dress still stuck to her back. Seeing her this way, he could visualize the measure of his own venality. It was more than rape, he told himself. It was an attack on her pride, her goodness, her conception of decency and honor, all things which he imagined he had debased. He felt sick with the knowledge of his own capacity to inflict such horror, but it gave him no feeling of expiation, no sense of the moment of truth, no release.

He listened to the sound of water running in the bathroom, imagining how she must feel as she administered to her abused body. He could feel his stomach knot and nausea begin, the retching rise in his gut as he dashed into the kitchen and put his head under the faucet of the sink, turning the cold water on his head. Then she was standing over him, watching. He turned the faucet off, feeling her eyes, the water dripping onto his shirt.

"I should never have come," she said. She was still pale, but she had recovered her equilibrium.

"Then why did you?" he asked. He wanted to sob, but found the strength to resist.

"I thought I could persuade you," she said calmly.

"You didn't." He cleared his throat, hesitated. "I took advantage."

"I asked for it," she said, her voice strong. "Consider the blame shared."

Who is the victim, he wondered? Had he been the manipulated or the manipulator? Once again he felt the nagging vulnerability of his age, of his generation and all its anachronisms.

"I was prepared to do anything to get that story printed," she said, shuffling into her coat.

"Where the hell is the morality in that?" he said, suddenly angry.

"The truth is worth any sacrifice."

"And I thought that I had abused you."

Her head moved from side to side, her blond hair soft and flowing with the movement. She started toward the door, turning, her hand on the knob.

"Despite this bungle, that story must be told."

"Bullshit," he shouted. "I decide that." A shadow of fright fell on her face as she let herself out the door.

"You had no right," he shouted after her, knowing that she was out of earshot, as he ran into the bedroom and flung himself down on the bed.

What he experienced then could not be sleep, since he was conscious of his sense of place, a sensation of floating on the pedestal-propped bed in the clear expanse of space. The glass of the large windows had become invisible and he was simply hanging in the Washington air, suspended near the blinking red lights of the neighboring television and radio antennas. There was some logic in his position. It was, after all, his own room, in his own apartment. The incongruity was Charlie's face sneering at him, disembodied, like one half of a helium-filled balloon. He could hear his own voice barraging Charlie's face with questions, although he could not make out what these questions were, only that they were becoming increasingly repetitive in tone and inflection; he was apparently asking the same question over and over again. It was maddening not to be able to make out the sound of his own question, or to find the substance of it even in his own mind. Worse, the face that was Charlie's did not understand the question, and it increased his agony to see that Charlie's face was almost flat and did not reach that place in his skull where the ears should be. So he was screaming, or so he thought, a question that he could not understand, even though he was the one who was screaming it, and which could not be heard since the face that was allegedly receiving the question had no ears. Only the clicking sound of typewriter keys, coming from somewhere in the distance, relieved what had become an interminable, hopeless, unbearable frustration. He knew that once he found the source of the sound, he could tap out his question and because the face of Charlie did have eyes, here at last might be a way to get through. He felt something inside himself leave his body in search of the typewriter, whose clacking keys grew louder, then faded, then grew louder again, until finally the sound of the keys disappeared completely and he knew he was screaming out a foreign sound. But his eyes were open now and he could feel a hand on his shoulder shaking him.

"You're having a nightmare." It was Jennie's voice. He could barely catch his breath and his clothes were bathed in sweat. "You were howling."

"What did I say?" he asked, exhausted. The memories of the dreamlike episode were clear. Perhaps she might unlock the mystery of the unheard question.

"Just odd noises. You must have had a bellyful of cheese." With her words came a faint odor of wine, champagne perhaps. "I've been writing my story." The source of the typewriter sound, he thought, looking at his watch. It was only eleven. She had dashed from the White House to the apartment to write her story, to get him to help.

"I was going to be a real rat and wake you," she said brightly, brushing back his matted hair. Sitting up, he felt a sharp pain in his loins, remembering. She flicked the switch, bathing the room in suffused light. Her hair smelled of cigarette smoke. Leaning against the headboard, he lit a cigarette, puffing deeply, looking around the room. Was he searching for Charlie's face in the air, noting the spot where it had hung, disembodied and scowling?

"Take a gander, salamander," she said, pushing the copy paper in front of him. He took it and started to read, the stilted awkward sentences assailing him like hurled rocks.

"What shit!" he said. He could see her mouth tighten, her eyes narrow.

"I seem to be particularly constipated tonight." She grabbed the lit cigarette from his hand and puffed, blowing the smoke out like gusts of anger. "I really saw it, too," she said. "The stupidity of the inane toasts.

The platitudes. That silly little Jordan king with his ramrod back and deep voice, a pint-sized Omar Sharif. The tacky dresses of the Cabinet wives, the oh-so-with-it show biz types, the whole media exploitation, another contrived happening. I tried to carry it in my head until I could get to a typewriter, and then I sat down and it all came out like dry little turds."

Normally he would have been gentle, praising her, making changes, merely rearranging words to give greater scope. But now he held the copy as if it were a disintegrating animal corpse. She looked at the face of the clock on the end table.

"I've got to get it down to the *Chronicle*," she said, holding out a copy pencil. He held the copy out at arm's length and dropped it in a pile on the bed.

"Don't tease, Nick," she said, reaching to retrieve the paper. When she had reassembled the pages, she handed it back to him. This time he flung it in the air, watching the papers float to the floor.

"Come on, Nick. Really, I haven't time." He watched her carefully, wondering how long it would take her to discover the reality. Again she started to retrieve the papers.

"Please, Nick," she said, holding the papers now as if she were hugging a child. "Stop playing." She reached out, copy in one hand, pencil in the other, her lips pouting, a contrived attitude of a cute little girl begging for a favor.

"You can't bake bread with horseshit," he said, smiling.

"Please, Nick. Pretty please." She stubbornly refused to accept his refusal, sure of her hold over him.

"Submit it the way it is," he said quietly. She looked at the first page of the copy again.

"They'll laugh at me, Nick. You're quite right. It's absolutely awful. The copy desk people will snicker over it. They'll tear it apart and tomorrow Margaret will know, Nick."

"What will Margaret know?"

"That you're not helping me anymore. I'll be at her mercy."

"There's always Myra."

It was said softly, but he could see it strike her like a tracer bullet. Her body actually moved backward as if it had been hit.

"Myra?" She looked dumbly at the copy in her hand. The pencil dropped to the floor. Perhaps she was contemplating the possibility of Myra's assistance, because she said, "Myra can't write. Can she?" Was it an attempt to twist the accusation, test the validity of his knowledge?

"Don't you know?" he asked, conscious of his own sense of control.

She watched him, unsure, looking at the face of the clock. "Please, Nick. Stop playing with me. I'll miss the deadline."

"They already have the guest list and the pictures."

"Nick, please."

"Story to appear in tomorrow's editions," he hissed, taunting her.

"Please, Nick. The other paper will have it. You're being cruel."

She was trying to recover from the reference to Myra, denying it to herself. He could see she was ravaged by panic. No more Pygmalion, he told himself. She stood watching him for a moment, her mouth twisting.

"You're really not going to do this?" she asked. She was trying a new tactic now, contrived contempt.

"Why should I?" he asked, enjoying his power.

"You owe it to me."

"That is absolutely the ultimate in egocentricity, Jennie."

She must have seen that her power had diminished extensively. "You're still mad at me," she said. "That's it. You're still pissed off."

"I'm nothing."

"You made me so damned mad, Nick. I just had to get away." Did she really understand how far off the mark she was? he wondered.

"It doesn't matter anymore, Jennie. I don't give a flying fuck."

It might have been the hurled obscenity, but he could see now that it was dawning on her. She sat down at the edge of the bed, the copy on her lap, her head nodding.

"I'm sorry, Nick," she said, her hand gripping a thigh, caressing. Even that won't work, he told himself, feeling his soreness as he shifted away from her. Not now.

"I was flattered," she said. "Myra needed someone, a woman, to talk things out with. What's wrong with that?"

"Knowing you, a great deal. I trusted you. I told you things."

"Nick, I swear," she said quickly, genuinely panicked now. "I didn't break our confidence."

"Bullshit."

"Believe me, Nick."

"Believe you?"

"Nick, please understand. It was a woman-to-woman thing. She needed someone."

"Loneliness at the top, I suppose."

"Yes, something like that."

"Then why the big secret? Why all the subterfuge?"

"We didn't want you to be upset, that's all."

"How kind." He could imagine their discussions, probings. What was the best strategy to manipulate old Nick? First Margaret. Now Jennie. The conspiracy of the sisters. He remembered Henderson's words. "I've given you my balls." What a joke. At this rate neither of them would have any balls to give.

"The king is dead, long live the queen," he said bitterly, watching her face for some reaction. He imagined he detected uncertainty, perhaps fright. Then he saw the inner workings of the subtle cover-up, the grave face.

"We had a mutual interest."

"You mean old Nick."

"As a matter of fact, it was for you," she said, her eyes misting.

"Come off it, Jennie," he said coldly. "Save it for the Academy Awards. We both know what you are."

She brushed away a tear and straightened. "Well, apparently the storm is over," she said. "You do owe me something for my time."

"You mean for the use of the flesh."

"Well, you've got to admit, I gave you the best of my talent."

"Your only talent."

"It is something."

"Then we're even," he said bitterly, feeling a whimper begin somewhere deep inside him. "You did me. I did you."

"Please, Nick. Do me now." She handed him the copy paper. His fingers refused to grasp it as it fell across his lap. "Just this once. Until I can get my bearing again. It's one small lousy favor, purely professional."

"Worried about your damned image?"

"Yes I am, Nick."

He knew she had reached the stage of total capitulation, an addict in need of a fix. It was the one last ploy and he could assess it dispassionately. He reached for the copy paper and started to read it again, searching for the pencil, which she found on the carpet near the bed, handing it to him. Getting up from the bed, he walked to the den, where the typewriter stood on its little desk. He punched out the butt of his cigarette and lit another one, put paper in the roller, and quickly began the rewrite. "You know, Jennie, you're almost an illiterate." He typed swiftly, reconstructing the story, inserting the subtleties, the little nuances that might reflect what she had told him about the ritualized shame of it. After each sheet was finished, he handed it to her.

"Make sure the names are right."

"Sure, Nick," she said eagerly, looking over the finished copy.

When he had finished, she reread the entire story again, reaching out and grabbing his upper arm, which he shrugged off.

"Slug it thirty," he said.

"Fini."

"The end."

She got up and started to the door, turning. He was expecting it, knowing how her mind worked now, her *modus operandi.*

"And tomorrow, Nick?"

"It's all right, Jennie. We'll make it look like a phase-out. I won't leave you hanging by your thumbs. We'll go to the game together tomorrow." He wondered if she realized that he was delivering her to Margaret's mercy. Surely she knew, and was even now imagining strategies, constructing scenarios, calculating a new method of survival in the newspaper business.

Objectivity, he sneered, as she crossed the threshold and closed the door quietly.

20

The sun burst against the cantilevered roof line of the
Robert F. Kennedy Memorial Stadium, a glistening
gem against a rare, deep-blue Washington sky. It was
still too early for the crowds to begin their invasion.
The only people around the stadium at that hour were
stadium workers, or diehard fans determined to catch
early glimpses of their heroes, or the special elite who
picked their way up to the private club, sleepy-eyed
but expectant. And then there were the lucky few, the
elite of elites, who like Nick were invited to the owner's
box, the one remaining stronghold of the imperial city.
Here the patron could exhibit his prize, the Queen of
the City, Myra Parker Pell, who reveled in her glory,
the tiara of her power clearly displayed, the mace of
her authority held high for the assemblage to admire
and, if necessary, kiss.

Nick had always observed the Sunday ritual with
some humor. But having bowed to the mace—indeed,
he thought bitterly, having shoved it up his ass—he
could see himself as having joined the vassals in the

imperial box, another fawning courtier. Which was apparently what Charlie was trying to warn him against from the depths of his inarticulate hell until he betrayed them all with that bullet and the splattered brains. Yet in an odd way Myra, too, was an innocent victim. Could she be blamed for wanting to accept the full measure of her inheritance, for taking what was hers? We are all innocent, he thought, although knowing it gave him little solace.

His mood was bleak as he waited for Jennie in the chill outside the stadium. It was all cross and double cross and double double cross again, everyone thrashing about in search of his private talisman—power, integrity, objectivity, honesty, truth, glory, admiration. Which was his? he wondered, not finding it in the catalog.

Despite the sun, the cold stimulated teariness in his eyes. He had told Jennie to meet him at the entrance, a gruff command, spat out between gulps of hot coffee as he sat with the New York *Times* spread over the refuse of his Lucite desk. The depth of the Sunday *Times'* reporting was overwhelming. By comparison the Sunday *Chronicle* was an inept rag, swollen with trivia. Today he had counted seven advertising inserts, gaudy-colored with, it seemed, row after row of panty ads. He had never imagined that there could be so many different styles and qualities of panties.

The city room was quiet at that hour. A single type-writer clacked and a news aide sleepily opened what remained of a mountain of press releases. The absence of vibration from the presses made the atmosphere particularly unreal, almost eerie. In the far corner one of the older reporters, named McGaren, nodded over his desk reading a book. A widower, he had no home except here. Like me, Nick thought.

A mailbag lay crumpled on the floor near Miss Baumgartner's desk. He stifled the urge to open the bag and poke through it, searching out the hate mail. But knowing it was there, the hallucinatory ravings, the focused anger, was enough. He would read the letters tomorrow and they would provide their bizarre reassurance.

He thumbed through the *Times,* seeking ideas for stories and editorials. Because of the game, he would miss the morning's editorial meeting. Of course, Monday's editorials were already tentatively programmed. He knew his search was merely a mask for his real intent. Like old Mac sitting in the corner over a book, he simply had nowhere else to go. His life had boiled down to this, at last. The final reality!

Ripping tearsheets from the *Times,* he checked story possibilities in red grease pencil and flung the remainder on the floor, revealing again the slightly soiled copy of Gunderstein's story. He glanced over to Gunderstein's empty desk, expecting to see the intense pimpled face, calm and myopic.

A news aide brought wire copy. The rest of the world was in motion now. The week had begun in other hemispheres, reality had descended, agony stirred, conflicts awoke, birth and death happened, pain began. Words! Everything was words. Media! He wondered if Martha Gates was scheduled to work that day, but he refused to look at the attendance roster.

When he had completed the tearsheets and written in grease pencil the names of the deskmen to whom he wished them directed, he walked out to the city room and handed them to a news aide. Returning, he caught sight of Bonville sitting stiffly in his office, a plume of smoke from steaming coffee rising in the quiet air. Bonville did not see him, could not feel his eyes watching, even as Nick stood in the doorway, casting a shadow. Bonville's concentration was beyond destruction. It was only when Nick banged his fist against the open door, knuckles against the wood, that Bonville looked up, expressionless.

"Still got a copy of that health insurance editorial, Bonnie?" Nick asked gently, as if the need to ingratiate himself were suddenly of primary importance. Bonville looked at him quizzically.

"Yes, I do, as a matter of fact." His long bony

fingers reached into a desk drawer. Unlike his own, the surface of Bonville's desk was neat and organized. Finding the copy quickly, he held it out for Nick to grasp. When he had not, he laid it carefully on the desk top as if it had been something delicate, fragile.

"I'm surprised to see you today, Bonnie."

"I'm rather surprised I'm here," Bonville said, his Adam's apple bobbing in his scrawny throat. "I mean that figuratively as well as literally." Nick could sense the beginnings of another confession. Please don't, he told himself.

"Frankly, I'm going through a bit of a crisis," Bonville said.

"You too?" It was a tribute to Bonville's insensitivity not to have caught the obvious. The man was totally within himself, Nick knew. He searched for the right moment to leave, but Bonville was continuing.

"I can't seem to make a dent. I feel I'm talking to the wind."

"You're the house radical, Bonnie. You keep us on our toes."

"I see the truth with such clarity," he said, avoiding Nick's eyes. "Sometimes I feel as if all my nerve ends were reaching out and finding the meaning, right at the heart of things. If only I had the power to persuade you, to verbalize the sense of truth."

"Come on, Bonnie. There's a hell of a difference between truth and ideology."

"That's exactly the point. I don't think of myself as an ideologue."

Nick found himself getting edgy. He hadn't meant to be drawn in. There was no point to it, no possibility of resolution. Bonville was a classic Leftist ideologian, handpicked by him to leaven the editorial committee.

"I really don't think I can continue to take the beating," Bonville said suddenly, his pain showing now.

"You take things too seriously, Bonnie." Would he sense the hypocrisy?

"Not seriously enough," Bonville said, looking at him as if for the first time. "The world is falling apart."

"Old Cassandra."

"There is injustice everywhere," Bonville said.

Another one, Nick thought. What is it about this business? he wondered. That damned sense of justice that ran like a stream through all of them. He felt engulfed by it. Enough!

"We'll discuss that health piece tomorrow, Bonnie," Nick said, escaping, conscious that he had left some of Bonville's words in midair.

Back in his glass cage, he could feel the day begin, as the room began to fill, actors taking their places, the play beginning. At the moment their audience was stirring in their warm beds, the prospect of a lazy Sunday before them, the expectation of the big game, which magnetized their attention. In his absence a news aide had piled on more copy, the columnists' filings, the overnights from around the world, the flood of words converging. He began to read, trying to pick up again the rhythm of his work, the exquisite balance, as comforting as a pair of old shoes that had grown to fit the contours of his feet. If only he could stay in his glass cage forever, never stirring from within its perimeter and the mental boundaries it symbolized. Here is where he wanted to live and here he wanted to die. Thank you for this gift, Charlie, he told himself, feeling the gratefulness of a loyal old dog who would not stir from its master's grave. The loss of this world would be his thirty, he knew, taking pride in the newspaperman's symbol, the origin unremembered. Telephones began to ring. Typewriters clacked. Voices hummed. The giant was stirring.

"Yes," he said into the mouthpiece of his own telephone which had rung.

"Nick." It was Myra. She seemed surprised. "I tried your apartment."

"Some loose ends," he said. He would not show her how much he needed to be here.

"Just wanted to be sure you wouldn't forget the game."

"Not a chance."

"And Jennie?" There was the slightest change of pitch, or had he imagined it?

"Jennie, too."

She had paused, her breath expelled, perhaps, in relief. He was certain now that Jennie had not confided, a mark of her own strategy for survival.

"And, Nick. I just want you to know how grateful I am for your attitude on Henderson. He called me late last night. I'm very thankful."

"He admitted it, Myra. He implied you also knew." It was important for her to know that he shared their little conspiracy. The pause was longer now, as she gathered her thoughts for some adequate response. She also knew the limits of her powers.

"He's our kind of guy," she said, ignoring the accusation. She could hear only the sound of her own drummer, he knew.

"Yes, Myra. He's our kind of guy." The words came out rippling, as if they were dragged over an old-fashioned washboard.

"It's going to be one helluva year," she said, girlish, gleeful.

"We needed an encore," he said. "See you later."

He had barely hung up when the telephone became persistent again, drawing his eyes away from the overnights. Finally he picked it up. It was Gunderstein's flat quiet voice, a slight quiver revealing a tenseness that might not be detected in a face-to-face talk.

"Will you be in for a while?" Gunderstein asked.

"I'm going to the game."

"I must talk to you." It was a confrontation he wanted to avoid. Could Gunderstein ever really be placated? The man's tenacity was superhuman.

"I'm leaving early." He knew then that he should just hang up the phone and run, as far as he could go. But there was no escape, not from the all-seeing myopic cyclops that was Gunderstein.

"Please, Mr. Gold. I can be there in ten minutes." The phone clicked off, leaving the receiver in a wet and trembling hand. When he had finally returned it to its cradle, Nick felt his concentration drain away. Moving his body in the chair, he looked into the city room again. Down the line of desks he could see the dark face of the Atkins girl, caught, he imagined, in the agony of nonobjectivity. Even at that distance she must have felt his eyes on her. She looked up, her head bobbing slightly, then returned to her typing.

The overnights seemed suddenly hollow, pretentious, as if the reporters were forcing themselves to fill space, injecting interpretations and stretching them to the point of pontificating. He was tempted to take his pencil and emasculate the copy, remove all the opinions and propagandizing, extract the spice of the newspaperman's art like a bad tooth. Usually it was impossible for him to see this kind of blatancy and do nothing about it. Sometimes he would excise a word, a paragraph, sometimes kill an entire story. This morning, though, he felt his powers ebb, a man caught in a neverending dream sequence reaching for an object that his fingers refused to hold. Media! The word buzzed in his head like an insect beating its wings against a light. Later, he knew, he would read the printed paper with growing anger as he viewed the words he should have destroyed. It wasn't enough that he had set the line, at best fuzzy and ill-defined except in his own brain, but policing the line was a special problem, requiring the alertness and vigilance of an army. It was impossible for one man's brain to monitor it all. If only the information would just stop coming for a single day. Even when there were strikes, and they knew they would skip publication, the information continued to come. It was always processed and kept in readiness for the moment when the public would be let in, the zoo reopened.

Gunderstein arrived breathless, the front of his hair sweaty, plastered to his forehead. Little red circles had already outlined his pimples, a sure guide to the state of his agitation. He looked furtively from side to side as if someone might be expected to intrude at any moment.

"I've refocused my story," he said, taking a sheaf of

copy paper from the side pocket of a rumpled jacket. The pages were folded vertically. He opened and smoothed them as he thrust them on top of the pile of dispatches.

"It's really a closed issue, Harold," Nick said looking blankly at the copy, refusing to stir his eyes to read it.

"I've actually cleared the major hurdle, Mr. Gold," he said. "Allison has agreed to be quoted. I assume that's your major objection."

"Allison?" He had barely remembered the man's name, although he had invoked the idea of his non-quotability as a major stumbling block to publication. Why couldn't Gunderstein let sleeping dogs lie?

"Yes. He has agreed to be quoted." Gunderstein pointed to the copy.

"He's not afraid?" Nick asked.

"He's frightened to death."

"Then why?"

"I paid him," Gunderstein said simply.

"You paid him?" The cadence of his words indicated that he wanted to say more. Gunderstein waited for the words that did not come.

"It was my own money," Gunderstein said, before Nick could protest that he had not authorized the payment.

"You're crazy, Harold," Nick said finally.

"Twenty-five thousand."

"You're crazy," Nick repeated.

Gunderstein smiled thinly, his meaning unmistakable. The story is everything, the means to acquire it merely incidental. They had been down that road before.

"You shouldn't have done that, Harold." He knew before it was uttered that it was an unworthy response, a naïve admonishment. "If it ever gets out . . ." He had heard that before as well. Indeed, he remembered having said it in just that way, fear and outrage curdling his guts while the mind sought adequate rationalizations.

"The story is everything, worth anything, the ethics

of the payment directly proportional to the necessity of the story's being told," someone had said. Had it been Gunderstein? Or Myra? Or himself?

"Is it really worth that much to you, Harold?" Nick asked.

"I guess it speaks for itself, Mr. Gold," Gunderstein said. "It simply must be told."

Nick looked dumbly at the pages before him, despite himself starting to read, then checking himself after the lead paragraph:

"A former CIA operative has accused Senator Burton Henderson, the Democratic front-runner for the presidential nomination, of being the principal engineer of the assassination of Diem of South Viet Nam in 1963," the paragraph began.

"Right out on the limb," Nick said.

"The limb will hold."

"And the concept of two sources?" Nick could barely dislodge the words.

"There aren't two sources, Mr. Gold. The Dallas and Los Angeles bullets took care of that."

"And Allison? The man's a drunk and frightened. He'll crack when the others start pressing him for motivation. He'll be sure to mention the money."

"It'll be too late by then. The story will be out. Besides, I doubt if he'll mention it."

"And if he does?"

Gunderstein shrugged.

"Sooner or later it all comes out."

They had gone over that ground, too. Who would finally be the first to tell the story of the quarter of a million? What will it matter then? The President was gone now. History had marched on. Was it he who argued for the price of the truth?

"In the end, Allison finally agreed with you," Gunderstein said. "He'd be safer with the story up front than hiding in the shadows, a potential victim."

McCarthy's words, too, cascaded downward from the vault of time. "Find out," he had said. "Whatever it costs, find out." It had echoed and reechoed in space and time.

"People will think this whole business of democracy is one gigantic license to steal, a fraud. Aside from Henderson's career, have you assessed the impact on this country?" The words sounded like his, familiar in the delivery, but their integrity seemed suspect, even to him. He wondered if Gunderstein could detect the hollowness, the false ring.

"It doesn't matter," Gunderstein said quietly. "That's not for us to contemplate."

"Only the story?"

"Only the story."

"And if I choose not to run it?"

"You can't," Gunderstein said.

"But I can," Nick protested.

"Not in good conscience."

"Good conscience?"

Gunderstein nodded. Was it an implied threat? He would never know unless he picked up the gauntlet.

What had all this to do with conscience? he wondered. Self-interest was the paramount reason for all things, self-protection. It was in the rhythm of the evolutionary process, a part of the figurative food chain. The powerful eat the less powerful, while each transforms, developing new coping skills. They create new kinds of power, new life forms, in which the more powerful eat the less powerful and so on. He hung now by a thin thread over the razor's edge.

"You could always take the story to the New York Times," Nick noted, hoping that the suggestion might take hold. It was not Henderson who concerned him. Henderson, the confirming other source.

"I could."

Would Gunderstein see a story in that, the refusal of the Chronicle to carry the story, the implied cover-up, that abominable word, by the world's most powerful newspaper? And then would come the story of the quarter of a million, the avalanche of names, payoffs, a whole new Pandora's box. Surely the Chronicle would respond with denials, would find, in the musty attic of the *Times*, something to prick the balloon of their unbearable self-righteousness. Then the two great newspapers would lock themselves in mortal combat, draining their energy in a great media war—an unlikely outcome. It was an axiom of the media never to attack a fellow purveyor, at least on a peer level. Economics, the old concept of property ownership, dictated as always the extent of media reach. He, Nick, might stand in the doorway, but in the end, as he now knew, Myra held the key. Okay, Charlie, he asked, the futility of the question heavy in his mind, what do we do now? Go crazy? Take the bullet? Or walk away, the prospect of a living death?

"I should submit it to the legal eagles."

"There's no libel here, Mr. Gold, not on our part."

"When did you start to practice law?"

"Between us we know more libel law than a brace of lawyers." It was the only visible sign of cockiness he had ever revealed. "A good reporter understands libel by instinct, because a good reporter only writes the truth."

"That is the biggest crock of shit I've heard all morning," he said, knowing it was the truth, knowing that there was no libel in the story. By now, he could only view himself with disgust, his own cowardice galling. But Gunderstein stood his ground, humility returning, the face impassive again, although the myopic eyes seemed to squint less and the red circles around the pimples had diminished.

"Have you shown this story to anyone?"

"No."

"Martha Gates?"

"No." His eyes had narrowed at the mention of her name. Had she told him? The outrage of it, he thought, the invocation of moral principles.

"I need more time, Harold." He had framed the words carefully, more in tone than in meaning. It was necessary not to appear as if he were pleading. There was always the chance that Myra would understand, that reason could prevail. He searched for signs of her pragmatism, found many, invested her with her father's intelligence and balance.

"Give me time," he said, as if it were Gunderstein's to grant. He could feel Gunderstein's awkwardness in the face of the plea. He was, after all, the editor, not Gunderstein. The younger man stood awkwardly before him, shifting his weight clumsily from one foot to the other. Physically, he seemed so bland, almost frail. Perhaps in his very lack of formidability lay the key to his character.

"Let me read the story carefully," he whispered, reaching for the telephone, his ultimate technique of dismissal. Gunderstein watched him for a moment, then turned and walked slowly back to the city room. When he had crossed the room and sat down at his desk, Nick reached for the story, refolded it, and put it in the inside coat pocket of his jacket. It was then that he called Jennie, the words belched like commands as she acknowledged them with glum assents.

Putting on his jacket and fur-lined leisure coat, which barely reached to the end of his jacket, he walked quickly from the city room, his eyes fixed straight ahead, refusing to acknowledge Gunderstein's eyes, which he knew followed him. His coat testified to his destination. Let him draw his own implications.

He could see her emerging from the cab, probing carefully for the curb, with panted legs. She was dressed in her own special version of what was expected for the game, a high-crowned fur hat, teddy bear jacket, a blaze of orange which he knew would match her lipstick. Seeing him, she moved gracefully, recalling for him the special moments of tenderness. He could have been quite content in his ignorance, he thought.

"Hail to the Redskins," she said, falling in step beside him as they passed through the door to the special entrance. In the elevator they huddled in the crowd, light-hearted and bantering, as the cab moved slowly upward.

Faces turned as they arrived at the private suite be-

hind the owner's box. The elite were crowded around
the bar, sipping Bloody Marys, the dominant personality Myra Pell, slender and carefully groomed in a
beige pants outfit. She had been talking with Swopes,
elegantly suited in a camel's hair sport jacket and soft
red shirt. Nick noted the familiar faces, the Chief Justice of the Supreme Court, Senator Jack Martin, a
long-shot presidential hopeful, Barry Halloran, the President's Press Secretary, the swinging Ambassador from
Iran, who sported a lovely wide-eyed showgirl type,
clutching at his arm. Ambruster, the head of the CIA,
his breakfast companion of a few days ago, Mrs. Hoffritz, the obligatory rich dowager hostess, recently wid-
owed, already slightly smashed, the ex-vice presidential
candidate Richard Melton, Melissa Haversham, the
actress of the current hit television show, daintily sipping champagne, John Packard, the oil lobbyist, tall
and stately with a deeply flushed face, and his pouchy
wife, bloated by too many cocktails and canapes, both
of them clutching large glassfuls of bourbon on the
rocks. But it was the blue eyes of Burton Henderson
that magnetized him for a moment, matching perfectly
the blue sky that peeked in the distance. He smiled
broadly into Nick's face as his wife worked at keeping
her eyes averted, the mantle of her past humiliation
still visible. Behind him was Biff Larson, the Secretary
of the Treasury, rakish in a shiny leather jacket. Nick
felt his hand being pumped and grasped as Myra moved
between him and Jennie holding each by the upper
arm, the attentive hostess.

"And here's Jennie," she said. Without seeing it, he
could assume that there was a special squeeze on Jennie's arm, a knowing signal.

"So you're the acid wit at the end of the by-line,"
the Chief Justice said, grabbing her hand. Jennie's eyes
flashed furtively at Nick.

"Pungent but attractive," the dowager said.

"It's me," Richard Melton said, grabbing Nick's
hand. "The old professional ex-pol."

"I wondered where I saw you before," Jennie said

brightly. Once in the crowd, her spirits had perked up. Perhaps it had been Myra's caress that stimulated her. She took a Bloody Mary from the bar.

"I'm great copy for the 'What Ever Happened to' columns."

"What ever did happen to you?" Jennie asked.

"I joined the Mafia."

"Well, at least you didn't change your occupation."

The Secretary of the Treasury laughed heartily, clinking glasses with John Packard.

"To the energy crisis, Biff."

"Long may you profit by it, you bastard," the Secretary of the Treasury said. Nick could not be certain if sarcasm was intended.

"Well, is that broken-down geriatrics ward going to win today?" Barry Halloran asked Swopes.

"Ask Melissa," he said. "She's just come up from giving the boys a pep talk."

"It was marvelous. I've never been in a football locker room before. I've never seen so much manhood in one place," she said winking.

"I'd say you must have inspired them," the Iranian Ambassador said in his charming continental accent. The actress wiggled her hips playfully.

Beyond their chatter, Nick could hear the sound of the crowd, cheering the men who practiced on the field. Henderson came over and pumped Nick's hand. He was relaxed and happy, oblivious to the ticket of his demise that bulged heavily in the inner pocket of Nick's jacket.

"A great day for a ball game," he said.

"Just great," Nick answered with some effort, the words ejaculated with more force than was required.

"I'm really happy that you fellows have gotten together." It was Myra's voice, quietly intruding.

"You've got one helluva guy here, Myra," Henderson said, the implied possessiveness not lost on him.

"We're pretty proud of him ourselves."

"I understand that you were Charlie Pell's best friend," he said, his blue eyes flitting between his and

Myra's face. It was one of those unexpected remarks. He could actually feel Myra blanch.

"Buddies, those two," she said cheerfully.

"I've heard fantastic things about him," Henderson continued. How could he know he was treading on what was painfully private?

Myra moved away, heading for Ambruster. They began to talk in hushed whispers.

"I'm sure he feels a bit relieved as well," Henderson said, his smile vanishing. "He's taken so much flak lately he must feel like a piece of Swiss cheese."

"Well at least he's not running for anything," Nick said. Henderson frowned briefly, then smiled.

"That's one saving grace," he said smugly, reaching out to catch Jennie's hand.

"Now here is one sharp kid," he said.

"That was quite a do the other night," she said. Nick watched her aim her sense of womanness. It was her instinct not to miss a chance at latching on to power.

"I looked over your future home last night," she said.

"So I read."

"It's real campy. Loved the backyard. And I do hope you change the cook."

"Definitely." He waved his wife over. Moving reluctantly, she sipped her drink as she came toward them.

"Jennie says we should change the cook in the new place." Nick noted that Mrs. Henderson's eyes seemed weary, glazed.

"His mousse was positively inedible."

"We'll have to look into it," she said, unable to carry off the required bantering response. Henderson looked at her sharply, disapprovingly. Nick could sense the tension between them. She upended her glass and walked to the bar.

In a corner of the room, white-jacketed black waiters removed the silver covers of the chafing dishes, signaling the beginnings of the buffet. The smell of eggs and sausage permeated the room.

"Mmm, smells good," the Ambassador's girl friend said, apparently relieved to have found a topic of conversation. Nick watched the Ambassador's hand slip down to caress a well-rounded buttock, caught his wink when he saw Nick watching.

"Soup's on," Swopes announced. None of the guests moved. It was considered gauche to be first in line. The slightly tipsy dowager came toward him. Nick braced himself, looking across the room at Myra, who winked playfully. Knowing what was to come, he tried to turn away, but she had already grabbed his lower arm.

"And how is Mr. Brezhnev's man in Washington?" she said, lisping. Once the reigning Washington hostess, she had been systematically destroyed as a media figure by the shift in the *Chronicle*'s coverage, when the Lifestyle section replaced the old Society columns. Charlie had always suspected that she, along with others, had paid the reporters for her coverage, if not in cash, in other ways: lavish gifts, trips abroad. It could never be proved.

"We'll freeze the bitches out," he had said, actually compiling a blacklist. "If I see the names of these cunts in our paper, I'll fire the lot of you," he had shouted at a meeting in his office with the two Society reporters, long gone now, as they sat, guilt-ridden and pale. He had written down a series of names which he had forced them to memorize on the spot. He had wondered if they would make an issue out of it with the Newspaper Guild, but it had all blown over. Occasionally he had let their names slip in. They were, after all, a bit of nostalgia and one couldn't avoid; for example, Mrs. Hoffritz's massive contributions to the Kennedy Center and whatever worthy causes were the current fad. Besides, she represented a kind of caricature that added spice to the Washington scene.

"I'm no longer working for Brezhnev. Mao has made me a better offer, Mrs. Hoffritz."

"There are lots of real Americans out there, just waiting for a chance to get you," she said. A remembered phrase echoed in his mind, suddenly solving the identity of the writer of one of his persistent hate letters. He felt a strange kinship with her. Fryer of my gut, he chuckled.

"So it's you," he said mysteriously, knowing she would never understand. Inviting her might be one of Myra's private jokes, he thought.

"Your dress is lovely, Mrs. Hoffritz," he said, winking at Swopes, who led her away to the buffet table.

"She owns half the real estate in town," Richard Melton said behind them. "In my day, all you had to do was knock Stalin and down would come a ten-thousand-dollar check for your campaign."

"I always wondered what you fellows did with that dough," Nick said.

"Don't knock campaign funds, Nick. It kept a lot of us in groceries."

"I know."

"Standard practice in the industry."

The buffet line had begun to form. Outside the din was increasing. He felt the bulk of Gunderstein's copy in his pocket. He searched for Myra. She was talking to Henderson, the two of them alone now. Mrs. Henderson glared at them from the buffet line. He felt no pity for the poor woman, wallowing in her humiliations and misconceptions, caught in the web of her husband's imagery. It was, after all, a comfortable misconception, since she could excuse her husband's infidelity if it was necessary for the cause. Perhaps she too had made that sacrifice herself. He heard Myra's familiar laughter. Starting toward them, he stopped, noted how banal it appeared, the two of them together, confident of their power. They seemed so innocent, two children at play.

"Ummm, delicious," the Ambassador's girl friend squealed as he spooned tiny chunks of scrambled eggs into her mouth. Beside her, Biff Larson in his tight-fitting leather jacket bent down and held his mouth open for a proffered bit of egg.

"Down his greedy gullet," the Iranian Ambassador said, smiling. "Double the price of the next piece."

"The Middle Eastern mentality at work," the Secretary of the Treasury said with mock sarcasm.

"Oh, you mean oil," the Ambassador's girl friend shrieked, proud of her knowledge of current events.

"You should let her negotiate with us," Biff Larson said.

"She drives a hard bargain," the Ambassador said, winking to Nick, who was listening idly to their chatter.

"I'll bet," the Secretary of the Treasury said, also turning to Nick. The Ambassador held a hand near his mouth and whispered in Nick's ear.

"She has an absolutely exquisite body," he whispered.

The Secretary of the Treasury, who had imagined what the remark might have been, said: "Bribing the press again, Mr. Ambassador?"

"It is an old Middle Eastern tradition."

"Bribing the press?"

"No. In my country we are the press." He turned to his girl friend and blew her a kiss.

"You're not giving things away again?" Melissa Haversham said. The Chief Justice, who had been talking to her, watched her hips move as she walked toward him.

"I'll take them both," the Secretary of the Treasury said. "Just wrap them up and deliver them to my home."

"In an unmarked brown wrapper," the Ambassador's girl friend said, apparently confused by their repartee, feeling the need not to be considered dumb.

Nick listened to the patter, the relaxed Washington talk. It represented a kind of special shorthand, understood, like Morse code, by both the sender and the receiver. On this stage nobody played for the audience, only for themselves, a tight little group, like the hardcore gamblers of a floating crap game.

Nick moved out of earshot, leaning against the far wall, balancing his plate. Outside the noise of the crowd grew louder. He ate by habit, tasting little, watching Myra circulate again, the Queen Bee offering herself for impregnation to the workers. He had the impression that she could feel his eyes on her, a laser beam, energizing her as she made her rounds. Henderson followed in her wake, the symbolism apt. Jennie completed the train, looking for a new place to roost now that she had lost him.

Again he felt for the folded copy in his jacket, rubbing its bulk, sensing the frantic beat of his heart beneath it. Myra was coming toward him now, a thin benign smile pasted on her lips.

"Are you all right, Nick?" she asked. He quickly removed his hand from his jacket.

"Fine." He cautioned himself. Was this the moment?

"There's a time to shut off the motor, Nick." It sounded like an order.

"Cut him adrift." He found himself saying it, despite the draining away of courage. But the players were being announced and the room had suddenly reverberated with the boom of the crowd, a wave of stamping and vibrations, drowning out intelligible sounds.

"What?" she said. But the noise persisted. He looked upward, watching the ceiling, waiting for the sound to die down. It seemed like the recurring dream of the unheard shout, the unreachable grip, where energy and motion defied real movement. If she had heard, would she have understood?

"Last call for drinks," Swopes shouted above the din as the group clustered around the bar.

"Who do you like in the game?" Henderson asked, casual, unruffled, confident. Behind him Nick could see his wife, stern and dour, a note of hopeless resolution in her glazed eyes.

"The Skins, of course," the Chief Justice said. "You can't drink the man's booze and do otherwise."

"Now there's an unbiased judge," Myra said, laughing, as the group proceeded into the box. He felt a tug on his arm, turned and saw Jennie.

"It's not who wins or loses, but how you play the game, right, Nick?" she said, then whispering, "Besides, who gives a shit?"

It seemed a clue to his own resolve. What did it matter, after all? Nothing would change. If not Henderson, it would be someone exactly like him, someone tinsel thin, media-created, able to rationalize the most bestial act in the name of country, or flag, or ideology, or some other self-conceived concept of morality.

Someone has got to become the watchdog of the public conscience, Mr. Parker had said that day, long ago. But who will watch the watchdog? he asked himself.

He who owns words owns the world, he repeated to himself as he filed into the box, the Imperial Box. The crowd cheered, a single mindless plaint from the immensity of the stadium. Each of them surely could feel the sense of their own specialness, as if the crowd were cheering for each of them. They, who had the power to control the callous inert crowd mind. In the antiseptic isolation of his glass cage, he had to imagine the sense of power, to create it in his brain, but here in this immensity of humanness, he could see it, feel it, smell it. We have no right to play with their innocence, he told himself, watching Myra's confident profile, her chin lifted proudly. He caught another glimpse of Henderson's blue eyes, sparkling with the moisture of the cold.

Then he felt the urge begin, seeing the distance between himself and the field, the low railing of the box, easily scaled, as Charlie might have seen the trigger of the hanging shotgun. Muscles tightened as they signaled for energy from the brain, but, at that moment the stadium became quiet, the humanity frozen as one voice rose above the rest in the rendition of "The Star-Spangled Banner," the ritualized words stilted and irrelevant.

A wrenching shiver seized him as he viewed the standing crowd, an amorphous indistinguishable mass, singing with innocent expectation. He could sense something expiring in this environment, a terminality in himself as well. Who will be left to watch the watchdogs? he asked again, wondering if his lips had moved soundlessly. Or will the watchdogs become the guardians, the threatened? Suddenly Myra's eye caught his, winked, a sign of her benign possession of him.

As he heard the last echoing strains of the National Anthem, the resurgence of the crowd's mindless babble, he knew he was misplaced in space, a straggler in an untracked jungle. He who kept the word must never leave the glass cage, never feel or touch or taste the humanness that could corrupt objectivity, destroy perfection.

Sounds of the crowd rang in his ears as he ran from the box, passing the black waiters who were clearing the imperial buffet. Outside in the glaring sun he flagged a cab and directed the driver to take him to the *Chronicle*.

The story, the word, in the end, was all, the only meaning. Reaching into his pocket, he pulled out the sheaf of paper, making mental notes of an appropriate headline, cursing Gunderstein as he read. The man was constantly splitting infinitives.

Bestselling Novels from POCKET BOOKS

KEEP ABREAST OF CURRENT AFFAIRS